Chrystle Fiedler seamlessly blends spine-tingling suspense and a passion for alternative health in these acclaimed Natural Remedies mysteries!

SCENT TO KILL

"A well-crafted mystery. . . . Devotees of natural medicine and aromatherapy will enjoy the tips that appear at the beginning of each chapter." —*Publishers Weekly*

DEATH DROPS
A DearReader.com Mystery Book Club pick

"An engaging investigative thriller . . . an enjoyable whodunit." —*The Mystery Gazette*

"Fiedler has a knack for detailing aspects of acupuncture, massage, yoga, and homeopathy . . . fertile ground for further adventures of an unconventional but eminently likeable doctor." —*Mystery Scene*

"As engaging as it is educational about natural remedies and full-body health." —*Herb Companion*

"Entertaining, informative. . . . *Death Drops* is a gem!" —Gayle Trent, author of *Killer Sweet Tooth*

"Absorbing and entertaining."
—Linda Bloodworth-Thomason,
r/producer of *Designing Women*

nise." —*Library Journal*

Also by Chrystle Fiedler

Scent to Kill
Death Drops

garden
of death

A Natural Remedies Mystery

Chrystle Fiedler

Pocket Books

New York   London   Toronto   Sydney   New Delhi

DISCLAIMER

This publication contains the opinions and ideas of its author. It is intended to provide helpful and informative material on the subjects addressed in the publication. It is sold with the understanding that the author and publisher are not engaged in rendering medical, health, or any other kind of personal professional services in the book. The reader should consult his or her medical, health, or other competent professional before adopting any of the suggestions in this book or drawing inferences from it.

The author and publisher specifically disclaim all responsibility for any liability, loss, or risk, personal or otherwise, which is incurred as a consequence, directly or indirectly, of the use and application of any of the contents of this book.

Pocket Books
A Division of Simon & Schuster, Inc.
1230 Avenue of the Americas
New York, NY 10020

First Pocket Books paperback edition April 2015

POCKET and colophon are registered trademarks of Simon & Schuster, Inc.

For information about special discounts for bulk purchases, please contact Simon & Schuster Special Sales at 1-866-506-1949 or business@simonandschuster.com.

The Simon & Schuster Speakers Bureau can bring authors to your live event. For more information or to book an event, contact the Simon & Schuster Speakers Bureau at 1-866-248-3049 or visit our website at www.simonspeakers.com.

Manufactured in the United States of America

10 9 8 7 6 5 4 3 2 1

ISBN 978-1-4767-4891-7
ISBN 978-1-4767-4892-4 (ebook)

To the village of Greenport, my paradise on the North Fork of Long Island. It's good to be home.

chapter one

Willow McQuade's Favorite Medicinal Plants

ALOE VERA
Botanical name: *Aloe barbadensis*

Medicinal uses: Aloe is a handy plant that no household should be without. This juicy, succulent plant features spiky leaves that contain a thick gel that you can use topically to soothe and heal minor burns, sunburns, and blisters and prevents scarring. You can also use it for insect bites, rashes, acne, and other skin conditions like eczema, poison ivy, and poison oak. Place this hardy plant on your kitchen windowsill or plant in your garden. Just make sure your aloe plant has sunshine, well-drained soil, and moderate water, and then watch it grow and reap the many benefits it provides!

Gardening is one of my favorite natural remedies. I can think of no better pursuit than plunging a trowel into the moist, brown earth, removing enough dirt to create a space for a beautiful, health-giving plant, and watching it grow.

It was the third Friday in June, and I was up to my knees in dirt and loving it. The last few weeks had brought pastel-blue skies, billowy clouds, and the delicious summery scent of sea air drifting in from the bay. In the tree above me, cardinals and catbirds twittered and cawed. It was a perfect day for gardening.

I finished digging, picked up a chamomile plant, gently placed it into the hole, shoveled in some earth, and patted the ground around it. Then I pulled off my gloves, sat back on my heels, and reviewed what I'd done so far that afternoon. I'd planted over a dozen plants in the garden's Medicinal Herbs for Heart Health section. The leaves and flowers fluttered in the sea breeze, but the roots of the plants were secure.

I dispense natural remedies, both as a naturopathic doctor and as the owner of Nature's Way Market & Café. The store originally belonged to my aunt Claire. But when Claire was murdered, I left Los Angeles for good and moved back to my hometown of Greenport, on the East End of Long Island. I knew I had to find Claire's murderer, which—to the local cops' surprise— I did. Almost as difficult was taking over Nature's Way. I couldn't let everything that Claire had worked so hard to build disappear. Now, a little more than a year later, I felt like an actual business owner. Nature's Way was operating in the black, and I was ready for a new project.

Last June I took a trip to London to visit a cousin, and while I was there I visited the Chelsea Physic Garden. Claire had often raved about it, but I had never had the chance to see it for myself. I was both enchanted and educated by the section with medicinal plants for various conditions.

Three months later, in October, I learned that the empty plot of land next door to Nature's Way, a little over two acres in size, had become available. The lot was completely overgrown with scrub and weeds and needed a lot of TLC, but I had the soil tested for pH and nutrient content and it was top-notch. So I jumped at the opportunity to re-create what I'd seen in London. I had my next project.

My garden, like the one in London, would show-case various types of plants and use them to educate the local community about the many health benefits of herbs that people can grow at home, such as aloe for burns, turmeric for arthritis, and fennel for indigestion. I planned to hold workshops in the garden and store to show people how to grow and use these herbs. Now, all of the classes were almost full and I planned to add more.

Tomorrow, on the first day of the annual Maritime Festival, all of Claire's friends would gather, and I would officially open the Claire Hagen Memorial Physic Garden. Since the festival first began in 1990, so many events had been added that we locals could barely keep track. But my favorites were the opening day parade, visits from tall ships, boat races, the clam chowder and best pie contests, and the annual pirate invasion, complete with treasure hunts and mermaids.

The whole week would be given over to festivities, the town filled with visitors. It seemed the perfect time to open the new garden to the public.

Qigong (pronounced *chee-gung*), my scruffy, black, gray, and white terrier, ran up and put his nose in the dirt next to me. He sniffed, decided something was hidden there, and started digging with his chunky little paws. I patted his head. "Thanks, buddy. I appreciate the help."

"Need help, hon?" Jackson Spade glanced over at me from the north end of the garden, where he'd been working with our new gardening assistant, Nate Marshall. They were putting down paver stones as a patio for our new outdoor teahouse. Nate, a recent graduate of Stony Brook's horticulture program, was tall and lanky, with owlish glasses that gave him a scholarly look. He also had a remarkable green thumb. Jackson said all Nate had to do was look at a plant and it would thrive, which was a bit of an exaggeration—but not by much. Fortunately, Nate had signed on to care for the garden throughout the summer.

Jackson told Nate he'd be right back and came over to me. Dressed in his old jeans, a Green Day T-shirt, and boots, he was covered with dirt from working all day in the garden, but it didn't matter. With his short cropped hair, just enough stubble to be sexy, and dreamy blue eyes, he made me melt.

Jackson and I met last year when he had come to Nature's Way looking for more natural remedies for his bad back. Aunt Claire had helped him feel better with the cures she'd recommended, and he was hoping for further improvement. Jackson was grateful for Claire's help and kindness and so he agreed to help me in my quest to find her murderer. The fact that he was an ex-cop, now on disability because of his back, had worked in our favor. We nabbed the killers and along the way, fell in love. Now, it felt as if we had been together forever.

"I'm okay," I said. "Qigong is doing a great job digging holes."

"I'll bet," he said. "I think he's a little jealous of Nate. Qigong wants to be your chief gardening assistant."

"No one digs a hole like you do," I assured the dog. Then I got up and pulled Jackson into a hug. "But you're the best. I couldn't have done all this without you." I gave him a kiss.

"Now you have dirt on your nose," he said, smiling. He pulled a bandana from his back pocket, gently wiped the dirt off, and kissed my nose. "Okay, you're all set."

I glanced at the sky that was suddenly full of clouds, blocking out the late-afternoon sun. "What time is it?" I asked.

Jackson checked his watch. "It's almost five. Time flies when you're having fun in the garden."

I pulled off my gardening gloves. "It sure does. But we need to get ready. Tonight's the big night. I get to see you in a tux." Jackson's wardrobe usually consisted of jeans, a T-shirt, and boots, but tonight we were going to the Land and Sea Ball, the opening event of the festival, and Jackson had promised to wear a tux. He looked good in anything, but I was certain he was going to be a knock-out all dressed up.

"And I get to see you in that gown that makes you look like Cinderella." He gave me a quick kiss. "I just need to clean up over there."

He turned to start back to Nate and the open-air teahouse. But before he could take a step, Qigong, done digging, dropped something at his feet. It was a rectangular object wrapped in what looked like an old dish towel.

Jackson bent and unwrapped the towel, revealing a small cardboard box. Or at least it had been. It was nearly flattened now, the cardboard thin with age and barely holding its rectangular shape. "Hmm . . . no wording on the box," Jackson observed. He lifted what was left of its lid, and I saw a glint of metal inside. "Why would anyone bury one earring?" he muttered.

"What do you mean?" I asked.

He brushed off some dirt, then held it out to me—a delicate gold earring with an exquisite heart-shaped setting. "There's only one in here," he said. "I wonder why."

"It looks really old," I said. "It's probably an antique."

"What kind of stone is that?"

I squinted at the colorless stone in the middle. Even under the cloudy skies, it had a sparkle to it. "There's so much dirt around the edges, it's hard to be sure. But I think . . . it might be a diamond."

"We should find the other one," Jackson said. He took my spade and dug into the ground, but even with Qigong helping him, he didn't find the other earring. "Nothing here, but I could get that one appraised."

"Go for it," I said. "If it's valuable, you can use the money for your animal refuge." A year ago, after Jackson adopted two abused dachshunds, he decided to open a haven for animals at his place in East Marion, which was five minutes from Greenport. He had plenty of space, enough for a garden and room for the animals to run free. So far, he had acquired a horse, two donkeys, a goat, five dogs, six cats, two rabbits, and a turtle—and three dedicated volunteers to help him run things.

"Are you sure?" he asked. "This could really be worth something."

"You know I'm not into jewelry," I said with a shrug. "But I do like helping your refuge. So keep it."

I handed him the earring, and he dropped it into his pocket. "Thanks, McQuade. That's very nice of you."

"No problem." I began to put my tools back into the gardening basket. "I think we're in good shape for tomorrow, don't you?"

"Well, the patio isn't done yet, but I think the garden is really impressive. You're ready."

I blew out a breath. "Good, so we can just relax and have fun tonight."

"Sounds like a plan. I just have to do some cleanup with Nate."

I picked up the basket and gave him another quick kiss. Even when he was covered with dirt, Jackson was ridiculously kissable. "If you hurry, we can shower together. It's really much more environmentally friendly."

"Sounds good to me. As you know, I can be very friendly," Jackson said, smiling.

"That's what I'm counting on," I said, smiling back at him.

. . .

Nature's Way Market & Café was located on Front Street, across from Mitchell Park. The building, a three-story yellow Victorian with red trim, had outdoor seating on the porch, which was ideal when you wanted to catch the sea breeze or the morning sun. A black wrought-iron fence surrounded the property, and brightly colored flowers accented the walkway.

The interior was whimsical and charming with chalkboard specials and aisles of natural cures and natural foods. Jackson had recently put up bookshelves, and I'd packed them with volumes on everything natural from yoga to meditation to superfoods.

Next to the bookshelves was an oversized bulletin board with postcards and photos from customers who had visited Nature's Way from places as far away as Russia, Japan, India, and Australia.

The walls were painted a cheery lime green with lemon trim, so the place had a bright, sunny feel even on a cloudy day. As always, the air was redolent with the smells of healthy food, excellent coffee, and homemade baked breads and pastries.

At this late hour, there were few occupied tables and no one behind the counter where we sold sandwiches, pastas, smoothies, soups, and salads along with gluten-free chocolate brownies, carrot cake, and cupcakes. I went into the kitchen, where my genius baker and second-in-command, Merrily Scott, was taking freshly baked bread from the oven. Merrily, who was twenty-three, had the energy of the Energizer Bunny, helped along by the caffeine in our organic coffee. Cute and perky, she wore the Nature's Way uniform of jeans, a white T-shirt, and a green apron, her short blond hair in tufts with tiny colored bands. The customers loved her food and her attitude. I couldn't have asked for a better employee.

"That smells amazing," I said.

Merrily gave a little start. "Oh, you scared me. I thought I was alone."

"Just on my way through." I held up the gardening basket. "I wanted to put this inside, and then I need to shower and get ready."

"I can't wait to see you two all dressed up." She slid the loaf of bread onto the counter. "You're both going to look great."

"I know Jackson will," I said, grinning. I walked over to the checkout counter and stashed the basket on a lower shelf. "I just wish you didn't have to serve the desserts." Nature's Way had agreed to provide the desserts for the ball this year, and Merrily had outdone herself.

"Actually," she said as she came over to me, "Nate invited me to go the ball with him, so Wallace is coming to handle the service. We'll help, too, if we're needed, don't worry."

I wasn't worried at all. Wallace Byron was a pro who had owned his own health food store until he retired, but I was surprised that she and Nate had hooked up so quickly. He'd only been here for a few weeks, and he was already dating my manager. Still, he seemed like a nice guy. "Well, you'd better get ready, too."

She took off her apron and slid it into a cubbyhole under the counter. "I was just waiting for the bread to come out of the oven. I'll see you there."

· · ·

After Jackson and I took a nice, long soapy shower together with fantastic smelling organic lavender bathing gel, we got dressed. I'd chosen a little black dress. Actually, it was a classic silk and lace strapless evening gown from the 1950s that looked like something Audrey Hepburn would have had in her closet. The strapless bodice was boned and the skirt made of three layers, sheer lace, sheer silk organdy, and black taffeta.

When I looked at myself in the mirror, I couldn't help but be reminded of how much I looked like my aunt when she was younger. Both of us were tall and blond, with blue eyes, high cheekbones, and good teeth, the teeth of the tiger, my aunt used to say. I felt a pang of sorrow over how much I missed her.

"Hurry up," Jackson said, through the bathroom door. "I want to see you."

I did a final check of my hair and makeup, opened the door, and stepped into the bedroom.

"Wow," Jackson said. "Wow." He came over to me. "You do look like Cinderella, that is, if Cinderella ever wore black."

"You don't look too shabby yourself," I replied. "In fact, you look incredibly handsome. Just like James Bond." He wore a classic black shawl-collar tuxedo jacket, shirt, and pants, along with suspenders and cuff links, topped off by a spiffy black bow tie that I bought at the same vintage store where I bought my dress.

I'd even managed to find black pointy toe winklepicker oxfords in his size to complete the look. The contrast between his rugged good looks and the formal ensemble made quite an impression.

He pulled me close and I felt his warmth. The smell of his coconut aftershave was sexy. "I want to take you to bed right now," he said, his voice husky as his hand ran up my leg. "I mean, right now."

"But we'll be late," I said, laughing. "And you know that Cinderella can't be late for the ball."

chapter two

Willow McQuade's
Favorite Medicinal Plants

ASHWAGANDHA
Botanical name: *Withania somnifera*

Medicinal uses: Ashwagandha, a woody shrub from the nightshade family, builds chi, or good energy, making the body more stress resistant. In Sanskrit, the name ashwagandha means "smell of a horse," but it has the strength of one, too. That's why it's good to use if you are recovering from an illness. This herb boosts immunity, nourishes and calms the mind, promotes sleep, and improves brain function in the elderly. Use for anxiety, exhaustion, memory loss, mental fatigue, neuroses, overwork, and stress.

Okay, we were a little late. When we arrived at the Maritime Museum, the parking lot was full and the place packed. The Land and Sea Ball was *the* place to be on the East End tonight for friends of the museum and their guests.

The museum was a nineteenth-century brick building nestled at the end of the Railroad Dock, right next to the slips for the Shelter Island ferry. While the inside was impressive, filled with maritime memorabilia and photos, it wasn't all that spacious. So to handle the overflow, the organizers had added an outdoor area for the jazz band and dance floor and a second bar. Surrounded by greenery and twinkling white lights, the "deck" looked out on Shelter Island across the bay.

The local paper, the *Suffolk Times*, had written up the menu for the Land and Sea Ball that morning. The "sea" portion of the feast would be seafood dishes from local restaurants and a clam and oyster bar. The "land" would be represented by favorite dishes from local eateries. Local wines would be served from Lieb Cellars and beer from the Greenport Harbor Brewing Company. Nature's Way had contributed three organic desserts: berry parfaits with whipped cashew cream, gluten-free almond cookies, and plum-raspberry-peach crisp with vanilla ice cream and a dash of cinnamon.

"This place looks really beautiful," I said, taking Jackson's hand. "I'm glad we came."

"Me, too. Would you like a drink?" Jackson had been sober for ten years, but he didn't mind if I had one or two.

"A white wine spritzer sounds great."

He kissed me on the cheek. "Be right back."

When he headed to the bar, I took a look around the outdoor area and spotted Merrily and Nate on the dance floor. Her dress was typical Merrily, crafty and funky, made out of black denim with metal stars embossed all over it. Nate wore a black vest, black tie, and black jeans. They looked good together.

Merrily spotted me and said, "Just taking a break."

"No problem. Have fun!"

I glanced at the serving area, where Wallace was busily getting ready for the dessert course. With his silver ponytail and small Ben Franklin specs, he almost looked as if he were in historical costume. The green suede Birkenstocks, though, which you could see beneath the white tablecloth, gave him away.

I took Jackson's arm and led him over to Wallace. "How is everything going?" I asked.

Wallace pulled out parfait glasses and lined them up. "We're doing okay. I think everyone is going to love what Merrily prepared."

"I really appreciate you helping out here," I said. "Don't forget to note the extra time on your sheet."

"I will, no worries."

Mayor Hobson went to the bandstand and took the microphone. "Thanks, everyone, for turning out tonight. This event kicks off our week of festivities that will delight locals and visitors alike. Tomorrow, as you know, we start the Maritime Festival with the opening day parade and the traditional blessing of the oyster fleet at the Railroad Dock."

I felt an arm slip around my waist and turned to find Simon Lewis smiling at me. Simon was a TV producer and writer, not to mention my ex-boyfriend. He had followed me from L.A. to Greenport a year ago, failed to win me back, but fell in love with and purchased a second home here.

Last September I helped him out of a jam when he was suspected of murdering another TV producer. This had earned me his undying gratitude and cemented my place in his life, whether I liked it or not.

I pulled his hand away. "What are you doing here?"

He gave me a boyish grin. Simon wasn't conventionally handsome, but he had an undeniable, irresistible charm. He also had a steady named Carly, a producer whom I'd met last September when she was here filming on location at the Bixby estate in Southold, just a few minutes east of Greenport. Now she was in the UK, busy working on a new movie.

"I can't just sit at home, and wait until *Vision* starts up," he explained. Simon's previous show, *Fast Forward*, had been canceled, but now he had a new one about a psychic who solves cases, inspired by the star of Carly's show, who investigated the haunted mansion on the estate. In the meantime, he was trying to write a novel, without much success. He came in to the café each morning with his laptop and mostly stared at the screen. "Besides, you know I'm into maritime history, especially pirates, so I had to come. And, Willow, I need to ask you for a favor."

Someone shushed us. "Later," I said, wondering what favor Simon needed this time.

Simon, ever impatient, proceeded to text me. My phone pinged. I glared at him, plucked it out of my purse, and without looking at the message, turned it off.

"Okay," Simon said, sounding defeated. "I'll wait."

The same someone shushed us again.

"Now, as for the prizes," the mayor went on, "we've got some great gifts that have been donated by our local merchants for a raffle. All of the money that we raise each year goes to the museum's children's program along with maintaining the Maritime Museum and Bug Light lighthouse in Peconic Bay. But this year, we're doing something new, providing a twenty-five-hundred-dollar scholarship for a Greenport High School student who plans to study marine biology."

The mayor checked his notes and continued speaking, "This scholarship is thanks to the generosity of the late Frank Fox, who also donated a tract of land in the heart of Greenport to the village when he died. The competition for the space was keen, but the Village Board and I chose to give this piece of land to Willow McQuade, the owner of Nature's Way Market & Café."

There was more applause but I also heard a few dissenting voices. The decision to award me the parcel of land was not without controversy. Most of the competing applicants were here tonight, I realized as I scanned the room. But there were also quite a few friends of mine and Aunt Claire's who waved to me, smiled, or gave me a thumbs-up. It felt good to have their support.

However, Kylie Ramsey, the head of the local farmer's market, who had also applied for the lot gave me a cool look. Harold Spitz, who organized flea markets and who also wanted the space, did not return my gaze. Maggie Stone, head of Advocates for Animals, who had wanted the land for a dog park, gave me a dismissive glance and whispered something to the man to her right.

Over at the bar, I spotted Charles White, M.D., an orthopedic surgeon, who along with his investors had wanted to build a high-end boutique hotel on the lot to cater to rich out-of-towners. White was talking to his friend Joe Larson, a local builder and village trustee who had championed White's plan and openly disliked me and what he called Aunt Claire's "wacky New Age ideas."

White's wife, Arlene, a sixty-something woman who looked ten years younger, thanks to an obvious face-lift, stood next to them, looking bored. Dressed in a fancy taffeta gown, she sipped what looked like a Bloody Mary. Arlene was not one of my favorite people. She had come into Nature's Way several times to try and convince me to give the land to her husband. Basically, her point seemed to be that they were entitled to it because they had more money than I did.

All of them seemed oblivious to the fact that they were standing next to Jackson, my boyfriend, who was clearly listening to what they were saying. Just seeing them brought back the stress of those weeks when we were all petitioning the Village Board with our ideas. I might never have created the garden if I'd known how many enemies I was going to make. Jackson must have seen the tension in my face from across the room. He gave me the peace sign, and I smiled.

Martin Bennett and his wife Sandra, who ran an organic dairy in Aquebogue, thirty minutes west of Greenport, came up to me. Sandra, a petite, energetic woman in her forties, had also applied for the lot so she could put in a creamery to make and sell artisanal cheeses, using the milk from her cows and goats.

I braced myself for more conflict. "Martin, Sandra, how are you?"

Sandra smiled. "We're doing fine. We just wanted to come over and show our support."

"We noticed that the other applicants were not exactly being friendly," Martin added. He was a trim, fit man, an amateur bike racer.

"No, they aren't," I said. "They still seem to resent the garden."

"Well, we all wanted the land," Sandra admitted. "So you've got to expect that everyone else would be disappointed. But honestly, I think the garden is a great idea. I knew Claire, and she would be ecstatic about what you're doing. We can't wait to visit."

"Thanks," I said. "I really appreciate that."

"Actually, we're going to be vendors in a spot on Front Street across from your store all weekend long," Martin said. "We could do it then, hon, you know, take turns taking the tour."

"That's a good idea, love," Sandra said, taking his hand.

Jackson walked back over with an iced tea and my wine spritzer. He handed it to me, and said hello to Martin and Sandra.

When they stepped away, Simon said, "That guy has had some work done."

"What do you mean?"

"I see it all the time in L.A. Didn't you notice how tight the skin was on his face? And his nose looks like George Clooney's."

"Maybe he wanted to improve his looks." I hadn't known Martin before so I didn't have anything to compare it to.

"They went too far," Simon said, finishing his cosmopolitan. "I'm empty. Time to go to the bar."

As he walked off, I turned to Jackson. "What did Dr. White and Joe Larson say about me?"

Jackson took my arm and pulled me to a neutral spot, away from prying ears and eyes. "Don't let those two get to you, Willow. You're doing a good thing for Greenport. Claire would have been proud."

But I needed to know. "What did they say, Jackson?"

He didn't answer at first.

"Jackson?"

He put his hand on my shoulder. "Promise me that you won't get upset."

I took a breath. "I'll try to be calm. What is it?"

"White was complaining that you had gotten the lot illegally, that you had cheated, did something to tilt the vote in your direction. Larson was telling him not to worry, that they would get the land for themselves eventually."

"Cheated? That's crazy!"

"I know that. You know that. They're idiots."

"He's right, Willow," Simon said, reappearing at my side, holding a pink cosmo. "You're doing an awesome job on the garden, and I can't wait to have a cup of tea on that patio that you"—he turned to Jackson— "and that guy, what's-his-name, are building."

"Nate, his name is Nate," Jackson said. "But that's nice of you to say, Simon." Jackson tolerated my friendship with Simon because he knew I loved him, and also because he kind of liked my ex, too. After the case last fall, Jackson had softened toward Simon. They were almost friends now.

The mayor, who had left the stage briefly to confer with an aide, now took the microphone again. "As I was saying, Ms. McQuade, uh, Dr. McQuade, that is, is in the final stages of completing the teaching garden and an open-air teahouse for everyone to enjoy. We're sure that her Aunt Claire would be pleased, God rest her soul."

I had a strong suspicion that it was Aunt Claire's influence that was the tipping point in the decision to award me the land. She had been incredibly well liked and did a lot for the community, especially when it came to helping homeless animals. I had used some of the proceeds from her bestselling Fresh Face Cream to set up the garden. To give back, I pledged 10 percent of all the profits from the garden and teahouse to the local animal shelter and to Jackson's refuge. But just because Claire had helped me didn't mean that I had cheated. I had gotten the lot, fair and square.

"Tomorrow, the Claire Hagen Memorial Physic Garden will be open to the public," the mayor announced. "If you can, please join us for the opening ceremony at noon."

There was more applause, but now, some loud grumbling, too.

White pushed away from the bar and headed toward the stage, with Joe Larson trailing behind him. "Everyone needs to know that Willow McQuade got that lot from Frank Fox illegally," White announced loudly.

"He's right," Joe Larson said. "We've got people looking into it. But I think that's all we should say for now."

"What is going on?" I felt my stomach knot. "What is he talking about?"

Jackson took my hand and squeezed it. "Ignore him. We won't let him take away the garden. Don't worry."

"I'll get my lawyers on it," Simon said. "The big guns."

The knot in my stomach twisted. "I don't want to get into a nasty battle over this."

"You have to protect your interests, Willow," Simon said.

Mayor Hobson cleared his throat, and said, "Joe, Dr. White, please keep your opinions to yourself. Now I know that there are others who also aren't happy with our decision about this land, but I hope everyone in the community will support Willow in her new venture."

"That vote was fixed and we're going to prove it!" Dr. White insisted.

"That guy needs to shut up," Jackson said.

White pushed his way through the crowd and over to us. "You talking to me? You're saying that I need to shut up?"

"You heard right," Jackson said, stepping in front of me. Simon stepped forward and shielded me as well.

"Oh, it figures," White said. "You're sticking up for your little girlfriend. Did she lie to you, too?"

"Dr. White, please! Control yourself!" The mayor checked his notes again, plastered on a fake smile, and said, "Enjoy the party, everyone, and thank you!"

But Dr. White wasn't done. He leaned around

Jackson until he was just inches from my face. His hot breath smelled of beer and cigars. "Enjoy your little project, Ms. McQuade. You won't have it for long."

"Why don't you tell me what you're talking about?" I said as calmly as I could. "Because you're wrong. I did not cheat to get that land. I would never do that."

"We have lawyers looking into the way that that vote came down. We know and you know that it wasn't right. And we're going to prove it. You'll see."

"Time to go," Jackson said, grabbing his arm. "Back away from her. Now."

"Yeah," Simon added. "You don't want to take us on, buddy."

White studied Simon carefully, and I had an awful feeling that he was seeing what I saw. While Jackson, an ex-cop, could hold his own in a fight, Simon had all the physical conditioning of a hamster. "Maybe I do want to take you on," White said. With a sudden movement, he wrenched his arm from Jackson's grasp and tried to punch Simon.

But before he could make contact with Simon's face, Jackson tackled him and pinned him to the ground. "That's enough," Jackson told him. "Like I said, time to go."

Merrily and Nate ran over. "Are you okay, Willow?" Merrily asked.

"I'm okay, thanks," I said, feeling anything but.

"It's all lies," Dr. White yelled. "And we're going to prove it!"

Jackson got him to his feet and pushed White toward the exit. "Let's go. You need to get out of here before you do something really stupid."

"Let me give him a good punch before he goes," Simon said. "I owe him one."

"Forget it," Jackson said, turning to look at Simon. "No way."

While Jackson was distracted, White seized the moment and pulled free. Jackson and Simon ran after him. This time, though, Dr. White lost his footing, and we watched as he tumbled over the low shrubs that edged the outdoor area and landed with a splash in the bay. A few people clapped. After a few moments, White sputtered to the surface, spewing expletives.

"Now, that's what I call a party," Simon said, smiling.

chapter three

Willow McQuade's
Favorite Medicinal Plants

<u>ASTRAGALUS</u>
Botanical name: *Astragalus membranaceus,
Astragalus mongholicus*

Medicinal uses: A pretty plant with pastel flowers, this important herb is often used in traditional Chinese medicine to support and enhance better immune function. In fact, in Chinese this herb is known as *huang qi* or "yellow leader," which refers to the root color and it's go-to status as a healing tonic. Astragulus is commonly used to prevent and treat common colds and upper respiratory infections. The root of the astragalus plant is typically used in soups, teas, extracts, or capsules. Astragalus is generally used with other herbs, such as ginseng, angelica, and licorice.

Jackson and I woke up early the next morning, surrounded by our menagerie, my dog, Qigong, Claire's kitties, Ginger and Ginkgo, both tabbies, and Jackson's long-haired doxies, Rockford and Columbo. After we'd played with them and scratched them all behind the ears, we showered, got dressed, and headed downstairs.

When I stepped outside, I could feel the buzz in the air from all the Maritime Festival activities. On Front Street, vendors on both sides were getting wares ready to sell, artists competing in the Nautical Art Show were setting up in Mitchell Park, and the marina was full of sailboats, motorboats, and yachts. Soon the blessing of the oyster fleet would take place at the end of the Railroad Dock across the inlet. The sky was a crystal iris blue without a cloud in sight, the temperature, a balmy seventy-two degrees.

It was so nice out that we decided to eat alfresco on the porch. We had a breakfast of Merrily's French toast along with fresh strawberries and coffee while we reviewed what still needed to be done that morning.

"You got the tables and chairs right?" I asked Jackson. We were borrowing them from his neighbor.

"In my truck," he said, sipping his coffee. "I'll set them up after we eat."

The Nature's Way booth would be right in front of the store, which would make things easier for us. "Thanks," I said. "I've got some great stuff to put out."

Jackson nodded. "You do. It's a smart idea to sell some of the plants that you have featured in the garden."

"I already texted Nate to remind him to pick up the

medicinal plants from Ollie's Organic Greenhouse on the way in. He'll get seeds, too. Hopefully, after people take the tour, they'll want to take plants and seeds home and start their own gardens. I'm going to offer paperback copies of Aunt Claire's organic gardening books, too." My aunt had been a prolific writer and author, and her gardening book *Gardening, Naturally* had been a national best seller.

"Did the other stuff come in?" Jackson popped a strawberry into his mouth. The dogs sat at our feet waiting for small bites of French toast. He slipped them each a snack.

"The gardening aprons, hats, tool belts, and plant stakes with the Nature's Way logo came in yesterday." I'd recently had the logo designed and was pleased with the result, which was the name, and an illustration of the store with the garden next door.

"If the clothes sell, you might want to think about carrying other items."

"I don't think I have room, although I'd love to carry Life Is Good, Good Karma T-shirts."

"You just need a rack to display them," Jackson said. "I'll build you one if you want."

"You are the best boyfriend," I said, and leaned over to kiss him.

As I did, Simon walked up the steps. "Ah, the love-birds." He took the seat next to me and squeezed my hand. "I need to talk to you, Willow."

I suddenly remembered the text I'd ignored the night before.

"I can help you and me," Simon began.

"What is it?" I asked suspiciously. I finished up my

French toast, giving another treat to the dogs. "You said, you could help you *and* me?"

"Exactly."

"This should be good," Jackson said, sitting back. Simon was a friend, but he was not known for his altruism.

"Okay, you know I have writer's block, right?"

"Yeah, I sort of guessed." I had noticed that Simon spent more time looking at his laptop screen than typing when he came in for breakfast.

Simon flashed me his very white Hollywood smile. "I came up with the perfect solution."

"Really? Do I have a problem?"

"The summer season is upon us and you need more help in the store and the café. I need to do something menial to free up my mind so I can get creative. You know, like Albert Einstein when he worked in the patent office and discovered relativity?"

I knew where this was going. "You want to work here?"

"Yeah, you know, being a waiter and stuff, something brainless to rest my mind. Two birds with one stone. Am I a genius or what?" Simon looked exceptionally pleased with his solution.

"That's great, Simon," Jackson said, knowing what I was in for. Simon could be helpful. He could also be selfish, self-absorbed, and unavailable. "It's also really nice that you think that Willow's work here is menial."

Simon clapped Jackson on the shoulder. "That's not what I mean, big guy. She's the boss. I mean the people who work for her." He turned to me, giving me a puppy dog look. "So, what do you say, Willow? I can start right now."

He was dressed in khakis and a white Izod shirt. He'd just have to put on a green apron. But could he be a waiter?

"Wait a minute, Simon," I said. "Have you ever done this type of work before?"

"In college, sure, for a month or so, until . . ." He paused and looked at us.

"You got fired," Jackson guessed.

"I'm a writer, I can't do work like this forever. But a week or so might help my creative process."

I did need the help, especially during festival week. I looked at Jackson, who gave the idea a thumbs-down. But Simon was a friend and really, how much trouble could he get into? So I said, "We'll do a trial period and see how you do. How's that sound?"

"Put me to work, boss," Simon said, grinning.

The first thing we needed to do to get our booth ready for the festival was to bring out the tables and chairs. While Jackson and Simon went inside, I decided where to set up everything. Minutes later, Jackson came out by himself, with a folding table under each arm.

I knew what he was going to say before he said it. "Are you crazy, letting him work here?"

"I have to give him a chance," I explained as we set up the first table. "I don't know if it will really help his writing or not, but Simon is a friend. Besides, I could use the help."

"You just hit on the million-dollar question," Jackson said. "Do you think Simon is actually capable of helping anyone besides himself?"

"He's got potential," I said carefully.

Jackson started setting up the second table, adjacent to the first one. "Willow, you need to think about what's best for you and your business. Simon's just going to get in the way. He's already going on about how working here is going to free up his mind and make him really Zen. He said he could already feel it already 'altering the vibration of his brain waves.' Talk about New Age blather . . ."

I shrugged, unsurprised. "So when he's unblocked, he'll leave. Hopefully, it won't take long." I spotted the Nature's Way van take a left at the light, which meant that Nate would arrive at any minute. "I see Nate, good timing."

"Don't change the subject. And if you have any illusions about Simon being a hard worker, he's only carrying one chair at a time." Jackson motioned to Simon, who was making his way down the stairs, a folding chair in one hand, a muffin in the other.

Simon put down the chair and took a bite of the blueberry muffin. "Merrily is an amazing baker. She even let me taste a sample of the peach pie that she's making for the contest in Mitchell Park this afternoon. Delicious!"

"Yes, she's very talented," I said. "Can you please get the other chair?"

It was already eight forty-five and the parade would start at eleven, which meant people would be congregating in front of the store soon.

"In a minute. I want to finish my muffin." Simon took another bite. "You know what? Coffee would go great with this. Want anything?" he asked as he headed back down the walkway.

"No, we're okay, but come back soon."

Simon, oblivious, waved and took another bite.

"Oh, yeah, he's going to work out just fine," Jackson said sarcastically, his eyes still on Simon. "Please tell me you're not paying him for this."

"Jackson, just accept him the way he is. Be Zen."

"No one is that Zen," Jackson informed me. "Not even you." He shook his head. "I'm going to check out the garden one more time." As he spoke, Nate parked the van, then took a flat of medicinal plants from the back.

"I'll meet you there after Nate and I set up," I told Jackson. "We need to put up the ribbon." I'd bought bright yellow ribbon from the hobby store and a new pair of oversize scissors to cut it with. "After that, I want to watch the parade at eleven."

"Sounds good," Jackson said, giving me a kiss.

So while Nate and I set out the plants, seeds, and merchandise, Jackson looked over the garden and Simon had coffee.

After we set up the tables, I got the ribbon and scissors from my office and went over to the entrance of the garden. I could see the procession for the parade lining up on First Street by the ferry and the Maritime Museum. The local high school band, horses, ponies, and rescues from the local animal shelter who always marched in the parade were already in place. Behind them, I glimpsed giant floats and after them, the first of the classic cars pulling into place.

I noticed Sandra and Martin's booth near the movie theater. I hoped that they would take a tour of the garden later. Other vendors, closer to Nature's Way, were selling everything from T-shirts to nautical crafts to hot dogs and lemonade.

Jackson walked over to me, brushing dirt from his jeans.

"Everything okay in the garden?" I asked, wanting things to be perfect. "Should I take a walk-through?"

"No need," he said. "I just had to replace a plant that some critter ate. But don't worry. Now it all looks great. We're ready."

Visitors crowded the sidewalk as the parade made its way down Front Street to Main Street. Kids shouted with delight as tractors pulling carts drove past with those onboard throwing candy to the crowd.

"Don't you just love mermaids?" Simon asked, as a colorful float with six mermaids rolled past.

"I guess so," I said. "I never really thought about it."

But I couldn't help being charmed by the parade. The local high school band had never sounded better, and even the dogs looked like they were having fun, wagging their tails, barking at their owners' sides. Everyone was having a good time.

"Looks like our old friend is here," Jackson said to me. He nodded toward a man in the crowd, standing beside his young wife and toddler son.

"Oh, great. My favorite person." It was Detective

Koren, my nemesis in all things murder. Even though I solved my Aunt Claire's murder and the mystery of who had killed a Hollywood producer last fall, he still resented my amateur sleuthing skills and my success rate. As always, he was dressed impeccably, but today he went for the casual look, khaki shorts and a polo shirt. Just to bug him, I threw him a wave. He pretended not to see me.

I turned my attention to the next float, which featured a plywood pirate ship, with a skull-and-crossbones flag and several menacing-looking pirates. They circled the ship and growled at the crowd as they sang "A Pirate's Life for Me."

Next up were antique cars of every size, shape, and color. Riding in the cars were the mayor and the Village Board, but I didn't see Joe Larson, who had championed White. I hoped this meant that he wouldn't be at the ribbon-cutting ceremony for the garden.

The parade ended at noon, and soon after that we all gathered in front of the garden gate. Merrily closed the store temporarily and came out, along with Hector and Allie, my in-house acupuncturist and masseuse, who took a break from their appointments to attend. Aunt Claire's boyfriend, Nick, our beloved yoga teacher, was there as well. Nick had encouraged me to fight for my garden project and ignore the naysayers. He'd become a good friend, especially now that Claire was gone.

It seemed everyone who had worked with and loved my aunt—from her pet-rescue efforts to her Scrabble club—turned out, and so did others who shopped at Nature's Way and considered her a friend. I knew she would have been very touched.

On the left side of the trellised garden gate, there was

a brass plaque that read: Claire Hagen Memorial Physic Garden: Forever in Our Hearts. Peace, Light, Love and Blessings to All Who Enter Here. The mayor and the trustees, except for Joe Larson, stood to the right.

"Thank you all so much for taking time out of your busy Maritime Festival weekend to remember a truly wonderful citizen of our beloved village," Mayor Hobson began. "Claire Hagen always had a kind word for everyone and never said no to a request for help, be it for people or our four-legged friends. So it is my great honor to introduce her niece, Willow McQuade, who is carrying on her work at Nature's Way and in the community."

The crowd clapped, and this time there were no dissenting voices.

I stepped toward the gate. "Thank you, Mr. Mayor. Thank you, everyone. I am very touched and moved by your show of support today. I know that it would have made Claire deeply happy. What would make her even happier is the fact that you'll learn so much by visiting this garden and hopefully take this knowledge and put it to use in your own lives.

"This garden is modeled after the Chelsea Physic Garden in London, which both my aunt and I visited. The Chelsea Garden was founded in 1673 by the Worshipful Society of Apothecaries so that their apprentices could study the medicinal qualities of plants. Today it is one of the most important centers of botany and plant exchange in the world. With the help of my team, especially Jackson Spade and Nate Marshall, I've modeled this garden on their vision. I hope you enjoy it!"

Jackson handed me the scissors, and I cut the ribbon as a photographer from the local paper snapped a shot. "I now proclaim the Claire Hagen Memorial Physic Garden open!"

The crowd cheered and Jackson pulled me into a hug. "Congratulations, Willow. You did it!"

"*We* did it," I said, taking his hand, feeling happy and proud. "Now everyone, let's take the tour of Greenport's new garden of medicinal plants!"

I walked under the arch and entered the garden, the crowd trailing behind me. The lot was generous, a little over two acres, and I'd designed it in a grid pattern and packed it with plants. There were two main pathways, one on the left and one on the right, with the entrance on Front Street and the teahouse at the north end. The entire garden was surrounded by a six-foot fence. It felt safe and secluded, an oasis from daily life.

"Here you'll find a wide array of plants that contain proven therapeutic compounds," I explained. "The beds are arranged according to area of treatment, from dermatology to cardiology."

I pointed to the first section on the left. "These plants produce compounds that have anesthetic or pain-relieving properties." I touch a long-stemmed herb with small, creamy-white flowers that bloomed from June to August. "For example, this is *Filipendual ulmaria*, or meadowsweet, which contains small quantities of salicylic acid, the active ingredient that is used in aspirin."

The crowd moved in and inspected the plants and the plaques in front of them, each with information about the Latin name, where the plant originated, and its properties.

Next, I moved on to the plant collection with anticancer properties, like *Catharanthus roseus*, or Madagascar periwinkle, which contains alkaloids used in anticancer drugs. I continued with my tour, introducing medicinal plants that had benefits for the skin, including aloe, which was for sale at our booth, as well as plants for lung disease, neurology and rheumatology, psychiatry, ophthalmology, and gastroenterology.

I headed to a sunny area of the garden next. When everyone gathered around, I said, "Here, we've planted a cardiology garden. I gestured to a tall plant with purplish flowers. "This is one of most well-known cardiac herbs. *Digitalis lanata*, or wooly foxglove, contains a cardiac glycoside known as digoxin that is extracted directly from the leaves and is used to control and prevent abnormal heart rhythms and strengthen the heartbeat."

I turned back to look at the plant and noticed that there was something on the ground behind it. I asked the crowd to wait a moment and stepped around the plant bed. It looked like a piece of pink cotton cloth, but when I knelt down and tried to pick it up, I found that it was attached to an arm. I started to scream.

The arm belonged to Dr. Charles White. Burgundy-red blood dribbled from a gash in his forehead down into his sightless blue eyes. His rimless glasses lay next to him, broken and twisted. The not-so-good doctor was very, very dead.

chapter four

Willow McQuade's Favorite Medicinal Plants

<u>BILBERRY</u>
Botanical name: *Vaccinium myrtillus*

Medicinal uses: Bilberry, a close cousin to the blueberry, is a tasty plant with bright blue berries and verdant green shrubbery, used in jams, pies, and wines. But this antioxidant powerhouse also has many medicinal and healing purposes. Since the Middle Ages, it has been used to treat diarrhea, scurvy, and other conditions. Today, the fruit is also used to treat menstrual cramps, eye problems, varicose veins, venous insufficiency (poor blood flow to the heart), and other circulatory problems. The fruit and leaves of the bilberry plant can be eaten or made into extracts or used to make teas.

It was a good thing that we were in the cardiac section of the garden, because my heart felt like it had just stopped. I looked at the body again, hoping it was just a bad dream. No such luck. "It's Dr. White. He's dead," I said, feeling light-headed. I stumbled backward, wanting to get away. But the crowd moved closer, anxious to see what was going on. A low murmur of whispers filled the air.

Jackson ran up to me, and I leaned on him as I pointed to the body. "You were just here," I said, trembling. It suddenly seemed cold. Had we really eaten breakfast outside on the porch this morning? "How . . . how did this happen?"

He pulled me into a protective hug. "I don't know. But obviously someone killed him, and it happened after I left, in the past hour or so. We'd better call Koren."

I tried to think clearly. "I just saw Koren at the parade."

Jackson pulled out his phone and quickly texted the detective. Within minutes, Detective Koren was pushing through the crowd, holding his badge high, a crime-scene tech behind him.

"Police, coming through. Move aside, people, please!" He spotted us and walked over. "Don't tell me that you've found another dead body, Ms. McQuade." He drilled me with a look.

I felt like crying and pressed my head into Jackson's chest.

"See for yourself, Koren," Jackson said.

Koren squatted next to the body and took a pulse. "He's dead, all right." His eyes scanned the body.

"Looks like he was whacked over the head. That's a nasty-looking wound." He stood up and gazed around the area. "It could have been made with something like that." He pointed to the shovel that leaned against the fence. "What exactly happened here?"

"I don't know," I said. "Whoever did this must have done it during the parade, after Jackson left the garden."

"What do you mean? Give me a timeline, please."

But before I could answer, Simon pushed through the crowd and came over to us. "What's going on? Are they hassling you again, Willow?"

"Stay out of this, Lewis," Detective Koren said. He had placed Simon under arrest last fall for the murder of a Hollywood producer. I had cleared Simon, but it didn't mean that Koren liked him. "You want to get yourself back in it again?"

"I just don't want Willow to say anything she shouldn't." This was ironic, as Jackson and I had counseled him to do the same last year. Simon pulled me to the side. "I'll call my lawyer. He'll take care of this. I owe you one, Willow."

"Thanks. I think I'm okay but I'll let you know." I composed myself and turned to Koren. "To answer your question, Detective, I was working on setting up our booth until the parade started."

"Yeah, she was with me," Simon said. "I'll vouch for her."

"Thank you, Mr. Lewis," Koren said, and scribbled something down in his notebook. "And you, Spade? Where were you?"

"I was in the garden, checking things out, making

sure everything was ready for the opening," Jackson said. "I spotted a plant that needed replacing, put in a new one, then went out to meet Willow to watch the parade. Whoever did this killed White between eleven, when I left the garden, and now."

The detective pointed to the shovel. "You used this to replace the plant?"

Jackson nodded. "Yes, and that's all. Don't get any wild ideas in your head, Koren."

"That's Detective Koren to you, Mr. Spade, and I heard about your fight with Dr. White last night." Koren put on a plastic glove, stepped over to the fence, and picked up the shovel. "Sure you weren't getting back at him for harassing your girlfriend?"

"Of course not. White was making a scene, and Willow was upset. But if you think I would kill a man because he was being a jerk, you're crazy."

Koren turned to the crime-scene tech. "Make sure you get this shovel." He pulled out his phone and texted someone, probably his partner, Detective Coyle. While he did, I puzzled over the murder scene. How had this happened? Why was Dr. White here, of all places? Had he intended to cause trouble during the dedication and something had happened?

Koren finished texting and turned back to Jackson. "Men do strange things in the name of love, Mr. Spade. Are you sure you don't have anything else to say?"

"Jackson, you don't have to answer his questions," Simon said. "Let me call my lawyer."

"Back off, Lewis. I'm not going to say it again," Koren warned him. "And I'm not going to hurt your ex-girlfriend's boyfriend. There's no need to call your big-shot lawyer."

"He's just trying to help," Willow said.

"Exactly," Simon said. "Willow can help, too, Jackson. Look what she did for me. She's a great amateur detective. She's solved two murders already."

It was ironic, but when we were living together in L.A. and I was working at a holistic clinic, Simon had been unsupportive and uninterested in my work. He began to look at me differently after I solved Aunt Claire's murder and later cleared him of murder charges.

"Hell, she's probably got a better track record than you do," Simon said to Koren.

The detective went up to Simon and poked him in the chest. "I told you to back off. Stop interfering with my investigation."

Mayor Hobson pushed through the crowd and went over to Detective Koren. "What's going on here? What's happened to the tour? I just stepped away to take a quick phone call. Has something happened?"

Koren turned to him and lowered his voice. "Yes, it seems that Dr. White has met an untimely demise in Ms. McQuade's garden."

"What?" The mayor's cheeks became flushed. "This can't be happening, not now, not this weekend, not when we've worked so hard to make it a success. This is going to ruin everything!"

"So you were close to the deceased?" Detective Koren said. "You seem really choked up about it."

The mayor turned on him. "Of course I'm not

happy that the man is dead, but this is the Maritime Festival, Detective! Something like, this, well, it's just a disaster."

Detective Coyle, also dressed in casual weekend clothes, came toward us with Joe Larson, my favorite—not—trustee behind him. Koren pulled Coyle to the side, while Larson zeroed in on the mayor. "Sorry I'm late. Did I miss anything?" He gave a short bark of a laugh. "Of course I didn't. This whole thing is a joke."

"Shut up, Joe," the mayor said. "White's dead."

"What are you talking about? Charles is *dead*?"

"Yes," Detective Koren said. "He's dead, Mr. Larson, please step back."

Koren said something to Coyle. After which, Coyle said, "Okay, everybody, I want you all to back up and head for the entrance in an orderly line but do not leave. We'll need to talk to all of you."

The crowd groaned but did as he asked. So much for my garden tour.

"This is all her fault," Larson said, pointing at me.

"How do you figure that, Mr. Larson?" Detective Koren asked.

"It's exactly what Dr. White said last night. Ms. McQuade got this land illegally, and now this tragedy is going to shine a very unfavorable light on Greenport during the festival."

"That is a blatant lie," I retorted.

"That's enough, Joe," the mayor said. "Leave it alone. Let the police do their work."

"I'll need to talk to you, Mr. Larson, and the rest of you," Koren said. "This garden is officially closed for the rest of the weekend."

"You can't do that," I said. "It will ruin everything. We have tours scheduled."

Tom Coster, a town trustee, a prominent local attorney, and a loyal customer of Claire's, who had advocated giving the land to me, said, "This seems capricious, Detective. This will ruin the opening weekend for the garden. Ms. McQuade and her friends have worked very hard to be ready for the festival. Surely you can work through the night and let her have the garden back in the morning, can't you? We're a tight-knit community here. Let's work together."

"You're just saying that because you liked her aunt," Larson replied, giving him a disgusted look. "Hell, that's why she got the lot in the first place. No one bothered to look further."

"Joe, I told you to leave it and I mean it," Mayor Hobson said, and pulled Detective Koren aside.

They spoke for a few minutes and then Detective Koren said, "Mayor Hobson and Mr. Coster are your new best friends Ms. McQuade. The garden will be closed but only until tomorrow morning. You can begin your tours again then."

The police staked out the garden, gathered evidence, and began to question everyone who had been in the garden for the opening. After they'd finished talking to Jackson, Simon, and me, we headed back to the store, first stopping to check the booth out front. Wallace and Nate were busy with customers, and I noticed that half of the medicinal plants and some of the merchandise was already gone.

Wallace finished chatting with a customer, handed her a bag, smiled, and wished her a good day. I tapped him on the shoulder. "How is it going?"

He turned to me and said, "How are you doing? One of the people on the garden tour told me what happened! Is it true? Are you okay?"

"It's true and we're okay," I said. "I'll tell you all about it later. Have you been busy? It looks like you've sold a bunch of stuff."

"We have," he replied as new customers made their way to the booth. "I don't think most people know what went on in the garden. In fact, we need more plants from out back."

"I'll get a pallet." Jackson grabbed the wagon and headed out back. Simon remained with me, which wasn't a surprise as he didn't enjoy manual labor of any kind. I wondered how long his stint at Nature's Way would last.

"I can go back to Ollie's later if we run out," Nate offered. With his friendly personality and Peter Parker good looks, customers loved him almost as much as Wallace. "I'll need to get some for tomorrow, regardless." He handed a healthy-looking aloe plant to a customer.

"Sounds good," I said. Perhaps there was hope for my medicinal garden after all. "Thanks, guys. I'll check on you later."

I looked at my watch and realized that it was already 1:25 p.m. I turned to Simon. "You and I are due at the Maritime Art and Photography exhibit in Mitchell Park at two. We'd better get something to eat and go." Simon and I had both been asked to be judges for the show, after which all the items would be auctioned off.

"Wait a minute," Simon said as we climbed the stairs to the store. "Aren't you going to do something? You know, investigate, like you usually do?"

Investigating this murder would be an absolutely crazy thing to take on, given that it was Maritime Festival week and that I was trying to get my new garden project off the ground, so to speak. But I had to admit that part of me was interested in solving another puzzle. I was good at it. As Simon had said, I'd solved two murders, both before the police. Still, I couldn't imagine immersing myself in an investigation with everything else I had going on.

Then again, if the cops went after Jackson, because of the argument he'd had with White, I would have no choice. I would have to act.

I put the key into the lock and opened the door to Nature's Way. For a moment, I couldn't remember why the store was closed but then I realized that Merrily was competing in the pie contest, also in Mitchell Park, until two o'clock. This wasn't a problem since all of the action was outside today. "I'm not sure what I'm going to do," I told Simon. "Right now, I'm hungry and I need to eat. How about you?"

"I could eat."

I smiled. "You can always eat." I went into the kitchen and proceeded to make lunch for the three of us. While I worked, Simon leaned across the kitchen counter and kept talking. "I mean, someone was killed in your garden and Detective Koren did seem interested in Jackson. It also doesn't make the garden or Nature's Way look so good. You need to solve this thing, and quick. I know you can do it."

"Thanks, Simon. I appreciate your confidence in my abilities," I said as I placed the organic cheese quesadillas topped with sour cream and guacamole, blue corn chips, a bowl of salsa, and three glasses of passion fruit iced tea on a tray. "But I need to talk to Jackson first."

"Talk to me about what?" Jackson walked into the kitchen.

"About investigating this case," Simon said.

I handed the tray to Jackson. "I haven't decided anything yet."

"Why don't we eat by the window?" Jackson carried the tray to the table near the plateglass window at the front of the store so we could see outside. Our booth out front was still drawing plenty of customers. After we sat down, he said, "How are you doing, McQuade?"

"Not so great," I admitted. "We all worked really hard to make the garden perfect for the opening and then this happens. And even though I never liked Dr. White, I feel bad for his family." I gave a shudder. "I have a feeling that I'm going to have nightmares about finding him like that."

Jackson nodded. "It's not the kind of sight you get used to."

Simon gave an impatient sigh. "Obviously you didn't want to find a dead body in your garden, but now that you have, what are you doing to do about it?

chapter five

Willow McQuade's
Favorite Medicinal Plants

BLACK COHOSH
Botanical name: *Actaea racemosa, Cimicifuga racemosa*

Medicinal uses: Native Americans were among the first to use black cohosh as a woman's tonic, while other tribes used it for fatigue, aching joints, and better kidney function. Historically, black cohosh has been used for rheumatism (arthritis and muscle pain), but has been used more recently to treat hot flashes, night sweats, and other symptoms that can occur during menopause. Black cohosh can also be used for menstrual irregularities and premenstrual syndrome. The underground stems and roots of black cohosh are commonly used fresh or dried to make strong teas (infusions), capsules, solid extracts used in pills, or liquid extracts (tinctures).

Jackson responded to Simon's question by drilling him with a look, and saying, "Willow isn't getting involved. The police can handle this."

"So you don't want her investigating?"

Jackson shook his head. "Of course not. Someone obviously wanted White dead, and we don't know that he, or she, is done killing."

"Agreed," I said, and took a bite of my quesadilla. "What bothers me is that Koren is obviously interested in you."

"And he doesn't like you for some reason, Willow," Simon added opening up two raw sugar packets and putting them into his tea. "It's probably because you're better at his job than he is."

"There is that," Jackson said. "He doesn't like me much either, and it's not good that I handled the shovel when I was replacing that plant or that I had that very public fight with White last night. Koren doesn't need much to go on, you know that."

"I have to do something," I said, picking up a blue corn chip. "It will be twenty-four to forty-eight hours until the autopsy results come in. We need to get ahead of this thing and fix it before it becomes a bigger problem for us and the store and garden. If we work together we can figure this out."

"Together?" Jackson raised an eyebrow. "You mean, the three of us? You have to be kidding."

"We did it before," I said. "Remember?" Last year when Simon was under suspicion for murder he had been surprisingly helpful with knowledge and ideas. While Jackson was my true partner, a little extra help couldn't hurt. "We can begin with the art and photography show this afternoon. I'll scope things out and maybe start asking questions. Simon can help. He has to be there anyway. You can come with us or stay here and scope out the scene."

"You want to work together?" Jackson repeated, not looking happy.

"Yeah, man, like the Three Amigos!" Simon said, putting his hand up for a high five. "Or the Three Musketeers!"

"Or the Three Stooges?" Jackson rolled his eyes. "I've got a bad feeling about this, McQuade."

After we finished lunch, Simon and I headed across the street to Mitchell Park to judge the art and photography show, while Jackson stayed behind to keep an eye on the police and what they were doing. The park was crowded with people enjoying the show, walking their dogs, relaxing on the grass, and riding the merry-go-round.

The park overlooked the harbor with a view of Shelter Island across the bay. The docks were packed with speedboats, yachts, and even a bright red tugboat. Over at the Railroad Dock, where the Shelter Island ferry picked up cars and passengers, visiting tall ships were moored. It was picture perfect. It made sense that *Forbes* magazine had declared Greenport "One of America's Prettiest Towns."

As we walked into the park, Merrily was on her way out, happily carrying the winner's trophy, a bronze apple pie on a bronze apple tree. It was almost as big as she was.

"Congratulations, Merrily!" I said. "You won! That's fantastic!"

"No surprise there," Simon said. "Your pie is the best."

She smiled. "Thanks, guys, but it was actually quite close. I thought the dessert chef from the North Fork Table was going to win with their rhubarb pie, but then they awarded me the trophy. It's going to look great on that shelf in the kitchen, if it fits."

"Good for you. I can't wait to taste your pie; that is, if there's any left."

Merrily smiled. "There's plenty. You know me, I made five pies and entered the best one." Her expression grew serious. "I heard about you finding White's body. What's going on with the police?"

"Still investigating, but the mayor convinced Detective Koren to let us open again in the morning."

"That's something, at least." She looked across the street at Nature's Way. "Well, I'd better go back. We might get some folks in for a late lunch. I'll see you later."

We said good-bye and headed down the path past the Little Miss Mermaid Contest being held in front of the carousel, where young girls dressed up in mermaid costumes were competing for DVDs of the movie. In the center of the park, beyond the fountains, was a colorful mixture of nautical photographs and paintings that Simon and I were here to judge.

I spotted Patty Thaw, the owner of Patty's Photo Shop, and the organizer of the event, at a table near the carousel. I went over to her to get our judging sheets. For the moment, I decided to put Dr. White's murder out of my mind and focus on the task at hand.

"Hi, Patty, we're here, ready to judge away."

Though Patty was in her late sixties, she was a

regular at Nick's yoga classes, and had a calm demeanor, not to mention a lean, toned look. She gave me a kiss on the cheek. "I didn't expect to see you here, Willow. I heard about what happened—Dr. White, dead in your garden! That's not the headline you wanted for opening day. How absolutely awful!"

I wasn't surprised that she knew. Good and bad traveled fast via the village grapevine. Someone who had attended the dedication must have told her what happened. "Yes, it was awful," I admitted. "I still can't believe it."

"But we made the commitment to help with the art show," Simon put in. "So we're here."

"Okay, then, I'm glad you are." She pulled two clipboards out of her green tote, grabbed two pens, and handed them to us. She pointed to the paper on the clipboard. "You just need to go around, check out each piece, and rate it on a scale of one to ten, based on originality, creativity, and execution. Afterward we'll auction them off to raise money for the North Fork Animal Welfare League, so we need to get the judging done by four at the latest. Harold Spitz and Maggie Stone are already making the rounds."

Harold and Maggie were two others who had competed for the lot. Harold had wanted it for his flea market and Maggie, the head of Advocates for Animals, had wanted it for a new dog park. I'd seen them both the night before at the ball, and they weren't exactly friendly. I explained to Simon who they were.

He gave one of his dramatic sighs. "And I thought we were going to have some fun."

"It's okay," I said. "Just be cool, no fighting."

"Something wrong?" Patty asked us.

"No, we're fine. Where should we start?"

Patty pointed to the artists and photographers set up near the fence that separated the park from Aldo's Café. "Why don't you begin over there? You can work your way around the green."

"Will do," I said, and we headed in that direction. "I hope Harold and Maggie aren't over there," I said to Simon.

"I thought you were going to investigate," he replied. "Maybe they know something."

"You might be right," I admitted. "Both of them knew Dr. White and wanted the land as much as he did. Talking to them might be a good idea."

"See, I'm being helpful already."

Simon needed constant reassurance and praise to be productive, so I said, "Right. Thanks, Simon."

We made our way down the first row of booths. Every artist had three "walls" of plywood with mesh on top to display their work. Unfortunately, most of them had painted or photographed local boats, lighthouses, beaches, and fish, but without much imagination or sophistication. I gave most of the entries fours or fives.

"This stuff is awful," Simon said, writing down his scores. "I'm giving them all a two, and that's being generous." One of the artists turned to give him a sour look.

"Shhh," I said. "We have to be diplomatic." I pointed to the row of artists whose booths were set up next to the water. "Let's head over there next." It was becoming hotter, and I wanted to cool off with the sea breeze. I noticed that Joe Larson seemed very interested in a painting in the last booth on the right, so we started at the opposite end.

When we came out of the first booth, I saw several pirate ships heading into the harbor. "Look they're going to do their pirate show." I pointed out the ships to Simon.

"What kind of show is it?"

"They do live reenactments with sword fights. They're even doing a treasure hunt for the kids."

"What a kick! Let's check it out. It might inspire me. I'm thinking of writing and producing a movie about pirates. Kind of like *Pirates of the Caribbean*, but more of a historical piece, with a real pirate like Captain Kidd."

"Chill, Johnny Depp." I tapped my pen on the clipboard. "We need to do our judging."

"Just a few minutes, okay?"

I said yes, because I really wanted to see it, too. We went over to the dock by Claudio's where they were landing. The place was packed. Pirates dressed in colorful garb docked the boats and then reenacted a fight, complete with swordplay and men overboard.

Meanwhile, the Thieves Market in the parking lot was doing a brisk business selling everything from pirate T-shirts to hats and plastic cutlasses.

My phone pinged and I looked at the text I'd received. It was from Jackson:

K & C still in garden. Nothing else new here. XO J.

I put the phone away and we continued watching the pirate show.

The fight now over, they descended onto the docks

and began mingling with the crowd and giving away "pirate's booty"—aka candy—to the kids.

I nudged Simon, "We'd better get back. Patty might be looking for us."

We headed back to the park, where I immediately noticed that Joe Larson was still planted in front of the same painting.

"Joe Larson is here," I told Simon. "He's been looking at that painting for the past twenty minutes."

"Good," Simon said. "I have a few things I want to say to him."

I grabbed his arm. "No, let's keep our distance." I pointed to the booth farthest from Joe. "Let's go back over there. We need to stay focused."

While we continued judging, I kept an eye on Joe Larson. He was still studying the painting, but when we were a few feet away, he spotted us, gave me an annoyed look, and moved off.

I couldn't wait to see the painting that Larson had been so interested in. But when I finally stepped in front of it, I couldn't figure out why Joe had been so riveted. The painting was unremarkable. The subject matter was a modest shop in a two-story green building. I recognized it at once. It was a store on Main Street, in Greenport, that sold cigars. Rumor had it that an apartment on the second floor was used as a men's club. The building was sandwiched between a cupcake store and a tea shop, and located a block from Claudio's restaurant, at the foot of Main Street overlooking Greenport Harbor.

The painting Joe was so fascinated by wasn't particularly good or interesting. But there had to be some reason for his interest. I pulled my phone out of my purse and whispered to Simon, "Cover me."

He looked at the painting. "You found a clue already? Great! What do you want me to do?"

"Just stand in front of me so no one can see, especially Joe Larson."

Simon stepped around me and played lookout. "Okay, go for it."

I took a few quick photos with my phone, sent them to Jackson, and slipped the phone back into my pocket just as the artist, a large burly guy with a beard, finished his conversation with a customer and came out of the booth. "You like that one, huh?" He pointed to the painting of the cigar store.

"Yes, it's . . . nice," I said. "Does it have some personal significance for you?"

"Nah, I just like cigars. I've been going to that place forever. Actually, I painted it on commission for the owner, but after I finished, he said he didn't want it."

I couldn't blame him. It was pretty dull for handmade art. Why was Joe Larson so fascinated by it? I thanked the artist, gave him a score of six, which was generous, and moved on to the next set of booths. On the way, Jackson texted me back:

Got pix, what is JL up to? K & C still here. J.

We spent the next hour judging the rest of the entries in the competition. Once we got into the groove, it became easier and, thankfully, the work got better. The photographers that I enjoyed the most captured the essence of the town and the area, like the one who had created a set of images of the wetlands near Jackson's house in East Marion, or the one who focused on close-ups of local flora and fauna in the nature preserve.

I pointed to a photograph of a single conch shell lying on the beach, the sun setting on the water beyond. "I like this one. It's simple but it works."

"I like the local landmarks best, maybe because I took the walking tour last week." Simon pointed to a painting of the Floyd Memorial Library on North Street. "This was built in 1917 by Grace Floyd in memory of her father, Charles Gelston Floyd, the grandson of General William Floyd, and a signer of the Declaration of Independence. There's a lot of history in this town."

"I guess I take it for granted."

"That's natural. You're from here. It's my adopted hometown. Besides I like architecture and history." He moved on to a painting of the Greenport jail in the historic commercial district, where he had been held last fall, and which featured barred windows and a brick exterior. "This I don't like. Too many bad memories, but you see this?" He pointed to the green light beside the front door. "It used to be called the Green Light Hotel because in the early days when someone was locked up, that light was turned on."

"Maybe that's where they got the idea for the Green Light Tour of Greenport."

"What's that?"

"Every Saturday in the summer and fall merchants put a green lantern out front if they'll be open after hours for customers. It's a way to increase business."

We walked over to the next booth where the paintings had a strong impressionist influence. One, a painting of the local farmer's market, was really good, and I stepped closer to examine it. As I did, I heard a cheerful voice saying, "See anything you like?"

It was Kylie Ramsey of the farmer's market, another one of my competitors for the garden lot. Kylie was in her early thirties and attractive, with long brown hair and green eyes. She was very tan from working in the sun. She gave me a look like she'd just sucked on a lemon. "What are *you* doing here? I heard about Dr. White. Don't the police want to talk to you?"

"We've talked to them. Simon and I are judges for the event."

Kylie shook her head. "Judging others might not be the best thing for you to be doing right now, Willow."

"What are you talking about?" I asked.

"I mean, a lot of people in this town are unhappy about the way you got the land. You really don't want to make any more enemies."

"Is that a threat?" Simon asked.

Kylie shrugged. "More like . . . a warning. I just think Willow should know how people feel about her."

"That's becoming very clear," I said. "But that doesn't mean I understand it. Kylie, I offered to share the space with you."

"That wouldn't have worked." She straightened the painting on its easel and wiped an imaginary spot of dust from the frame.

"Fine," I said. "You don't like me, you don't think I deserved the lot. I don't know what I can do to change your mind. But do you have any idea about who would want Dr. White dead?"

Kylie's eyes narrowed as she studied me. "I'm not talking to you. I know what happened last year at the Bixby estate. You're a snoop who causes trouble."

"What happened last year was that she solved the murder," Simon said. "She saved my life."

Kylie gave a Simon an overly bright smile. "Good for you."

Simon's eyes narrowed as he studied Kylie's artwork. "This is the painting that you're entering in the competition? It's pretty pathetic, isn't it Willow?"

"No, Simon. Actually, it's good," I said honestly. "And we need to score it appropriately."

"Well, I won't hold my breath," Kylie replied, as she turned on her heel, and headed over to a potential customer.

We jotted down our scores and headed for the last row of exhibitors. That's where we found our fellow judges, Harold Spitz and Maggie Stone. Both of them had wanted the lot as much as Kylie had. I braced myself for yet another confrontation.

"Enjoying the judging?" I said.

Harold mumbled something, and Maggie said, "Yes, we are. Everyone is so talented here."

"Obviously they didn't see the stuff we saw," Simon whispered in my ear.

"Hush, Simon," I said, and leaned in to look at a painting of the Bug Light lighthouse. It was very realistic, so much so that it almost looked like a photograph. "I like this one."

Harold mumbled something else. "We don't," Maggie

said. "It's too realistic, and so pedantic, a bore, really." She wrote something down on her scoring sheet.

"Oh," I said. "I hadn't realized that realism was a negative thing."

She gave me a look. "If you don't mind me asking, what are you doing here? We heard about the trouble in the garden."

"We made a commitment to Patty."

"So that's why we're here," Simon added. "Is that a problem?"

Maggie shivered in the hot afternoon sun. "Not at all, but murder is, well, so unsavory, and it does seem to follow you around, Willow. That's what I told them."

"Told who, Maggie?" I asked.

"Mayor Hobson and the Village Board, of course. I simply told them that you weren't a good risk when it came to the lot because of all the murders you find yourself involved in. Unfortunately, they didn't listen to me. Maybe they will now."

"*All* the murders?" Simon echoed. "Before Dr. White, there were two. Exactly two."

Actually, there had been three, but I didn't say so.

Maggie shrugged. "And now Dr. White makes three. That's a lot of murders to come your way in what—a little over a year?"

The way she put it made me uneasy. It was a lot of murders. But I knew they didn't have anything to do with me. "Look," I said, "I just try to help out where and when I can, especially when it comes to my family and friends. Right now, I'm wondering who wanted Dr. White dead. Do you or Harold have any ideas?"

"Not a clue," Maggie said.

Harold mumbled something to Maggie.

"What did he say?" Simon asked.

Harold said something else to Maggie.

She turned to us. "Harold says that there was no shortage of people in the village who wanted that man dead."

chapter six

Willow McQuade's
Favorite Medicinal Plants

BORAGE
Botanical name: *Borago officinalis*

Medicinal uses: Borage leaves, flowers, and seed oil can help you feel happier and can even inspire courage. In 1597 herbalist John Gerard quoted in his writings an old saying: "*Ego borago gaudia semper ago*," meaning "I, borage, always bring courage." In fact, the flowers have long been used to bolster courage; perhaps the fact that they nourish the adrenal glands explains why. In medieval times the flowers were even embroidered on the mantles of knights and jousters to give them courage. Borage was also snuck into the drinks of prospective husbands to give them the courage to propose!

Borage leaves and flowers have also been used in treatments for anxiety, mild depression, grief, heartbreak, and worry. As a flower essence, borage is

used to lighten mild depression and ease discouragement. Borage helps bring joy, optimism, enthusiasm, and good cheer, improves confidence, and dispels sadness.

"Like who?" I asked Harold. "Who wanted Dr. White dead? Did that include you?"

But Harold just shrugged and moved on to the next booth.

"Leave him alone," Maggie said. "He didn't get along with the man, but he certainly didn't want him dead."

"Who do you think had it out for Dr. White?" I asked. "I find it hard to believe that you have no opinion."

"Me, too," Simon said.

Maggie blew out a sigh and gave me a look that suggested that we were both incredibly tiresome. "Dr. White wasn't well liked, not by his wife, not by his patients. God knows what kind of people he got involved with when it came to those real estate deals. Joe Larson, for one, is no saint. The two of them together made sure that none of us had a chance for that lot. But they couldn't figure out how to stop you." She checked her watch. "Now, if you'll excuse me. As you know, we need to finish up by 4 p.m."

She walked over to Harold. She said something to him, and he seemed to get angry. Suddenly, his face became as red as a raspberry. She tried to placate him, but he stormed off.

"What's going on over there?" I wondered aloud. "He seems really upset."

"And she's buzzed," Simon said. "Her breath smells like vodka."

"I thought you couldn't smell vodka on someone's breath."

"Most people can't, I can. My mother and father drink vodka martinis every day at five o'clock." Simon's parents were retired, wealthy, and lived on the Gold Coast of Long Island. His father had been a thoracic surgeon to New York's elite.

"If what they said is true, then we have a pretty large suspect pool. Harold might even have had a reason to want White dead. This is going to be a difficult puzzle to piece together."

"Yeah, but you're up to the challenge," Simon said breezily. He studied a truly awful painting of a tall ship on an easel. "Now, what do you want to give this masterpiece—a one or a two?"

We finished judging by four o'clock and helped Patty tally the scores. Within an hour, we had our winner, second and third place, and three honorable mentions. Patty asked the entrants and the public to gather around the stage behind the merry-go-round for the results and subsequent auction.

The first-place winner was Kylie Ramsey. Even though Simon had given her a low score, the rest of us had agreed that her painting was the best. Patty handed her the award, a sculpture of a seagull on a boat pier.

The crowd applauded. Kylie threw me a strange look that I couldn't decipher.

Second place went to the photograph of the seashell on the beach that I liked, while third place went to the guy who painted the cigar store. He placed because of the generous scores given by Maggie and Harold. I wondered why they were helping him.

After the *Suffolk Times* photographer took photos and everyone had been congratulated by friends and family, Kylie walked over to me, holding her trophy. "Thanks for being fair about judging me. This means a lot."

"You're lucky that Willow is nice *and* fair," Simon said.

"Thank you," Kylie said.

"You're welcome."

She turned to go, but stopped herself. "I'm sorry for what I said about you and your snooping. I'm just upset about losing the chance to give the farmer's market a permanent home in the village."

"I meant what I said about sharing. You're welcome to use the outdoor teahouse space anytime. Or you can set it up in the parking lot behind Nature's Way."

"Thanks, but I think we'll stay put at the church annex parking lot for now. They've been nice and don't mind us being there on a Saturday morning. I think it was just my ego that made me want the lot. You know, I wanted to make the farmer's market bigger and better."

She looked at the trophy but seemed to be deciding whether to say something else. "You were asking about Dr. White. I didn't know him well, but I wouldn't have chosen him if I needed surgery, that's for sure. Too many of his patients are suing him for botched surgeries, including a friend of mine. She's still in pain and it's been five years since her surgery. Doctors like that shouldn't be allowed to practice medicine."

"Well, if it's the surgery that caused the pain, I agree," I said. But I knew that pain was complex and surgery couldn't always cure it. "Can I ask who your friend is?"

Kylie looked at me suspiciously. "You think she had motive to kill him?"

"I have no idea," I said honestly. "I'd just like to ask her about Dr. White. It might lead to something."

Kylie thought it over. "I'd have to check with her first before giving out her name."

"I understand," I said. "But if you think of anything else please call me." I pulled a business card out of my wallet and handed it to her.

After she left, Simon said, "Why didn't you push her for her friend's name? Pain can make people do desperate things. She could be the one who killed White."

"I know that, but if I pushed Kylie too hard, she would have clammed up completely. Now, I can gently ask her again. Or find out some other way."

"Okay, Nancy Drew, if you think so."

The contest over, volunteers began setting up for the Maritime Festival auction. I used the time to quickly text Jackson and tell him what we were doing. He didn't reply but showed up just before the auction started at six. We told him what had happened and what Kylie had said.

"I hate to say it, but Simon's right. You could have pressed her for the name."

"My gut said no," I explained. "But I'll get the name. Don't worry. By the way, what did you make of those photos of that painting? It snagged third place." I pulled out my phone, scrolled to the photos of the cigar-store painting, and showed it to Jackson again. "Did you notice anything unusual?"

He shook his head. "No, but I've heard that there's a men's club on the second floor made up of local businessmen, the mayor, and the Village Board. Sounds cozy."

I had hoped that Jackson might have spotted something in the painting that I had missed. Obviously, I would have to do some digging. "Is everything okay at the store? What about Koren and Coyle? Are they still there?"

"Not too many customers in the store. Unfortunately, our friends are still in the garden."

"As long as they're gone by morning," I said. "Is the booth still busy?"

He nodded. "You're almost sold out. Nate's handling it. He told me that you made about twelve hundred bucks today. That's good news at least, right?"

I blew out a breath. "It sure is."

Maggie, from the dog park, took the stage, announced that the auction was starting, and that all proceeds would go to benefit the animal shelter in Southold. I spotted Joe Larson on the opposite side of the crowd. "Larson is over there." I nodded in his direction. "Let's see what happens."

Half an hour later, Maggie began the auction on the ugly cigar-store painting. Joe Larson found himself bidding against two other people, but when the price reached $250, they dropped out and he won the painting easily.

He paid for it and quickly hustled it away before we could talk to him. We watched as he climbed into a silver Mercedes and drove off.

We crossed the street and headed back to Nature's Way to get ready for the Green Light shoppers. But before we went inside, we went to the garden to see what was going on. The ribbon from the opening had been replaced by yellow crime-scene tape and an officer stood sentry.

"Is Detective Koren here?" I asked him.

The officer, who had beads of sweat running down his face, gave me a grim look and said, "He left. What do you want?"

"I'm Willow McQuade, the owner of this garden and of Nature's Way and I wanted to see—"

He stopped me before I could finish. "You can't come in here."

I reminded myself to breathe, and said, "Will Detective Koren be back?"

"Don't know. You better move along. This is still an active crime scene."

"But the mayor said it would be open by tomorrow morning."

"It'll take as long as it takes, miss."

"But he told us that it would be done by then, and if he thinks—" Jackson took me by the arm and led me away before I could finish. This was good judgment on his part, as I was quickly becoming frustrated. "Koren had better keep his word. We've worked so hard, and I've got tours of the garden booked all weekend."

"Don't panic yet. Let's go upstairs and see what's going on."

We went to my bedroom, and while Jackson played with the dogs, I grabbed the binoculars, went out on the balcony, and trained them on the site of the murder. There, a group of crime-scene techs were working the area. The body of Dr. White had been removed.

"Techs are still working, body is gone, and no Koren in sight," I reported. "Do you think he's coming back?"

"Yes."

"How do you know that?" I kept the binoculars trained on the scene.

"Because it's dinnertime and he probably just went to grab something. Believe me, he'll be back. This is a big deal." The two doxies, Rockford and Columbo, were now on their backs side by side as Jackson scratched their bellies.

I watched as the techs examined the south end of the garden. I hoped they were being careful around the plants, but I knew that wasn't their top priority.

As I trained the binoculars on the path, Koren and Coyle came into view. Both of them were carrying cups of coffee and brown bags; dinner, no doubt. Koren had his phone pressed to his ear, a stressed look on his face.

"You were right. Koren and Coyle are back."

"I won't say I told you so." Jackson got up, took the binoculars, and trained them on the cardiac section. "But Koren doesn't look happy."

"No, he doesn't. He must be under a lot of pressure from the mayor and the festival organizers to solve this quickly. I hope that he doesn't zero in on you."

"That makes two of us."

chapter seven

Willow McQuade's
favorite Medicinal Plants

CALENDULA:
Botanical name: *Calendula officinalis*

Medicinal uses: Calendula is a hardy, long-blooming plant with radiant yellow flowers that will brighten your garden. But there's more. Calendula also has amazing healing properties. Antiseptic and anti-inflammatory, this flower helps to promote cell repair and growth. You'll find calendula in many items at your health food store such as lotions, salves, and creams that treat everything from cuts and scrapes to insect bites, varicose veins, and athlete's foot. Calendula also is a nourishing and cleansing tonic for the lymphatic system, which helps to improve immunity. It also aids digestion, helps to ease throat infections, and is used in children's ear drops. Inside the body and on the skin, this is a helpful herb that speeds healing and improves health.

Since we were all working late, I closed the store for an hour so we could eat together. After we were finished, we worked on getting Nature's Way ready for the Green Light tour and the workshop on how to plant a healing garden. This involved moving the tables in the dining area and putting out delectable gluten-free chocolate cake and organic lemonade. But now it was past eight and no one had shown up.

"I can't believe this is happening," I said to Jackson. "When we sold out today in the booth, I figured that we would be busy tonight."

"But things were slow in here today, Willow," Merrily said. "I think we only had three or four tables. They're all out there eating clam chowder and pizza and hot dogs."

"Plus, Peter Tork, you know, from the Monkees, is giving a concert on the green," Wallace said.

I looked around the empty store. "Well, nothing is happening here, so if you want to go to the concert, you can," I said. "Have fun. You worked hard today."

"Are you sure?"

"Yes, go. Merrily, you can go, too. Check out the concert and enjoy the rest of the festival."

"Great, thanks. Now I can go meet Nate," Merrily said, and grabbed her purse from under the counter. "I'll come in early to clean this up. Hopefully the cops will be gone by then, and you can start giving tours of your garden again." She came over and gave me a hug.

"I hope so. Thanks, Merrily."

Simon went over to the cake table. He ran every morning, which is why he could eat whatever he wanted, and he took full advantage of this fact. "Since the party isn't happening, I think I'll get a cup of coffee and a piece of that cake to go, if that's all right. I'm going to go home and try to write. The caffeine will help keep me awake."

"Enjoy," I said. "I hope the writing goes well. As for this workshop, I'll just have to reschedule for another night."

Jackson squeezed my hand and gave me a sympathetic look. "It's not your fault. When things like this happen, people stay away. It's not like with Claire when there was some question about how she died. It's obvious that the man was murdered. Someone knocked him on the head, in broad daylight in Greenport, during the Maritime Festival, when fifty thousand-plus people are in town. Word spreads fast."

I brought in the green lantern, closed up Nature's Way, and we went for an evening stroll with the dogs. The band was tuning up on the stage in the park, and the audience was finding seats on beach chairs and blankets on the circle of grass that faced them.

The sunny day had cooled into night and a fresh, salty breeze drifted from the bay across the green. It was almost cool, and I was glad that I had brought along a light sweater.

We headed north on Main Street to do our window shopping, since that's where most of the art galleries and boutiques were. We followed the green lanterns to the end of the block, taking in paintings, sculptures, drawings, mosaics, and stained glass. There were still plenty of tourists and locals crowding the streets. I thought I knew why they had stayed away from my store, and it didn't feel good.

When we walked up to the Tolle Gallery, we found Harold and Maggie inside, talking to Rhonda Rhodes and her partner, Ramona Meadows. The two women were in their early fifties and recently retired from practicing law in the city. For phase two of their lives, they dreamed of opening a retail garden center and had also applied for the lot. Right now, there was only one place in town to buy flowers, a small florist's shop that sold exotic flowers. Things were okay between us but I knew that they, too, were disappointed about not getting the space.

Ramona spotted me, excused herself, and came to the door. A pretty redhead, she wore a shift dress with a flower pattern and orange Crocs, the shoe of choice on the East End in the summer. "I heard about what happened on your garden tour. Wow, are you two okay?" She leaned down and began to pet the three dogs.

"I think so," I said. "But it was a terrible thing to find. I just feel bad for Dr. White's family."

"I feel sorry for his son," Ramona said. "He's in his twenties, teaches at City College, and he's a decent guy. But White and his wife were on the verge of divorce. She might not be all that broken up about it."

"I didn't know that." I couldn't help wondering if maybe his wife was the one who wanted White dead. If money was the issue, would she get a better settlement as a widow than as a divorcée?

"What about your garden tours?" Ramona asked. "Is that all off now? That would be a shame."

Rhonda, trim, with short, cropped strawberry-blond hair, and also wearing a shift, came to the door. "Ramona, who are you talking to? I want to show you something." She saw us, and said, "Oh, it's you."

"I'll be in soon." Ramona watched her go then said, "Don't mind her. She just really wanted to build that garden center."

"I'm sure you can find a spot that's just as good," Jackson said.

"You'd think so, Jackson, but it's not that easy with the zoning laws. And not everyone wants a garden center with all of that traffic as a neighbor. You got lucky, Willow. I hope you appreciate that."

"With everything that's happened, I don't feel very lucky right now," I admitted. "But I know what you mean. So what are you going to do?"

"For the time being, we're leasing land from the Coventry Cooperative in Southold, and selling our veggies at the farmer's market with Kylie Ramsey. She's done an amazing job with the market, and we do really well there. You should come by. We've got some great stuff you could sell at the store, unusual organic produce, like celtuce."

Jackson grinned. "Is that a cross between celery and lettuce?"

"You sound skeptical," Ramona said, smiling. "You should try it."

"I will," I said. "You sell wholesale, right?"

Ramona nodded. "Sure. Why don't you come by tomorrow? We've got a lot of produce that might do well in Nature's Way."

"Sorry, tomorrow won't work," I said. "We're going to be fixing the damage to the garden from today."

"All those cops trampling your plants," Ramona said sympathetically. She glanced inside the gallery, and Rhonda waved her over. "Well, I'd better go. Maybe we'll see you at the market?"

"I'll do my best." As she walked away, I said, "Well, Ramona seems pretty reasonable about everything, but did Rhonda seem pissed off at me—or was I imagining it?"

"Rhonda didn't actually say much," Jackson reminded me. "Still, I'd say she and Ramona obviously wanted the lot very badly. So I don't know if they'd do anything actively hostile, but right now, I wouldn't consider them friends. Rhonda may be yet another sore loser. Greenport seems to be full of them."

"Let's go home," I said, suddenly exhausted. I hated thinking that half the people in town were potential enemies. I started walking back down Main Street, but stopped as Qigong sniffed the grass around a telephone pole. Columbo and Rockford quickly joined in.

Jackson took my hand. "When we get home, I'll draw you a nice, hot bath. You can put your aromatherapy stuff in it—lavender or whatever—and you'll feel better."

"That sounds comforting, which is just what I need. Thanks, Jackson."

We continued past the two-story white building that housed the East End Historical Society, and the Arcade department store parking lot. I loved Greenport, but the town was becoming an increasingly uncomfortable place to live. "All I can think is that getting the lot has caused nothing but trouble," I said. "White is dead, business is off, everyone is upset, and no one likes me. Worst of all, you may be a suspect in his death. I think I may have made a mistake in going after the lot."

Jackson gave me a swift, sweet kiss. "Don't even waste your time thinking that way, because there's nothing you can do about it now."

I shook my head, wondering if I would ever be able to feel good about the garden again. "You're right about that."

When we got home, the police were still working in the garden. Thanks to the big klieg lights, we could still watch most of what was happening with the binoculars. They had moved out from the area where White's body was found and were now searching other sections. I wondered if they had found anything so far, and if so—what?

I decided to take Jackson's advice and take a hot bath. I added my favorite organic lavender and lemon balm bath salts and settled in for a nice, long soak.

A little while later, Jackson came in, got undressed, and slipped into the oversized tub. We kissed, hungry for each other, perhaps even more so now, since so much had changed in the past twenty-four hours. But making love in a tub isn't easy, so we soon switched to shower mode. Afterward, feeling clean and satisfied, we got dressed, me in my T-shirt and undies, him in his sweats, no shirt.

Our evening routine was to read before we went to

sleep while the dogs and cats snoozed next to us, and tonight was no different. I settled into bed and picked up my copy of Agatha Christie's classic mystery *Body in the Library*, while Jackson grabbed Michael Connelly's latest. I felt safe and secure, and pushed out of my mind any thought of tomorrow.

We stayed like that for about an hour, after which Jackson closed his book, took mine, and put them on the nightstand. "I want to tell you something." He pulled me close and I snuggled into his body and his warmth.

"What is it?" I asked warily. "I really don't want to think about tomorrow."

"I know, but I have to say it. I agreed to rigorous honesty in AA, and I abide by it."

I nodded, understanding.

"It isn't like you to have second thoughts," Jackson began. "Not when you were so sure about your decision to apply for the lot and all the work that you did to get it. Even though some bad things have happened, it doesn't mean that you were wrong or that you made a mistake." He gave me a gentle kiss. "Try to separate yourself from what's happening and what people say, and listen to yourself. You created this garden—"

"With your help, and Nate's."

"We helped, yes, but you've been the driving force all along. This was your idea, your baby. You can't turn away from it now."

"I know," I said, and kissed him back. I did know he was right, but I felt so weary. As if this wonderful idea of mine had turned into a hike up the Himalayas, instead of a walk in the park.

Ginger woke up, stretched, and changed position, right above Jackson's head, and began to purr loudly. He gently picked her up and put her back on the foot of the bed, and snuggled next to me again.

"I wonder what Aunt Claire would say about all this if she were still here. Would she have applied for the lot, like I did?"

"Definitely, Claire was a sharp businesswoman, I guarantee that she would not have ignored this opportunity, even if it meant ruffling some village feathers. You were meant to do this, Willow. It's going to work out. Trust me."

chapter eight

Willow McQuade's
Favorite Medicinal Plants

<u>CHAMOMILE</u>

Botanical name: *Chamaemelum nobile* (Roman chamomile, syn. *Anthemis nobilis*), *Matricaria recutita* (German chamomile, formerly *Chamomilla recutita*, syn. *M. chamomilla*)

Medicinal uses: Since the times of ancient Greece, both types of chamomile have been used medicinally in the same ways. Tiny but mighty, chamomile is rich in nerve- and muscle-relaxing nutrients such as calcium, magnesium, potassium, and B vitamins that help promote relaxation, easing stress and anxiety, encouraging the movement of chi or good energy, and promoting sleep. It is has also been approved in many countries to treat inflammation, indigestion, muscle spasms, and infection.

Sleep did not come easily, and I woke up just about every hour. While Jackson and our animals snoozed, I grabbed the binoculars and padded over to the window. The cops were still in the garden. It seemed that they were moving in a grid pattern, so when I woke up at 2 a.m., they were working around the anti-inflammatory plants. An hour or so later, I spotted them working the ground in the analgesic plants area. I worried that with every step they were destroying what Jackson, Nate, and I had worked so hard to build.

Finally, at 4:30 a.m., I heard several cars start up on the street. I went to the window and looked out, and the garden was finally dark. For now, the cops were gone. After that, I fell into a deep sleep.

On Sunday morning, we got out of bed at seven. I skipped my usual morning meditation and yoga practice, threw on shorts and a Nature's Way T-shirt, and headed out to the garden, fearful of what I might find there. The morning air felt dewy, soft, and salty. Out in the harbor, deckhands on one of the tall ships were raising their flag. The Shelter Island ferry headed for the Greenport dock, leaving whipped-cream waves in its wake. Early risers were out strolling in Mitchell Park and walking their dogs.

When Jackson and I walked up to the garden gate, the yellow crime-scene tape was gone. "So that's it," I said, "They're done investigating."

"In the garden maybe, but I'm sure Koren will be back to talk to us—me, specifically. My prints are on that shovel. I wasn't wearing gloves."

"That doesn't mean that you killed White."

"Of course not, but you and I both know that

we're in for round two with Detective Koren." Jackson
pushed open the gate. "But for now, let's see what the
garden looks like."

I sucked in a breath. "I'm really worried about what
we might find."

"Hopefully, it's not another dead body."

I gave him a look. "That is not funny."

He put his arm around me. "Whatever we find,
we'll fix it, don't worry."

At first glance, it seemed as if the police had been
careful; the damage looked minimal. But as we went
from section to section and plant to plant, we saw foot-
prints all over the beds, torn leaves, smashed plants,
and broken branches. If my garden had been a painting, it was as if someone had splattered red paint across
my beautiful creation. I felt like crying.

"Steady, Willow," Jackson said as he pulled me into
a hug. "We can fix all of this. Nate will be here soon
and the three of us will go through it section by section,
plant by plant, and prune, replant, replace, and water.
If we're not done by the time we open at noon, I'll keep
working with Nate while you start the tours. They can
see us in action."

We decided to begin working in the cardiology area,
since that's where Dr. White had died and where inves-
tigators had spent most of their time. Here, plants were
uprooted and leaves ragged from handling. The path
was also a mess; most of the cedar chips were gone. We
had a lot of work to do.

I pulled on my gardening gloves and grabbed my

favorite pair of shears. "I knew Koren didn't like me, but this is ridiculous."

"He's trying to find a killer, Willow," Jackson gently reminded me. "I really don't think it's personal."

"You're right, but the sooner this is fixed and yesterday is erased, the better."

"Agreed." Jackson kissed me and headed to the potting shed. "I'll get a couple of new bags of mulch for the walkway while you figure out what needs to be done." While I surveyed the damage, Jackson brought over a bag of cedar mulch, split the bag with his pocket knife, and poured it over the area in and around the cardiology plants. Immediately, the smell of cedar filled the air. "Hmmm, that smells really good. It's almost like aromatherapy."

Jackson smiled. "I like it, too. Maybe I should get some cedar aftershave."

"Then you'll smell like mulch."

"That won't work. I'll have to think of something else to get your motor going."

I smiled at him. "I have faith in you. You'll think of something."

He put the bag down, came over to me, pulled me close, and gave me a good, long kiss. We had been together for a year and a half and it still felt new and electric between us.

We were interrupted by Nate. "Hey, guys, uh, sorry."

"No problem, Nate," Jackson said, "Help me get the rest of the mulch to repair the path."

While they worked on the pathway, I turned my attention to the plants. The foxglove bush that Dr. White had been lying behind was completely uprooted, but it would survive. I replanted it, added organic fertilizer, and watered it thoroughly. "Guys, I'm going to need mulch around this plant, too."

Nate grabbed a bag of mulch and came over and gently spread it around the plant. The three of us worked together and very quickly, things began to look better.

But as usual, when one thing goes right, another can go wrong. Or as the fourth-century Taoist sage Chuang Tzu said, life is ten thousand joys and ten thousand sorrows. An hour later as I was working in the section that featured plants for mental and emotional well-being, such as St. John's wort for mild to moderate depression and kava-kava for anxiety, Detectives Koren and Coyle returned.

"We need to talk to you two," Koren said as he walked up to me. He was wearing a black suit and a tie with a geometric black-and-white pattern, while Coyle wore a rumpled brown linen suit and a tie with a golfer on it. He really needed some of Koren's fashion savvy.

Jackson had just finished spreading the mulch two sections over. He saw the detectives, put the bag down, said something to Nate, and came over to us. "What is it now, Koren?"

"The autopsy results are in. Dr. White died from massive head trauma to the front of his skull, delivered by your shovel. Big surprise, your prints are all over the handle."

For a moment, I couldn't breathe, and the world began to spin. I felt myself heading for the ground, but Jackson noticed my reaction and grabbed me before I could fall. "It's okay, Willow," he said, his voice steadying me. "Yes, I told you that I used the shovel to replace a plant," Jackson told the detectives, his tone was calm and confident. "I wasn't wearing gloves. I'm sure that mine wasn't the only set of prints on it either."

"No, you're right, they weren't," Detective Koren admitted. "Let's go over your movements again."

Jackson sighed. "As I already told you, I replaced the damaged digitalis plant just before 11 a.m. Then I went out to Front Street to watch the parade with Willow."

"And you, Ms. McQuade? You were at your plant stand before the parade, right?"

"Right. I was working with Wallace Bryan and Nate Marshall, who is over there." I pointed to Nate, who was getting something out of the potting shed.

"Okay, Spade, so you're saying that Dr. White came in after you left and so did the person who killed him? That's a lot of activity for you not to notice."

"Normally, maybe," I said. "But the parade passed by in front of the garden, and as you know, since you were there, it was quite loud. It would have been really easy for anyone to get into the garden from the other side, on Adams Street. They would just have to hop the fence."

"Yeah, I tried that," Detective Coyle said. "It wasn't exactly easy, but it could be done."

"There you have it, Detectives. Can we finish our repairs to the garden?" Jackson looked at Detective Koren. "We still have a lot to do before Willow can open up again."

"Your people weren't exactly careful in here," I said. "They did a lot of damage."

"Too bad," Detective Coyle said. "It's a crime scene, Ms. McQuade. We're trying to find a killer."

"Calm down, Coyle," Detective Koren said. "We're sorry about any inconvenience you may have experienced."

"That sounds real sincere," Jackson said. "Now can we get back to work?"

"For now," Detective Koren said. "But don't leave town."

"Me, leave? I'd miss you too much."

"Knock it off, Spade," Koren said. "And stay local."

"Yeah, we're watching you," Coyle said.

As they walked away I said, "You shouldn't aggravate Koren. He wants you to slip up."

Jackson grinned. "I know, but he just makes it so easy. Let's get busy, McQuade."

I finished up the section I was working on and moved on to the next one. Once I was on a roll, the process seemed to go faster, and with every repair I made, I felt as if I was getting my life back in order, too.

Two hours later, around nine-thirty that morning, I took a break and went inside to get us something to drink. I found Wallace and Merrily slammed with a full house inside and out, and no Simon.

I shouldn't have been surprised, but I was. Since Merrily desperately needed peppers, artisan cheeses, fresh bread, and eggs, someone needed to go to the farmer's market. I called Simon and got his voice message: *"I'm where my muse takes me. Do what you do."* The phone beeped.

"Simon, it's Willow. You need to put your muse on hold. I need your help at Nature's Way *now*. Call me!"

"I really need that stuff, Willow, especially the bread," Merrily said, looking worried. "Otherwise, we won't have sandwiches."

It seemed that I didn't have a choice. Jackson and Nate would have to work without me for a while. The garden didn't open again until noon, so we had time. "I'll go. Give me the list."

After I brought some fresh-squeezed organic lemonade and buttered blueberry muffins to Jackson and Nate in the garden, I took one for myself and headed over to the farmer's market. It wouldn't take long and, to be honest, I needed some time alone to get my head straight about all that had happened. Koren hadn't taken Jackson down to the station, but it didn't mean that he wouldn't be back.

Their visit had jolted me into realizing that I had to stop feeling sorry for myself and find the killer. And that was exactly what I was going to do.

The farmer's market was held each Saturday and Sunday morning in the parking lot behind the church annex on Main Street. Vendors set up trim, white tents, where they offered everything from gourmet coffee, hummus, and Moroccan condiments, to sunflowers, zinnias, and goat cheese.

I decided that since I was here, I'd check out Ramona and Rhonda's produce, and more important, ask some questions about the case. For all I knew, they might know something or even be suspects. But before I could get that far, I spotted my wannabe waiter.

Simon was wearing a navy Izod shirt, white linen

shorts, boat shoes, and Prada sunglasses. He looked ready to step onto a yacht. I watched as he chatted up the girl at the Honeybee Yum! booth. I walked up behind him and tapped him on the shoulder. "Did you get my message?"

He whipped around. "Willow! Leah, this is Willow. She's the one I was talking about. She runs Nature's Way in town."

"Nice to meet you, Leah. Simon, can I talk to you for a moment, please?"

He pushed his sunglasses onto the top of head and smiled. "Something going on with the case?"

I pulled him away from the booth. "No, you were supposed to help us out at the store this morning, and now we're super busy."

"That's good," Simon said.

"Where were you?"

"I couldn't make it down because the muse was calling me. I think it had something to do with that murder. It got my juices going again last night. I couldn't type fast enough. I mean, the ideas were flowing! I got up early this morning and kept going. I feel reborn."

"So, now that you're not blocked, you don't want to be a waiter anymore?" Good, old Simon—reliable and a good friend one minute and completely self-involved and oblivious the next.

"Hell, no! I've got to keep writing! I just came down here to pick up some of my favorite java to give me a caffeine fix and then I'm back at it." He leaned in and whispered in my ear. "However, I do still want to help you with the case."

"That's something, at least," I said. So, while I picked up bread and cheese, I told him everything that had happened and my plan to talk to Ramona and Rhonda again.

"You might want to talk to Kylie again, too. She's here and she's been chatting it up with this chick who I think is selling something here, too. Maybe she's that friend who was a patient of Dr. White."

"That would be too easy."

"They were up there." He gestured to the right. "Talking at the info table."

I glanced that way and spotted Kylie, but she was sitting alone at the table, which was covered with leaflets, talking on her cell phone.

"I don't see the friend, Simon."

"She was just there. Let's take a walk around and we can look for them."

We circled the lot, looking for Kylie's friend and Ramona and Rhonda. We found the couple's booth first, at the back of the lot off Carpenter Street, although no one was behind the table. The banner above read: Ramona and Rhonda Heirloom Veggies: The Most Unique Produce on the North Fork! While we waited for someone to show up, I checked out the produce, which looked fresh and delicious. I knew that I'd bring some of it home to Merrily.

Moments later, Rhonda rounded the corner and came up to the booth. She wasn't happy to see me, and she barely hid her displeasure. "What can I get for you?"

"I'll take a couple of squash, some celtuce, and four of the heirloom tomatoes. Everything looks really good."

"Glad you think so." Her tone was cool and detached. She quickly rang up my purchase and put the items into a brown paper bag. "It wasn't easy to find a place to garden, but we managed."

"Yes, Ramona mentioned that. I'm glad things worked out for you two." I handed her ten dollars.

"Things didn't work out, Willow," she said sharply. "We made the best of a bad situation. Dr. White was right about you. If it hadn't been for your aunt, some-one else—like us—would have been able to use that lot."

"Hey, wait a minute," Simon said. "Willow got that lot fair and square, and she's done a great job on the garden. It's really beautiful."

Rhonda handed me my change. "I haven't seen it, so I can't say, and now that Charles—Dr. White—was found dead there, I'm certainly not going to go."

"Were you two friends?"

"I wouldn't say that, but when we first moved out here, he used to be my doctor."

I thought about what Kylie said and wondered if she was another disgruntled patient. "*Was* your doctor? Did something happen?"

"That is none of your business." A group of people began to crowd around the booth. "If you don't mind," Rhonda said, "I need to take care of my customers."

"She's a frosty one, isn't she?" Simon said as soon as we were out of earshot.

"Sub-zero." I glanced at Kylie, who was still on the phone. "Let's try to find her friend."

We circled the parking lot, but Simon couldn't point out the woman whom Kylie had been talking to.

We decided to try and talk to Kylie again, but before we could, she put her phone away, got up from the table, and hurried out of the parking lot, but not before glancing in my direction.

"Should we follow her, see what's up?" Simon asked.

I checked my watch. We'd only been gone from Nature's Way twenty minutes. We had to get back to Merrily with the food, but we could probably take a little more time. And I wanted to make some progress; we still didn't have a single reasonable lead.

I wasn't sure what to do. But then, as Kylie reached First Street, before she scurried away, she turned and looked at me, again.

I grabbed Simon's arm. "Let's go."

chapter nine

Willow McQuade's
Favorite Medicinal Plants

<u>CRANBERRY</u>
Botanical name: *Vaccinium macrocarpon*

Medicinal uses: Historically, cranberry fruits and leaves were used for a variety of problems, such as wounds, urinary disorders, diarrhea, diabetes, stomach ailments, and liver problems. Today, cranberry products have been used in the hope of preventing and treating urinary tract infections or *Helicobacter pylori* infections that can lead to stomach ulcers, and to prevent dental plaque. Cranberry has also been reported to have antioxidant and anticancer activity. The berries are used to produce beverages and many other food products, as well as dietary supplements in the form of extracts, teas, and capsules or tablets.

Clearly, Kylie's errand had something to do with me. So we followed her as she walked briskly toward the harbor on Main Street. The Maritime Festival was already in full swing, and the sidewalks were jammed full of people while motorists vied for available parking spots.

Beyond the bank, the road was closed to traffic. After we walked past the Greenport Historical Society building, Kylie headed into the center of the street. We followed her as she threaded through the many vendors selling everything from nautical T-shirts to nautical CDs. At the Capitol One building, she moved to the sidewalk, but we stayed in the middle of the road, pretending to look at T-shirts and sun visors. A few yards later, she stopped at the Cheese Emporium, a cheese store and café, and went inside.

"Now what?" Simon said.

"We walk casually past the café and try to see inside. C'mon." But moments after we crossed the street, Kylie came out of the Cheese Emporium with a bottle of juice and a cheese roll and sat at a table for four out front.

"So much for being casual," Simon said. "What do you want to do?"

"I want to see who she's waiting for. Maybe it's that friend you saw—or someone else." I glanced at the Coronet Diner on the corner, a Greenport institution. "Let's go to the Coronet, get some coffee, and see who joins her." I looked in my bag for the small pair of binoculars I always carried.

"Roger that. I'm gonna get a peanut-butter-and-banana sandwich for my breakfast. It's good for a hangover."

"I thought you were writing last night." I grabbed the binoculars at the bottom of my purse and took them out.

"I *was* writing. And then I had a few drinks to celebrate. Got to reward yourself when you do good."

Simon certainly didn't have a problem with that. When he got the job as executive producer on his first TV show, *Parallel Lives*, he bought a beach house in Malibu; and when he sold his first nonfiction book for six figures to a major publisher, a loft in Soho.

Simon had been born into money and had earned millions more. When we lived together in L.A. he showered me with lavish gifts. I wound up with a closet full of designer clothes and boxes and boxes of Jimmy Choo shoes that I donated to charity when I decided to stay in Greenport. I didn't miss Simon's money. Jackson gave me so much more than Simon ever could.

We went into the Coronet, snagged a window table, and I used the binoculars to look across the street and watch Kylie. She was still sitting alone at the table, and she had an annoyed expression on her face. "What is she doing here instead of being at the market?" I said.

"She's obviously waiting for someone," Simon said. "It must be something important for her to step away like this."

We settled in and ordered. When our iced teas came, Simon's theory proved right. Kylie was joined by Rhonda's girlfriend, Ramona. "Simon, is that the woman you saw Kylie talking to at the market?"

Simon glanced across the street then shook his head. "No, she had dark hair and a better body. She was much younger."

Ten minutes later, Harold and Maggie, our fellow judges from the art show, rounded the corner by Sweet Indulgences with a man I didn't recognize. The three of them went over to the Cheese Emporium and sat down at Kylie's table.

"Good friends meeting for breakfast?" Simon suggested.

"No. It doesn't look that casual. It looks like they're having a meeting of some sort," I said, training the binoculars on each in turn.

We watched as Maggie started talking while the others listened intently. She put a file folder on the table, opened it, and handed a piece of paper to Kylie, then Harold and Ramona. They each looked it over.

They talked a little while longer, but before the waitress could take their order, all five got up and took off in different directions. Maggie and Harold crossed the street and walked over to the Coronet. I wondered if they'd notice us inside. But they were absorbed in another task. Maggie pulled out a sheet of paper, Harold handed her pieces of tape, and she taped the paper on the window next to the other announcements for plays, concerts, and charity events.

"What the heck is that?" Simon said.

Before we could get up and see, my phone pinged and I saw a text from Merrily.

How close are you? We need bread!

As we headed toward the door, I texted her back:

On my way.

Simon opened the door and we went outside to look at the flyer that had been posted in the middle of the big window opposite the counter. It read:

Petition!

To: The Greenport Village Board
From: Shop owners and citizens of Greenport

SHUT DOWN THE GARDEN OF DEATH!

Recent events at the new medicinal garden on Front Street, namely the death of Dr. Charles White, have convinced us, your local merchants, that the Village Board of Greenport made a grave mistake in awarding the Fox parcel of land to Nature's Way, and the owner, Willow McQuade, ND.

It is patently obvious that the publicity from this event will hurt business now and in the future and threaten the livelihoods of every Greenport merchant.

Furthermore, we also believe that the selection method that granted Ms. McQuade the Fox lot was seriously flawed and that she was awarded the lot was because of the previous "good works" of her aunt, Ms. Claire Hagen, and not on her own merit.

We think that there is but one choice: take back the medicinal garden from Ms. McQuade and declare the land the Dr. White Memorial Park. We want to make this a neutral green space in the heart of Greenport that everyone can enjoy, instead of leaving it in the hands of a shop owner who is clearly irresponsible. If you stand with us in this fight, please sign below and leave your address and contact information. We will present this petition at the next board meeting.

I stood there, too shocked to speak or even move.

Simon put a hand on my shoulder. "I'm so sorry, Willow."

"This can't be happening," I said, as anxiety squeezed my chest. I felt like I couldn't breathe. "I knew that most of the applicants were bitter, but this is really low. And Kylie and Ramona . . . I didn't think they were so completely against me."

Simon snatched the sign off of the window, crumpled it into a ball, and threw it into a nearby trash can. "We're not going to let them do this to you. I'm calling my lawyer."

This time I didn't stop him.

Simon worked fast. As we walked back to Nature's Way, he got on the phone with his über-lawyer, the one who had defended him last fall when he was accused of the TV producer's murder. I only heard Simon's end of the conversation, but he told him to get on the case, no matter what the cost.

Moments later, Simon clicked off his phone. "He'll take care of it. He says its harassment, pure and simple. He'll squash the motion and that petition by issuing a cease-and-desist notice today. He says it's a piece of cake compared to my problem last year." He put his arm around me. "So don't worry, it's going to be okay."

But I was worried. I thought I had a full plate before, between the opening of the garden and running Nature's Way on Maritime Festival weekend. But now, solving Dr. White's murder, and this action by the shop owners that threatened to destroy everything we had built, seemed like too much to handle.

Simon walked me back to Nature's Way. It was almost eleven, and the tours started at noon, so I really hoped that Jackson and Nate had been able to get most of the work done.

After I brought Merrily the bread, eggs, and other goods from the farmer's market, we went to look for Jackson and found him in a section at the front of the garden that had plants with healing properties for the skin. The misty morning had evolved into what was going to be a humid and hot day, and Jackson had worked up a sweat. I watched as he gently extracted a plant from its plastic pot and set it into the ground. Meanwhile, Qigong was "helping" by digging small holes in the section.

When we walked up, Qigong scampered over to greet us, nose covered in dirt, while Jackson firmed up dirt around the new plant and pointed to a patch of calendula. Calendula was one of my favorite remedies. Its bright orange and yellow petals were used in an essential oil that was an astringent, an antiseptic, and an anti-inflammatory. It was good for everything from rashes, cuts, and wounds to insect bites and even a soothing facial.

"I had to replace two of the calendula plants, but the rest of it was okay," Jackson told me. "Nate's almost done in the back and then he's setting up the booth in front with Wallace, so I think you're in good shape for your garden tours and merchandising. I'm going to work on the patio next, after I fill up these holes. Qigong's good company, but he does like to dig."

But when he saw the look on my face, he knew something was very wrong. We told him what had happened and what Simon had already done to fix it.

Wordlessly, Jackson put down the spade he had been using, took off his gloves, and wrapped me in a big bear hug. He knew what this meant and how hard we had both worked on the garden. The idea of it being destroyed was simply unbearable.

Since no one was around, I let myself cry, knowing that it would bring healing. Jackson held me while I did, until I was calm again. When I was done, I pulled a few tissues out of my bag and wiped my face. I picked up Qigong and he happily licked the rest of my tears away.

"It's going to be fine. Simon and I will make sure of it."

"You two, you're going to work together?"

We had collaborated on the last case at the historic Bixby estate and fortunately, everything had ended well, but I was still a little surprised by how positive he sounded about their new partnership. But when I thought about it, it made sense. Jackson loved me, and so he was putting my welfare first, even though Simon drove him crazy at times.

"Sure, we're the Three Musketeers, right?" Jackson said. "Simon will take care of the lawyer stuff, and I'll make sure the garden is in good shape, while you give tours and take care of Nature's Way."

"And solve the case," Simon said. "Don't forget that."

I smiled at them, feeling supported, relieved, and much calmer. "You can count on me."

chapter ten

Willow McQuade's Favorite Medicinal Plants

DANDELION
Botanical name: *Taraxacum officinale*

Medicinal uses: Dandelion is one of the planet's most famous and useful weeds. Historically, it has been used to treat liver disease, kidney disease, and spleen problems. The entire dandelion plant is useful as a medicine and a food. Dandelion greens are edible and a rich source of vitamin A, iron, calcium, and minerals. Dandelion is also often used as a mild diuretic for fluid retention, and a liver tonic to help purify the blood. Dandelion can also be used to help clear the body of old emotions such as anger and fear that can be stored in the liver and kidneys. In addition, dandelion can be used to treat mild digestive problems and various skin conditions.

As a flower essence, dandelion reduces tension, especially muscular tension in the neck, back, and

shoulders. It fosters spiritual openness and encourages the letting go of fear and trusting in your own ability to cope with life. Use the fresh or dried leaves and roots of the dandelion, or the whole plant, in teas, capsules, and extracts. Try putting dandelion leaves into your salad, use it as a cooked green, and even use the flowers to make wine.

Much as I wanted to find Dr. White's killer, we only had about an hour before tours started, and I needed to turn my focus to more immediate things—finishing up repairs on the garden. But I was interrupted by the arrival of Sandra and Martin Bennett.

When Simon spotted them he grabbed my arm and whispered in my ear, "That's the woman that Kylie was talking to at the farmer's market."

"Really? Are you sure?"

Simon nodded. "Very. They were having a pretty intense conversation. This one here was even crying at one point."

"That's good to know," I said, puzzled. I turned my attention to the couple. "Hi, you two. Come to see the garden?"

Sandra tucked a strand of dark hair back into her ponytail and smiled. "We thought we'd take the tour since we're not busy yet. Is it too early? The sign says you don't open until noon."

"That's the plan," I said. Even though I was pressed for time, I felt glad that some of the other merchants wanted to see the garden.

"Do you have time to show us around?" Sandra was

wearing jeans and a T-shirt with their logo, a happy-looking cow and the words: Organic Artisanal Cheese Fresh Daily! Maybe it would turn out that we could work together, I thought with a glimmer of hope. Maybe she and Martin would oppose the petition to close the garden.

"Sure, I can squeeze in a quick tour."

"Nate and I will make sure everything is good to go," Jackson said.

So, while they kept working I gave a tour through the front sections of the garden. Simon trailed along with the tour. Sandra and Martin seemed both interested and impressed with the work we'd done. Sandra was especially interested in the section of plants for pain—like feverfew for migraines, cramp bark for menstrual cramps, and arnica for muscle aches.

"It's amazing that this little flower can help stop a headache," she said, examining the feverfew plant, which had small daisylike heads. "I've had bad migraines for ages now. I wonder if it would help me."

"Are your migraines connected with hormonal changes?" I asked.

"My gynecologist thinks they are."

"Then I can suggest some good supplements that might help."

"Great. I'd also like to pick up some arnica. I broke my shoulder in a fall a few years ago, and I had to wait almost a month to have the surgery, and then . . . it didn't go well. So now I'm left with chronic pain. I tried talking to that doctor about natural remedies, but he was very dismissive. Long story, short: he's no longer my doctor and I'm looking for alternatives to handle the pain, besides relying on prescription pain-killers."

"I think that's smart. Can I ask—who was this doctor?"

"I shouldn't say." She turned to Martin and said something that I couldn't hear. "He's local."

"And a real jerk," Martin added.

Sandra squeezed his hand. "It's okay, honey."

Simon shot me a look and I knew we were thinking the same thing. What were the chances that the doctor was Charles White—an orthopedic surgeon—and that Sandra was the one who'd been suing him for the botched surgery?

As we headed toward the back of the garden to continue the tour, Sandra surprised me by saying, "Where did they find Dr. White? I have to admit, I'm a real true-crime junkie. I read about it and watch it on TV."

"Does she ever," Martin said, rolling his eyes.

I hoped that the rest of my visitors weren't interested in the same thing. But I took them over to the cardiac section and pointed out where I had found the body. "Dr. White was right there, next to that fox-glove plant."

"How creepy," Sandra said with a shudder. "Why in your garden? I mean, of all places. It seems strange."

"We don't know."

"Do they know who did it?" Martin asked.

"We don't know that either, but some of the local merchants are circulating a petition to shut down the garden. Have you seen it?"

"We heard about it, but of course we'd never sign

something like that. Right, love?" she said, and took her husband's hand.

Martin gave me a sympathetic look. "No, of course not. I mean, we wanted the lot, too, but that feels too much like revenge."

"It doesn't matter," Simon said. "My lawyer will shut them down. He's working on it as we speak."

"Good. It was a mean-spirited thing to do." The wind blew a pink and white flower toward us, and Sandra caught it in her open palm.

"That's hawthorn," I said. "It's good for the heart—calms palpitations."

"Well, maybe those other merchants should try it," Martin muttered. "I don't understand why they can't let this go. They're a bunch of hypocrites, too. They'll all go to White's wake this afternoon, even though they didn't like him. No one did."

"I heard that one patient sued him."

"True," Sandra said. "And she wasn't the only one."

"Are you two going to the wake?" Simon asked.

She shook her head. "No way. Besides, if the festival is anything like yesterday, we'll be slammed this afternoon. We nearly sold out of everything we had brought."

"Working the booth is definitely a two-person job," Martin added. "And today we made sure to bring more cheese and yogurt."

"Where is the wake being held?" I wondered if I should attend—or if I could even get away to go. Or if they'd let me in. Still, if I did go, it might help me zero in on a few suspects.

"At Jellico's in Southold, by the monument," Martin said. "The wake is from four to six, today and tomorrow, and the funeral is Monday at the Catholic church, also in Southold. The Whites lived down by Laughing Water, in a big house, you know, by the beach."

While Martin talked, Sandra crouched down and carefully examined the section where Dr. White had been found. "How did he die?"

"Someone hit him on the head with a shovel."

"That had to hurt," Martin said.

"Yeah," Sandra said. "How weird."

What was weird was her fascination with Dr. White's death. But before I could press her for answers about her relationship with him, Nate ran up to us. "Jackson wanted me to come and get you. He's found something really cool in the garden!"

We followed Nate back over and found Jackson in the section of plants that had psychiatric properties, like St. John's wort for depression and valerian for anxiety. He was on his hands and knees, digging up something with Qigong's help.

"What's going on? Did you find something else?" I explained to Sandra, Martin, and Simon that we had found an antique earring in the garden Friday afternoon.

"Nate found a bunch of new holes in this section, probably courtesy of Qigong, and a valerian plant that had been uprooted. I was helping him fill in the holes and replant, and I found this." He showed me a long, narrow object wrapped in a dirt-covered towel.

"Well, unwrap it, man!" Simon said impatiently.

Jackson carefully unwound the towel, revealing what looked like an old sword. The blade was long and looked hand-forged, as if it had been beaten into its shape. The hilt was wrapped with the remains of what had once been leather, and at the very top of the sword, a dark red, glittering stone was set in the pommel.

Simon peered at it more closely. "I don't think that's a piece of glass," he said, with something close to awe in his voice. "You'd have to get it appraised, but I'm guessing you just found a sword set with an unusually large ruby. If I'm right, the stone alone will be worth a small fortune."

I couldn't believe it. "Come on, Simon. The whole thing is probably a fake."

Holding it by the hilt, Jackson turned away from us and swung the sword experimentally. "It's got an awfully nice weight and balance for a fake," he said. "I think this thing was meant to be used."

"That's why you need an appraiser to look at it," Simon said.

"Fake or not, how did it wind up in your garden?" Jackson asked. "It looks ancient. Where do you think it came from?"

Simon shrugged. "Maybe it's pirate treasure. In the 1600s pirates frequented the East End."

Jackson looked at him. "You're kidding, right?"

Martin leaned in to stare at the sword.

"No, not at all," Simon continued. "When Captain Kidd found out that the British government had declared him a pirate, he sailed to New York on his boat, the *Adventure Prize,* in June 1699, and buried some of his treasure on Gardiner's Island. The authorities recovered a portion of it, but not all. To this day, people are still searching for it. What you found could be pirate's booty from Kidd or someone else. Stranger things have happened."

"Isn't that a little far-fetched?" Martin asked, raising an eyebrow. "I mean, it's more likely that this thing is a reproduction or—"

"There's a way to find out," Simon said. "An expert is giving a lecture about Captain Kidd at the Maritime Museum tomorrow night, as part of the festival. I was planning on going since I want to develop a project about pirates, maybe even Captain Kidd himself—a more realistic version than the Depp movies. We could check it out and show the expert this sword. He should at least have an idea of whether or not it's authentic to that time."

"If what you say is true, this could be Captain Kidd's sword," Sandra said, sounding excited. "Wouldn't that be something?"

"Except how did it get here?" Jackson said, still clearly bothered by its appearance in the garden.

Martin checked his watch. "We'd better go back to the booth," he said to Sandra. "It's getting busy again." He gestured out to the street, where crowds were starting to gather.

"Right," she said. "But let us know what you find out, okay? This is better than true crime."

"Stop by the store and I'll help you with those supplements, too, if you like," I offered.

"I'll do that. Thanks."

After they left, Jackson went over to the tool shed, found a clean towel, and wrapped up the sword again. "I kind of wish Sandra and Martin weren't here when we found this," he admitted. "I have a feeling that the fewer people who know about it, the better. We should probably ask them not to mention it to anyone—at least not before we know whether we're dealing with a real artifact or a reproduction."

"I'll tell them," Simon said. "I want to talk to Sandra again anyway. She seemed unusually interested in Dr. White's death."

"She said she's a true-crime junkie," I reminded him.

"Or maybe she's the patient who sued White," Simon suggested.

"What do you mean?" Jackson asked.

Simon told Jackson what she said earlier about White. "To top it off, I saw her with Kylie at the farmer's market. Sandra could be that friend that Kylie was talking about yesterday."

"And you're thinking that she killed White and was returning to the scene of the crime?" Jackson said. "Those things don't always happen in real life, Simon."

"I know, but I still think it's worth checking out."

"Me, too," I said. "We need to find out more about her—and about what else might be buried in this garden. Do you think that's why everyone wanted this lot? Not for their businesses but to find treasure?"

"If there was a rumor about this as a site, yes," Simon said. "People do strange things when it comes to money. All those merchants could even be working together to get whatever's buried here."

"That's an unsettling thought," I said. "But, if it's true, then their determination to take the garden away from me suddenly makes an awful kind of sense . . . I think we need to go to that wake later on this afternoon. We could go after the garden closes and before the sea shanty concert tonight."

Jackson shook his head. "I'll skip the wake. I saw enough death when I was a policeman. Besides, I want to work on the patio and the teahouse, make sure it's open by next weekend before the festival is over. Why don't you go, Simon? Keep an eye on Willow. We can go to the concert when you come back."

"Will do," Simon said. "I doubt I'll be able to write today after all of this."

Jackson grinned. "Does that mean you want to be a waiter again?"

"Uh . . . let me think about it."

"You do that," I said. "Shall I take the sword inside?"

Jackson handed the towel-wrapped sword to me. "Put it in a safe place until later."

I put the sword on the top shelf of my closet under some sweaters next to Aunt Claire's diaries, papers, and books. But before I did, I unwrapped the towel and took a closer look at the sword. The metal blade was tarnished, and I couldn't tell what the metal was—some kind of steel? Beneath the eroded leather wrappings, the hilt seemed to be carved of wood. And the pommel, it, too, was made of a tarnished metal. I grabbed a washcloth from the bathroom and ran it under the tap, then dabbed at the dark red stone, cleaning dirt off all of its facets, making it shine.

The result was an impressive blood-red jewel. But it was still difficult to believe that it was a genuine ruby as Simon had said. After all, rhinestones made of glass had plenty of glitter. But somehow, it didn't seem like a rhinestone. It seemed like the real thing. "You didn't actually belong to Captain Kidd, did you?" I asked. The blood-red stone seemed to wink back at me. "We'll find out," I told it. "Soon enough."

chapter eleven

Willow McQuade's
Favorite Medicinal Plants

ECHINACEA
Botanical name: *Echinacea purpurea*

Medicinal uses: The echinacea plants that line the walkway in front of Nature's Way are some of my favorite flowers. Not just because they come in a variety of dazzling colors, or because they make me smile, but because of echinacea's many health benefits. Purple cornflower, the most commonly used and the most potent, has traditionally been used to shorten the duration of colds and the flu and to ease symptoms like fever, cough, and a sore throat.

A study in the *Journal of Clinical Pharmalogical Therapy* in 2004 showed that taking echinacea at the first sign of a cold can ease symptoms and shorten sick time. University of Alberta researchers found that volunteers who took echinacea experienced 23 percent lower symptom scores than those who did not. Echi-

nacea works by increasing the levels of a naturally occurring chemical in the body known as properdin, improving immunity. The aboveground parts of the plant and roots of echinacea are used fresh or dried to make teas, juice, and extracts for medicinal use.

For the first garden tour that afternoon, the group was small, just eight people, but thankfully they were interested in medicinal plants, not Dr. White's murder, and I finally felt as if I was fulfilling my mission in creating the garden.

I gave the tours on the hour and things continued to go well until Harold Spitz and Maggie Stone showed up, just before my 4 p.m. tour. I braced myself for more conflict. This was quickly becoming exhausting.

"We know what you've done," Maggie said, sounding angry. "You're not going to get away with it."

"What have I done?" I asked, reminding myself to breathe and remain calm no matter what.

"We've already had calls from Simon Lewis's high-priced lawyer," Maggie said furiously.

I shrugged. "I saw that lovely little petition you started to take the garden away from me. Did you really think I was going to just give it up?"

"If you want a fight, you'll get one," Harold vowed, his voice rising.

"Lower your voice," I said, and motioned them farther away from the queue forming at the garden gate. "I'm not looking for a fight. I'm worried about keeping the teaching garden open for the community, and I'm going to do everything I can to make that happen."

"You can't stop us," Harold said. "It's the will of the people."

"Oh, please," Simon said, walking up to us. "It's the will of some jealous merchants who can't stand the fact that they lost and someone else won and is doing a great job and giving back to the community."

I blinked. "Where did you come from?"

"I told you I was meeting you back here to go to the wake." Simon glanced at his watch and smiled at me. "I'm early."

"I wanted that lot for a dog park," Maggie went on, as if Simon had never spoken. "That's giving back to the village, too."

Simon pointed to Mitchell Park across the street. "There's a whole park right there that you can use."

"It's not the same thing," Maggie snapped. "You wouldn't understand anyway. You're an out-of-towner."

"Excuse me, but I own property in Greenport and I've been living here part-time for the past couple of years."

An African American woman in her seventies wearing a flowered shirt and shorts and a sun hat stepped out of the queue and came over to us. I quickly recognized her as one of Claire's animal rescue friends, Alicia Carter. "Harold and Maggie, you two should be ashamed of yourself, circulating that hateful petition and hassling this dear, sweet girl who is just trying to carry on Claire's legacy and help the community."

"Stay out of this, Alicia," Harold snapped. "This is not your business."

"It's everyone's business—everyone who loves Greenport and wants to support Willow's efforts to make it a better place." She took my hands. "The good people in this community don't agree with what they are doing, Willow. You can count on us."

"Thank you, Alicia," I said. "I really do appreciate it." It felt good to have her and the rest of Claire's friends on my side. I gave her a quick hug and she rejoined the line again.

Harold and Maggie were whispering to each other; probably figuring out their next move. But I had had enough. It was almost four and I needed to start the tour. "Are you two done? I have people waiting."

"Little old ladies won't save you," Harold said, giving me a nasty smile. "Enjoy it while you can."

"You, too," Simon said cheerfully.

Maggie couldn't resist taking the bait. "Enjoy what?"

"Your last day of freedom. As of tomorrow, my lawyer is going to keep you so wrapped up in red tape that you won't be able to breathe without filling out notarized forms. I do hope you enjoy being deposed—and that you both have excellent lawyers of your own. Because for you, this is going to get very expensive, very fast," Simon promised. "If I were you, I'd save myself a lot of time, money, and frustration and just give up now."

"We'll see about that," Maggie said. "Let's go, Harold."

We watched them cross the street and stomp into the park. I could almost see steam coming out of Harold's ears. "Thanks, Simon," I said.

He gave me a rueful grin. "I know, I know. It's obnoxious to use my money to push people around. But sometimes . . . it's just fun. Now, when are you going to be done so we can scope out that wake?"

"It usually takes me about forty-five minutes to do a tour, and then I'll need to change. Why don't you walk around and play tourist? I'll meet you inside at five."

"A-okay," Simon said. "Go get 'em, girl."

We arrived at the funeral home in Southold at five fifteen. The parking lot was packed with mourners' cars. As Martin had predicted, the fact that White had not been well liked didn't seem to matter. Everyone wanted to make an appearance, for whatever reason.

I managed to squeeze my mint-green Prius into a tight spot in the back by the garage. The car had been a gift from Green Focus, the company that made Claire's Fresh Face cream, a thank-you for finding the formula after she had died.

I'd changed into a plain black shift dress and flats. Simon wore khakis and a navy blue blazer over a white button-down, no tie. We entered through the back door and found a long line snaking down the hallway. I was suddenly feeling jittery, as if I'd had several cups of espresso. I tried to concentrate on my breathing to calm my nerves as we headed to the front of the room, what would have been the living room, in this converted house.

While Simon skipped paying his respects and made small talk with some of the attendees, in particular a good-looking brunette, I walked up to the coffin. Dr. White looked plastic and very dead. I quickly moved on to look at the wreaths and arrangements of flowers and the collages of family photos.

Arlene, his widow, sat in the front row next to a

young man, whom I guessed was her son. On her other side was Joe Larson, and beside him, the man we had seen at the Cheese Emporium.

Larson handed tissues to Arlene as she cried and at one point pulled her into a hug. I wondered what their relationship was—family, friends, or something more?

Arlene was wearing an elegant black jacket and skirt. From what I knew of them, she and her husband had always been among Greenport's wealthiest. But it occurred to me that she now had plenty of money that was hers to spend any way she wished. Of course, this would have occurred to the police, too. I knew that they were probably checking the Whites' finances, making sure that Charles White had not been killed for his insurance.

Arlene finally stopped sobbing, and Joe Larson left her sitting there with her son. He circulated around the room and ended up talking to members of the Village Board and the mayor. But when Maggie and Harold entered, he quickly excused himself and went over to them. I wondered if he was working with the merchants to shut my garden down as well—and whether he, too, had heard from Simon's lawyer.

Maggie spotted me and said something to Joe, who shot me an angry look, said something else to her and Harold, then headed over to me. Fortunately, Simon chose that moment to reappear at my side.

"I think we'd better leave," I said. "I don't want trouble."

"It's your call," Simon said.

I braced myself as Joe Larson strode up to me. "You have no right to be here," he began. "You were never a friend to Charles or Arlene. I think you'd better leave."

He grabbed my arm and tried to pull me toward the door.

"Don't touch me." I tried to yank my arm away, but he was strong and gripped me tightly.

Simon put a hand on Larson's arm. "Let go of her now," he said in a quiet voice, "or my lawyer will sue you for assault . . . Willow, is that a bruise I see on your arm?"

Larson released me at once. "This is a private wake. I think you two should leave now. You'll only upset Arlene." He took out a handkerchief and wiped his forehead. It *was* hot in here.

I glanced over at Maggie and Harold, who both had smug looks on their faces. Obviously, they thought they'd won this round of the battle.

"Are you working with them to close the garden down?" I asked Larson.

"I don't know what you're talking about."

"I think you do. I think you want that lot and will do anything to get it, and—"

"That's over," Larson broke in. "I've moved on to other things."

"Like Arlene?" Simon asked.

"That's preposterous. Charles was my business partner and my best friend. Now, you two need to leave."

The truth is, I would have been happy to get out of that stifling room. But I also wanted to find out more about the grieving widow, and I knew this was probably my best chance to talk to her.

"Okay, we'll go," I said. "But first, I just want to express my condolences to Arlene."

"Not going to happen, lady. If you want me to call the police and have them escort you—"

But before he could finish, Arlene spotted us and scurried over, with the man from the meeting and her son, close behind. "You have a lot of nerve showing up here," she began in a furious undertone. "My husband was killed in your garden."

"I know, and I just came to tell you how sorry—"

"If you're really sorry," she said in a much louder voice, "then you'll shut down the Garden of Death."

I stared at her, suddenly understanding. "You're the one who started that petition, aren't you?"

"She's not discussing that," the man said. Up close his face looked like a weasel, with a narrow jaw and beady, dark brown eyes.

"I certainly was, and I'm not afraid to admit it," Arlene said. "And if you have a problem with that, this is my new lawyer, Michael Yard. He's overseeing everything now."

"Well, he's not going to succeed," Simon said. "My lawyer will see to that."

"You may find that high-powered, out-of-town lawyers aren't welcome in this community," Yard said. "We have a different way of doing things on the East End."

"You mean skirting the law and slandering good, hardworking people, like Willow?" Simon countered.

Arlene's son spoke up. "Mother, let's go back and sit down." He steered her back to her seat, with Yard following.

"We're done here," Larson said.

"For now," I agreed.

Simon and I headed out. The jittery feeling I had before was gone, and in its place was a sadness I hadn't expected. I'd never liked Charles White, but I wasn't happy that he was dead, and it was awful knowing that he'd died in my garden. And it wasn't much better knowing that his widow somehow blamed me for his death and was trying to turn the rest of the town against me.

"Hey, Willow, it's going to be okay," Simon assured me as we crossed the parking lot to my car.

"It doesn't feel okay," I told him. "It feels like this whole thing is far from over."

chapter twelve

Willow McQuade's
Favorite Medicinal Plants

ELEUTHERO
Botanical name: Eleuthero (*Eleutherococcus senticosus, E. gracilistylus*), formerly *Acanthopanax senticosus,* and *A. spinosus*

Medicinal uses: Eleuthero has been used by tribe peoples of Siberia and the Chinese for over four thousand years. An ancient Chinese proverb is: "I would rather take a handful of eleuthero than a cartload of gold and jewels." In the frigid regions of China, Russia, and Japan, reindeer, a symbol of strength and endurance, consume this plant.

Since 1962, Russian cosmonauts have been given rations of eleuthero to help acclimate to the stresses of being weightless and living in space. Athletes, deep-sea divers, rescue workers, and explorers all use it to nourish themselves during stressful situations. More than a thousand studies have been conducted on this

**herb, which can also help if you experience fatigue,
exhaustion, weakness, or anxiety.**

It was relief to get back to Nature's Way after such a
hostile environment at the funeral home. The village
of Greenport, the store, and my comfy home on the
third floor made me feel safe and secure, even more so
now that Jackson was in my life. Since Claire had died,
I had taken over her business, continued to grow it, and
established myself as a member of the community. I
belonged here, and no one was going to run me out of
town, certainly not Arlene White and Joe Larson.

Simon had gone home, presumably to write, and
since it was almost six thirty, I went into the kitchen to
get something to eat. The smell of fresh baked goods
filled the air.

I peeked inside the oven and saw three peach pies.
Merrily was making her award-winning dessert for our
customers. She'd placed her trophy on the shelf above
the counters, so she could see it while she worked.

I went to get a frozen organic pizza from the freezer
to bake and eat with a green salad—and found Merrily
and Nate, their arms around each other. They jumped
apart when they saw me. "Don't mind me," I said
quickly. "Just getting something to eat. How are things
going?"

"I'd better get back outside and help Jackson clean
up," Nate said. "I'll tell him that you're back." He
quickly dashed outside.

"I didn't mean to interrupt you two. Is everything
okay?"

"It was crazy busy from three to about five, but we're okay now. I was just going to close up. Wallace and Nate brought in all the merchandise from the booth. They sold a bunch of stuff again, so that's good."

"Merrily, I meant with you two."

She smiled. "We're doing really great. Nate's so sweet, and he's such a good listener."

"Just go slow," I advised. Before Merrily started working for Aunt Claire she had ended an abusive relationship; she hadn't really dated much since then. Last year, she was infected with Lyme disease and that took its toll on her social life. When Nate was hired a few months ago, the two became friends, and now it seemed the relationship had deepened.

"I am, don't worry. Nate understands that I need to take it one step at a time. Can I get you something to eat?"

"Don't bother. I was just going to heat something up."

"Nonsense, I just baked a spinach and mushroom quiche." She went over to the counter and pointed to it. "I was just letting it cool. I'll make a fresh green salad to go with it. I've already fed all the animals." She put the pizza back into the freezer and closed the door.

"Then I'm going to take a quick shower. I'll be back down to eat in a few." I wanted to scrub myself clean of the bad vibes from the wake and my run-in with Joe Larson. I went upstairs and visited with the dogs and cats before I jumped into the shower. Afterward, I changed into jeans and one of my favorite old, soft sweatshirts. When I stepped back out onto the landing, the door to Allie's massage room was open. She was at her desk, opening a box and pulling out big bottles of massage oils.

I knocked on her open door. "Got anything new and interesting?"

"Hey, Willow. Yes, a few. Check out this new massage oil from Mountain Rose Herbs. It's called Rose Moon Massage Oil." She opened the bottle and took a whiff. "Want to try it?"

I took the bottle and inhaled. "I smell a hint of geranium."

"Good nose. It also contains organic lavender, calendula, chamomile flowers, sweet almond oil, and even real rose petals. Very therapeutic."

"I'll bet your massage clients will love it."

"I hope so." She put the cap on the bottle and turned her attention to me. "How are you doing? I hear it's been a rough couple of days."

"Well, I'm taking a break tonight. I'm going to grab something to eat, and then Jackson and I are headed over to the sea-shanty concert."

"Simon told me that you're investigating again. Is that really necessary? I mean, after what happened up at the estate last year?"

"I have to, Allie. The detectives are interested in Jackson. They found his fingerprints on the murder weapon, a shovel in the garden." I gave her the rundown on Koren and Coyle's visit, the merchants' plan to try and shut us down, and the freaky wake I'd just attended.

She gave a low whistle of amazement. "They're calling it the Garden of Death? That couldn't be more opposite from what you wanted to create."

"No kidding . . . Allie, do you think I've made a mistake in opening the garden? Do you think Claire would have done the same thing?"

She nodded. "I do. You can't help it if some nut is on the loose. Sometimes things just happen. Keep your chin up. You'll get through this."

I nodded, but I did feel a little better. Something about talking to Allie always cheered me up. "So, what are you up to tonight?"

"Well, this weekend has been crazy busy with clients, not that I'm complaining. So I'm just going to hang out with some of the people in my building and watch movies. I got *North by Northwest* and *Sex and the City: The Movie* on DVD."

"That sounds like fun, but where's Hector?" Hector, my acupuncturist extraordinaire, lived with Allie in a beautiful loft apartment on Main Street. Hector was gay and Allie was straight. Both of them were looking for boyfriends.

"He's in Bridgehampton, seeing clients and staying with a friend at her beach house for the next couple of days."

"Well, I'll be glad when he's back." Both Allie and Hector had been with me since I took over the store. In fact, they moved out here from NYC to help me make it a success.

Allie and I hugged, then I made my way downstairs to the second-floor landing where I met Jackson, who was on his way up.

"Good shower?" he asked.

"Good shower. But it would have been better with you there."

"We can't always conserve water," he said, giving me a kiss. "So how did the wake go? Any trouble?"

"Plenty," I said, and told him what had happened.

"So the widow White is behind the petition . . . I thought the two of them were getting divorced. What gives?"

"Good question."

"If I know you, you'll figure it out." He gave me another kiss. "I'll hop in the shower and meet you downstairs."

At seven thirty Jackson and I grabbed two lawn chairs and a blanket and headed across the street to the park. The concert didn't start until eight fifteen, but we wanted to make sure we got a good space. We found one on the lawn facing the stage and were close enough that Jackson could take a few photos. The night air was crisp and clear, without a trace of humidity, and an almost full moon dominated the sky.

Personally, I wasn't that crazy about sea shanties, but once Jackson heard them at his first Maritime Festival years ago, he'd become a fan. He even listened to sea-shanty CDs in his truck.

Since he was into them, I'd learned a lot about them, too. For example, I knew that sea shanties were work songs that were sung on sailing ships, used to keep a good rhythm during work and make sailors more productive. A typical shanty featured a shanty man, who would call out a verse, and the rest of the sailors would respond.

There were long-haul shanties and short-haul shanties,

respectively, for long– and short–rope pulling, and others for other onboard tasks. The only constant was that songs about life at sea were sung as the sailors left for places unknown, and songs about home were sung as they headed for land. Shanties weren't performed anymore except for shows like this and in the movies.

"This is going to be good," Jackson said as he set up the chairs. "I've been looking forward to this concert for weeks."

Obviously, he wasn't the only one. The park was quickly filling up with couples, friends, and families eager to see the show. I glanced around, scanning the crowd, wondering if I'd see Kylie or Maggie or any of the others who were joining forces against the garden.

"See anything interesting?"

"Not so far."

"Why not take a break?" Jackson asked gently. "There's plenty of time for all of that later."

He was right. I needed to work on the case, but time away to clear my head was good, too. "Okay, I'm officially taking a break."

"Good, you're going to enjoy this. I know you don't like sea shanties as much as I do, but this concert could change your mind."

I took his hand and smiled at him. "Consider my mind open."

Fifteen minutes later, the lights dimmed and Mayor Hobson introduced Manly Men Singing Sea Shanties. The group was a perennial favorite, and when they took the stage, the crowd erupted in applause.

There were five singers, all of whom looked like they had just come off a fishing trawler. The group started with "Blow the Man Down," and people began clapping and singing along. Jackson joined in and was having a grand time. For a little while any trouble that the two of us had melted away.

"This is 'Spanish Ladies,'" Jackson said as the group started a second tune. "It's a capstan shanty sung on homeward-bound journeys. You'll like it."

"We'll drink and be jolly and drown melancholy," the song began.

"There's a lot about drink in these songs," I noted.

"I'm sure a lot of sailors had the sea version of cabin fever," Jackson said. "If you were stuck on a boat for months, with bad weather, backbreaking work, and no way to communicate with anyone at home, alcohol was probably one of the few comforts. Most of them probably could have used AA." Jackson had joined Alcoholics Anonymous years ago, and it had changed his life. Before AA, he had been prone to bouts of depression and got into fights when he was drinking. It had even affected his performance on the job. After the police department put him on probation, he joined AA and began recovery.

Six months later, though, he was injured when he slipped on black ice chasing a suspect. He was never able to return to his work as a police officer, but with treatments from Allie and Hector and the supplements and dietary changes that Aunt Claire and I suggested, he felt much better.

The group finished the song and moved on to "Blood Red Roses," a shanty about going around Cape

Horn that I recognized from one of Jackson's CDs. While he enjoyed the show, I scanned the crowd again. I couldn't help myself; a lot was at stake, for all of us.

This time I spotted Sandra and Martin Bennett on the far side of the lawn, sitting with her friend Kylie Ramsey and, surprisingly, with Maggie and Harold as well. So, Sandy and Martin wouldn't sign the petition to shut my garden down, but were still friendly with their fellow business owners. A few feet away, Ramona Meadows and Rhonda Rhodes, the heirloom vegetable growers, sat on a blanket with their two black Labs.

During the next hour or so, I split my attention between the singers and the group to my left. But their attention seemed to be on the show. Finally, the lead singer announced that they'd come to their last song, and began to sing, *"When I was a little boy, my mother always a told me that if I did not kiss the girls, my lips would grow all moldy."*

"Now, that is just weird," I told Jackson.

"I agree, but the song is really just about a sailor's adventures with women from all over the world until he finds the one who is 'just a daisy.'"

"Okay, that is super corny, but I have to ask: Am I your daisy?"

He leaned over and kissed me. "You bet."

Rhonda got up and walked across the lawn. I told Jackson that I'd be right back and got to my feet.

He tugged on the hem of my sweatshirt. "McQuade, what are you doing?"

"I'm following Rhonda. She might be up to something."

"What happened to taking a break?"

I gave him a kiss. "Break's over. But I'll be back soon, I promise."

I followed Rhonda as she made her way through the crowd and to the path that ran along the dock's edge. A few moments later, she stopped outside the camera obscura, a building that resembled the bottom layer of a lopsided cake with what looked like a periscope on top. Rhonda leaned against the side of the building and stared out at the water. Was she waiting for someone?

While the band kept playing, Rhonda kept waiting. Finally, Joe Larson came around the corner and approached her. I walked around the camera obscura to try and hear what they were saying, but could only catch snippets. Rhonda's voice was high-pitched and anxious as she said, "You promised me!"

Larson replied, "You have to be patient," and something that sounded like, "It'll happen soon" or "I'll have it soon." But then, unfortunately, he glanced around the corner and spotted me. He said something to Rhonda and she hurried away.

"What are you doing—following me?" Larson demanded.

"Don't flatter yourself," I said. "This is a public space."

"Where's your bodyguard with the high-powered lawyer?"

"Simon's a good friend, that's all." I looked over at where Jackson had been sitting. He was on his feet now, searching the crowd for me. I needed to get back. The group began to sing the last chorus of the song.

Joe looked at the camera. "You ever been inside this thing?"

"Yes, a few times."

"Our tax dollars at work. What an eyesore."

The camera obscura was one of Greenport's quirkiest attractions. Basically, it's a darkened room into which light enters through a small opening, and is then reflected by a mirror through a lens onto a viewing table. So even though you're standing inside a dark room, you can see images of Greenport projected onto the viewing table. Rotating the camera allows you to see in all directions. I loved the camera obscura. Its images were vibrant and serene and always made me appreciate the scenic beauty of the area even more.

"Clearly, you're not an art lover," I told Larson. "Leonardo da Vinci did experiments with the camera obscura. Vermeer used it as a drawing aid in the seventeenth century, and Canaletto used it for his paintings of Venice. There are only five of these cameras in the U.S. and about fifty in the world."

"Fascinating. I gotta go."

"Can I ask you something?"

"Make it quick."

"How do you benefit if the town shuts me down? Odds are, you won't be able to build anything else on the lot."

"I've got my own reasons and they're none of your business."

I thought about what Simon had said about the find in the garden. "Like pirate's treasure?" I suggested

Larson gave me a skeptical look. "You're nuts, lady. Stay away from me." He walked off into the crowd.

The song ended, and the crowd called for an encore. But as I walked back over to Jackson, someone took me by the shoulders, spun me around, and shoved me inside of the camera obscura. I landed on my knees on the wooden floor as the door closed and made a decisive clicking sound.

There was no light seeping in now. I was in a totally black space, and I couldn't help the feeling of dread that was slicing through me. I keep a small flashlight on my key chain, but I didn't have my keys on me now. I got to my feet, brushed off my pants, and waited for my eyes to adjust to the darkness. But that didn't help. With almost zero light filtering in from the night sky, the darkness was thick and black.

This must be what it feels like to be blind, I realized. Walking slowly with my arms outstretched in front of me, my fingertips finally found a wall. I felt around frantically for the seams of the door and then the door-knob. I turned and pulled. It was locked, of course. I ran my fingers over the lock but couldn't find any mechanism to unlock it. I pulled at the knob again and shouted for help but the noise of the concert, which I could hear faintly through the wooden walls, drowned me out.

Calm down! I told myself, trying to beat back a rising wave of panic. I knew that Jackson would come looking for me, but when? And would he be able to hear me?

I felt around the walls for a light switch but there was none. Carefully, my hands outstretched, I moved back toward the center of the room until I touched the viewing table.

But the only things I could see were the lights from the docks and the inky black water in the marina. It wasn't light enough to make a difference inside and I continued to fumble around in the dark. I went back to the door and pounded on it. The crowd erupted in more applause. I waited to see if the band would play another song and when they didn't, I started yelling.

"Help!" I shouted. "I'm locked inside the camera! Someone please open the door!" I banged on the door and shouted until I was hoarse.

No one came.

chapter thirteen

Willow McQuade's
Favorite Medicinal Plants

EVENING PRIMROSE
Botanical name: *Oenothera biennis*

Medicinal uses: The evening primrose plant features shamrock-shaped yellow flowers on slender green stems. This delicate beauty hides the fact that evening primrose oil provides an important nutrient called gamma-linolenic acid (GLA), an essential fatty acid required by the body for growth and development. The oil is extracted from the seeds of the evening primrose and is usually put into capsules for use. Evening primrose oil has been used since the 1930s for eczema (a condition in which the skin becomes inflamed, itchy, or scaly because of allergies or other irritation). More recently it has been used for other conditions involving inflammation, such as rheumatoid arthritis. Studies show evening primrose oil can

be helpful for PMS and the breast pain associated with the menstrual cycle.

Moments later, the fireworks started. I stopped my shouting long enough to watch the images of the flashing colored lights play out on the viewing table before I went back to the door and yelled and pounded some more. What seemed a very long time later, the fireworks finally ended, but I kept at it. I was starting to feel claustrophobic, as if the room were getting smaller and I couldn't get enough air into my lungs.

Suddenly, I heard Jackson yelling for me. "Willow? Are you in there?"

"Yes," I said, stifling a scream. "Get me out!"

He jiggled the lock. "This isn't opening. I'll be right back! Hold on!"

I took some deep breaths and tried to calm down. Jackson returned moments later and banged at the lock with something. It came loose after a few tries, and he threw the door open. "Are you okay?"

I ran into his arms. "I am now."

Jackson held me close, as if he didn't want to let me go, and I was very happy to stay there, wrapped in his arms. "You're shaking," he said at last. "Let's go home. I'll make you some hot tea, and you can tell me what happened."

But I shook my head. "I need to be outside. Let's go to Aldo's and sit on the patio. I can have some tea there."

We walked out of the park and took a quick right into the coffee shop. Because of the festival, the place was busy and Jackson stood in line to get his decaf coffee and my tea while I went outside to the patio. I breathed in the night air and thankfully felt my panic subside.

Jackson came out a few minutes later with our order, and after I told him what had happened, we sat companionably side by side, not saying much, trying to reach equilibrium again. The one other couple on the patio got up and went inside and we had the place to ourselves. Jackson reached over and took my hand. "Feeling any better?"

I took another sip of my calming chamomile tea and nodded. "Much. Thanks for saving me, again."

"I'm getting used to it." He gazed out at the harbor. "But I don't like it. Seriously, I think you need to throttle back on this investigation." He pointed to the camera obscura. "When things like this start happening, it means more trouble is on the way."

"You're still a suspect and those merchants are still trying to shut me down. Like it or not, we really don't have a choice."

Jackson took a sip of coffee. "Then we both need to be a lot more careful."

"We will be."

"Who do you think locked you in there?"

"Joe Larson is the most obvious suspect. He'd been right there minutes before, and our conversation wasn't exactly friendly. But Rhonda was there, too—they were talking together before he saw me—so either one of them could have done it." I rubbed my arm where I'd been grabbed. "Whoever threw me in there was strong. I'm guessing it was Joe."

"Or it could be someone else entirely," Jackson pointed out.

"Well, the park was packed with people, so I guess anything is possible. But my gut tells me that it's someone from that little group that's made it very clear that they want to shut down the garden."

We finished up and headed back to Nature's Way. Most of the crowd from the concert had dispersed by this time, but people still lingered in the park and strolled along Front Street.

As we headed up the path to the door, I said, "Let's check out the garden before we go inside. I'm worried that someone has been in there again. After all, we've been gone all night."

He pulled a penlight out of his pocket and we walked over to the gate. Jackson opened it but stopped me before I could go in. "I just saw a flash of light near the patio. I think someone might be inside. Stay here."

He ran off down the path. Moments later he yelled, "Hey, you, stop, stay right there!"

I took off after Jackson and ran down the path through the darkness to find out what was going on. I found Jackson in the not-yet-completed outdoor teahouse. "There was someone in here," he reported breathlessly. "He had on black jeans and a black hoodie and had a black backpack, but he went over the fence before I could grab him. He dropped this." Jackson trained his flashlight on the ground, revealing a small shovel, covered in dirt, and a new hole in front of the patio.

"We need to show this shovel to the police," I said. "Maybe there are fingerprints or they can figure out where he bought it."

Jackson pulled a bandanna out of his pocket and picked up the shovel. "Fingerprints are doubtful. I think he was wearing gloves." He checked out the label on the shovel. "It's from Home Depot, one of thousands, I'm sure. They'll never be able to trace it."

By this time I had my keys out, the tiny flashlight on. I saw something else on the ground. "What's that?"

We both stared at another object wrapped in tattered cloth. I knelt and unwrapped it, careful to keep hold of the dirty cloth, so I wouldn't get my fingerprints on whatever was inside.

"A *goblet?*" Jackson asked a moment later.

"Seems to be," I murmured. "It's some kind of metal, tarnished." It was set with what looked like red coral and turquoise, and like the sword, looked seriously old. "This is bizarre," I said. "Who buried all this stuff on this lot?"

"And what else is here?" Jackson wondered.

I looked up at him. "This is really starting to spook me. If all this stuff is real, and someone knows about it and wants it . . ." I turned and looked at the patio. "But I thought they were looking in the garden. What was he doing over here, in the teahouse?"

"Who knows? Maybe they're working a grid pattern."

"At least he didn't touch the plants."

Jackson gave a heavy sigh. "We've got to show this to the police as well. And we should probably show them the sword and earring, too."

I nodded. "But it's not an emergency, and I'm exhausted. Let's call them in the morning."

Jackson gave me a long look. "Hopefully we can convince them to let us hold on to these pieces for a day or so. I want to show all this stuff to the expert who's talking at the Maritime Museum tomorrow night."

"Me, too. If we find out this really is pirate treasure, it could go a long way toward helping us figure out why Charles White was killed here—and maybe even by whom."

"It might be a good idea to research the history of this plot of land as well. Maybe something significant did happen here."

"Good point. In the meantime, we've got to keep this garden closed and protected after hours."

"If you really want to keep everyone out, then you need to install a lock and put barbed wire on top of the fence."

I winced. "That's not exactly in keeping with my idea of a community garden. What else can we do?"

"Install an alarm system, and put up surveillance cameras, but all that high-tech stuff costs money. You could use a guard at night, too."

"I hate the idea of doing any of that, but I'll think it over. Maybe as a first step, we can put a lock on the gate. I'll call the locksmith in the morning, and then we'll see what happens."

Early Monday morning, around 8 a.m., while Jackson went home to tend to his rescues at his farm with his team, I returned to my daily routine of yoga and meditation in the yoga studio on the second floor. Nick, Aunt Claire's boyfriend, wouldn't hold his yoga class until eleven, so I thought I'd have the place all to myself.

But I'd just settled into my routine, starting with several sun salutations, when Allie came in with her tablet, an anxious look on her face. "Sorry to interrupt your practice, but I thought you should see this." She handed the tablet to me.

The screen showed a Web site titled: Shut Down the Garden of Death. On the home page was a photo of the garden with the spot where Dr. White's body had been found circled in bright red. There was also a black-and-white photo of him when he was alive. The text chronicled what had happened and then urged visitors to sign the online petition, which so far had seventy-five signatures. Arlene White and her minions had been busy.

"I can't believe they're doing this, especially after Simon's lawyer contacted them."

"It's probably not illegal," Allie said.

"Probably not," I agreed with a sigh. I clicked on the arrow that took me to the petition and found Arlene White's name in the number-one spot, followed by Harold Spitz, Maggie Stone, Kylie Ramsey, Ramona Meadows, Rhonda Rhodes, and Joe Larson. I recognized some of the other names from Greenport; others were new to me.

I clicked on the Comments button. "Ouch," I said as I read a list of comments ranging from, "lot was awarded unfairly" to "better off as a public park" to "we need a dog park, not a private garden" and "how about a memorial garden for Dr. White?"

"I didn't want to upset you, but you needed to know about this. I couldn't figure out who set it up. It just says Greenport Merchants United at the bottom. I guess that's the group of people you were talking about."

"I'm sure it is." I closed the site and handed the tablet back to her. "I need to call Simon." I got up and went over to the stack of sticky mats where I'd left my cell phone and rang his number. When he answered I told him what had happened. We talked for a few minutes and I hung up. "He's going to call his lawyer again and ask him to shut down the site. If he can."

Allie gave me a sympathetic look. "Well, if he can't, keep in mind that seventy-five signatures aren't any kind of official mandate."

"I know. But if the petition goes viral . . ."

"Try not to think about that." She gave me a quick hug. "I've got an early appointment or I'd stick around to talk. But we can talk later if you want. In the meantime, call Jackson. He'll make you feel better. Gotta go." She threw me a wave and was out the door.

My yoga and meditation practice forgotten, I called Jackson and told him what had happened. "I looked at the seventy-five names, but only twenty or so were familiar. Who are all these other people who hate me so much?"

"They don't hate you. It's probably friends and relatives of the Whites and the merchants who wanted that lot. Don't let it get to you, okay? Focus on what you need to do today, like running the store and giving tours of the garden. And don't forget to call a locksmith and remember we're going to see that pirate expert tonight. It's a good chance to get some real answers."

"When are you coming back? We need to call Detective Koren about the intruder and that shovel you found, not to mention the goblet."

"Already done. They're meeting me in the garden at 10 a.m. You don't have to be there."

"Of course I'll be there."

"Okay, I'll see you then. Love you."

"Love you, too. Bye."

I forced myself to focus, as Jackson had said, on the day ahead. The Maritime Festival was still in full swing, with foodie tours, events at local restaurants, lectures and readings at the museum and libraries, and more nighttime concerts. There would even be a two-day yard sale and antique show. All of this activity would lead up to the finale of the festival this coming weekend, with the arrival of more Tall Ships, boat races, more pirates, a chowder contest, and a production of *The Tempest*.

But for now, I kept my attention on the present moment and on my yoga and meditation practice, knowing that it would restore balance and provide peace and serenity. Afterward, I showered, dressed, and headed downstairs, Qigong trailing behind me.

After I checked in with Wallace, who always arrived early and had opened Nature's Way at eight for breakfast customers, I made myself some organic buttermilk pancakes and tea, and went into my office.

The space felt like a hug, with cozy chairs and

couch. I loved the Peace sign above the door and the bookshelves containing vegetarian cookbooks as well as volumes on natural remedies and medicinal herbs. On the walls were hand-drawn pictures of healing herbs and various yoga positions, photographs of Aunt Claire's native Australia, and London, where she once worked as an editor for British *Vogue*.

I sat down at my desk and ate my breakfast while I flipped through the latest issue of *Natural Health*. Qigong jumped onto the couch and quickly fell asleep again. I needed to take him for a walk.

I finished eating and put the plate aside but continued to sip my green tea while I checked my e-mail. Nothing out of the ordinary there, which was reassuring. Just the usual newsletters from natural product stores, confirmations of orders that Wallace had placed, and an e-mail from my mother, who was vacationing in Tuscany with my sister, Natasha, the doctor, and having a great time. My mother, sister, and I got along best when we saw each other infrequently, since neither of them really understood my passion for all things natural. I'd definitely taken after my Aunt Claire and I didn't regret it, even with the latest turn of events.

I'd just written back to my mom when the phone rang. "Hey, it's me," Simon said. "Long story short: my lawyer can't shut down the petition. He says anyone can start a petition. There's nothing illegal in that. But if they try to take it further, to the Village Board or whatever, he'll take care of it."

"Thanks," I said, unsure of whether that was actually good news.

"No problemo," Simon said. "Anything else happening?"

I briefly told him about the intruder in the garden the night before and the goblet Jackson found. This of course interested him. "No wonder everyone wants your garden. You may be sitting on a gold mine."

"You could be right. I cleaned off the stone on the sword and it looked pretty real to me, but I'm no expert."

"I think it's real and I think that someone used your lot to hide some kind of treasure, ancient or not. Remember to bring what you found to the lecture tonight. With luck, this expert will know whether this stuff dates back to the time of Captain Kidd."

"I will unless the cops want them. They're coming by at ten this morning to get the shovel. I'm dreading it. I just hope they don't take Jackson in."

"I wouldn't worry. If they do, just let me know and we'll take care of that, too. Besides, you're an ace detective. You'll figure this out soon."

I appreciated Simon's faith in me, but I was also feeling confused—and scared. I was clueless as to who had murdered Dr. White. But I also knew that things could change quickly, and I'd have to be ready if they did. As Louis Pasteur said, "Chance favors only the prepared mind." If I paid attention, the answers would eventually become clear. At least, I hoped so.

chapter fourteen

Willow McQuade's
Favorite Medicinal Plants

FEVERFEW
Botanical name: *Tanacetum parthenium, Chrysanthemum parthenium*

Medicinal uses: Feverfew has been used for centuries for fevers, headaches, stomachaches, toothaches, insect bites, infertility, and problems with menstruation. Recently, feverfew, a member of the daisy family, has become known as a migraine preventive. It works by helping to stop blood platelets from releasing too much serotonin and histamine, both of which can dilate blood vessels and lead to migraines. In Britain, migraine sufferers chew a leaf of feverfew each day to help prevent attacks. A systematic review of research in the medical journal *Public Health Nutrition* showed that feverfew is effective and safe in the prevention of migraines. The dried leaves, flowers, and stems of feverfew are used to make supplements

found in capsules, tablets, and extracts. Choose a high-quality supplement to ensure botanical integrity.

After I called a locksmith about the garden gate, I decided to take Qigong for a much-needed walk. I also wanted to clear my mind before Detective Koren and Detective Coyle arrived with more questions.

As we strolled down Front Street, I could see that Maritime Monday seemed to be paying off big-time for local merchants. The sidewalks were crowded with shoppers carrying bags from various stores. I hoped they would visit Nature's Way as well.

Qigong and I headed down Front Street to Main, where we took a right and headed for the docks. Here the streets were crowded, too. When we got to the middle of the block, I remembered the painting that Joe Larson had been so eager to buy.

The two-story Victorian-era building depicted in the painting was on the left side of the street, sandwiched between a cupcake store and a tea shop. The ground-floor windows were covered with brown paper and a sign that read: Marion's Antiques Coming July 4th! On the top floor was what looked like a residential unit. The cigar store was gone.

I crossed over to that side of the street to take a closer look. The green paint on the building was faded and flaking, and several tiles from the roof had fallen into the alley.

I noticed that there was a separate entrance on the north side of the building, so I slipped into the alley and went to see if it was open. It wasn't. I was headed back to the street when I heard a noise from the other end of the alley, by the old shipyard. I turned to see what it was.

As I did, I saw someone in black pants and a hoodie with a black backpack slip out of sight. Qigong began to bark frantically and started to run, dragging me along. Was it the same person Jackson had caught in the garden last night?

I raced after Qigong. My heart was pounding by the time we reached the mouth of the alley. I looked in both directions, but there was no one. The stranger in black had vanished.

Qigong tugged me toward the shipyard, and I didn't think twice. I raced into the yard, the dog at my side. Panting, I looked around, but again, there was no one except us. Qigong stopped barking and starting sniffing the ground.

The shipyard was deserted, and even though it was morning, I suddenly realized that adrenaline was not my friend. It was making me take risks that I shouldn't be taking. Silently, I chastised myself for taking a chance that might land me in trouble just like it had the night before, and we quickly started back toward Main Street.

I made it back to Nature's Way by nine fifty-five and put Qigong on the couch in my office for a nice snooze before going out to the garden. There, I found the locksmith, busy putting a lock on the gate, and Koren and Coyle talking to Jackson.

Jackson pointed to the fence while he explained what had happened. Coyle was holding the shovel, which had already been bagged.

"Ms. McQuade," Detective Koren said. "It's nice of you to join us. Your boyfriend was just telling us about what happened. What may I ask prompted you to look in the garden last night in the first place?"

I told him about being locked up in the camera obscura in Mitchell Park and how it had unnerved me. "When we got back here I just wanted to make sure that the garden was okay. We've been finding holes in the garden, like someone is looking for something."

"Looking for what exactly?"

"We don't know," Jackson said. "But we've found several objects that may be artifacts. We've been told that they may have been left by pirates."

"Pirate treasure? That's a new one," Detective Coyle said with a laugh. "What do you think of that, Koren?"

"Not much," Detective Koren replied. "I think Ms. McQuade couldn't resist snooping around the murder scene, like she usually does, and it had nothing to do with these supposed pirate artifacts. Isn't that true?"

"It's my property, Detective."

"She has point," Jackson said.

"From what I've heard, certain people want to take the lot away from you, especially after what happened with Dr. White," Detective Koren said. "So you might not own this land for long."

"Yeah, and if we find out that Jackson here had anything to do with the doc's murder, that's just going to make it that much easier," his partner added.

"Jackson had nothing to do with Dr. White's murder. We told you what happened."

"Right, and now all of a sudden you've got this

mystery suspect in a black hoodie that's supposed to take the attention away from him." Detective Koren scribbled something in his notebook.

"The man was here, Detective. In fact, I think I saw him again this morning over by the shipyard."

Jackson gave me a questioning look. "You saw him?"

"I can't be certain it was the same guy, but he was dressed the same way you said the man was dressed last night, and he ran when he saw me."

Detective Koren turned to Coyle. "Check it out. Ask around at the shipyard, see if anyone has been hanging around."

"This doesn't mean you're off the hook, Spade," Detective Coyle said.

"Go," Detective Koren told his partner. "And give me the shovel."

Coyle handed it over but not before giving Jackson a nasty look.

Still, it was good that they hadn't been interested in the artifacts. This meant that we could take them to the lecture tonight.

"He's right," Detective Koren said as he turned to leave. "We're not done with you yet."

With Koren's warning ringing in our ears, Jackson returned to his work on the patio, and I went back inside to see how many people had signed up for the garden tours this afternoon. The hourly tours from twelve to two were full, with fifteen people each. After that, interest seemed to fall off, and no one so far had signed up for the tours at three and four. Perhaps more people would sign up as the day went on.

Regardless, I had enough to keep me busy and my mind off the case until tonight when Jackson, Simon, and I attended the lecture at the Maritime Museum. We needed answers, especially after Koren and Coyle's ominous warnings, and I really hoped that this expert could provide them.

I'd finished up the first three tours, but when there was no one waiting at the garden gate by 3:10, I texted Merrily to see if anyone was coming. When she didn't reply, I headed up the path to Nature's Way, past Nate, who was busily selling merchandise and plants, to see what was going on.

I opened the door to find the place packed. Merrily and Wallace looked totally overwhelmed. Both of them were speed-walking from the kitchen to the café, carrying platters of food, while a line of customers waited at the checkout counter.

I hustled over to the counter and began to check people out. Some of them were paying their bills from the café; others were buying staples like quinoa and organic peanut butter. Most of those waiting were patient and pleasant, but a few were downright nasty, complaining about the wait. Quite a few supporters stopped to tell me that they had heard about the petition and that they were on my side.

After I'd helped everyone, I went into the kitchen and found Merrily pulling two quiches out of the oven. "Are you okay?"

Merrily put the quiches on the counter and took off her oven mitts. "I didn't expect us to be this busy, but

I think between the yard sale and the news about the murder, people wanted to check us out."

"Great," I said. "Sales are through the roof due to morbid curiosity."

"We did sell a lot," she pointed out.

I sighed. "Did we get any more sign-ups for the tours? I texted you but you didn't respond. Now I understand why."

Merrily pulled her phone out of her pocket and looked at the screen. "Okay, the garden tour at four is almost full, but no one so far for three." The front door opened and two groups came in looking for tables, followed by four women who started browsing the shelves, and yet another group that lined up by the counter for baked goods. Wallace poked his head into the kitchen. "Willow, can you stay for a little while longer? We could really use your help."

"Of course," I said, and went to work. I directed one of the women to the section with homeopathic tinctures, then grabbed menus and went over to the door to greet the new customers. Since there were no empty tables inside, I suggested that they have lunch on the porch. Both parties agreed, and I went back outside and got them settled at two separate tables.

As I did, I spotted Kylie Ramsey, of the farmer's market; heirloom veggie growers Ramona and her partner, Rhonda; and Sandra Bennett across the street in Mitchell Park. The four merchants were chatting and laughing as they strolled along the boardwalk toward the Shelter Island ferry terminal and the Maritime Museum. I wanted to believe that Sandra wasn't in on the effort to shut down my garden, but the fact that she seemed so chummy with these women made me wonder.

Since confronting them wouldn't do any good, I went back inside and returned to the counter. I'd checked out another half dozen people when Nick followed his students downstairs after his afternoon yoga class and stopped to see me. "Hi, sweetheart," he said as he gave me a kiss on the cheek. "Are you all right? Allie told me about that nasty Web site."

"I'm okay," I said. "Though sometimes I wish I could crawl back under the covers and pretend none of this was happening."

"That's not your style," Nick told me gently. "You'll fight for what you believe in. Claire would expect nothing less."

As he spoke, Nate rushed into the store. "Willow, you'd better come outside," he called.

"What is it?" I asked, stepping out from behind the counter.

"A bunch of people are picketing in front of the garden."

I stood there, stunned. "They're doing *what?*"

"Protesting the garden. No one can even get near the tables. We're going to lose all our sales. You've got to do something!"

Nick squeezed my arm. "Go get 'em, girl. I'm right behind you."

I told Merrily that I'd be right back, and Nick and I went out to the garden. As we rounded the corner, I could hear the chanting: "Shut down the Garden of Death! Shut down the Garden of Death!"

Then I saw them, a group of a dozen or so people I didn't recognize led by Maggie and Harold. They were holding signs with the same slogan and marching in a circle in front of the garden.

My heart sank—this display certainly wouldn't help make my garden a success. What I couldn't understand was how something so beautiful could be so maligned. But I'd heard that if you don't understand someone's motivation, it probably has to do with money and greed. I had the feeling that this was the motivation here, but were they after the lot or what might be buried here?

"You'd better call Simon," Nick said. "And where's Jackson?"

"Working on the patio," I said, trying to calm myself with a few deep breaths. "Can you please go get him?"

Nick nodded, pushed his way past the protestors, and went into the garden. As he did, Ramona, Rhonda, Kylie, and Sandra all crossed the street from the park. They grabbed signs from the pavement and joined the group. None of them looked my way.

I took a few steps back and texted Simon and told him what the situation was. He immediately texted me back:

Will call lawyer. B there soon. Stay calm!

I called the police and asked them to come over, put my phone into my pocket, and walked up to the protestors.

Maggie and Harold stepped out of the circle and came over to me. "We don't give up," Harold said, a smug tone to his voice. "And you can't shut us up."

My phone pinged and I pulled it out:

Judge will issue order asap. Stay strong! S.

"Actually, yes, I can. A judge is about to issue an order prohibiting this demonstration."

"On what grounds?" Maggie said, annoyed.

"I'm not sure, but you should leave."

"No way," Maggie said. "Keep going, people!" She and Harold began pacing in a circle again, shouting along with the other protestors. Sandra marched along with them, avoiding my gaze.

Jackson pushed the gate open, and he and Nick came over to me. "You okay?"

"I just got a text from Simon. The lawyer is handling it, but until he does, this is making the garden and Nature's Way look really bad. I called the police."

"Time to move out," Jackson told the protestors. "The cops are coming, and you people need to go home. This is private property."

"The sidewalk isn't," Harold said, waving the protestors over. "We're not leaving."

A Southold town cop car pulled up, and two uniformed officers got out and asked what was going on.

"These people are picketing in front of my garden, and I want it to stop," I explained. "My lawyer has asked a judge to stop this. Can you make them leave?"

Maggie gave me a toothy smile. "I don't think your lawyer's going to have much success. There's a little thing called the Constitution. We're exercising our rights to free speech and the freedom to assemble."

But Jackson pulled one of the cops aside and said something to him. The cop conferred with his partner then said, "You're disturbing the peace. Besides, this is making the town look bad during the Maritime Festival. The mayor would appreciate your cooperation. Please leave."

"We are not leaving," Harold insisted. "Keep marching, everyone!"

"Wait a minute," Simon said as he walked up to us. "I just got a text from my lawyer. You are to cease and desist immediately." He held out his phone so that Harold and Maggie and the cops could all see a copy of the signed order.

One of the cops nodded. "He's right. Move it along, folks."

The crowd grumbled but began to disperse. But not before Maggie said, "You can't stifle free speech, Mr. Lewis."

"This has nothing to do with free speech. You're just trying to cause trouble for Willow—which I'd call harassment. Now get lost."

"Thanks, Simon," I said as they left. "I owe you one."

"I'm not keeping score," he said. "I'm just trying to help." We watched as the cop car pulled away. "By the way, what happened with the detectives this morning?"

"We tried to tell Koren and Coyle about what we found in the garden," Jackson said. "But they didn't believe us, let alone consider the artifacts as motive for White's murder."

"So you still have the earring, the sword, and the goblet?" Simon asked.

I nodded. "All three."

Simon grinned. "They actually did us a favor. Make sure and bring all three with you tonight to the lecture. I predict that Professor Albert Russell is going to find them extremely interesting."

chapter fifteen

Willow McQuade's
Favorite Medicinal Plants

FLAXSEED
Botanical name: *Linum usitatissimum*

Medicinal uses: Flaxseed is the seed of the flax plant, which is believed to have originated in Egypt. Flaxseed contains lignans (phytoestrogens, or plant estrogens), which can help with hot flashes during menopause. Flaxseed also contains soluble fiber, like that found in oat bran, and is an effective laxative. Whole or crushed flaxseed can be mixed with water or juice and is also available in powder form. Flaxseed oil is available in liquid and capsule form. I like the nutty taste and add it to my organic yogurt along with granola and whatever fruit is in season.

That night, lights were streaming from every window of the museum when we arrived. Inside, there was a display featuring an oversized map of the East End on a corkboard and a table with copies of Professor Russell's new book, *Pirates of the East End*. People milled around, checking it out, along with the exhibits about the maritime heritage of the area. There were displays on the Greenport fishing industry, the oyster industry, and the huge lighthouse lens that dominated the west end of the museum.

The only person I recognized was Harold. He appeared to be alone, no Maggie for once. The last thing I wanted was a confrontation, so I watched from a distance as he browsed the maritime photos in the gallery. Fortunately, none of the other protestors were there, and for that, I felt grateful.

Simon found us seats in the third row, and I sat between him and Jackson. Jackson had brought the earring, sword, and goblet in a duffel bag. I was also grateful that there weren't any security guards in the museum checking bags. But the Maritime Museum was small; it didn't really warrant a security staff.

A few minutes before eight, a petite woman in a red suit headed to the podium. With her was a tall, slightly balding man, sporting horn-rim glasses, a bow tie, and a day's growth of beard.

"Good evening to you all. I'm Sarah Peterson, the director of the Maritime Museum. Tonight I am pleased to welcome Professor Albert Russell, author of *Pirates of the East End*, to our museum." The crowd, which by now filled every chair, applauded. "We're all very excited to learn more about your research, Professor."

"Thank you for having me," Professor Russell began, opening a notebook on the podium. "I'm a native of Shelter Island, and it's good to be back on the North Fork. My interest in pirates started in my teens when I first learned that pirates frequented the East End. In college and grad school at Columbia University, I became a history major. I was particularly captivated by course work on merchants, pirates, and slaves in the seventeenth century. My new book evolved out of my teaching history at Columbia and a recent series of articles that I wrote for the *New York Times*.

"I think we can all agree that pirates are fascinating," the professor went on. "I guess that's why you're all here." He smiled and a few people laughed. "My talk tonight will center on the pirates who frequented Long Island, and the most famous pirate of all—Captain William Kidd and his visit to Gardiner's Island."

He began by defining the difference between piracy and privateers. Privateers, captains of privately chartered ships, were licensed to capture enemy ships and give a portion of the loot to the government, while pirates made their own rules, stealing from whomever they chose and keeping it all.

"In the seventeenth century, eastern Long Island, with bays and inlets on one side and the Atlantic Ocean on the other, was a favorite playground and battleground for pirates," Russell explained. "One of the most frequented places was Gardiner's Island, just off the East Hampton coast, settled in 1639 by Lion Gardiner after he received a grant from King Charles I of England.

"The island, a part of the town of East Hampton,

has been owned by the Gardiner family for nearly four hundred years. Sixty years after the Gardiner family settled there, Captain Kidd—privateer and reputed pirate—sailed his ship, the *Adventure Prize,* into one of the island's many harbors. He was on his way to Boston to clear his name after being accused of piracy.

"With permission from Lion Gardiner's grandson Jonathan, Kidd buried thirty thousand dollars of treasure in a ravine between Bostwick's Point and the Gardiner Manor House. To the best of our knowledge, this treasure consisted of gold dust, silver bars, gold Spanish coins, rubies, and diamonds.

"Before Kidd left, he warned the Gardiners that if the treasure was stolen, he would kill the entire family. But when he arrived in Boston, he was captured, sent back to England for trial, and later executed."

Jackson leaned over to me. "It sounds like Kidd's treasure was just on the island."

Professor Russell continued. "When the governor of New York ordered the Gardiners to deliver the treasure, some of it was missing. The rest has never been recovered."

I whispered in Jackson's ear, "See, some of it is still missing."

"Today, a boulder with a bronze tablet marks the spot where Kidd's treasure was buried," Russell went on "There is also some evidence that leads us to believe that Kidd may have buried treasure at the foot of Montauk Point, in two small ponds named Money Ponds. That, also, was never recovered." The professor closed the notebook in front of him and said, "Now, I'm happy to answer your questions."

We sat through the question-and-answer period without saying anything, waiting for everyone else to leave. It was bad enough that Sandra and Martin knew about the sword. Now that she had bonded with Greenport Merchants United, I was sure that the entire group, including Maggie and Harold, either already knew about it—or would soon know. I didn't really want to let anyone else in on our find.

Nearly twenty minutes later, Professor Russell said, "I think that's all the time we have for questions, so—" But then he stopped and pointed to someone in the back. "Go ahead, sir."

I turned around to look and saw that it was Harold. He stood up and said, "Thank you, Professor. You mentioned the pirate treasure on Gardiner's Island and in Montauk, but I was wondering if this type of thing has ever been found here on the North Fork. There are rumors to that effect. I've been hearing them since I moved out here twenty years ago."

I grabbed Jackson's hand and squeezed. Did he know about what we'd found? Had Sandra or Martin told him?

Professor Russell smiled. "I've heard those rumors, too, but so far, there isn't any proof that pirates buried anything in Greenport."

"Thank you, Professor," Harold said. I turned to look at him again, and he gave me a smug smile.

The professor ended the Q and A, then signed his books for the long line of people who had purchased them. We waited until the book signing was over and everyone had left before we got up and approached the professor. Jackson put the duffel bag on the table, where it landed with a soft *thunk*.

"What do we have here?" Professor Russell asked.

"We need your expertise, Professor," Jackson said. He took the earring, sword, and goblet out of the bag and set them on the table. "We found these items buried in Willow's garden, and we need to know if they could be pirate treasure."

"This is Willow McQuade, by the way," Simon said quickly. "And this is Jackson Spade, and I'm Simon Lewis."

The professor gave us all a nod of acknowledgment, then carefully picked up the earring. He examined it then moved on to the sword and the goblet. When he was finished, he said, "You say you found them in your garden? Where is this place exactly?"

"It's located in Greenport, next to Nature's Way Market & Café on Front Street," I answered. "The land is to the west of the store, actually. We've been working there since this spring, digging it up and planting medicinal plants. That's where we found them."

"That's quite a story." He picked up the sword again, peering at the pommel and its blood-red gem.

"There's more," I said. "Since then, we've discovered several holes in the garden and last night, someone was in the garden, but they got away before we could find out who it was. He or she left a shovel behind, which we've turned over to the police. They're investigating, since a local doctor was murdered in the garden on Saturday morning."

The professor's expression sharpened. "Dr. White, that's who you're talking about, right?"

"Did you know him?"

"Unfortunately, yes. He was my mother's orthopedic surgeon. She fell in her kitchen and broke her arm. It took forever for him to do the surgery, and after he operated, she was left with chronic pain that was very debilitating. She suffered until the day she died."

"My condolences," I said.

"Thank you. Dr. White was supposed to be here tonight, you know. I wasn't looking forward to seeing him. But if he had come, he would have gotten a piece of my mind, I'll tell you that. My mother suffered greatly because of him. Of course she was just a number to him. He never even used her name when he treated her."

"We've been told that he wasn't a very nice man or very well liked," I said. "So why was he coming to see you?"

"From what I could gather, Dr. White studied anthropology in college before he switched to orthopedics. But he continued to pursue the field in his off time, you know, taking vacations to historic dig sites, museums, and the like. He said he had something he wanted to talk to me about."

"But he didn't tell you what it was?" Jackson asked.

"No, he didn't. Now that he's dead, I can't help wondering what he had on his mind."

"Me, too," Simon said.

"I'm afraid it will have to remain a mystery." Professor Russell picked up the sword again. "But perhaps I can help you. The sword and the goblet might be artifacts from the era when pirates visited the East End."

"Might be?" Simon echoed.

"Exactly. The goblet is possible but doubtful. It isn't quite the right style for that era, but the sword is. If it's the real thing, it should be in a museum. On the black market, it would be worth a fortune. That's why there are so many good fakes out there." He leaned in and examined the stone. "The only way to know for sure is to send all of these items to a lab to have them analyzed. The wood, metal, and these stones can be verified and, hopefully, dated. But I just can't make any guarantees simply by looking at them."

"What about the earring?" Jackson asked.

"Not seventeenth century," the professor said. "I'm guessing it's either Victorian or Edwardian, but again, you need to have it professionally appraised to get any sense of its true history and value."

Simon looked disappointed. "So you can't tell us if the sword and goblet are from Captain Kidd's missing treasure?"

"Not simply by looking at them, no. You might take them into Christie's or Sotheby's in Manhattan," he suggested, naming two major auction houses. "Their experts might be able to help you."

Simon looked annoyed. "Last time I brought something into Sotheby's for an appraisal, it took weeks for them to get back to me. We don't have weeks. We need to sort out this out quickly."

Professor Russell glanced at his watch. "I'm afraid I need to be going. But let me think about it overnight. Why don't you call me in the morning?" He pulled a card from his jacket pocket and handed it to me.

"That sounds great," I said. "Thank you so much for your help."

"Don't thank me," he said, giving me a warning look. "I'm afraid that you may be involved in something far more complicated than you know. If people think there is something of value in your garden, you'll find no peace. People act very strangely when it comes to buried treasure. There has already been one murder in your garden. There's no telling what could happen next."

Outside, Simon headed for his car, while Jackson and I walked back to Nature's Way. "Well, that was interesting," I said as we strolled past the Blue Canoe restaurant on Third Street. "Not only what the professor had to say, but Harold as well. I think he knows. He gave me such a smug smile after he asked that question."

"Word spreads fast in a small town, especially about something like pirate treasure. Or maybe he already knew."

"If that's the case, maybe he and Dr. White were both looking for the treasure in the garden, they fought, and Harold killed him."

Jackson shrugged. "Harold's an arrogant ass, but I can't quite see him as a murderer. But maybe they were partners and they had a falling out. These things happen. Regardless, that intruder last night proves that whoever it is isn't done looking."

"Which means they'll probably be back tonight." We came to the light on Front Street, took a right, and headed past the movie theater.

"Let's hope the lock on the gate will dissuade them, but what you really need is a twenty-four-hour guard."

"That's not the image I'm trying to project."

"Maybe not, but it might be necessary until we figure this out. Let me see if I can find someone to help you, just at night, to patrol and keep any interested onlookers away."

"Okay," I said, relenting. "You know best about security matters."

He kissed me. "Thank you." He pointed at the garden up ahead. "At least it's quiet right now."

But as we got closer, we could see that someone had spray painted graffiti all over the fence and the garden gate in huge, ugly neon letters: Shut Down the Garden of Death and Evict Nature's Way Now!

"This is so hateful," I said, beginning to tremble. "So awful."

"It's really getting out of control," Jackson agreed. He pulled out his penlight and stepped closer to examine the damage.

"Who would do something like this? The garden was supposed to be a haven, a restful place in the heart of Greenport."

Jackson pulled me into a hug. "It's going to be okay. It's nothing that can't be covered with some black spray paint."

"And then what? First, Dr. White is murdered, then someone digs up the garden, then the petition and that horrible Web site, the intruder last night, those protestors, and now the graffiti. What's next?"

"Let's not jump to conclusions. Take a deep breath. You need to calm down. Don't borrow trouble."

"I've got plenty right now." The graffiti was a

reminder that I couldn't ignore. "I can't look at this. Let's go inside."

I changed into my sweats and a T-shirt and got into bed, where Jackson was already playing with the dogs. Jackson gave me an appraising look and said, "You need to turn your mind off, McQuade. You've had a long day."

I took a tube of honey and grape seed oil hand cream from my night table and began rubbing it in. "I just keep thinking that I really made a mistake in creating that garden. Look at all the trouble it's caused."

Jackson scratched Qigong behind the ears, then in turn, Rockford and Columbo. "Greedy people are causing this trouble, not the garden."

"Maybe we should close it down."

Jackson gave me a surprised look. "What do you mean—just give up? That's not like you, Willow."

"I don't want to fight with anyone," I said. "I'm tired of having half the town against me, trying to take the garden. Maybe I should just give it to them."

"I think you'd regret that," Jackson said. "Especially since Professor Russell might be the key to figuring this whole thing out, and he told you to call him tomorrow. You just need to keep putting one foot in front of the other."

"And maybe Professor Russell will leave me just as stuck as I am right now. He couldn't tell me anything definitive tonight, so I'm not going to count on him having some miraculous key to the case."

Jackson thought for a moment before he said, "You

know what, you're right. Why don't you just give up? It's definitely the easier thing to do. It's not like there's anything at stake—like your business and all the hard work you put into the garden. Let them win."

He picked up his book, opened it and began reading. The dogs quickly arranged themselves, Qigong on his shoulder, Rockford on his stomach and Columbo at his feet.

"I thought you wanted me to be safe. If I quit, I'll be safe."

He used the book flap as a bookmark and looked at me. "Of course I want you to be safe. But if you quit, if *we* quit, there's a good chance that we'll still be in danger. Someone wants what's in that garden, and they won't stop until they get it. But if you want to quit, go ahead. It's up to you." He opened the book and began reading again. Qigong looked up at me, yawned, and put his head back down. I had to admit that they all looked pretty cute together.

"Are you using reverse psychology on me?"

Jackson smiled but kept reading. "Is it working?"

"Yes, it's working. You're right. There's too much at stake to give up. Besides," I said reluctantly, "I never give up."

He closed the book and gave me a kiss. "That's my girl."

"I'll call Professor Russell first thing in the morning, on my way to get black spray paint."

"You always were a good multitasker. I'll contact my security guy and meet you in the garden. I need to work on the patio, so you'll have your open-air teahouse." He took the hand cream away and put it on the nightstand. "Now, what can we do to pass the time until then?" He gently moved the dogs to the side of the bed, where they snuggled next to each other and promptly fell asleep again.

"Gee, I don't know. Got any ideas?"

He pulled me to him. "Just one."

chapter sixteen

Willow McQuade's
Favorite Medicinal Plants

GARLIC
Botanical name: *Allium sativum*

Medicinal uses: Garlic is an edible bulb from a plant in the lily family, and one of the superstars of medicinal plants. It has been used as both a medicine and a spice for thousands of years. Antiseptic, antibacterial, and antimicrobial, garlic stimulates the production of white blood cells, improving immunity and helping to speed healing from colds and flu. There is a reason Grandma's chicken soup makes you feel better! Garlic also is effective at lowering high cholesterol and blood sugar levels. You can eat garlic cloves raw if you're feeling brave or add them to your next soup or stir-fry.

Tuesday morning found me out in the garden, spraying black paint over the ugly graffiti. When I'd started, I was furious that I had to repaint the fence at all, but gradually, as the graffiti disappeared, I felt better about things. It was just after 10 a.m., and I'd just covered the last of the neon lettering, when my cell rang. The caller ID read Albert Russell.

"Professor Russell, thanks for calling me back," I said.

"Not at all. I'm glad you phoned."

"I realized I have a lot of questions I didn't ask you last night," I began. "I was wondering if you could stop by this morning. Or I could come to Shelter Island, whatever you prefer. Is that possible?"

"It is, and I can come to you," he said. "I need to pick up a few things from your store. I have my sister staying with me, and she only eats organic food. My cupboard is bare."

"We've got plenty of that here. When were you thinking of coming over?"

"Within the hour. I think it's important that we discuss your artifacts further."

"My *artifacts*? Does that mean you think they're the real thing?"

"We'll talk about it when I get there. Expect me by eleven."

I walked over to tell Jackson about our visitor. He and Nate were working on the patio at the north end of the lot. They seemed to be making progress, but it was difficult to be sure. "How are things going, guys?"

"It's going," Jackson said, wiping his forehead with

his glove. "We had to take two steps back, but now we're moving forward."

"What do you mean?"

"I mean that despite the new lock, someone was in here again, digging around."

"Yeah, they even moved the pavers," Nate said as he lugged over a gray paver stone and set it on the ground. "So we had to fill in the holes, smooth it out, and make sure the ground was level before we could put these back. What a pain."

"It's fine, Nate. Stop complaining." Jackson threw him a look.

"Why didn't you tell me?" I asked Jackson.

"You have enough to think about."

"I still need to know. Can I talk to you for a minute?"

"Sure," Jackson said, taking off his gloves. "Nate, start prepping the next paver. I'll be right back."

Nate didn't look too happy about being left on his own, but he didn't say anything.

When were out of earshot, Jackson said, "I am getting really tired of his complaining."

"Really? He seems fine to me. What's going on?"

"When we started to work together, Nate was enthusiastic and capable; he did everything I asked without complaint. But lately, he's got a poor attitude and productivity to match. I'm not sure what to do about it."

"Me either," I said, dismayed. "But I can't fire him now. We still need him to maintain the garden and to help you finish the teahouse."

"Don't worry, I'll make it work. But enough about Nate. Did you talk to Professor Russell?"

As we continued to walk to the front of the garden I told him about our phone conversation. "He's coming over at eleven. Do you have time to meet with him?"

"I'd like to, but we're way behind and I really don't want to leave Nate alone any longer than I have to. Why don't you report back?"

"I could do that."

"I'll look forward to it." He stepped closer. "You know, you look really pretty today."

I'd just thrown on a multicolored sundress made of organic cotton and flip-flops and put my hair in a pony-tail, but I was glad he liked it.

Jackson pulled me to him and nuzzled my ear, and then planted baby kisses all along my neck. My spine tingled, along with other more interesting places. I wanted to stay but I needed to go.

"We'll finish this up later," I said, pulling away, but not before giving him a long, soulful kiss.

"I'll be here."

Inside, things were running smoothly at Nature's Way. I'd forgotten that Merrily was off this morning, but Wallace was doing fine all by himself. I retrieved the artifacts from the bedroom closet, brought them downstairs, and put them on the couch in my office, where Qigong was chewing on a bone. I knew that no one would be able to take the treasures with him there.

As promised, Professor Russell showed up at pre-cisely eleven o'clock. He had several empty cloth

shopping bags in one hand and a long list in the other.
Today he was dressed more casually, sort of, in jeans, a
long-sleeved denim shirt, and a paisley tie.

"Hi, Professor, looks like you're ready to stock up."

He smiled. "My neighbor shops here and she raves
about the selection, so I came prepared."

"What do you need?"

"Here's my list." He handed me the piece of paper.
"My neighbor assures me that you carry all of these
items."

I quickly scanned the list. On it were things like
gluten-free bread and cookies, rice cereal, and organic
peanut butter, along with NoFo Crunch, one of our
customer favorites, made with granola, dried fruit,
nuts, and organic raw kombucha. "We sure do. Why
don't you let me put the order together for you?"

"That would be grand," he said. "I can check my
messages on my phone while I wait. I had quite a nice
response to my talk last night. I'm hoping that it will
help book sales."

"I'm sure it will. It was very informative." I scanned
the café; there were a few open tables. "You can sit anywhere you like. Would you like something to eat or drink?"

"A cup of Earl Grey tea would be lovely."

He took a table next to the window, and I went into
the kitchen and made him his tea. When I came back,
he was staring intently at his phone. "I think I've found
an appraiser for your items."

"That was fast. Who is it?"

"Another expert on Gardiner's Island and Captain Kidd's treasure, someone who knows even more
than I do."

His food list temporarily forgotten, I took the seat across from him. "Who is this person? Can he or she help us?"

He took a sip of tea, then said, "First, let me explain the chain of events. As I was leaving last night, your friend Simon Lewis approached me and told me what happened in your garden, the fact that Jackson is a suspect in Dr. White's murder, and about the merchants who have been harassing you and trying to shut down your venture."

"So, you know," I said.

"Yes, and I'm sorry for your trouble."

"It hasn't been easy," I admitted.

"Simon was very insistent that I help you. It's obvious he really cares for you."

"We used to be a couple but we're better off as friends," I said with a smile.

"That is often the case." The professor took another sip of tea. "It seems Simon has done his own research on the pirates that frequented the East End, for some movie project, he said, and he's convinced that the artifacts that you've found are lost treasure. He asked me to help you, and I told him that I would consider it."

"I was already inclined to do so, as I indicated at the museum. When I got home, I did some research on you and the two cases you've solved. I take it that you are trying to solve the mystery of Dr. White's murder as well?"

"I have no choice," I said. "I have to clear Jackson, myself, and my business for being at fault."

"Clearly, you are not at fault. I think forces beyond your control are at work here, and perhaps I can help you."

"It would be wonderful to finally get some answers. I feel as if I've been going up one blind alley after another."

The professor shrugged. "Well, I doubt I can tell you who killed Dr. White, but I may be able to help you identify the sword and goblet. Simon could be right—the sword, at least, may indeed be from a pirate ship. It may even be Captain Kidd's treasure, and the goblet may be perhaps a hundred years more recent. As I said last night, some of that treasure was never recovered. I'm hoping that my Captain Kidd expert, Dr. Travis Gillian, who works with the East Hampton Historical Society, will be able to help identify your items. I called him this morning, and he has just agreed to see us. Are you free to go over there today, to East Hampton? I've texted Simon and he can obtain the services of a helicopter pilot who can take us to there and we can even fly over Gardiner's Island on the way, if you are willing."

I checked the calendar on my phone. I didn't have any tours scheduled for that day, and everything else on my to-do list could wait. "Let's go."

I contacted Simon, who called his pilot, the one who took him to parties in the Hamptons, and made the arrangements. We agreed that the professor, Jackson, and I would meet him at the airfield in Mattituck, a North Fork town twenty minutes west of Greenport.

Two hours later, we were up in the translucent blue sky, flying east down the length of the North Fork, over the glistening aqua-blue Peconic Bay. It was a spectacular view of verdant wetlands, sprawling farms that produced everything from pumpkins to potatoes, and numerous vineyards that crisscrossed the land, along with the homes and the villages that made up Cutchogue, Southold, and Greenport. The North Fork, east of Cutchogue, was to me the "real" East End.

Professor Russell sat in front next to the pilot, while Simon, Jackson, and I sat in the back. We all wore helmets with microphones, so we could talk with each other.

I leaned around Jackson and said to Simon, "Thanks for helping me with this, Simon. I really appreciate it."

"We both do," added Jackson, who had the bag of artifacts on the floor between his feet. "And thanks for the scenic tour."

"This isn't the most direct route to the island, but I thought you'd enjoy seeing the East End from this vantage point," Simon explained.

Moments later, we passed over the Maritime Museum and the ferry terminal. Professor Russell said something to the pilot, and he turned north and flew over Nature's Way on Front Street. "There's the store," I said, pointing out the open window. I quickly scanned the medicinal plant garden. From this distance everything looked peaceful and serene. Today, there were no protestors. "All quiet."

"That's nice for a change," Jackson said.

The pilot continued flying over Greenport, past Mitchell Park and the harbor and the shops and restaurants and the dozens of tourists and locals clogging the streets. Today was the Maritime Festival Foodie Tour.

You could buy a wristband for twenty-five dollars and visit all the local restaurants and sample their offerings.

The pilot flew across the neighborhoods north of the village, those around the Stirling Harbor Marina, before heading East again, toward East Marion, where Jackson lived. I dug my binoculars out of my purse and handed them to him so that he could see his house, which was on the north side of the road just before the Orient Point causeway that transected the wetlands and the bay.

Within minutes, we flew over his two-and-a-half-acre property with the rambling farmhouse that was an ongoing restoration project. The property also contained a huge barn and a generous paddock for his rescued animals, which included horses, donkeys, and goats, along with dogs and cats.

It was a beautiful day, so most of the animals were outside. Some of them were munching grass and hay and others were playing with the volunteers or lounging in the sun.

"It looks like things are fine at your house, too," I said.

"The interns and volunteers are doing a great job. The animals are all thriving."

"Thanks to you."

"I'm glad to be able to do it. I just applied for another grant from the state, and chances are good we'll get it. If we do, I want to expand the paddock and the barn so they all have more room."

"You're a good man, you know that?" I would have kissed him, but my helmet prevented it, so I had to settle for squeezing his hand.

"By the way, I found a guard for you."

"Really, who is it?

"Bob Cooper. He's an old cop buddy of mine from up the island. He's retired out here and does this type of thing for extra bucks, but he's reasonable. He'll be there at seven tonight, before it gets dark. Hopefully, he'll discourage any fortune hunters."

"I hope so."

We continued East over the Causeway and into Orient, with its old money and stately mansions and newcomers building and renovating homes. Finally, when we reached Orient Point and the Cross Sound ferry terminal, the pilot informed us that if we looked south, we'd see Gardiner's Island in the distance.

The helicopter flew over the water toward one of America's largest privately owned islands and oldest family estates, four hundred years old, in fact. Featuring thirty-three hundred acres and twenty-seven miles of coastline, Gardiner's Island was closer to the South Fork and part of the town of East Hampton but really, it was a kingdom unto itself.

It felt exciting to be so close to this mythical place with so much history. I squeezed Jackson's hand. "This is amazing. I just wish that we could land on the island and go explore."

"Can't put down there," the pilot said. "They don't like visitors, unless you're invited, but I'll try to get close so you can get a better look."

"Believe me, I tried to get us access," Simon said. "Maybe when I have a production deal for my pirate movie, and I need to do research, it'll be a different story."

"Maybe not," Professor Russell said. "The inhabitants like their privacy. You can't really blame them. Even their electricity is produced by their own generators."

As we neared the island, the copter descended and we skimmed above the brilliant blue of Gardiner's Bay. "I know the island has been in the Gardiner family for more than four hundred years," I said, "but who owns it now?"

"Until 2004, Robert Charles Lion Gardiner, the sixteenth lord of the manor, as he liked to call himself, owned it with his niece, Alexandra Creel Goelet. Now that he's gone, it's hers. The two didn't get along."

"It was pretty contentious," Simon said. "He said that she wanted to develop the island, which wasn't true. He even tried to adopt a distant relative in Mississippi to maintain control, but that didn't work out."

"That's a pretty desperate move," Jackson said.

"It was. Rumor is that Gardiner didn't do his part to take care of the island either. Now, that's all fallen to Mrs. Goelet," Professor Russell said. "But it's worth it to her. Aside from its historical significance, the island is her family home. Recently the family came to an agreement with the village: no development until at least 2020. I hope it stays that way."

Minutes later, the helicopter hovered over the pristine shores of Gardiner's Island. The scenery was spectacular, majestic sandy cliffs, green rolling fields dotted with red barns and crisscrossed by dirt roads, untouched wetlands, sparkling ponds, and birds in flight. "Wow, this is absolutely beautiful," I said.

"It sure is. The original Lion Gardiner got a good deal," Simon said. "He bought this from the Montaukett Indians for a large black dog, blankets, a gun, powder, and shot, right, Professor?"

"That's right. But just to make sure, he obtained a land grant from King Charles I of England."

"Guess he wasn't taking any chances," Simon said.

"The Gardiners have always hedged their bets," Professor Russell said.

"Simon, we're just about to fly over Cherry Harbor," the pilot said.

Simon pointed down at the island, where we could see a cutout of a harbor and several motorboats moored there. "When the family or anyone else comes from East Hampton, they take a launch to this spot. See that road?" He pointed out a dirt road that tracked over the land. "That leads to the Manor House, and there's the windmill. They just had it painted."

The white windmill stood on a promontory overlooking the harbor. I used the binoculars to scan the road to its destination and there, in the middle of the island, was the red brick Manor House. "That looks pretty impressive."

"The original Manor House was built by Charles Gardiner in 1774, but it burned in a fire in 1947 after a guest fell asleep while smoking," Professor Russell explained. "They built the current Manor House, a twenty-eight-room Georgian estate, that same year. Beyond the mansion there are one thousand acres of old-growth forest. It's the largest stand of white oak trees in the Northeast, untouched by man."

"It's like a time capsule, the way the East End would

be if it had never been developed," I said, amazed at what I was seeing.

"Indeed, there are also one thousand acres of pristine meadows, with rare birds, Indian artifacts, and structures that date from the seventeenth century," the professor said.

"There are no natural predators, so there are huge herds of swans here, too," Simon said. "The ospreys here have nests right on the beach for the same reason."

"This is all fascinating, but I have to ask, where did Kidd bury his treasure?" Jackson said.

"Coming up," Professor Russell said. "With Lion Gardiner's grandson's permission, Kidd buried thirty thousand dollars of treasure in a ravine between Bostwick's Point and the Manor House."

"Including swords and goblets?" Simon asked.

"It's possible. We know it included gold dust, silver bars, gold Spanish coins, rubies, and diamonds," the professor answered. "There's a small stone marker on the spot, right about there." He pointed out the window to a spot near the northwest shore. "It's believed that all of the treasure was removed, but there is no way to know for sure. Your sword, and even the goblet, could have belonged to Captain Kidd."

"And we're about to fine out," Simon said, smiling.

chapter seventeen

Willow McQuade's
Favorite Medicinal Plants

GINGER
Botanical name: *Zingiber officinale*

Medicinal uses: Ginger, like garlic, is a powerful medicinal herb. Ginger is used to alleviate postsurgery nausea, as well as nausea related to chemotherapy and pregnancy. Research shows that ginger is even more effective than Dramamine for curbing motion sickness without causing drowsiness. I always take along candied ginger when I'm traveling. Ginger contains compounds that also help reduce the inflammation and pain of rheumatoid arthritis, osteoarthritis, and joint and muscle pain, and improves digestion. The roots of the ginger plant are used in cooking, baking, and for health purposes. Common forms of ginger include fresh or dried root, tablets, capsules, liquid extracts (tinctures), and teas.

You can also apply ginger topically in a compress

**to joints, bunions, and sore muscles; to minor tooth-
aches to relieve pain; over the kidneys to relieve the
pain and assist in the passage of stones; on the chest
and back to relieve asthma symptoms; and on the
temples to relieve headache. Along with garlic, this
versatile herb deserves a place in your natural medicine cabinet.**

The helicopter landed in East Hampton Airport, and
Jackson, Simon, and I climbed into the back of a black
Lincoln town car; Professor Russell sat in front. The
driver headed into East Hampton, past the Town Pond
with its three-hundred-year-old cemetery, and into the
quaint and charming village, the main road lined by
majestic old elms.

I had assumed that we would be meeting in one of
the offices belonging to the East Hampton Historical
Society. But we drove past the Osborn-Jackson House
on Main Street, the Town House, and the Hook School-
house.

When the driver took a left on Main Street and
glided past the historic English Hook Windmill in the
center of town, heading east toward Springs, I became
concerned. "Professor, where exactly are we going?"

He turned around to face me. "I thought we needed
a place that was somewhat private. Dr. Gillian is waiting for us at the Pollock-Krasner house in Springs.
It's one of the historic buildings that he oversees as a
curator for the Stony Brook Foundation. The museum
is closed on Mondays, so we'll have the place to ourselves."

"I thought this expert was with the East Hampton Historical Society," Jackson said.

"He works with them from time to time, but he also works with the Stony Brook Foundation. Believe me, no one knows Kidd and that era better."

Ten minutes later, we drove past a simple cedar shake house with a wide front porch, perfect for summer afternoon lounging, then pulled into the driveway and parked.

"It's a pretty unassuming property," Professor Russell said. "You'd never guess that this used to be home to the undisputed leader of the abstract expressionist movement."

"When did Jackson Pollock move out here?" I asked as we all got out and stretched our legs.

"In 1945, after he and fellow artist Lee Krasner were married. They purchased the property with a loan from art dealer Peggy Guggenheim."

"Great view of the creek," Jackson said.

"Yes, that's Accabonac Creek, and if you're wondering, Gardiner's Island is that way." He pointed to the east. "And this is where Mr. Pollock worked, or I should say created."

He began to walk toward a barn in the backyard. As he did, a tall, academic type who could have been Russell's older brother opened the barn door and stepped out. He had a neatly trimmed gray beard and wore a white linen shirt, cream-colored trousers, and loafers without socks. When we met, he shook Russell's hand and said, "Good to see you, Professor, and your friends, too. Hello, everyone. I'm Dr. Travis Gillian. I have to admit, I'm curious about what you've found. But first, let me give you a quick tour of the studio. That is, if you're interested."

"Very much so," I said. Jackson and Simon agreed, and Professor Russell made quick introductions as we walked into the barn.

There, Dr. Gillian asked us to take our shoes off and put booties on. "We're going to be in his studio, where Pollock worked," Dr. Gillian said. "We need to preserve the art."

After we'd changed he led us down the hall to a bright open room. There was a horizontal window at the top of the rear wall. Below that, small black-and-white photos lined the wall above metal cans filled with paintbrushes. To the right and the left were oversized photos of Pollock as he worked, and one of Lee visiting him in the studio, sitting on a wooden chair. The walls were a dingy white with paint speckling everywhere.

The floor was easily the most interesting aspect, covered in swirls, droplets and smudges, and layers of paint, the leftovers from masterpieces. On top of a small stepstool were the boots that Pollock used when he created, covered in layer upon layer of paint.

"The whole studio seems like it's frozen in time," I said.

"I know," Simon said. "It almost feels like Pollock could walk in at any moment and begin painting again."

"Yes," Dr. Gillian said. "It does have that feeling." He turned to us. "Now that you've seen the studio, I guess it's my turn. I'm eager to see the artifacts that Professor Russell mentioned."

"I'll get them," Jackson said, heading for the car. He'd left the bag of artifacts in the trunk for safekeeping.

"Good," Dr. Gillian said. "We can sit outside and I'll take a look."

We sat down at the rustic picnic table in the backyard, the professor and Gillian on one side, us on the other. Jackson returned moments later and set the bag in the middle of the table.

Dr. Gillian pulled a pair of thin Latex gloves from his shirt pocket and carefully put them on. Chagrined, I realized that we all should have been more careful when handling these pieces.

As if he read my mind, Professor Russell said, "Don't worry about touching the artifacts. It won't affect anything."

"He's right," Dr. Gillian said. "This is just a habit of mine. I'm sure they're fine." He carefully opened the bag and slowly pulled out the first item, which happened to be the goblet. He examined it, then put it on the table. "No damage done here."

"What do you think? Is it pirate treasure? Is it Captain Kidd's?" Simon asked as he leaned in to get a closer look.

"The goblet is very old, easily from the sixteenth or seventeenth century. Whether it's pirate treasure or not, I can't say."

I felt a pang of disappointment. I was hoping for some definitive answers. I needed to know why everyone seemed so interested in my medicinal garden.

"But let me look at the rest." He repeated the procedure with the earring. "I'd say this is from the late 1800s, and there's a good chance that's a diamond. The design and workmanship are Victorian, so it's probably not pirate treasure and, since you only have one of a pair, it's worth may be restricted to whatever you can get for the stone and gold."

"I think you'll be intrigued by the last item they have," Professor Russell said.

Dr. Gillian pulled the sword out of the bag. Startled, he sucked in a breath and immediately put it down on the table. Nervously, he stroked his beard. "I can't believe it."

"I thought so," Professor Russell said. "I had a feeling it might be the same one."

"What are you two talking about?" Simon said, impatient for answers.

Doctor Gillian carefully picked up the sword again. This time, he examined it from every angle. "I never thought we'd see this again."

"What do you mean?" I said, now feeling just as impatient.

"The East Hampton Historical Society sponsored a special Maritime Exhibit in June 1999 to commemorate the three-hundred-year anniversary. This very sword was the star of the show."

"What kind of anniversary?" Simon asked.

"To mark the date of Captain Kidd's visit to Gardiner's Island," Jackson answered.

"Very good, yes." Dr. Gillian put the sword down gently on the bag. "You are correct, Jackson. Kidd's Long Island adventure was in June 1699, right before his capture. He was on his way to Boston to prove his innocence in the charges of piracy. He stopped at Gardiner's Island for three days. During that time—we don't know exactly when—he buried treasure worth about thirty thousand dollars back then at Cherry Harbor, in a ravine between Bostwick Point and the Manor House."

"While he and his men were there, he asked Mrs. Gardiner to roast a pig for him," Professor Russell added. "Kidd enjoyed it so much that he gave her a piece of gold cloth, a small piece of which is still in the East Hampton Library. Supposedly, the cloth came from a Moorish ship captured by Kidd off the coast of Madagascar."

"Wow, this guy really got around," Simon said. "Amazing."

"Indeed," Dr. Gillian said. "But this was to be his last trip. After Kidd was arrested in Boston, Lord Gardiner delivered the buried treasure to the authorities. Supposedly, there were bags of gold dust, bars of silver, pieces of eight, rubies, diamonds, candlesticks, and some other items."

"Like a sword?" I squeezed Jackson's hand.

Dr. Gillian nodded. "Yes, at least they thought so. A sword like this one was put into the archives of the East Hampton Historical Society and subsequently removed and shown at the exhibition. It was never definitively proved to be part of Kidd's treasure, but its age, workmanship, materials, and general style made that theory plausible. A month later, on the last day of the exhibit, the sword was stolen, never to be seen again."

"And you think this is the same sword?" Simon asked.

"I'd have to do some tests and research to be sure, but it certainly looks like it."

"Okay, say it is Kidd's," Jackson said. "How would it have gotten to Greenport? And does that mean there's more treasure in the garden?"

"I don't know. But I can see why you have had interested parties trying to find out. The earring and goblet may not be from Kidd, but they're still valuable. If this becomes known, I think you're in for some more trouble. I know you've already got your hands full, what with Jackson being a suspect in that doctor's murder."

"I hope you don't mind, Willow and Jackson, but I thought it best for Travis to know the entire story," Professor Russell interjected.

"Not a problem," I said. "We need all the help we can get."

"I hope I can help," Dr. Gillian said. "But for now, you two need to be very careful, at least until you figure out what exactly is going on."

"I've just hired a nighttime guard for the garden," Jackson said.

Dr. Gillian nodded approvingly. "I think that's an excellent idea. You could also hire an expert to use a metal detector on the garden, but that may cause more problems. You can have false or mixed readings and end up digging up areas without profit. I assume that's not something that you'd want to do in a newly planted garden."

"No, we wouldn't," I said. "But we need to stop what has been going on."

"I understand. In the meantime, I'd suggest putting these items in a safe place. If you'll allow me, I'd like to keep the sword and have some tests run on it, to make sure it's the real thing. I'll give you a receipt, of course. If it is the sword that was stolen, we could restore it to the East Hampton Historical Society."

I looked at Jackson. "What do you think?"

"I think that this is an ongoing murder investigation, and the sword may play a role in some way we're not aware of yet. I think the best idea is for Dr. Gillian's experts to check it out and let us know what they find. In the meantime, we keep following leads."

"Then we'd better get back," I said. "The Maritime Festival is still on all this week, and there's a lot going on. At least it's good cover for investigating."

"Professor Russell told me that you've done this before," Dr. Gillian said. "But please be careful. Buried treasure can often mean buried secrets. And that can mean big trouble."

chapter eighteen

Willow McQuade's
Favorite Medicinal Plants

GINKGO
Botanical name: *Ginkgo biloba*

Medicinal uses: Ginkgo is the oldest tree species on the planet and was common even when dinosaurs roamed the earth. It has a high resistance to disease, insects, and pollution. In humans, it helps relax blood vessels, improving circulation and the delivery of nutrients, including oxygen and glucose, throughout the body, including the brain.

Today, versatile ginkgo leaf extract is used to treat a variety of ailments and conditions, including asthma, bronchitis, depression, fatigue, and tinnitus (ringing in the ears); to improve memory; and to relieve neuropathic pain. In Europe it is one of the best-selling medicines and used in the treatment of a wide variety of disorders associated with aging including dementia, memory loss, and senility, and to promote recovery from stroke. It is an antioxidant, which means it helps to neutralize cell-damaging free radicals, and a good cerebral or brain tonic.

Extracts are usually taken from the ginkgo leaf and are used to make tablets, capsules, or teas. Occasionally, ginkgo extracts are used in skin products. Numerous studies of ginkgo have been done for a variety of conditions. Some promising results have been seen for Alzheimer's disease, dementia, and tinnitus.

The helicopter dropped us off at the Mattituck Airport, and we returned to Greenport late Tuesday afternoon. Simon went home and Jackson, the professor, and I all went back to Nature's Way. There, Jackson headed for the garden to check things out while we went inside to work on Professor Russell's shopping list.

The store and café at Nature's Way was pretty quiet when we came in, with only Wallace on duty. He emerged from the kitchen, drying his hands on a dish towel. "You're back. Did you have fun?"

I had told him that we were going for a helicopter ride with Simon, but nothing more than that. "It was amazing to see the East End from up there. How are things here? Where's Merrily?"

"Nate took her home. She said she had a migraine."

I had never known Merrily to have migraines. So the fact that she had gone home with one was a bit of a surprise. I wondered if maybe she'd actually wanted to spend time with Nate. But I kept this to myself and said, "I hope she feels better."

I went over to the cash register, opened it, and plucked Professor Russell's grocery list out from under the money tray. "Wallace, do you have time to help me put together Professor Russell's order?"

He threw the dish towel onto the counter. "Sure, what do you need?"

"I'll get the bread, cookies, cereal, peanut butter, and quinoa." I tore the list in half. "Can you get the rest? It will go faster."

Between the two of us, we were finished in fifteen minutes flat. We packed up the order in two boxes, and the professor and I headed for the Shelter Island ferry.

Since Professor Russell wanted to try and make the five thirty boat, we took the shortcut through Mitchell Park, which was again buzzing with activity. This time is was because organizers were setting up for the two-day Annual Maritime and Nautical Yard Sale and Antique Show.

Cars and trucks were lined up on the south side of the street, where normally there was no parking. Two police officers were helping to coordinate the traffic and the drop-off of items, which included ships' lanterns, telescopes, diver's helmets, wooden ships' wheels, anchors, barometers, and fishing tackle.

"What do we have here?" Professor Russell asked. "More maritime festivities?"

I nodded. "It is a weeklong celebration. Tomorrow is the first day of the yard sale and marine antique show to benefit the museum and several local animal charities."

"How nice," he said. "I'll have to come back over and see what they're offering."

As we walked toward the carousel and beyond that, the boardwalk, I noticed Maggie and Harold. Both of them were holding clipboards and were on their phones while gesturing to people, trying to indicate where they should put their donations.

Kylie and Sandra were also nearby, helping out. After their protest in front of Nature's Way, I had no interest in speaking to any of them, but I decided I'd stop by the next day to see if I could uncover anything connected to Dr. White's murder.

The docks were absolutely packed with yachts and other pleasure boats, and teeming with visitors. When we rounded the corner onto the boardwalk, we found actors rehearsing lines. Behind them, the production team worked on building the set.

"Are they putting on a play as well?" Professor Russell asked.

"Yes, it's *The Tempest*. It opens on Friday and runs through Sunday. The Shakespeare productions here are usually good. You might want to come see the show as well."

"I may do that. Are you going to go?"

"I plan to, but it depends on how busy we are."

We continued walking along the boardwalk as it snaked its way past Mitchell Park and the Blue Canoe restaurant. When we reached the dock on the Greenport side, the ferry from Shelter Island was heading in. "There's your ferry," I said. "I really appreciate you coming over. Thanks for all of your help, Professor."

"You are very welcome, Willow," he said. "I'm glad to help. I just wish I could do more. Do you think the police will be back to see Jackson again?"

"Unfortunately, I'm sure they will."

"Do they have any other suspects?" We stepped inside the ferry building. Through the window, we could see the ferry pull in and then heard the thud when it touched the dock.

"Not that I know of, but I keep hearing that the doctor was not well liked. He seems to have enraged half his patients. There could be a long list of people who wanted to do him harm."

Russell put down his carton to buy a ticket from a vending machine. "One that I may be on, I'm afraid. White really was a terrible doctor, and not a nice person either. As I said, he treated my mother horribly."

He reached into his pocket for some coins. He had some trouble putting them into the machine because his hands were shaking. He continued, his voice getting louder, more urgent and angry. "Not just because he didn't help her, but because he was always so condescending to her. He never treated her with respect. He made her feel small. I can't say that I'm sorry he's dead, Ms. McQuade."

He finally got the coins in and a ticket ejected. He stuffed it into his pocket and kept his hand there. It seemed that the more he talked about his mother and Dr. White, the angrier he seemed to get.

"I can guarantee that you are not the only one that feels that way."

He gave me a sad look. "I'm afraid that's no comfort."

We said good-bye and I watched as he boarded the boat, holding his boxes. As I mulled over our conversation, I couldn't help but wonder if perhaps he had wanted Dr. White dead as well. Was he really interested in helping us with the artifacts—or did he just want to keep track of what was going on in the investigation because he was the killer?

I thought it over. Staid and nerdy Professor Russell, a murderer? No, I decided, that seemed very unlikely. Besides, I had far more plausible suspects to pursue.

When I got back and went into the garden to find Jackson, though, I had second thoughts. *Maybe I will mention Professor Russell to him.* At this point, no one could really be ruled out.

I'd have to dig further to winnow down my pool of suspects, which right now included Sandra Bennett, and any other disgruntled patients of Dr. White; his best friend, Joe Larson; White's wife, Arlene; the guy in the black sweatshirt; and any number of nameless treasure hunters. I still hadn't figured out if Harold Spitz and his friend Maggie Stone or Ramona and her partner, Rhonda, wanted him dead.

But as I went into the garden, all thoughts of my private investigation vanished. In the back, by the yet-to-be-completed teahouse, I spotted Jackson, who was hunched over and twisted like a pretzel. A huge paver stone lay at his feet. I felt my adrenaline spike as I ran to him. I was ready for fight, flight, or whatever was needed to help him. "Jackson, what happened to you?"

"I was trying to move one of the larger pavers by myself, since Nate is AWOL. I guess I picked it up wrong. I think I pulled something in my lower back."

"Oh, no. How bad is it?"

He frowned. "About a seven or eight on a scale of one to ten," he said, referring to the pain assessment scale used by doctors.

I looked at my watch. It was 5:46 p.m. "Dr. Lewis's office will be closed by now, however, I can try to treat you here." I hadn't yet set up my practice as a naturopathic doctor, with everything that had happened, but I hoped to do so next year. In the meantime, I could use my acupuncturist's office upstairs. "But, Jackson, if your pain is unmanageable, we'll have to go to the emergency room." Conventional medicines are often needed to manage severe, chronic pain. Jackson's doctor and I worked together to treat Jackson more effectively.

He shook his head. "I have the meds I need along with your remedies. I just need to lie down and rest. If it's not better in the morning, I'll call my orthopedist." He tried to straighten up but let out a groan.

I could feel his pain. "Let's get you inside, honey. Wallace can help us." After I pulled out my phone and called Wallace, I put my right arm around Jackson's waist to try and help him walk. *Stay calm*, I said to myself. You need to be *his* rock right now.

We made our way out of the garden and onto Front Street. But when we reached Nature's Way and headed up the walkway, Detective Koren was waiting for us on the porch.

"Koren is here," I whispered.

Jackson looked up and groaned again. "That's just what we need."

Koren looked spiffy in a sharp black suit, a white shirt, and a black tie. His eyes narrowed as he took in

Jackson holding onto me for support. "What's going on here?"

"I hurt my back, again."

Slowly, we made our way up to the porch. Koren came down to meet us. "Can I help?"

"We've got it, thanks," I said. "What can we do for you, Detective?"

"We followed up on that guy you said you saw in the shipyard, and he must be in the wind, 'cause we can't find him."

"That is not good news," I said.

"Not for you, Jackson. You're still our prime suspect."

"I'm touched," Jackson said. "But you have nothing on me, nothing that will stand up."

"We'll see." Koren pulled a notebook from his inside jacket pocket. "I heard from a friend of mine that you took a sudden trip over to East Hampton this afternoon. Is this something you want to tell me about?"

"How did you hear about that?" I pushed open the door to Nature's Way and helped Jackson inside.

Koren followed us. "I have my sources. So, want to tell me what you were doing? Leaving town like that, it's well, suspicious. That along with the murder—"

"We went over to tour the Jackson Pollock museum," Jackson said.

"And you had to go by helicopter? That seems . . . unusual."

"Simon Lewis, as you know, is very wealthy. He set it up and invited us to go along. Now, I really need to go lie down."

"That's fine," Detective Koren said. "For now. But

maybe when you're feeling better you can come down to the station and answer some more questions."

"I'll be bringing a lawyer, Koren, no freebies."

"That's your right. I'll be in touch."

After he left, I waved Wallace over and we made our way up the three flights of stairs to our bedroom. Jackson wanted to handle it on his own, but he needed help to maneuver from step to step, so it was slow going.

Unfortunately, it also gave me time to think. On top of my worry list was Detective Koren's visit, which as usual was unsettling. He kept digging, which was his job, but he also disliked Jackson, which could lead to erroneous conclusions.

Complicating matters was the fact that for the time being, Jackson couldn't do much to help me clear him of Dr. White's murder, and I didn't know how long he would be out of commission. I certainly couldn't wait, so I'd have to forge ahead. Maybe Simon could fill in.

Further down on my worry list was that with Jackson's injury, he would no longer be able to help in the garden, especially if we had to make repairs because of vandals. Having a guard would help but he couldn't be here 24/7. I wished I could count on Nate, but he seemed to be increasingly flaky and difficult.

When we got to the third-floor landing, we met Allie, who was coming out of her massage office. "Oh, no, what happened to you, Jackson?"

"He pulled something in his lower back," I said. "He's going to rest it and see how he feels in the morning."

"You've been doing so well," Allie said, tucking a strand of red hair behind her ear. "I can give you a treatment—at least loosen up the muscles—and I'm sure Hector can work on you, too, when he gets back in town."

"Thanks, but right now, I want to lie down with a heating pad."

"Okay, just let me know." She squeezed me on the arm and went downstairs.

Wallace and I got Jackson into the bedroom. Immediately, all three dogs trooped down the doggy stairs next to the bed and rushed us, tails wagging and wanting attention. "Hey, boys," Jackson said. "You can keep me company."

Thankfully, the bed was made. "Let me just get the heating pad and you can lie down." I went to the closet and plucked out the pad and plugged it in. Slowly, we moved him onto the left side of the bed, and he lay down, flat on his back.

"How does that feel?" Wallace asked, grabbing Jackson's book and his Kindle and placing them on the nightstand.

"Not great," Jackson said. "But thanks, Wallace."

"No problem," he said, and went back downstairs to close up.

I helped the dogs up onto the bed and they snuggled next to Jackson. "I feel awful that you hurt yourself because of me." I could feel tears welling up, but I didn't want to cry in front of him. He felt bad enough as it was.

"I wanted to help, remember? It's not your fault. Can you please grab my muscle relaxants and some ibuprofen from the bathroom?"

I did as he asked and returned with them and a

glass of water. He took the ones he needed and put the bottles on the nightstand.

"Do you want to watch something?" I went over to my DVD collection on the bookshelf next to the bed and picked out the fifth season of *The Murdoch Mysteries*. Jackson and I were both fans of the show that featured cutting-edge Victorian science, circuitous plots, and an appealing Canadian detective.

"No, that's okay. I'll probably just go to sleep. But before I forget, can you please call Denver and tell him what happened? He'll be okay to stay overnight and keep an eye on things."

Denver Hale was the only paid member of Jackson's staff at the animal sanctuary. The rest were volunteers. Jackson paid him with some of the grant money he'd received. It wasn't much, but Hale was like Wallace, retired and well off, so it didn't matter. He just loved animals and wanted to help them.

"I'll do that, and help Wallace close up. I want to get some arnica to help you heal. You can take a shower if you want and eat when you wake up. We've got some of Merrily's pie for dessert." I leaned over and gave him a kiss. "Try not to think about all this other stuff. Just let your mind rest."

Now if I could just do the same.

chapter nineteen

Willow McQuade's
Favorite Medicinal Plants

<u>GINSENG</u>
Botanical name: *Panax ginseng* (Asian ginseng),
P. quinquefolium (American ginseng)

Medicinal uses: Asian ginseng has been used in Chinese medicine for six thousand years to strengthen the body, reduce inflammation, improve immune function, and speed recovery from illness. Ginseng, which is known as the king of herbs, is highly valued for its restorative and energizing properties. American ginseng has properties similar to those of Asian ginseng, but it is milder.

Ginseng of either variety is packed with powerful phytonutrients, which act as antioxidants that protect the body. Ginseng enhances mental alertness, boosts energy, helps relieve stress, and provides a feeling of well-being. This herb also improves stamina, reaction time, and concentration, which make it useful if you

are studying, taking tests, long-distance driving, or meditating. The root is the primary medicinal component of the plant, and is dried and used to make tablets or capsules, extracts, and teas, as well as creams or other preparations for external use.

When Jackson woke up early Wednesday morning, he was still in pain, although after he took his medications and I rubbed his back with arnica oil, he was able to get out of the bed with help and take a shower.

Once he was dressed and back in bed, I went downstairs to get us all breakfast. He wanted buckwheat pancakes and turkey bacon, and since that sounded good to me I made it for us both, along with a fresh pot of coffee, and put it all on a large tray.

I was just about to go back upstairs when there was a knock on the door. It was Bob Cooper, our new night watchman. He was dressed in jeans, a Yankee sweatshirt, and matching cap and sneakers.

I flipped the locks and he walked in. "Hi, Willow, I'm just going off shift and wanted to report in."

"Thanks," I said as I walked back over and picked up the tray. "I was just about to bring Jackson's breakfast up to him."

Bob smiled. "I wish my wife would bring me breakfast in bed."

"Jackson put his back out and he's having trouble moving around; that's why I'm bringing it up. But I would do it anyway."

"Do you have a twin?" He smiled even wider.

"Sorry, but why don't you come up? I'm sure Jackson would like to talk to you. Do you want coffee?"

"No, I'm good, but let me take that for you."

We went back upstairs, where we found Jackson on his cell phone. He waved to us and said, "Okay, Doc, I'll stay on my usual meds and call you if I don't improve." He listened for a moment, then smiled. "Yes, she's been watching over me. I'm lucky to have you both on my team. Thanks a lot." He clicked off, and said, "Hey, Cooper."

"What have you done to yourself now, Spade?"

"I had a fight with a paver and I lost. How did it go last night?"

"It was pretty quiet—"

Jackson interrupted him. "See, I told you, McQuade. Hiring Bob was the right thing to do."

Bob cleared his throat. "Spade, you didn't let me finish. It was quiet until about midnight. That's when I noticed this guy, dressed all in black with a black rucksack, scoping out the back of the garden."

I sucked in a breath. "It must be the same guy you saw, Jackson." He nodded. "What happened?"

"The minute he saw me, he took off. I didn't get a clear look at his face."

"It's a good thing you were there," Jackson said. "It'll be interesting to see if he comes back tonight."

"I'll be back at seven. We'll see what happens."

After Bob left, I gave Jackson his breakfast. "Now, what did the doctor say?"

"Doc says to just rest it, and if I don't feel better in a day or so to come in." He put a generous pat of butter on the pancakes, then added syrup. "He definitely wants me to be treated by Allie and Hector, though. He thinks massage and acupuncture will definitely help. I think so too."

"Me too," I said, glad once again that Dr. Clifford had an open mind about alternative treatments.

"He also asked about the murder. He knew White from the hospital—they both had admitting privileges there—and the men's club in town."

"Maybe it's the same men's club that meets in that building in Joe Larson's painting."

"It probably is. I can't imagine there's more than one in a town as small as Greenport. Anyway, he said that Dr. White wasn't liked by most of the members there, including the partners in his medical practice, the mayor, and most members of the Village Board."

"No wonder he didn't get the lot."

"Doc said that he lobbied hard, and was not happy about the outcome; more like furious."

"That, we know. Did he say anything else?"

"Nope, that's it."

"Well, when I walked Dr. Russell back to the ferry we talked about how badly Dr. White treated his mother. He's pretty angry, too."

Jackson grabbed his fork and tucked into the pancakes. "So you think he could have killed White?"

"I don't know, but I never really followed down that angle, after I talked to Sandra that day in the garden. I got distracted by all the pirate treasure stuff."

"Easy to do. These are excellent by the way. Thank you."

"You're welcome." I sat on the edge of the bed and

we had breakfast together and gave tidbits of pancake and bacon to the dogs as treats.

"So what's your next move? What do you have planned for today?" Jackson said between bites.

"First I have to check to see if I have any garden tours, and then I think I'll stop by Dr. White's office and see what I can find out. Next, I'll go over to the yard sale. Maggie and Harold are running it, and Sandra and Kylie are helping. I might find out something from them if I'm lucky. I also want to do some research on the lot, if I can, and put the earring and the goblet in a safe-deposit box."

"Sounds like a full day. Maybe Simon can go with you. I'd feel better if you had someone around."

We finished up and put our plates on the tray again. "If it makes you feel better, I'll call him. He can some-times be helpful." I rummaged through my purse for my phone.

"When he's not driving you crazy." Jackson took a sip of coffee and smiled. The dogs, knowing that treat time was done, curled up next to each other and fell back asleep. "I just wish I could help you in some way today."

I found my phone and spotted my binoculars at the bottom of my purse. I plucked them out. "You can use these to watch the garden." I moved the overstuffed chair to a spot opposite the balcony. "You know, when you get up to stretch your legs."

"You mean do a *Rear Window* like Jimmy Stewart?"

"Why not?" I gave him a kiss. "You never know what you might see."

. . .

I put the earring and goblet we'd found into my oversized bag to bring to the bank, gave Jackson a kiss good-bye, and headed downstairs. When I got to the second floor, I took a peek into the yoga studio, where Nick was leading a class in hot yoga. Everyone seemed to be sweating yet serene.

Nick noticed me and came out onto the landing. He wiped his forehead with a handkerchief and said, "How is Jackson doing today? Allie told me what happened." Nick wore a sleeveless T-shirt and tight black yoga pants. He was in incredible shape, especially considering that he was in his late sixties.

"Better. His doctor told him to rest and see how he feels in a day or so."

"I can give him some gentle stretches that might help." Nick glanced back into the studio. He'd left the students in Downward Dog. "How is the investigation into Dr. White's murder going? Any progress?"

I gave him a quick recap on our helicopter ride over Gardiner's Island and to East Hampton. "Since Jackson's not feeling well. I'm going to convince Simon to keep me company as I continue to investigate today."

He put his hand on my arm. "Willow, I need to tell you something, and I know it won't make you happy."

I braced myself. What now?

He gestured through the window to his class. "One of my students told me that there is some kind of negative campaign on Facebook trying to shut down the garden."

I groaned. "Not that, too. I'm still upset about that awful petition online, and the fact that they picketed the garden."

"If I know you, you'll fix it." He gave me a quick kiss on the cheek. "I'd better get back in there and move them on to a new pose. I hope things go well."

As I continued downstairs, I pulled out my phone and searched for the site on Facebook. Sure enough, someone had created a page called Shut Down the Garden of Death! with a photo of the gate to the garden and one of Dr. White when he was alive, smiling and happy. It already had eighty-four likes.

There was also a conversation between Arlene White and someone named Jessica B. who wrote: "I'm with you Arlene! That garden is a blight on the village of Greenport!"

Feeling thrown off balance, I speed-dialed Simon, who answered on the fourth ring. "Speak."

"We've got a problem."

"Another one?"

I told him about the Facebook page. "It looks a lot like the online petition site. It must be Arlene's handiwork again." I tried to breathe consciously to calm myself down. "Simon, it's just so hateful. Why are they doing this?"

"They're jerks. Send me the link, and I'll call the lawyer. He may not be able to shut it down—freedom of speech and all that—but it's worth trying."

"Thanks." I pushed Send on the text with the link. "Also, Jackson hurt his back, and he wants me to have company today as I investigate. Can you come with me, please?"

Simon was quiet for a minute. "Listen, Willow, I'm really sorry to hear about Jackson, but I'm trying to write. That trip yesterday inspired me, and I'm making real progress on my new screenplay about pirates. I think it's got potential to be a summer blockbuster. I'm thinking Hugh Jackman would be perfect for the lead. Can it wait? . . . Hold on a sec." I heard his keyboard clicking furiously as I reached the bottom floor, headed into the store, and checked the clipboard to see if there had been any requests for garden tours. Eight people had signed up for the ten and eleven o'clock tours. My heart lifted. At least some people had an open mind.

"Yes, it can wait, but just until noon. I've got two tours to give this morning and then we can go. I want to check out Dr. White's office then go to the yard sale and antique show on the green, and a couple of other places."

He stopped typing and there was a long silence.

"Simon, you said you wanted me to investigate. I need your help. Detective Koren came by yesterday, and Jackson is still his chief suspect. Will you go with me?"

He sighed and finally said, "Of course. I'll be there."

After the garden tours, both of which were well received with, thankfully, no mention of the murder, Simon arrived. His lawyer had called him back on his way over to Nature's Way and told him that the site on Facebook had been removed. He had somehow been able to convince Facebook that it was harassment. It was nice to hear some good news for a change.

Merrily, who was due in at eleven, was late. I had called and left her a voice mail, asking where she was and whether she was okay. I didn't mention the fact that she'd left early yesterday and my suspicions about Nate leading her astray. Meanwhile, I had no doubt that Jackson would keep an eye on Nate from the window, at least as much as he could.

After Jackson, Simon, and I ate lunch, we set off for Dr. White's office. Simon had Googled the address, which turned out to be in Feather Hill, a shopping complex on the main road in the center of Southold.

We arrived ten minutes later and parked in a spot in front of the medical office, which was located in a two-story rustic building, across from the Southold post office. The wooden sign out front read: East End Orthopedic Specialists, and featured White's name embossed in gold paint, followed by Dr. Joseph Cohen and Dr. Todd Plummer.

"How are we going to play this?" I asked as we got out of the car. "Should we be honest?"

"That probably won't work."

"What, then?"

He thought about it for a moment. "Remember that brunette I was chatting up when we were at the wake? She's White's office manager. I think her name is Brigitte."

"And you didn't think to mention this before? Did she tell you anything?"

He shook his head. "We only talked for a few minutes. Besides, I have a girlfriend."

"Okay, so what do you want to do now? Use your charm to weasel information out of her?"

"You read my mind."

We entered the office and found two people in the waiting room. Behind the desk sat a pretty brunette, wearing a fuchsia shift and a name tag, that said Juliette. Well, he had been sort of close on the name. She spotted Simon and gave him a big smile. Simon had this effect on women.

"Simon, what are you doing here?" she practically purred.

"I came to see you. I didn't have your number, so I had to track you down," he said, giving her a dazzling smile.

Juliette got up and came around the desk. "You left the wake so soon, I didn't have time to give it to you." She scrutinized me. "And you are?"

"This is Willow. She's a friend of mine."

"Oh, nice to meet you." She seemed to relax.

"Can you get out of here for a few minutes? Maybe take a coffee break?" Simon suggested.

"Let me check." She went back to the desk and pressed the intercom button on the phone. "Mary, can you cover the front desk? I need to go out for a few minutes."

"Be right there."

Five minutes later, we were sitting in a booth in the Just Donuts café, sipping coffee. "Juliette," Simon began, "we're hoping that you can help us."

"Help you . . . with what? I thought that you just wanted to see me and get my number, you know, for later." She reached out and touched his hand.

"That would be great, but for now we need some information about Dr. White."

"Wait a minute," she said, withdrawing her hand. "What is this?"

Despite what Simon had counseled, I decided to go

with honesty. "Dr. White was killed in my garden, which is in the lot next to my store, Nature's Way, in Greenport. My boyfriend, Jackson, is being blamed for his death, and he didn't do it. I'm trying to clear him."

Juliette stood up. "I've heard about you and the Garden of Death. Mrs. White says you're a trouble-maker."

"Juliette, please sit down," Simon said. "Willow is a good person, and she and Jackson are being treated unfairly, especially by Arlene White."

She paused, thought about what he'd said, and finally sat down again. "I know what she's done. She asked me to help her but I said I was busy. So she got Mary to set up that Web site and the Facebook page."

"Why didn't you want to help her?" I asked.

"Because I worked for her husband for over three years, and I knew how he could be. He was no saint, and he had a lot of enemies. I almost quit a half a dozen times, but I need the money."

"Is it true that some of his enemies are former patients?"

"He didn't treat patients any better than he treated us. He was rude and dismissive. Worst of all, he was a bad doctor. The list of people who were suing him is a long one."

"Was one of them Sandra Bennett?"

She nodded. "Yes, she was suing him. It still isn't settled. Those things take forever. I heard him talking to his lawyer once, and he instructed him to drag it out for as long as he could. He had no sympathy whatsoever for the patients who were suffering because of his incompetence. Even if they were friends, like Mr. Larson."

"Joe Larson?" I glanced at Simon, who raised an eyebrow.

"Yes, they've been friends for years. Joe was helping him get that lot of yours. He used to come in here all the time. Dr. White kept patients waiting so he could talk to Joe. It was frustrating, for them and us, in terms of his schedule."

"What was wrong with Joe Larson?"

"His knee. He hurt it skiing and Dr. White did a knee replacement, but Joe's still having a lot of problems. He still has to wear a brace."

I realized that Joe Larson had more than one reason to want White dead. He may have coveted his wife, and now this.

"What about Mrs. Russell? Her son complained about Dr. White and the way he treated his mother."

"Did he ever! Mr. Russell used to call or come by several times a week to try and speak to Dr. White, but he kept avoiding him. The last time Mr. Russell was here, he threatened to file suit. I was sorry to hear that his mother passed away last year."

I nodded. "Yes, and he's still upset over how she was treated," I said. "Do you think that either Professor Russell or Sandra were angry enough to murder Dr. White?"

Juliette thought a minute before answering. "They were angry, yes, but murder? It's hard to imagine either one of them committing murder. Then again, who really knows what someone else is capable of?"

Juliette had confirmed my suspicions about both Sandra and Professor Russell, but the news about Joe

Larson was new and added to the mystery of who killed Dr. White. We arrived back in Greenport and went over to Mitchell Park to try and find answers.

The weather was sunny, with a slight breeze, and the park was filled with locals and visitors alike. A large banner that said: Annual Maritime and Nautical Yard Sale and Antique Show to Benefit the North Fork Animal Shelter framed the entrance, and the entire green was filled with tables and booths, selling all kinds of maritime and nautical antiques.

We started out at the east end of the park, by Aldo's Café and walked south toward the docks, checking out the wares and looking for suspects.

Simon picked up a brass diver's helmet and examined it. "This would look great on the shelf in my office in L.A." He asked the seller a few questions and Googled it to find out what it was worth before handing over his credit card and paying for it. As we moved on, he said, "He said it's an antique, and my research online confirmed it. I was lucky to get it. Next, I need a ship's wheel, so keep on the lookout for that."

"We're investigating, remember? Not shopping."

"No reason we can't do both." As we headed toward the docks, he zeroed in on a table displaying weathervanes, anchors, harpoons, and buoys. Simon examined one of the nautical charts and said, "I'm going to get this, too, and frame it for my office. It'll remind me of the East End while I'm away."

"When are you going back to L.A. anyway?"

"In August, that's when we start production. Until then, I can communicate via cell, e-mail, and Skype with my writers who are working on *Vision* episodes.

Like I said, I'm making progress on the screenplay so I want to ride it as long as I can before I have other responsibilities."

"That makes sense."

"And also help you solve this case, of course. I don't want Jackson going down for Dr. White's murder. I know what it's like to be behind the eight ball, and thanks to you, I got out. I owe you, and him."

While he paid for his purchase I checked my phone for any messages. I'd missed one text from Jackson that read:

Nate is here. Talking on phone, not working . . . JS

The JS, I figured, was for Jimmy Stewart. He hadn't lost his sense of humor.

At least Jackson was able to get up and walk around a bit. As for Nate, maybe he'd do some work when he finished that call. One could only hope. The teahouse was supposed to be finished by this weekend, for the closing of the festival, but that didn't look like it was going to happen.

I shoved the phone back into my pocket and glanced around. I noticed Harold Spitz talking to a vendor near the carousel.

"Let's try to talk to Harold," I said. "He's over there, and Maggie isn't in sight. Maybe we can actually get him to say something useful."

"What does this guy do anyway? Why did he say he wanted the lot?"

"He organizes yard sales. That's why he wanted the lot."

"But in actuality, he may have wanted it so he could dig up pirate treasure."

"Could be. If he runs yard sales, he's probably got an eye for antiques and knows what old things are worth. If he'd heard rumors about pirate treasure, that might seem like the ultimate get-rich-quick scheme."

We walked toward the carousel and stopped at a table where Harold was talking to a vendor who sold nautical jewelry. Harold, dressed in an immaculate white suit with a vest and pocket watch, and a straw hat, looked the very picture of a country gentleman.

"Hi, Harold," I said in my friendliest tone. "You did a really great job organizing this."

He looked at me suspiciously for a moment before saying, "Thanks, but I had help from Maggie, Sandra, and Kylie. It takes a village."

He turned to go, but Simon stepped in front of him and showed him the diver's helmet. "I just picked this up. What do you think? Since you're an expert at antiques, I mean."

"I'm no expert on antiques. I organize yard sales," he said, but despite this, he took the helmet and looked it over carefully. "This is a nice piece. In fact, I have a buyer who might be interested. I pick up things for him now and then. I could give you a good price for it."

"Sorry, not interested," Simon said.

"What is your buyer looking for?" I asked.

"He likes one-of-a-kind maritime and nautical items."

"Like pirate treasure?" I said.

Harold tried to hide it, but the question caught him off-guard. "I wouldn't know anything about that. Please excuse me." He pulled out his phone and dialed. Since he was next to me, I could see the name

"Ramona" come up on the screen. He was calling Ramona, of Ramona and Rhonda Heirloom Vegetables. "It's Harold."

I wondered why he was calling her. Perhaps he needed some special veggies from their farm—or he was planning another attack with his team on my business.

But I wasn't done talking to him. "Interesting question that you posed at Professor Russell's lecture," I said. "You know that rumor about pirate treasure on the East End? Is it true?"

He stopped and told Ramona to hold on, and turned to look at me. "I should be asking you that question, Ms. McQuade. From what I hear, if anyone knows about pirate treasure, it's you."

chapter twenty

Willow McQuade's
Favorite Medicinal Plants

HOPS

Botanical name: *Humulus lupulus* (syn. *H. americanus*)

Medicinal uses: This unusual plant with pale green, cone-shaped flowers is best known for giving flavor to beer, but its medicinal properties go far beyond this, helping to improve health and well-being. Hops can help to calm the spirit, stabilize nerves, ease anxiety, and improve sleep thanks to a compound called lupulin, which is considered a strong but safe, reliable sedative. It's easy to make a sachet with this calming aroma to insert in your pillowcase. Just fill a five-by-five inch sachet with hops and tie tightly with a ribbon. Both King George II and Abraham Lincoln slept with hops pillows to aid sleep. Hops flower essence can help inspire you to follow and progress along a spiritual path in life.

Harold gave me a smirk, put the phone to his ear, and walked away before I could respond. Although there wasn't much I could say. He was right. I just wished that he didn't know.

"So Sandra told him," Simon said.

"Or Martin. Or maybe he already knew about the treasure because he's the one who killed Dr. White and was digging up the garden."

"But how did these people find out about the treasure in the lot in the first place?"

"Good question," I said. "Jackson suggested that we research the history of Frank Fox's lot to try and find answers, and I think the best place to do that is in Village Hall. That's where we're going next."

But as we headed out of Mitchell Park, Arlene White and Joe Larson were on their way in. Arlene spotted me and walked over. She wore a black short-sleeved dress with a gold belt, classy widow's weeds. Arlene looked as if she was spoiling for a fight.

"Arlene, don't do this," Larson said as they approached us. "She's not worth it."

"You," she said, and poked her finger in my direction. "What were you doing at my husband's office?"

That didn't take long. Mary must have asked Juliette who we were and then passed the information along to Arlene. "Who told you that?"

"That's none of your business."

"I'll bet it was Mary, your Web site and Facebook helper."

"I have a right to express myself, especially now, in my hour of grief."

"Your Web site and that Facebook page are not about expressing yourself," Simon said. "The Facebook page was defamatory, and that's why it was taken down."

"He's right," I said. "It also wasn't very nice."

"Nice! How dare you talk to me about nice? You're responsible for my husband's death, you and your boyfriend."

"Lady, you're misinformed," Simon said. "Keep spewing these invectives and I'll get my lawyer to sue you for libel."

"It's not libel if it's true!" Then she began to cry. I watched her, unable to tell if the weeping was genuine or an act. I tried to give her the benefit of the doubt; after all, her husband had been murdered less than a week ago.

Joe put an arm around her and gave her a tissue. "Come on, Arlene," he said gently. "You're just getting yourself upset again." He led her away from us, and I noticed for the first time that Joe favored his right leg and walked with a slight limp. Juliette had been right about him.

I blew out a breath. "Let's get out of here."

We began to thread our way out through the vendors' tables. When we reached Front Street, though, Sandra was there, clipboard in hand, monitoring the traffic going in and out. As opposed to Harold's carefully considered appearance, her hair was up in a messy bun, and she wore a T-shirt, shorts, and sneakers.

"I need to talk to you," I said.

"Maybe later," she said. "I'm busy now."

But at that exact moment, the traffic through the

gate lagged. "Not right now you aren't," Simon said. "Let's go."

We stepped to the side, out of the earshot of any vendor or visitor, and I said, "We just talked to Harold, and I got the impression that he knows about what we found in the garden. Only a few people knew about that, besides Jackson, Simon, Nate, and me."

"That would be you and your husband," Simon said. "So did you tell him?"

Flustered, Sandra said, "No, I didn't, and neither did Martin."

"Maybe you told Maggie?"

Her face slowly turned bright red. "I might have mentioned it. I didn't know it was a secret."

"I didn't know that you and Maggie were friends. But after seeing you picketing with her and Harold and Kylie in front of my garden, I have to assume that you are. What happened to staying out of it, Sandra?"

She sniffed. "After talking to Maggie and Harold, I realized that they were right. Dr. White would never have been murdered right here in town if it wasn't for your garden. If the board had given the lot to one of us, this never would have happened."

"Do you actually believe that?" Simon asked. "Chances are it would have happened no matter who owned it."

"You don't know that."

"And you don't know that it *wouldn't* have happened if someone else owned it," Simon said. "That's a ridiculous thing to say."

"Besides, I thought you didn't like Dr. White," I said. "Wasn't he once your doctor?"

"I never said that!"

"You didn't have to. Kylie said she had a friend who was suing Dr. White. You talked about a doctor that you didn't like when you visited the garden."

Sandra made a face. "That could have been any friend and any doctor."

"No, Sandra," I said. "We just got back from his office, and his assistant confirmed that you were one of his patients and that you were suing him. But maybe that wasn't enough for you. Maybe you killed him."

"How could you even think such a thing?" Sandra looked genuinely horrified by the idea. "He was murdered in your garden, and it made the village look bad. It could hurt business for everyone. That's why I joined Harold and Maggie and Kylie."

Simon looked around the green. "Given the crowds all week long, I'd say business is booming, wouldn't you, Willow?"

"Well, I've had my problems, thanks to the murder, but the rest of the village seems to be thriving."

Sandra looked confused. "I don't know. It seemed to make sense at the time."

"Sandra," Simon spoke in an overly patient tone. "Why do Harold and Maggie really want to shut down Willow's garden?"

Sandra bit her lip and said, "I don't know."

"She was helpful," Simon said sarcastically as we left Sandra on the village green and walked over to Village Hall to do some research. "It was like she was reciting talking points. Is she really that stupid or was that all an act?"

"I'm not sure," I admitted as we turned the corner onto Third Street and headed north. "But I'm beginning to think that Sandra's extremely malleable. Whatever they say, she believes."

"She doesn't seem angry enough to have killed Dr. White," Simon noted. "But for all we know, she's after the treasure, too." He pointed at the parking lot behind the stores on Front Street. "Let me put this stuff in my car so I don't have to carry it."

We walked over to his red and black Mini Cooper and he popped the trunk. As he did, I noticed Rhonda Rhodes hurrying up Third Street. "I wonder where she's going. I just saw Harold call her partner, Ramona."

Simon carefully placed the diving helmet and maps on top of a clean towel in the trunk. "Who are they again?"

"Rhonda and Ramona are partners and they grow heirloom vegetables. We talked to her at the farmer's market on Sunday, remember?"

Simon thought about this. "No."

"You know, the table in the back, by the church. She wasn't very friendly. You didn't like her."

"Oh, right, no, I didn't." He slammed the trunk shut.

"Maybe Harold called Ramona, and she called Rhonda."

"To do what?"

"I don't know."

"Let's find out."

We caught up to Rhonda on the steps of Village Hall. She wore a flowered shift dress and flip-flops, like the one she'd had on Saturday night when Jackson and I had seen her at the art gallery with Ramona.

She threw me a wave and tried to hurry inside, but I caught the door and said, "Hi, Rhonda, how are you?"

She mumbled something and headed through the door to the left and down a hallway that led to the section of the building where you could pay your utilities.

"Maybe I was wrong about her being up to something." I pointed to the sign on the wall to the right of the elevator that said Map Room: Basement. "We go this way." I pushed the button for the elevator.

The elevator arrived and we rode it downstairs. We reached the basement, and the doors opened to a room with file cabinets covering just about every square inch. In front of the files there was a middle-aged, balding man working on an outdated computer. "Damn!" he said, and pounded the desk.

"Problem?" I asked.

"Oh, hello. Sorry about that. It's just that it takes forever to download files on this thing. I'm Larry. Can I help you guys?"

"I own Nature's Way at 528 Front Street, and recently, the village awarded me the lot next door. I was wondering if it was possible to research the history of the lot."

"Everyone wants to know about that lot. I just had a lady down here asking about it about an hour ago."

"Who was it?" I asked.

"She didn't say."

"Well, what did she look like?" Simon said.

"She was kind of tall, and she had on a flowered dress."

"I'll be right back," I said, and hurried back up to the first floor. But when I got there, Rhonda was gone. Perhaps she'd come to do research *and* pay her bill and had forgotten about the latter and come back, and that's when we saw her.

When I got back downstairs, Simon and Larry were across the room, peering into the open drawer of a lateral file cabinet. Larry was thumbing through documents. He found what he needed and pulled it out, then put it on top of another map. "Since the village of Greenport is so small, they still keep all the maps of all the lots this way. I found yours and the one next door. Follow me."

We walked over to a table shoved into the corner of the room with a large fluorescent light overhead. Larry put the map onto the table and smoothed it down. "Here you go."

Simon and I examined the maps. The one for Nature's Way showed the building and gave the dimensions of the lot and a list of utilities on the property.

"Look," Simon said. At the bottom of the map, tiny lettering read Property of Claire Hagen.

"I guess they never changed it when I took over."

"Oh, we're behind on all of that stuff," Larry assured me.

I ran my finger along her name.

"You miss her," Simon said.

"I really do. It never goes away."

He squeezed my arm. "Let's take a look at the other map." He pulled it out from under the stack and put it on top. "Look, there was originally a house on the lot."

"I didn't know that. I mean I figured there had been something there, but I didn't know it was a residence."

"It was owned by Frank Fox," Simon said. "It says so right here." He pointed to the name below the map specifications. "And it was a double lot. You see this line?" He pointed to a vertical line that transected the piece of land.

"It looks like there was some kind of outbuilding or a shed on the eastern side," I said.

Simon shrugged. "Doesn't tell us much. We knew Frank Fox owned the land; he's the one who donated it to the village."

I turned to Larry. "Do you have any information about the history of the lot, who lived here and when?"

"I knew you'd ask that. Everyone does."

"And what do you tell them?"

Larry shook his head. "It should be on the microfiche."

"*Should* be?" Simon said.

"That particular roll of microfiche is gone."

chapter twenty-one

Willow McQuade's
Favorite Medicinal Plants

<u>KAVA-KAVA</u>
Botanical name: *Piper methysticum*

Medicinal uses: Kava-kava is an ancient remedy used by Pacific Islanders to treat nervousness and insomnia. It is often used in the islands ceremoniously as a religious ritual, to welcome guests (including Captain Cook in the 1770s) and to honor births, marriages, and business deals. Kava-kava calms the mind, heart, and body, and eases anxiety and mild depression without compromising mental clarity. Taking kava-kava before bed can help induce pleasant sleep and vivid dreams. Kava-kava is fat soluble, so when I prepare it as a tea, I add coconut milk to the steeping solution to help the infusion assimilate kava's compounds.

I couldn't quite make sense of Larry's answer. "What do you mean, that roll of microfiche is gone? Where did it go?"

Larry shrugged. "Your guess is as good as mine."

"How does a roll of microfiche disappear?" Simon wanted to know.

"Usually someone borrows it and doesn't put it back—or maybe puts it back in the wrong place. But I've searched. This one is gone."

"When exactly did it disappear?" I asked.

Larry looked perplexed. "That's a good question. I don't know when it vanished. All I know is that for the last month or so, I've had a lot of inquiries about that lot—and a lot of people asking to see that roll of microfiche. And it's not there."

"So it's been gone at least a month," I said. "Great. I think we just hit another one of our blind alleys."

With no microfiche to give us answers, we returned to the maps of each lot, scanning them for any new information. While we did, I told them about Rhonda and my theory about why she'd come back.

Half an hour later, not having had a Eureka! moment, we thanked Larry for his help and took the elevator back upstairs. The doors opened on the first floor and we found the mayor in a heated discussion with Joe Larson, without Arlene White.

"We've made a decision and were sticking with it," Mayor Hobson said.

"Even though you're wrong," Joe Larson said, giving us a hostile look.

"I think you'd better leave, Joe," Mayor Hobson said. "We'll talk about this later."

Larson yanked the door open and stomped down the stairs.

"He doesn't seem too happy," I said, stating the obvious.

"He's not. He and several other prominent local businesspeople want us to change our minds about Fox's lot."

"We know about that," I said. "I hope you don't."

"I think your garden is a great addition to the village, but I'm getting a lot of pressure to change my mind."

"Stick with the side of the angels, Mayor," Simon said, slapping him on the back. "You won't be sorry."

We said good-bye and stepped outside, but the mayor waved Simon back in. While they talked, I quickly texted Jackson to see how he was doing.

He replied that Allie had given him a massage and he was feeling much better. This was really good news, because back problems can take a long time to resolve. I texted back that I had to go to the bank and would be back soon. I'd just put my phone away when Simon came out, and we headed back to Nature's Way.

"Spill," I said. "What did he want?"

"He invited me to this club for local businessmen."

"No women?"

He shook his head. "The mayor and most of the Village Board are members, along with people like Larson, he says. He thought it might be a good idea for me to attend."

"Why? You're not a local businessman. You're a Hollywood producer."

He shrugged. "I get the feeling that he's trying to help you. Maybe he thinks I can do that by going."

• • •

We decided that Simon should go to the meeting. Perhaps, in a relaxed setting like the club, he would be able to learn something to help us piece together the puzzle of Dr. White's murder.

Before we went back to Nature's Way, we stopped off at the bank and put the earring and the goblet into a safe-deposit box. I gave one of the keys to Simon. He went home and I returned to the store right before 3 p.m.

Merrily had finally shown up and was stocking the dry goods shelves with boxes of quinoa, a protein-packed grain that also contains iron and has a delightfully nutty taste. Wallace was in the kitchen, and four tables were full in the café, while several customers browsed our shelves.

"Hey, Willow," Merrily said as she grabbed two packages of quinoa from the box at her feet. "How was the sale?"

"Interesting, Simon found a few things. How are you feeling today?"

"I'm okay," Merrily said as she shoved the packages onto the shelf. She wore the typical Nature's Way uniform of a white shirt, green apron, and khakis, but her hair, which was usually up in neat tufts with colorful rubber bands, looked frizzy and flyaway. She was also chalk white, and had purple-black smudges under her eyes.

"Wallace said you had a migraine yesterday, and that's why you went home."

"Oh, that," she said. "I'm better now."

"But you don't look well. Merrily, are you all right?"

"I'm fine, Willow, really. I just had a hard time sleeping last night."

"Because of Nate?"

"No," she snapped. "We're good." She put three more packages onto the shelf and picked up the empty box.

Since I'd known Merrily, she had never lost her temper, so this surprised me. "It's just that you seem upset and distracted, and I'm wondering if it's because of your new relationship with him. Things are kind of crazy right now and with the murder and—"

"I'm not distracted," she said, interrupting me. "It's just like you said—there's a lot going on. I'm focused, don't worry. In fact, I just made three new apple pies. Do you want a slice? Jackson had two."

"Are you trying to get me to change the subject?" I asked.

Merrily looked at me as if I'd lost my mind. "Willow," she said patiently, "I told you about the pies for one reason: you love pie."

"True," I admitted, feeling sheepish. "Especially your pies."

"There's one on the counter. I'll be right back. Just have to put this in the recycle bin." She carried the box to the back.

It seemed obvious that she didn't want to talk about what was going on. I decided to leave it alone, for now.

The pie was, of course, delicious, but I was too worried about Merrily to really enjoy it. When I was done, I went upstairs to check on Jackson.

I found him in the chair I'd placed by the balcony, with his binoculars trained on the garden. Qigong, Rockford, and Columbo had been sleeping, but immediately ran over to me, tails wagging. I petted each in turn, and went over and gave Jackson a kiss.

"Hi, hon." He put the binoculars on his lap.

"Something interesting must be going on down there."

"Nate's been on his phone almost the whole time you've been gone. That's when he's actually in the garden. He also left for a half an hour twice. I think we need to let him go."

Frowning, I said, "That's a shame. He was such a good worker when he started this spring."

"When he's supervised, he works but complains. And when he's alone, he's completely nonproductive. Do you want to do it or should I?"

"I'm worried about how Merrily will take it. I just spoke to her and she's irritable and doesn't look well at all. Maybe we should talk to him first, give him one more chance?"

Jackson picked up the binoculars and trained them on the garden again. "I guess we'll have to. He's gone again."

I updated Jackson on my progress investigating and checked to make sure he had what he needed before heading back downstairs to work in my office. But when I got there, Merrily was gone again. I went into the kitchen to talk to Wallace, who was busy cleaning the display cases. The man was a marvel.

"Hey, Wallace. Where's Merrily?"

He shrugged. "Nate came in and she left with him."

"Does this happen often?" I poured myself a cup of organic coffee and added half-and-half and two packets of Truvia, a natural sweetener.

"All the time. Don't get me wrong, I think Merrily is great, but lately . . ."

"I know." I walked over the bay window and looked out, but she wasn't there. "I don't see her. Can you ask her to speak to me when she returns? I'll be in my office."

I settled in at my desk, took a sip of coffee, and opened my e-mail. Most of the messages were confirmations of orders that Wallace had placed, for things like supplements and body-care products.

I still couldn't get over how much easier my life was ever since Wallace arrived. He'd taken over the bulk of the management duties and went above and beyond whatever else was needed. It was because of him that I'd been able to even consider creating the garden.

Merrily, on the other hand, was a shadow of the worker she had once been. She'd been sick with Lyme, yes, but that hadn't even been much of a problem when it came to her productivity. No, it wasn't until Nate arrived that the problems started. I decided that I would have to let him go, without delay. She might object, and be upset, but once he was gone, maybe things would go back to normal.

Of course, she could still see him outside of work, but it might help to put some distance between them. And if things didn't improve, much as I hated to consider it, I might have to think about letting her go as well.

I finished going through the rest of my e-mail, then turned off the computer and headed outside to the garden to check on things.

The garden was beautiful; late-afternoon sunlight streaked through the trees and dappled the grounds. But as I made my way down the path, it became clear that something was wrong. Spades and clippers had been abandoned on the path, while a bag of mulch had been pushed into a flower bed and was partially empty. I took out my phone and quickly texted Jackson:

Something wrong in garden. Is someone here? That guy in black?

I waited for his response. It took a few minutes, so I guessed that he had gone back to bed. But moments later, he returned my text:

Think Nate is hurt . . . by pavers. M there. B careful . . . Shd I call cops?

I texted back:

Let me check out first . . .

I slipped the phone back into my pocket and yelled, "Merrily? Are you out here?"

"Willow?" Her voice sounded tenuous and strained.

"I'm coming. Is Nate hurt?"

"Yes, he needs help. Hurry!"

chapter twenty-two

Willow McQuade's
Favorite Medicinal Plants

GREEN TEA
Botanical name: *Camellia sinensis*

Medicinal uses: It's the polyphenols, a type of flavonoid containing catechin and proanthocyanidins with antioxidant properties, that have earned green tea such a well-deserved reputation for imbuing good health. I try to have at least a cup each day, especially when I need an energy boost. Green tea helps to lower cholesterol levels, keeps blood sugar levels moderate, stimulates the metabolism, and can help with weight loss.

The other thing I like about green tea is that it contains one-third to half as much caffeine as coffee, and because of its makeup, the side effects—jitteriness, irritability, and, after the effect has worn off, fatigue—are minimal compared to other caffeine sources. This may explain why Zen monks rely on green tea to help

them remain alert yet calm during long periods of meditation.

One of the widely researched components in tea is the alkaloid theanine, an amino acid that has been found to decrease anxiety, aid in sleep, and promote mental focus. In folkloric traditions tea is burned as an incense to attract prosperity and carried to impart strength and courage. Green tea extracts can be taken in capsules and are sometimes used in skin products. Leaves from the _Camellia sinensis_ plant are brewed to produce green tea. Why not have a cup right now?

I ran down the path and found Nate and Merrily by the unfinished teahouse. Nate lay on his back, in the dirt. Around him were several newly dug holes, and a shovel lay next to him on the ground. He had a nasty bloody gash across his forehead. Merrily was kneeling over him.

"What happened? Why didn't you call us?"

"He didn't want me to," Merrily said, crying. "But I can't get him up by myself."

I leaned over Nate. "Are you okay? Can you stand?"

His eyes fluttered open. "I don't know . . ." His eyes closed.

"Nate, what happened to you?"

He opened his eyes, and said, "I—I was moving another paver over and I lost my footing and landed face first on the patio."

I went over to the patio. "Where did it happen?"

"Over there. I don't know." He closed his eyes again.

Chances were good that he had suffered a concussion. If so, we needed to stop him from going to sleep.

"Merrily, keep talking to him. Keep him awake!" Quickly, I examined the immediate area but didn't see any blood or signs of an accident. The fact that there were freshly dug holes and a shovel, though, made me question his story. Was he lying? Had he been looking for artifacts now, too? Did the man in black attack him?

"Nate, wake up!" Merrily yelled.

"He needs to be seen at the emergency room. Help me get him to his feet," I said as I went over to him and grabbed his right arm. Merrily took his left arm, and slowly we got him to his feet. But he was as wobbly as a newly born fawn.

I worried that he might have a severe concussion and maybe even brain damage. I sucked in a breath. I hated the thought of an employee of mine being injured. After all, it was my fault he had been in the garden in the first place.

"Nate, we're going to walk you over to the bench by the entrance and I'll stay with you while Merrily gets her car."

So for the second time in as many days, I helped and injured man out of the garden. I'd have to put firing Nate on hold, for now.

After a restless night's sleep, I woke up Thursday morning just before seven and headed down to the yoga studio for my daily practice. With everything that had happened, I really needed to clear my mind.

The night before, Merrily had called from the ER to say that Nate *had* suffered a concussion and needed several stiches in his forehead. The doctor had released him with the caveat that he not be alone, so she was taking him home and staying the night.

The situation in the garden had gone from bad to worse. I didn't know whether to believe Nate or not, but my gut told me that something untoward had happened to him in the garden. Perhaps whoever was looking for pirate treasure had become bolder, or maybe more desperate, since he or she was searching the garden and attacking people in broad daylight instead of waiting until dark. I could see no other solution but to close the garden until this person was caught and the case was closed. I didn't want to open myself to a lawsuit.

How did such a good idea become such a nightmare? I could feel my stomach churning with sadness, fear, and flat-out dread. It was definitely time for yoga. I took a deep breath and began a series of sun salutations. I was just about to move on to the warrior pose when my cell phone buzzed.

It was an e-mail from Professor Russell:

Good morning, Willow—I'm planning on coming over to Greenport for the yard sale and antique show today. Are you free? No word on the sword yet, but I have some books about pirates on the East End you might find interesting, which I can bring along.

After what Juliette had said, I definitely wanted

to question him further about Dr. White, so I quickly
e-mailed back.

Sure, how about 11? I'll meet you at the entrance.
Bring the books! Thanks!

He replied:

I'll see you then!

Twenty minutes later, I'd finished my practice and
gone back upstairs, where I found Jackson getting
dressed.

"How are you feeling today?"

"Better."

"I was thinking that we needed to close the garden,
at least for now, after what happened to Nate."

"That would be admitting defeat, don't you think?"
He grabbed his work boots and went over to the bed to
put them on.

"Maybe. But I'm worried about someone suing us
if something else happens. I can't afford to have anyone
else injured in the garden."

"You've got a point," Jackson said. "But I still think
we need to finish what we've started—and I definitely
want to finish that teahouse."

"That's the last thing we have to worry about right
now. There's no way it's going to be completed by the
end of the festival. Too much stuff has come up this
week. The real question is, how do we keep the garden
safe?"

Jackson didn't hesitate. "I say we put a twenty-four-hour guard on it to keep any interested parties out." He laced up his boots, but not without difficulty, and then slowly got to his feet.

"Jackson, do you really think it's a good idea to work in the garden today? You look like you're still recovering."

"I think I can get Bob to help out in the garden. Since he retired, he works part-time with his son's construction company, so he knows what he's doing. I'll ask him to find someone else to help guard the garden while he's at it."

"But what do we do about Nate?"

"We wait until he's better then talk to him. Maybe give him a second chance, considering what's happened."

"Okay." My phone rang with a number I didn't recognize. "Hello?"

"This is Michael Yard. You may remember me from Dr. White's wake?"

"I remember you." Why was Arlene White's attorney calling me? I quickly put the phone on speaker so Jackson could hear him.

"I'm calling on behalf of my client Nate Marshall."

I stared at Jackson. "Your client?"

"Yes, Mr. Marshall sustained serious injuries yesterday when he was in your employ, and he's suing you for damages."

"I don't want to minimize what happened, but I was told that it was a concussion and he had a few stiches on his forehead."

"It was a severe concussion, Ms. McQuade, and he's likely to suffer long-term neurologic damage. He's dizzy and disoriented. You're his employer, you're responsible."

"Believe me, I feel bad about what happened, but a lawsuit isn't the answer."

"We think it is. I suggest you contact Mr. Lewis, Ms. McQuade, and ask him to find you a good personal injury lawyer." I could hear him shuffling papers around on his desk. "One more thing. I'll be bringing suit on Mrs. White's behalf as well." He hung up.

I looked at Jackson. "What are we going to do?"

He came over and gave me a hug. "It's going to be all right. Knowing Nate, he's exaggerating his injuries. We'll get our own doctor to examine him to confirm what he's saying. For now, call Simon immediately."

"What about Mrs. White?"

"Let's solve the murder first. If she's guilty, she won't be suing anyone."

At eleven o'clock, Jackson and I crossed Front Street to meet Professor Russell in Mitchell Park. But I left Nature's Way feeling uneasy. Merrily had texted me to say she needed to stay home and take care of Nate. She said nothing about Michael Yard and the fact that Nate was suing me.

The fact that Merrily was again not available meant that Wallace would have to handle the store and the café on his own. He told me that he'd call his niece,

Lily, who worked at another café in town, to see if she could fill in.

Jackson had been able to reach his friend Bob, our nighttime guard, and told him the situation. Bob had arrived before we left. The plan was that he would watch the garden until a friend of his, Tony, another retired cop with time on his hands, came in at seven that evening to take over. Until things returned to normal, they would switch off every twelve hours. When Jackson was working in the garden, Bob could help him out, too.

Because we needed a guard on duty before I could give tours, I told Wallace the situation and that we hoped to have the tours running again on Friday. To compensate for any inconvenience, I decided that anyone who bought a ticket for a garden tour could bring a friend along for free.

When Jackson and I got to the entrance of Mitchell Park, Professor Russell was waiting for us. He wore a black backpack, which reminded me of the one the intruder wore, but this one probably held the books he'd mentioned.

"Morning, Professor," I said. "How was your ride across?"

"Lovely," he said. "I always enjoy the view of Greenport when I'm on the ferry."

"Has there been any word about the sword?" Jackson asked.

"No, not yet, I'm afraid. Dr. Gillian did tell me that it could take some time. We'll just have to be patient. In the meantime—" He took off his pack and pulled out several books. "All of these focus on pirates who frequented the East End in the seventeenth century. Their indices make no mention of Greenport. Still, you may find some helpful information."

"Thanks," I said, taking the books as we started toward the green. "So, are you looking for anything specific today? There's going to be a huge amount of stuff at the yard sale and antique show."

"That's what Harold said."

"Harold?"

"Yes, Harold Spitz. The two of us chatted a bit after my lecture at the Maritime Museum, and then he called me the next day—when I was on my way over on the ferry to see you, in fact. He wanted to know if I might be interested in one-of-a-kind items from the seventeenth century, since that's my field of interest. He also suggested that I come over for his yard sale."

"What kind of items? Like pirate treasure?"

He laughed. "No, Ms. McQuade, of course not. More like antique furniture and interesting objets d'art. I've just moved into a new house with a lot more space, and I need to fill it. Anyway, I told him yes, and he said to find him when I came over for the sale today." He looked around the green.

"Do you see him?"

While he kept looking around, I glanced at Jackson and I could see that he was also thinking about what this might mean. Were Professor Russell and Harold working together? Was Professor Russell helping him find treasure, specifically whatever might be in my lot? Had the whole trip to East Hampton to see Dr. Gillian been just a ruse to get us out of town?

I looked around the green and spotted Harold at a table near the docks. "He's over there."

"Oh, good, I'll go over and say hello. Do you want to come?"

"We wouldn't miss it," Jackson said. "Let's go."

We began to walk across the green, but Martin Bennett intercepted us, and he looked angry. "I need to talk to you, Willow. Alone."

Professor Russell gave us a quizzical look.

"Why don't you go ahead, Professor?" Jackson said. "We'll be right there."

"If you say so." He walked off, but not without giving us a puzzled backward glance.

"I need to talk to her, not you," Martin told Jackson.

"I'm staying," Jackson said. "Get on with it."

"I want you to stop bothering my wife. She was very upset when she got home yesterday. She said you and your friend Simon bullied her into talking to you—demanding answers to questions about who her doctor was, and the pending lawsuit, and even her relationship with her friends. What makes you think that this is any of your business?"

"Because we're trying to figure out who murdered Dr. White," Jackson said.

"That's what the cops are for," Martin said, pointing his finger at me. "You need to back off."

"It happened on my property, Martin," I said. "And it's causing me a lot of trouble. I can't afford to wait until the police catch the killer."

"Oh, right. I forgot. You're the amateur detective who can't resist a new case. Are you having fun investigating?"

I tried to hold my temper. "This isn't a game for me."

"Or for Sandra," Martin said. "You can do as you like, but leave my wife alone. Understand?"

"Why don't you just hold off on the threats," Jackson said. "We're going to do what we need to in order to solve this, but we'll try not to involve your wife, if we can."

"You'll do more than try. I'm warning you."

I was getting really tired of this. "Martin," I said. "Your wife had a motive for wanting Dr. White dead. She's a legitimate suspect. The cops may want to talk to her as well. You won't be able to stop it."

"The cops?" Martin looked so upset by that idea that I actually felt sorry for him. "This is crazy. Sandra is the kindest, gentlest person I know. She did not kill White."

"Then she's got nothing to worry about," I said, even though I knew it wasn't strictly true. Jackson definitely did not kill White, and he had plenty to worry about.

Martin shook his head, then raised his eyes to meet mine. "Okay, no threats. I'm just telling you the truth. If anyone comes after Sandra, I guarantee that they'll be very, very sorry."

"Lovely guy," Jackson said as Martin walked off toward a taxidermist's booth where pink salmon, blue marlin, and yellowfin tuna specimens were on display. They weren't local fish, but I guessed it was true to the theme of the day.

We continued on our way over to Harold and Professor Russell. "Look who's with them," I said, slowing.

"It's Maggie of the almost dog park," Jackson said. "And their discussion looks pretty heated."

They hadn't noticed us yet, so I said, "Let's hang back a bit and see if we can overhear what they're saying."

So we headed over to a table about three feet behind and pretended to browse a truly extensive collection of miniature sailboats, yachts, and pleasure craft. The day was calm, so their voices carried easily.

"I don't understand," Professor Russell said. "I thought you were going to bring the item with you. It's why I came over."

"That wasn't possible," Harold said. "Not here."

"I'd like to see it for myself," Maggie said. "I think you're making it up."

"Shut up, Maggie," Harold said. "It's real, believe me."

"I hope so," Professor Russell said. "We're running out of time."

"He's right. Even you can't keep this up much longer," Maggie said. "You've been lucky so far, but that only lasts so long."

"When you have a goal, you work toward it," Harold said. "That is what I'm doing."

"Work faster, please," Professor Russell told him.

"Fine, I understand. Now, if you'll excuse me, I need to get back to my duties. I'll be in touch, Professor. Enjoy the sale."

I grabbed Jackson's arm and we walked away from the table, back toward the entrance to the park. "It sounds like Harold found something," I said.

Jackson nodded. "Yeah, and it's probably from the garden. Harold is about the same size as the intruder was. He could be the guy."

chapter twenty-three

Willow McQuade's
Favorite Medicinal Plants

LAVENDER
Botanical name: *Lavandula angustifolia*

Medicinal uses: Lovely, purple-hued lavender is appealing to people, bees, and butterflies. It's certainly one of my favorite herbs. Not only does it look beautiful and smell wonderful, it's a very versatile medicinal plant. Lavender's name comes from the Latin *lavare*, which means "to wash." Historically, lavender was used as an antiseptic and for mental health purposes. Today, lavender is popular as a spirit-lifting, nerve-relaxing, calming fragrance. You can use lavender for conditions such as anxiety, tension headaches, irritability, nervousness, restlessness, upset stomach, and insomnia.

Taking eight to ten sniffs of lavender essential oil from the bottle will help to calm your emotions and relieve stress and mild depression. You'll find lav-

**ender in bath salts, soaps, sachets, potpourris, sleep
pillows, creams, lotions, essential oils and other aro-
matic products. Try one, try them all!**

Back at Nature's Way, I looked at the books Professor
Russell had lent me on East End pirate lore. They all
looked well worn and much used, and I had to figure
he'd already pored over them himself looking for clues
to undiscovered pirate treasure, so I didn't expect
much. But for my own peace of mind, I'd have to do my
due diligence and scan them, just to make sure I didn't
miss anything.

I wasn't sure why he'd brought the books over;
probably to continue the "I'm a nice guy" routine. But
now Jackson and I knew that he was up to something
with Harold and Maggie. More than likely he had
pointed Harold in the right direction for digging, and
Harold did the work and they shared the prize. He
must have been flabbergasted when he saw the sword,
and goblet that we'd already found. More than that, he
wanted them for himself.

I left the books in my office then checked in on Wallace and Lily, his niece. Lily was intelligent, motivated,
and a hard worker, much like her uncle, and planned
to go to culinary college when she graduated from high
school. To thank them for all their help, I invited them
to come with us and Allie, as our guests, to the Maritime Festival's annual old-fashioned fish fry that night.
Wallace declined, explaining that he was busy helping
out with the sets for *The Tempest*. Lily, however, said
she'd meet us there.

A little before seven, I tucked a flashlight into my purse—I'd been meaning to do that ever since I got locked in the camera obscura—and Jackson, Allie, and I headed over to meet Lily at the fish fry. We all dressed casually, me in a pink Life Is Good T-shirt and jeans, Jackson in a white tee and jeans, and Allie in an azure-blue sundress, her red hair in a ponytail. When we arrived Lily was already there, having gone home first to take a shower and change into a pink shirt, navy shorts, and sandals.

We presented our tickets and got in line. The smell of frying flounder and french fries filled the air, along with roasting veggies and macaroni and cheese. Other side dishes included coleslaw, German potato salad, pasta salad, barbecued baked beans, and corn bread. Dessert consisted of blueberry, apple, and peach pies. Okay, it wasn't organic, but it sure looked and smelled great. We grabbed trays and set to work filling our plates with goodies. Luckily, we found a table with a view of Main Street and sat down to enjoy the meal.

I had taken exactly two bites when I got a text from Simon:

Going to men's club at 8:00. Meet you after. S.

"This is fantastic," Jackson said as he surveyed his plate. It was chock-full of just about everything offered.

"It really is," Allie said, and smiled. "This is why we live on East End, right?"

"Sure is," Lily said, squeezing lemon on her flounder. "It's so easy to get amazing food here." Next to us, Ramona and Rhonda sat down at a table. Lily noticed them and rolled her eyes.

"Something wrong?" I said.

"It's just my old bosses, Ramona Meadows and Rhonda Rhodes. I worked for them last summer at their farm. I don't like to talk badly about anyone, but they really are the worst. I lasted six weeks and then I quit."

"Why, what did they do?"

"What didn't they do? They made us work from six to six and paid us pennies, only gave us twenty minutes for lunch, and if you called in sick, you got fired."

"Isn't that illegal?" Allie said.

"They didn't care. We had to produce, or else, and we did. But it seemed like they never had any money. Rhonda, especially, was always complaining about their finances. She and Ramona fought about it all the time. I'm so glad I'm not working there this summer."

"We are, too," I said, and smiled "Then you wouldn't have been able to help us."

"Glad to do it," Lily said, getting up. "I need more of that corn bread."

"I'll go with you," Allie said.

Once they left the table, I turned to Jackson. "What did you think of what Lily said—about Rhonda and Ramona's money problems?"

"I think that it's pretty likely that if they found out about the pirate treasure in your lot, they'd be extremely interested."

"Rhonda was at Village Hall and the clerk said that she checked the records on the lot. Could she be the person in black?"

"Why not? She's about the same height as Harold, so it could have been her."

"Maybe I should try talking to Kylie again. She was more willing to talk to me after the art show."

"But if she knows that you were talking to Sandra and it upset her, she won't be sharing anything."

"I'm still going to try."

"I know you will," Jackson said. "Just don't go alone."

Since so many people were waiting to eat at the fish fry we had dessert and gave up our table. Lily went off with her friends, Allie called it a night, and Jackson and I decided to take a walk along the waterfront.

I still hadn't heard from Simon and was anxious to hear what he'd learned, and hoped to meet up with him soon. In the meantime, we headed down Main Street toward the traffic circle by Claudio's restaurant.

But our stroll was interrupted when Jackson got a text from Detective Koren. "This probably isn't good news," Jackson said, staring at his phone.

"What does he say?"

"Just that he needs to talk to me and to call him tomorrow morning."

"Do you think he wants to question you—or arrest you?"

"If he was bringing me in, he would be here, instead of texting me. Either he's learned something new or he has something specific he wants to ask me about." He shoved the phone into his pocket. "I'll deal with him tomorrow."

We crossed Claudio's parking lot and walked past the tackle shop and into Mitchell Park. There we followed the path that ran along the dock's edge at the south end of the park.

We passed the stage where actors, in period dress, were rehearsing *The Tempest*. The sets were terrific and, appropriately enough for the Maritime Festival, seaworthy, with an ocean backdrop, a beached sailboat, and the bow of a ship. I didn't see Wallace but figured he was backstage somewhere.

We'd just sat down on the bench in front of the carousel when I got a text from Simon:

Just got out of meeting. Where R U?

I texted back:

In Mitchell Park. Where do U want to meet?

End of Scrimshaw restaurant dock. Now. S.

"It's Simon," I told Jackson. "He wants to meet us." I texted back that we'd meet him there, and we headed for the Scrimshaw.

Simon was waiting for us at the end of the dock. Beyond the dock's end, the water was inky black, except for the lights from the Shelter Island ferries as they crisscrossed the bay, and the crescent moon above us.

"Hey, guys." Simon had dressed up for the meeting and was wearing a blazer over a blue T-shirt, khakis, and sneakers.

"You look nice," I said.

"Believe me, I was underdressed," Simon said. "The rest of those guys had on these purple robes with hoods, and wore these elaborate necklaces. I felt like I was in a Harry Potter movie."

"So what happened there?" I asked.

"Well, it was . . . weird. The place was all decked

out to look like a like a woodsy cabin, with knotty-pine walls and floors and this massive fireplace. There were these portraits of past and present leaders on the walls, as well as framed studio photos of the present members— incredibly cheesy—and there was this strange diamond-like diagram painted on the floor.

"Once everyone introduced themselves, they had this induction ceremony for me. Apparently, I'm a new member. Mayor Hobson read from this book, and I had to take this pledge."

"What did you pledge?" Jackson asked, sounding amused.

"Oh, loyalty, fraternity, secrecy, insanity, avarice. You know, all the usual stuff."

My eyes widened. "Insanity and avarice?"

"I'm teasing," Simon said with a grin. "Anyway, after the pledge, the treasurer and the secretary gave their reports, and they took care of club business, like voting on getting premium cable service. Next, Joe Larson did a presentation on how to make money investing in real estate. It was mind-numbingly boring."

"Sounds like they're Freemasons and that the club is a lodge," Jackson said. "It's like a fraternity of businessmen."

"I guess. They said they wanted to schedule a time for me to get my photo done for their wall, but I said I was too busy right now."

"Their loss," I said, and smiled. "So, who are the other members?"

"I didn't meet everyone, but Dr. White's partners in his medical office were there, and that trustee that helped you keep the garden open, Tom Coster. Oh, and Harold Spitz was there, but of course, he didn't talk to me."

"Did anything else happen?" I asked.

"Not really. After the presentation, they served refreshments and everyone hung out for a bit. The mayor and Tom Coster introduced me to White's partners so I could try and find out something to solve the case. Like I told you before, I think they're both trying to help you."

"I think we may need a lot more help," I said glumly. "I've been feeling seriously outnumbered. So, Simon, did you learn anything?"

"More like confirmation of what we already knew. White's partners told me that White was absolutely obsessed with getting your lot. They said he talked about it constantly. He was determined to build a high-end boutique hotel there and, despite the rocky state of their marriage, Arlene was counting on running it. He hated medicine, and the hotel was going to be his way out. Both he and Arlene were sure it was going to be a gold mine for them."

"Maybe because they knew what was buried on the property," Jackson said. "Anything else?"

"I did see that painting that Joe Larson bought at the art show," Simon said. "The one of the building where their meetings are held, but back when there was a cigar store on the ground floor. I still think it's not much of a painting, but they had it hanging right above the fireplace mantel in a place of honor. I asked Mayor Hobson why it was so special, and he didn't know. So when no one was looking, I got up close and examined it. And I found something interesting . . . If you look really closely, you can see numbers on the curb in front of the store."

"Sure, street numbers," Jackson said.

"Can't be," I said. "We don't have those here."

"Exactly," Simon agreed. "Besides, they were Roman numerals, XLIX, with XL being forty and IX being nine, so we get forty-nine."

"You actually remembered all that from school?" Jackson asked.

Simon winced. "I had to look it up on my phone."

"Who cares?" I said impatiently. "The real question is, what does it mean?"

"I don't know," Simon said. "But you have to admit, it's strange."

Jackson started guessing. "Maybe it's a date—a year. Or someone's age? Or the number of a player on a sports team? Or part of a license plate or a lottery number?" He shrugged. "Hell, it could refer to just about anything."

"It is strange," I admitted. "But like everything else in this case. I think we've just come to the end of yet another blind alley."

chapter twenty-four

Willow McQuade's
Favorite Medicinal Plants

LEMON BALM
Botanical name: *Melissa officinalis*

Medicinal uses: An official herb of many an apothecary, lemon balm was widely used in ancient Greece and Rome. Avicenna, the great Arabic physician (980—1037), said that lemon balm caused "the mind and heart to be merry." You'll find bees buzzing around this important member of the mint family. Out of the garden, this handy herb calms the heart, eases anxiety, boosts energy, improves concentration, cleanses the liver, improves chi circulation and sleep, and lifts the spirits.

German studies indicate that lemon balm's essential oils help protect the brain from excess external stimuli. Research also shows that lemon balm's citral and citronellal volatile oils help to calm nervous exhaustion and stomach distress. Inhale this essential

oil several times daily to ease mild depression. A delicious tea, it can also be used as a culinary herb. I like adding it to salads, soups, and smoothies for a tangy lemon flavor.

None of us knew what to make of the Roman numerals in the painting, but we hoped it would make more sense later. I thanked Simon for his help, and he went home to write, while Jackson and I strolled back to the store. There was a pleasant salty breeze that helped offset the humidity in the air. The streets were buzzing with people, who had been at the fish fry and were now window shopping or going on to a bar or restaurant to have a drink. The village seemed alive, and full of promise. Despite the light rain that had begun to fall, the Maritime Festival was kicking off the tourist season in a big way.

But when we arrived at Nature's Way, any hopeful or idyllic notions I'd had were crushed. There, in the front yard, were Qigong, Rockford, and Columbo, wandering around, alone in the dark. I never left them outside without supervision, day or night, and everyone knew this. Something was clearly very wrong.

"What are you guys doing out here?" I said, opening the gate and stepping inside the yard. They rushed to me and wagged their tails. From what I could tell, they hadn't been hurt, which was a relief. I hoped that the cats, Ginger and Ginkgo, were also okay.

Jackson looked at the front door, which was wide open. "Either someone left your bedroom door and the front door open, or you've had a break-in. I'm going to call Tony, in the garden."

He pulled out his phone, dialed, and put it on speakerphone. "Tony, it's Jackson. We just got home and the front door is wide open. Have we had a break-in?"

"Yeah, you did." Tony spoke in a low voice. "I was patrolling in the garden and about five minutes ago I heard noises coming from the house. I'm inside now. Come in, but be careful. I don't think anyone else is in here, but I haven't searched the whole place yet."

"Did you call the cops?"

"Not yet. My first instinct was to just get in here and catch the creep, and if I do—" Tony, the night guard, was in his early sixties and another ex-cop. I knew he worked out, and I knew he carried a gun.

Jackson turned to me. "You'd better stay out here with the dogs while we check things out. And, I hate to say it, but you'd better call 911."

"I'm worried about the cats." Suddenly, I felt cold, and shivered in the damp night air. "They were looking for the treasure, weren't they? They obviously didn't know that we gave the sword to Dr. Gillian, and put the goblet and earring in the bank."

Jackson shrugged. "Could be. Just call the police and wait here. I'll look for the cats." He set off for the house at a run.

I pulled out my phone and sighed. The last thing I wanted right now was another visit with Detectives Koren and Coyle. But before I could call 911, my phone rang. It was Jackson.

"Listen," he began. "The cats are fine and who-ever was in here is gone. I can't tell if anything is missing—they trashed the place pretty badly. They were definitely searching for something. Explain all that when you call 911. Tony and I are going to take a quick look around the outside of the store. We'll meet you inside."

"Okay," I said, and made the call. My hands were trembling.

"What's your emergency?" the operator asked.

"It's not an emergency, it's a break-in," I replied, and gave her all the details.

"Well, it's going to be awhile before we can send anyone over," she told me. "There was a big fight near the brewery tonight—locals and out-of-towners. Everyone in the station was called out."

I thanked her and hung up. Then, with the dogs following me, I started toward the store, bracing myself for whatever was inside.

But before we reached the door, Rockford ran over to the fence that ran parallel to the driveway and the garden and started to bark frantically.

"What is it, boy?" I followed him over to the fence. The other two dogs shot ahead of me, and within sec-onds all three of them were barking.

I pulled the flashlight from my purse and shone it on the fence and around the garden. There! Someone raced through the garden toward the front gate, opened it, and let it clang shut. I ran over to the fence at the front of the yard and yelled. "Hey, I see you! Stay out of my garden!" The person—who was dressed all in black with a black rucksack—dashed up Front Street and into the night.

I heard the sound of running, and then Jackson and Tony were at my side moments later. "What happened?" Jackson asked.

"Someone was just in the garden. The dogs started barking and he ran out. He was dressed in black and wearing a black backpack. I think it was the same guy."

"You stay here," Jackson said. "I'm going to take a look." He grabbed his flashlight and headed over to the garden.

I watched him and the beam of his flashlight travel from the entrance to the back wall of the garden.

"Nothing," he reported as he came back to us. "Not even a footprint."

"Do you think the person who broke in and the guy I saw are the same person?"

"That would be my guess," Tony answered. "Unless you have two or more people working together. Maybe one guy took the garden and someone else took the store and house."

"Let's get these dogs inside." Jackson picked up Columbo. "I'll take this guy upstairs if you can help Rockford."

I picked up Rockford, and he licked my face. "What I want to know is how they got downstairs. Qigong could do it, but two dachshunds? They'd be too scared to go down three flights of stairs."

"Uh, that was me," Tony confessed. "When I saw the door to the store was open, I raced inside. The dogs were barking like crazy, and I knew I had to search the place, so I took them out—just in case there was still someone up there. I didn't want them to get hurt."

"A man after my own heart," I said. "He thinks of the dogs first. Thank you, Tony."

Once we were inside Nature's Way, we put the dogs down and they scampered around, checking out the smells in the store. I went over to the checkout counter. Someone had pulled everything off the shelves beneath the register. "This is a mess." It felt invasive that someone had done this, without any concern for how it would make me feel.

Tony gave me a sympathetic look. "So is your office, I'm afraid."

The office had indeed been ransacked. The desk drawers were open and askew, papers were scattered on the desktop and all over the floor. Books had been pulled from the shelves and the cushions had been removed from the couch and ripped open; stuffing was everywhere.

My space had been invaded, and it would take hours to make it right. It felt like the proverbial straw that broke the camel's back, but I wouldn't, couldn't let it. Still, my hands began to tremble again.

Jackson stuck his head in the door. "You don't even want to see the third floor. As far as I can tell, nothing's missing. Unfortunately, the bedroom's a disaster." Seeing that I was upset, he pulled me into a hug. "But, listen, Willow, it's going to be okay. We'll fix it."

"I'm just glad that the animals are safe," I murmured into his shoulder. I lifted my head up and looked at him. "Are you sure that Ginkgo and Ginger are really all right?"

"They're fine. They were sleeping on the beds in Allie and Hector's old place. But their offices and your bedroom are a wreck. Whoever broke in really wanted to find that stuff."

"I hate this," I said. "I hate having the store—and my home—violated this way. I have to start cleaning up or at least putting things back in their places."

Jackson put a hand on my arm. "You can't. It's all one big crime scene. You have to leave it for the police."

I called 911 and spoke to the operator again, who told me that the police were still sorting out the disturbance by the brewery. It would be hours before anyone could respond to a nonemergency call.

"I don't think they're coming tonight," I said after I hung up. "What if we just clean up the bedroom? I don't think I can sleep in it the way it is."

"How about you let us take photos first?" Tony asked. "That way we can at least document what we found."

"That's a good idea," I admitted, calming down a little.

Jackson and Tony took photos of the mess that was the bedroom. The thief had opened all the drawers, pulled everything out of the closet, taken the cushions out of the chair. He even tore the sheets and blankets off of the bed. We did a bit of straightening in Allie and Hector's offices, but I wasn't looking forward to telling them what happened. I'd have to clean up my office in the morning, which also wouldn't be an easy task.

The only bright spot was that when I was putting things back into the bedroom closet, I discovered several old journals that had been Aunt Claire's. So, after we finished cleaning up, I made myself a cup of chamomile tea, got into bed, and began to read them. One of the journals chronicled the early years of Nature's Way. Others were filled with photographs and doodles of her favorite herbs and flowers, the germs of new book ideas, her goals, her feelings, her dreams, and even a travel journal, which I hoped contained notes about her trip to London's physic garden.

I'd had no idea that she had been so dedicated to writing about her life. But now that she was gone, these books felt like a gift, a second chance to learn more about her. This, to me, was real treasure, and I knew absolutely that she would want me to read them all, especially now, when I needed answers.

My dearest wish was that I'd find some clue to her intentions for the future of the business. Would she have lobbied for the lot as I had, or would she have stepped aside when the process became so contentious, especially with Dr. White? And what would she think about everything that had happened since then? Claire was no pushover, but she'd had gift for—how did she put it?—calming troubled waters. It was hard to imagine that she would have let things get so antagonistic. And dangerous.

My tendency was to dig in my heels and fight, and I wondered now if this had been the wrong approach. However, perhaps it was this aspect of my personality that enabled me to find answers when it came to murder.

Still, if I could find something to indicate that she would have approved of the direction I'd taken, I'd feel a whole lot better about everything.

• • •

I fell asleep before I could read all of her journals, and woke up the next morning at seven thirty-five, with Jackson's arms around me and the books on the floor. The rain, which had started out as a drizzle, was now a downpour, and I immediately worried about the tender, new plants in the medicinal garden.

On another front, it was Friday, and every merchant in Greenport knew that this rain would be the deciding factor as to whether the Maritime Festival this weekend was a washout or a success. Of course, I had other more sinister factors determining my fate.

So while Jackson and I ate a breakfast of oatmeal and blueberries at the window table in the café, I took out my phone.

"What are you doing?"

"Checking the weather for this weekend. I'm worried about the garden."

"Isn't rain good for plants? Or am I missing something?"

"Some rain is good, but a torrential downpour could wash out plants that aren't firmly established. That means more work and more money to replace them." I brought up the weather site and put in our zip code and got the forecast for the weekend.

"What does it say?"

"It says there'll be rain all day and tonight with clearing tomorrow, supposedly by noon. Sunday looks like a beauty, though, with sunny skies and temperatures in the midseventies, perfect weather for the last day of the festival."

I put the phone on the table. "At least it won't last for days, but I'm still worried." As I said this, the rain began to come down in sheets, completely obfuscating the view. "Is Bob here now?"

"He was supposed to come in, but he may not. He'll let me know. It's unlikely anyone is out there in this weather anyway. What are your plans for today?"

"I want to talk to Kylie about Harold, Maggie, Ramona, and Rhonda, and find out what they're really up to."

"What makes you think she'll talk to you?"

"Because I think she trusts me since we talked the day of the art show. She saw that I did what was right in awarding her first place, regardless of whether she was helpful to me in the case or not. I think she wanted to tell me about Sandra and her problems with Dr. White, but because Sandra was a friend, she held back."

Jackson gave me a skeptical look. "So what's different now?"

"I just don't think she's as close to Harold and the rest. She may open up to me this time. Anyway, I have to try. I also think we should tell Detective Koren about Dr. Gillian and the sword, the break-in, and our suspicions about Harold and the rest. It may get him on our side and off of your back."

"If he believes us. He didn't before." A thumping sound came from outside, and Jackson glanced out the window. "I think Bob's here. I told him about the break-in. I hope there aren't any more problems. It's not even 8 a.m."

The door opened and Bob stepped inside. He took off his raincoat and came over to us and sat down.

"Would you like some breakfast, Bob?"

"No, I'm good. I just wanted to check in about the weather. I've been out there for an hour and if it stays this way, I just don't think I'm needed today. Do you want me to stay?"

Jackson shook his head. "Go home. It's too wet for intruders or to get any work done in the garden. We need to clean up in here anyway."

"They made a mess of things, huh?" He gestured to the counter, which still needed to be reorganized.

"There's that, and the office, plus my practitioners' offices on the third floor," I said.

"Can I help?"

"I think we're okay," Jackson said. "But we'll really need you over the weekend. I'd like to finish up the patio for the teahouse, and Willow would like to lead tours if she can."

I looked at him. "Should we really be giving tours with all of this going on?"

"During the day you'll be fine with Bob around. What do you think, Bob?"

"No problem. Tony will watch the garden from 7 p.m. until I come back on shift in the morning." He got up and prepared to leave, but then he turned back to us. "You should know that as good a guy as Tony is, he's also a gossip and there's a very good chance that he's talked all about your break-in to cop friends of ours. You may want to get ahead of this with Detectives Koren and Coyle."

chapter twenty-five

Willow McQuade's
Favorite Medicinal Plants

LICORICE
Botanical name: *Glycyrrhiza glabra* (European licorice), *G. lepidota* (American licorice), *G. inflata*, *G. uralensis* (Chinese licorice)

Medicinal uses: Known as the "great harmonizer," licorice is one of the most commonly used herbs in traditional Chinese medicine, and is often added to herbal formulas I sell at Nature's Way. Licorice contains glycyrrhizic, which cools the inflammation of a sore throat, strengthens the vocal cords, and eases stomach irritation.

I've found that licorice tea and tinctures also do a great job of supporting the work of the adrenal glands to produce and eliminate hormones from the kidney and liver. In addition, licorice helps induce feelings of calmness, peace, and harmony. Some of my customers tell me that it enables them to deal with

stress more easily and rebound faster from stress-related fatigue. Peeled licorice root is available in dried and powdered forms. Licorice root is also available as capsules, tablets, and liquid extracts.

But before we could call the police for the third time—no one had ever shown up the night before—Detectives Koren and Coyle walked in, dripping puddles of rainwater all over the floor. Bob said hello and excused himself, while the two men hung up their overcoats and came over to the table.

"We were just going to call you," I said as the sky darkened and rain poured onto the porch.

"Is that so?" Detective Koren gave me a neutral look, giving away nothing.

"Yes, can I get you two some coffee?" Maybe if I was gracious they'd be nicer.

Koren looked at his partner. "Sure, why not? Two cream, no sugar."

I went into the kitchen and poured two cups of freshly brewed coffee, added cream, put a few banana muffins on the tray, and returned to find Koren and Coyle still standing. "Would you like to sit down?"

"We have something to tell you," Jackson said.

Koren sat down and threw his police notebook onto the table. "Save it, Spade. We already know about the break-in." He looked at the ransacked counter. "Was anything stolen?"

"Not that we can tell," I said. "But the only room we've cleaned up is the bedroom."

Koren gave me an annoyed look. "Didn't anyone

ever tell you that you're not supposed to touch a crime scene?"

"There's plenty of crime scene for you to examine," Jackson said. "That counter, for instance, and Willow's office. And before we cleaned up the bedroom, we took photos, documenting everything."

"We'll have a look at the office," Koren said. "And we'll take those photos."

"I'll get you the memory cards," Jackson said, and left the room.

"We tried to get in touch with you," I explained. "I called 911 twice last night. The operator told me she didn't have anyone to send out on a nonemergency call. You were all at a fight—or something."

The two detectives exchanged glances. Then Coyle took a bite of his muffin. "What is this? It doesn't taste like a real muffin, but it's still pretty good."

"It's gluten-free, Detective," I said. "I thought you might enjoy it."

"Whatever." He took another bite.

"A fight broke out by the brewery last night," Koren told me. "It started with some high school kids getting rowdy and then it escalated. Things got out of hand fast—and yeah, we were all on the scene until late, and then we were all down at the station house taking statements from the property owners, witnesses, and the guys we arrested." Greenport was a small town with a small police department. It didn't take much to tie up the entire staff. "It was a long night," Koren finished. "So why don't you just tell us what happened here?"

Jackson returned, handed Koren the memory cards

from the cameras, then walked them through the timeline of the break-in, from when we arrived to the intruder in the garden and the mess left behind.

"What do you think they were looking for?" Detective Coyle said, taking out his notebook and preparing to write.

"Pirate treasure," I said.

Detective Coyle put his pen down. "You've got to be kidding"

"We tried to tell you that we found things in the garden, and you didn't want to hear it," I reminded him. "You didn't believe us."

"So about our trip to East Hampton on Tuesday," Jackson said. "We weren't exactly forthcoming."

"Really," Koren said. "You, withholding? What a concept."

I ignored that and said, "We went to a lecture Monday night at the Maritime Museum given by Professor Russell, who is an expert on pirates who frequented the East End."

Coyle groaned. "C'mon. What does this have to do with Dr. White's murder?"

"We don't know yet," Jackson said. "But the next day, Dr. Russell called Willow and told her he had an expert who could appraise the artifacts, someone who knew even more than he did."

"So that's why we went over to East Hampton," I said. "We went to see Dr. Travis Gillian, from the East Hampton Historical Society. When we showed him what we'd found—"

"Which was what?" Koren said, interrupting.

"We found an earring, a goblet, and a sword," Jackson said.

"A sword?" Koren echoed.

"Yes, and Dr. Gillian thought it might be pirate treasure, Captain Kidd's in fact—a sword that was stolen from an exhibition at the East Hampton Historical Society in 1999. He's evaluating it now." The rain made a *rat-a-tat* sound on the windows, and the wind pushed against the branches of the rose of Sharon bushes in front of the porch.

"What's this expert's name again?" Coyle asked. I told him and he wrote it down. "We'll need to talk to him."

"Go ahead," Jackson said. "As of yesterday, Professor Russell said there's no word on whether the sword is authentic or not."

"What about the goblet and the bracelet?" Coyle asked.

"It was a single earring, and both Russell and Gillian think it's Victorian, not pirate treasure. And they didn't seem all that excited about the goblet either," I said, for the first time wondering why not. "The earring and the goblet are in a bank safe-deposit box."

Koren ran his hand through his hair, looking exasperated. "So what does this have to do with the murder of Dr. White, and why shouldn't you, Spade, be our prime suspect?"

"Because we think that Dr. White was murdered because of what was buried in the garden," I said. "We also think that Professor Albert Russell, Harold Spitz, Maggie Stone, Ramona Meadows, and Rhonda Rhodes may be involved, and maybe Joe Larson, too."

"So you're saying that this Professor Russell, who was helping you, as well as four local business owners and a Village Board member, may have been involved in Dr. White's murder?" Detective Koren was looking at me as if I'd just told him that it was sunny out.

I shrugged. "Except for Joe, we've heard that they may all be working together to find the treasure, but he may also be after it."

"So basically, they've all lost their minds," Coyle said.

Koren's eyes narrowed as he regarded Jackson. "If you ask me, Spade, that's a stretch. For all we know, you still have the sword yourself."

"I don't, and it's not a stretch. At least, it's no more of a stretch than you thinking I killed White because he wasn't nice to Willow at the Land and Sea Ball," Jackson said.

"You don't get to decide that, Spade," Detective Koren said, getting up. "We do."

We followed the two detectives upstairs and then back downstairs and into my office to examine the mess the perpetrator had left behind. Koren immediately called for a tech to try to lift prints, and then told us to stay out until their guys were done with it.

"That didn't go particularly well," I said to Jackson when Koren and Coyle finally left. "Are you okay?"

"I'm fine," Jackson said. "I have faith that you and I can solve this before they do. We'll just have to focus."

"Let's get more coffee and go back to the bedroom," I suggested. "We can brainstorm up there."

We had finished pouring more coffee when I got a text. "It's from Merrily. She isn't coming in today either."

"She's probably still taking care of Nate."

"I can understand that, but we need her here, too," I said.

The front door opened and Wallace came in. He stared wide-eyed at the counter. "What happened here?"

"We had a break-in last night," I said. "Nothing seems to be missing, but everything is a mess."

"But why? Is this about Dr. White's murder?"

"We think so," Jackson said.

"How can I help?"

"I just heard from Merrily and she isn't coming in. Can Lily fill in this afternoon?"

"I'll call her right now. But I thought you needed to see this, too." He pulled the latest issue of the *Suffolk Times* from under his arm and handed it to me. "Go to letters to the editor. I'm really sorry, Willow."

He went to hang up his raincoat and I flipped to the editorial section. I skimmed the page, my eyes coming to rest on a headline that read "Shut Down the Garden of Death!" and the letter below it, and quickly skimmed it. As I did, I reminded myself to breathe.

"Who wrote it?" Jackson asked. "Wait let me guess—was it Greenport Merchants United?"

I nodded.

"What does it say?"

"Basically, it repeats the information on that petition they tried to circulate—that Dr. White's death proves that the village made a mistake in granting the lot to me, how the publicity from the incident will hurt business in the village now and in the future and threaten the livelihoods of every Greenport merchant, etcetera."

"They want concerned citizens to write to the mayor if they agree, and the letters will be presented at the next board meeting in July." I put the newspaper down and shook my head. "They're not going to give up."

"Neither are we," Jackson said. "It's all the more reason to solve this thing and clear my name and yours. You said you wanted to brainstorm, so what's next?"

"First, I'm going to call Kylie Ramsey. Maybe she can tell us what Harold and his gang are up to." I looked up her number on the farmer's market Web site and called her, but she didn't answer, so I left a message asking her to call me.

"And your next move?"

"I don't know yet."

We went upstairs, played with the dogs and cats, and brainstormed ideas back and forth, but each one was more impractical than the next. After an hour, we took a break and went back downstairs to watch the police techs dust my office for prints.

The techs didn't seem too optimistic. But when they left, they told us we were free to clean up in there, which was the first good news I'd had that day.

An hour and a half later, when we were almost finished, Simon walked in and flopped onto the couch that Jackson had just put back together. At least he'd taken off his raincoat.

"You look awful," I said.

"Thank you, I feel awful."

Jackson shoved the last cushion into place behind Simon's back. "What's the matter? Writer's block again?"

"Exactly. I went home last night, thinking I could get something done on the screenplay, but I'm dry. I didn't sleep much either."

"That's not good, but we've got bigger problems," I said, tossing him the paper. "Go to letters to the editor."

He found the letter and said, "This is total BS."

"It gets worse. Someone broke in here last night. We think they were looking for the artifacts. Detectives Koren and Coyle were here this morning. We told them about the artifacts in the garden, the trip to East Hampton, and our suspicions about Harold and company—all to try to change their mind about Jackson."

"Did it work?"

"I doubt it," Jackson said. "Koren's going to call Dr. Gillian and circle back to me, I'm sure. You know what's interesting?" he mused. "The fact that neither Russell nor Gillian were interested in the goblet or the earring."

"They said the earring was Victorian," I reminded him.

"Exactly. It was made long after the pirates' era, yet someone buried that in the garden, too. It was in a box wrapped in cloth; clearly, it didn't end up in the garden by accident."

"Exactly," Simon said, "So who buried it?"

"I don't know," Jackson said. "But whoever buried the earring—and the goblet, which also postdates Kidd by at least a hundred years—wasn't a pirate. I'm not sure what that means exactly, but I do think we need to contact Dr. Travis Gillian, too, to try and get ahead of this thing." Jackson began to put the last few books back on the bookshelf across from my desk.

"Okay," I agreed, "but I'll need that receipt with his number on it, and I think it's with the goblet and the earring in the safe-deposit box."

"Google him," Simon said.

I got on my computer and looked up Travis Gillian, PhD. "I found the Web site for the historical society. Now I just need his e-mail or phone number." I went to the page where staff was listed and scrolled down to his name, which took me to a separate page. "Okay, here's his bio and his photo." I sucked in a breath. "Guys, we've got a problem. Look at this."

Jackson and Simon came over and looked at the monitor. "This is supposed to be a photo of Dr. Gillian," I said, pointing to a black-and-white photo of a genial-looking, white-haired man in his seventies, wearing a cardigan and a bow tie.

"That's not the man we met at the Pollock museum," Jackson said.

"And gave what could be Captain Kidd's sword."

"This is not good," Simon said, stating the obvious.

"The question is, did Professor Russell know, and are the two of them in this thing together?"

"I'll call him," I said, grabbing my phone. But I got his answering machine, too, and left a message. "Professor Russell, I need to talk to you about Dr. Gillian as soon as possible. Please call me." I'd just put the phone down when Detectives Koren and Coyle along with two uniformed police officers entered my office.

"That was fast," Jackson said. "What's going on?"

"I need you to come into the station to answer some questions, Mr. Spade."

I pointed to the computer screen. "We know about Dr. Gillian being a fake, but we didn't know before. You need to talk to Professor Russell. He'll confirm our story." But I wondered if this was true, given his friendship with Harold and Maggie. "There's no reason to take Jackson in."

"No reason? We talked to Professor Russell and he told us that Mr. Spade lied about the trip to East Hampton, and the meeting with Dr. Gillian. He also told us that the stolen sword, a priceless artifact, has gone missing. For all we know, you have it."

"That trip was real, and I can produce the flight log to prove it," Simon said.

"Can you prove that you actually met with Dr. Gillian?"

"Yes, I have a receipt for the sword," I said, beginning to panic. "I—I just have to find it."

"Even I know that's lame," Detective Coyle said. "You're stalling."

"He's right," Detective Koren said. "We can't believe anything either of you say, especially that business about Harold Spitz and Joe Larson. That's classic misdirection. Maybe you wanted Dr. White dead for personal reasons, Spade, or maybe you fought over that sword and he died. But you're going to answer for it." He nodded to the police officers. "Take him in."

chapter twenty-six

Willow McQuade's
Favorite Medicinal Plants

NETTLE
Botanical name: *Urtica dioica, U. urens*

Medicinal Uses: Nettle is one of the most versatile
herbs you can know, grow, and use. The ancient
Greeks and Romans planted and cultivated more
acres of nettle than any other crop for use as food and
medicine, and even clothing. Nettle is chock-full of vitamins and minerals, including iron and calcium, and
makes a nourishing tea and tonic to help strengthen
your body and ease creaky joints. And there's more.
Nettle works as an antihistamine to remedy allergies
and hay fever, nourishes and tones the veins, reduces
inflammation, and helps prevent blood clots. Nettle
also helps curb the appetite, cleanses toxins from the
body, and boosts energy. You will often find nettle in
PMS formulas and other remedies for menstrual, fer-
tility, and menopausal issues.

Note: If growing nettle yourself, be sure and wear gloves to protect your hands from the needlelike protrusions. An old folk remedy suggests rolling down a hill of stinging nettle to ease the pain of arthritis, but I wouldn't recommend doing this!

They snapped cuffs on Jackson and I felt my heart constrict. How could this be happening? I wanted to cry but didn't want to make it more difficult for Jackson, so I tried to hold it together. But then my hands began to shake, so I shoved them into my pockets.

Simon promised him that he would put his lawyer on his case. "In the meantime," he said, "don't talk to the police."

Jackson shot him a look. "I was a cop, Simon. Don't you think I know that?"

"Let's go Spade," Detective Koren said. "Say goodbye to your girlfriend."

Jackson turned to me and mouthed *I love you*.

I nodded and mouthed *I love you, too*. I took a step toward him, but Detective Koren waved me off.

Detective Coyle snickered and marched Jackson out the front door, followed by his partner and the other cops. When they closed the door, it felt like life as I knew it had ended.

Simon called his lawyer and I went back into my office. I sat at my desk and allowed myself to completely fall apart. Five minutes later, Simon came in and hugged me. I wiped my tears and quickly pulled myself back together again. "What did your lawyer say?"

"I told him that I wanted him in Greenport by this afternoon, and that I'll pay for his representation of Jackson. He's not available, but he's sending a new partner at the firm named Shawn Thompson, who is Harvard educated and a top-notch attorney. Thompson specializes in criminal matters and has won some really big cases in the city. Actually, he's the hottest lawyer in NYC at the moment."

"Thanks, Simon."

"No problem, but he also said to stay away from the jail right now. Jackson knows not to talk to Detectives Koren and Coyle until his lawyer arrives.

"Once Thompson hits town, he'll call us on the way to the jail and we can meet him there. He'll be with Jackson during any questioning and hopefully get him released. In the meantime, I say we follow up on what I learned about that painting last night, maybe research its history—and the history of the men's club."

I nodded. I wasn't sure how—or if—the men's club was connected to Dr. White's murder, but at this point, I was willing to follow any lead. "Okay, but first we need to go the bank and look at that receipt to see if it provides any clue to Gillian's real identity, and if it does, tell the police."

"I've been thinking about something else. Since I couldn't write last night, I used the time to go over the chain of events, and I realized that an important piece of the puzzle is missing."

"What is it?"

"Why that guy donated the lot in the first place."

"Frank Fox?"

Simon nodded. "Exactly. Did he do it to be a nice guy or did he have another motive? Maybe there was a reason he gave it away rather than profit from it."

"That's a good point. Fox might have had his own agenda."

Simon smiled at me. "I've never met a person who didn't."

Fifteen minutes later, we were in my bank, in one of the little rooms where they let you examine the contents of your safe-deposit box. Once the bank manager left, I opened the box. Everything was still inside, including the receipt from "Dr. Travis Gillian." But I could tell immediately that it wouldn't help us.

"It's just his name and the address of the East Hampton Historical Society, not even a phone number. He signed it as Dr. Gillian, but that doesn't mean much. It's obviously a fake. He could have had this printed anywhere."

"We should still show it to the cops, though."

"I guess, but we need more. I'm going to try Kylie Ramsey again." She didn't answer, so I left another message. "Now, we need to research that painting and the history of the men's club. Maybe we should go and talk to that artist again."

"I'll find him," Simon said, taking out his phone.

"And how are you going to do that?"

"I'm going to put in the description of the painting and see if I get a hit on his name." He punched a few keys. "Here he is. His name is Fred Monsell, and he shows his work at the Seaside Gallery. I can't believe this guy's stuff is in a gallery."

"Me either, but that's right near the men's club. Let's see what Fred has to say."

By the time we left the bank, the rain had lightened to a fine drizzle. We headed south toward Claudio's and the docks, then walked past the cupcake shop, the men's club, and the tea shop until we reached the Seaside Gallery.

We were in luck. Fred was there, clean shaven and wearing clean overalls rather than the paint-spattered ones he had on at the art show. He was explaining his work to a customer. The series of paintings he had on display in the gallery were all surprisingly good, various seascapes in the impressionist school, vibrant with light and swirls and dots of color.

The customer left and he turned his attention to us. "Help you, folks?" He went over to a little desk in the corner and pulled out a cigar. "Let's stand near the door so I can enjoy this bad boy. You want one?"

"No, thanks," I said. "Where are you buying your cigars, now that the cigar store is closed?"

He pointed out the rain-spotted window. "They moved over there when the new owners took over." The cigar store was now next to a Mexican takeout place. "Rent was cheaper. You've got to sell a lot of these babies to make any money."

"We wanted to ask you about the painting that you sold to Joe Larson at the art show," I said. "Was it by chance a part of a series, like your seascapes?"

"No, that one was special for the owner, Jerry."

Fred clipped the end off of the cigar, lit it, and took a few puffs. "I painted it last year."

"Last night I attended a meeting at the men's club, the one that's upstairs from where the cigar shop used to be," Simon said. "They put the painting on display there, above the fireplace."

"That's fitting," Fred said, and took another puff on his cigar.

"How so?" I said.

"It's the same building, right? That's why Joe wanted it, he said, for the club. He and Jerry were both members and they were friends, too. At least someone there got some use out of it."

"I examined the painting last night at the meeting," Simon said, "and I wanted to ask you about something. On the curb outside the building there are some numbers."

"Yeah, those Roman numerals."

"They add up to forty-nine," Simon said. "What does that mean?"

"Can't tell you, folks, 'cause I don't know."

"But you painted them," I said. "How can you not know?"

The phone rang in the back of the room. "Hold on, folks."

While he went over to take it, I said, "This is really strange. You would think he would know about all the elements in one of his own paintings."

"Maybe the owner, Jerry, told him to put the numbers in," Simon said. "Ask him."

Fred finished his conversation and came back over. "Sorry about that. Now you were saying?"

"We were wondering if maybe Jerry, the owner of the building, told you to put those numbers in."

"No, it wasn't him, it was his friend Frank."

"Frank Fox?"

"That's him. He came down when I was working on the commission. This was before he went up to live in the nursing home, but he was already pretty frail, and he told me that Jerry wanted those numbers put in. Since he was a friend, and a member of that club, too, I went ahead and did it. Never did find out why."

"Would Jerry know?" I asked. "Maybe we could ask him?"

"Hard to do that." Frank took another puff on the cigar. "Last year he died of lung cancer, right after he sold the business to someone else, and they moved it across the street. I'd just finished the painting but his wife didn't want it, said cigars killed her husband, and left it with me."

"Where to next?" Simon said as we stepped out onto Main Street. "Should we go to the library to research the men's club?"

"No, we need to talk to Joe Larson," I said. "I think he wanted that painting because of Frank, and we need to find out why."

"He may also know why Fox gave your lot away to the village."

I nodded. "Exactly, and I think Joe Larson works as a real estate agent for Country Living Real Estate. Their new office is on Front Street, right around that corner." I pointed to the intersection of Front and

Main street. "But first, please call that lawyer, Shawn Thompson, and find out where he is. I'm worried about Jackson."

Simon took out his phone and put it on speaker. Shawn Thompson answered after one ring.

"It's Simon Lewis. I'm here with Jackson Spade's girlfriend, Willow McQuade. We were wondering how close you are to Greenport."

"Hold on, please." We could hear him talking to his driver. "We just passed the exit for the Stony Brook Hospital. We should be there in an hour. I've talked to Detective Koren, though, and he knows that Jackson isn't answering any questions until I get there. I'll let you know once I hit town. We'll get him out, don't worry."

"Thanks, Shawn. Talk to you then."

"He sounds good," I said.

"I told you. Now, let's talk to Joe Larson."

A few minutes later we entered the upscale office of Country Living, all whites, grays, and clean lines, with glossy photos of available properties mounted on the walls. Joe, we were told, had gone out to show a listing.

We found out where and headed to a house in Arshamomaque, a hamlet off of Route 25, between Greenport and Southold. Fifteen minutes later, I pulled into the driveway of the property, a pink one-story beach house with a giant starfish on the garage, right across from Mill Creek.

Simon frowned. "It doesn't look like anyone is here."

We got out and walked around the house, but he was right. "Now what?" he asked.

I wasn't sure, but kept driving toward the boat

launch at the end of the street. The launch was used to put small boats, canoes, and rowboats into the creek, an idyllic place surrounded by woods and tributaries that fed into Peconic Bay.

Today the scenic area wasn't as charming, though. The rain had almost stopped but stray raindrops splattered the steel-gray surface of the creek. As we got closer, I spotted Joe Larson leaning on his truck, his phone pressed tightly to his ear.

I parked and we walked over to him. He wore a sky-blue suit and shirt with a navy striped tie. When he saw us, he quickly shoved the phone into his pants pocket and turned to face us. "What do you want, Ms. McQuade? I'm working."

Simon spoke up. "Last night's meeting was very interesting, Joe. I found your talk quite educational."

Joe looked wary but thanked him.

"I really liked the painting that you bought at the art show," I said. "We talked to Fred Monsell, the artist, and he told us about Jerry from the cigar store and selling the painting to you. He seemed to think it had found a good home since you, Jerry, and Frank Fox were all members of the club."

At the mention of Frank's name, something in Joe softened. "Frank was a good guy. He was a credit to our membership." His eyes narrowed as he looked at Simon. "I can't say I have high hopes for you, Lewis. You couldn't even commit to having your photograph taken."

"It's just that I'm in L.A. for most of the year. I won't be able to attend many meetings or really get involved."

"I'm sure you're a very busy man," Joe said with a smirk.

I tried to steer the subject back to the investigation. "Is there something special about that painting?"

Joe shrugged. "Not that I know of. I just thought it belonged in the club." He seemed to be telling the truth. I decided not to discuss the numbers on the curb. We needed to keep that information to ourselves until we knew what it really meant.

But Simon plunged ahead, saying, "Last night, I noticed that there are these Roman numerals on the curb in front of the store. Fred Monsell said that it was Frank Fox's idea to add them. Any idea what that might mean?"

Joe's eyebrows rose in surprise. "I never noticed that," he admitted. "But Frank was one for puzzles. Maybe it was a secret message to Jerry. But he's long gone now. Frank, too."

"Can you tell us a little bit more about Frank Fox? What was he like?" Two white swans traveled in a leisurely fashion downstream toward us. I wished I had some bread crumbs for them.

"Frank was a loyal guy, hardworking." Joe pointed west across the trees. "He owned a potato farm on the North Road, ran it for thirty years. That's all gone now. He was also a good husband and a good friend. You could always count on Frank to do what was right."

"Is that why he donated the lot to the village— because he thought it was the right thing to do?" I asked.

"Frank wanted to give something back to the village he loved. But then it all went wrong when you were given the lot, and Charles was murdered."

"So you think that it was because Willow got the lot that your friend was killed?" Simon said. "That doesn't make a lot of sense. Think about it, Joe."

Joe stared off into the distance and was silent. Several moments later, he surprised us with his answer. "You know, you're right. It probably wouldn't have mattered who had the lot. It might have happened anyway."

"I wish you would tell that to Harold and Maggie and the rest of that group. They really have made my life miserable."

"I know, I saw the letter in the *Suffolk Times*," Joe said. "Listen, Greenport is a small town. We all know each other. But that doesn't mean I condone what they're doing now."

"But you wanted that lot, too," I said. "You were even talking to Mayor Hobson about it the other day at Village Hall."

"I admit that I tried to influence the mayor and the other members of the board to give the lot to Charles. And now I like the idea of a memorial garden dedicated to Charles. So what? I didn't do anything wrong."

"You didn't push me into the camera obscura and lock the door?"

He had the grace to look embarrassed. "I felt like you were stalking me—and Rhonda and everyone else—and I got pretty annoyed about it. I'm sorry. That wasn't a good thing to do. But I did come back later to make sure you got out okay. Which you did."

"How considerate," I murmured.

He pushed off of the truck, shifted from foot to foot, and rubbed his knee.

"I'm surprised that you were still so friendly with Charles White," I said. "After all, he was your surgeon, and clearly you're still suffering."

"He did the best he could. I don't blame him for what happened."

"Why was Dr. White so interested in that lot?" Simon said. "Is it because everyone, including you, is looking for the same thing—buried treasure perhaps?"

Joe laughed. "Buried treasure? I don't think so. Charles wanted the lot so he could build a high-end boutique hotel there, and Arlene would have been the manager. Me, I figured that it was a good investment, a chance for us all to turn a nice profit." His phone rang. "I have to take this. I'm closing a deal." He got into his truck, started it up, and drove away.

chapter twenty-seven

Willow McQuade's
Favorite Medicinal Plants

<u>OATS</u>

Botanical name: *Avena fatua* (wild oat), *A. sativa* (cultivated oat)

Medicinal uses: While we're used to eating oatmeal from ripe grains for a heart-healthy breakfast to lower cholesterol, this is just the beginning of the medicinal benefits that oats provide. First of all, the alkaloids in oats nourish the limbic system and motor ganglia, increasing energy levels and a sense of well-being. Oat straw (the stalk) contains silica and other important minerals that help nourish and build strong bones, nails, hair, and teeth. The milky green top of oats contains compounds that soothe and strengthen the nervous system and help to treat anxiety, mild depression, exhaustion, insomnia, nervousness, and post-traumatic stress.

As a flower essence, oat is helpful for those who
are filled with uncertainty and dissatisfaction and are
unable to find their life's direction. Topically, oats can
help ease the pain and inflammation of sunburn, skin
irritation, and itchiness. So the next time you have
oatmeal for breakfast, think about everything else it
can do!

Note: Those with gluten allergies should use oats with
caution.

Simon and I drove back to Greenport, and since both
of us were hungry, and we hadn't heard from Jackson's
lawyer, we decided to stop and have a quick lunch at
Nature's Way. Wallace and Lily were busy, since the
rain had stopped, so I went into the kitchen and made
us organic falafel pita wraps with tahini and yogurt dip,
then grabbed two gluten-free chocolate chip cookies
and two Honest Teas. We took them into my office,
where we sat on the couch.

"Well, Joe didn't tell us all that much," Simon said,
chewing thoughtfully. "The weird thing is, though, I
believed him."

"Me, too," I said. "He's not exactly likable, but
he's honest. And I kind of admire him for being a loyal
friend to Charles White. He might be the only person
in this whole town who was."

"So what's our next move?"

"Shawn should be here soon, so I think we should
wait."

"I'll call him after I eat," Simon promised, and

opened his iced tea. "Do you think it was a mistake to mention the Roman numerals to Joe Larson?"

"It's hard to say. But if it's important and he figures it out before we do, we've got a problem." I took a bite of my wrap and the tahini dribbled down my chin.

Simon handed me a napkin. "Great sandwich, but messy."

We'd just finished our lunch when he got a call from Shawn, Jackson's lawyer. Simon put it on speaker. "Shawn, where are you?"

"I'm here. I just arrived at the jail. I wouldn't come over just yet, though. They're going to make me fill out forms before they let me see him. It's going to be a wait. I'll call you when I know I can get in there."

Simon hung up and turned to me. "Sounds like it will be awhile."

I nodded. "Let's go over our list of suspects and who we've talked to so far. We just spoke to Joe Larson."

"Sandra wasn't much help, and neither was Harold, but you did leave a message for Kylie."

"Right, and if she doesn't call me back, we can find her at the farmer's market, along with Ramona and Rhonda. That just leaves Professor Russell and Maggie Stone."

"Where would we find him?"

I thought a moment. "He did seem interested in seeing *The Tempest* in Mitchell Park, so what if I call him to remind him about it? I can at least leave a message."

"Do it."

"After that we can go see Maggie. Usually she's supervising Southold Town's dog run."

"Right, then we can circle back to see Jackson."

• • •

Professor Russell didn't answer my call, so I left another message. Fifteen minutes later Simon, Qigong, Rockford, Columbo, and I all arrived in Peconic, a small hamlet west of Southold. I figured they would enjoy an outing, and I also hoped that my animals might soften up Maggie.

We found the dog run on the east side of Peconic Lane. Fenced in with trimmed green grass and several park benches, it was a nice place to spend time, although not many people and their pets were around, since it was midafternoon. Maggie, though, was there, dressed in jeans and a sweatshirt, a whistle around her neck. I waved to her, but she didn't wave back.

Undeterred, Simon and the boys walked toward her. Qigong wagged his tail and greeted her while Columbo and Rockford hung back, since they were more afraid of strangers. She bent down and petted him. "Hi, sweetie. I didn't know that you had three dogs, Willow. They're adorable."

"Thanks, I have two cats, too. All of them are rescues."

"You know, you and Willow actually have a lot in common," Simon pointed out. "You both really care about animals. She's on your side, Maggie."

"If that were true, we would be talking in Greenport's new dog park, instead of here." She turned to scan the park, checking on the other dogs, a black Labrador, a collie, a boxer, and several mixed breeds.

"I'm sorry you feel that way, Maggie."

She gave me a sour look, and scratched Qigong behind the ears. "What do you want?"

"We're investigating Dr. White's death and—"

"That's a good one. He died in your garden."

"Yes, I know that," I said. I hesitated, choosing my words. "Look, I know you're still angry about not getting the lot. And I'm not trying to bug you. I just have one question—do you know anything about Harold's relationship with Professor Russell?"

"If I answer, will you leave?"

Neither of us said anything.

She blew out a breath. "Albert Russell is a client of Harold's."

"Is Harold procuring items for him, possibly out of my garden?"

"I don't know anything about that."

"The other day at the yard sale and antique show, it seemed like you did. You three were having a pretty intense conversation."

She shrugged. "You misinterpreted. And I agreed to answer one question, not a chain of them. Now, why don't you take your dogs for a nice walk and go home?" She turned away from us and headed toward the other end of the field.

Simon looked at me. "That went well."

We waited in the lobby of the police station for over an hour before Shawn Thompson, Jackson's new lawyer, stepped out to talk to us. Handsome, in what looked like a very expensive suit, he sported day-old stubble, manicured nails, and a gold Rolex watch.

"Simon, good to meet you," he said, shaking his hand. "And you must be Willow?"

"Yes, how is Jackson?"

He glanced around the room and at the burly cop on duty at the desk, and said, "Let's go outside."

"I thought you were going to be able to get him released," I said once we were out on the steps.

"Not until tomorrow. The police have the right to hold him for twenty-four hours, and that's what they're going to do. I think they're hoping that they can find something so they can charge him by then."

"But he didn't do it," I said. "This is ridiculous."

Shawn stated the obvious. "They don't have anyone else for it."

"Well, we're looking into it," Simon said.

Shawn smiled. "That's what Detective Koren told me, and he didn't seem exactly pleased about it."

"He never is," I said.

"But if you think you can do something, you'll have to work fast. If Jackson's charged, I can get him out on bail, but you definitely don't want it to get to that point."

"We've run down all the leads we can, for now," Simon said. "I don't know—"

But I interrupted him. "That's not true. We've got the play tonight—Professor Russell may be there—and plenty of suspects to talk to at the farmer's market in the morning. There are still plenty of things we can do to help figure out who really killed Dr. White."

Shawn smiled again, but this time his expression was tense. "Then I suggest you do them."

Friday night, Mitchell Park was abuzz with electric energy. The weather had finally cleared that afternoon, and now it seemed everyone had turned out for Shake-speare's *Tempest*. The area was already crowded with theatergoers, clutching programs and carrying beach chairs, vying for space in front of the stage.

Even though we had come a half hour early, we had to settle for a damp square of grass in the back by the docks. I'd brought along a blanket and an umbrella, not quite trusting that the rain wouldn't return. The air was still heavy with moisture and clouds filled the sky around the harbor. The set was the same as when I'd first seen it—an ocean backdrop, a beached sailboat, and the bow of a ship—but was now dimly lit until the play began.

"Cool set," Simon said. "Have you seen this play before?"

Disbelieving, I turned to look at him. "We saw it together."

Simon looked at me blankly.

"When we were living together in L.A.?" I reminded him. "It was at the Actor's Playhouse in Santa Monica. You wanted to see this actor you were considering for *Parallel Lives*, your show. You don't remember?"

"I don't think so. What's it about?"

"It's the one with Prospero, the Duke of Milan?"

"Not ringing a bell."

"He conjures up this storm to lure his brother Antonio and the king of Naples to his remote island? Chaos ensues?"

"Nope."

"Forget it, we've got to find Professor Russell," I said, and pointed to the ferry terminal behind us. "If he does come for the play, he's going to get off of the ferry and take the boardwalk up to the park. We've got watch for him, and Harold, too."

"You think they'll show up, even though they know you'll be here?"

"It's a big crowd. And I don't think either one of them is afraid of me."

Simon and I both scanned the park intently. A few minutes later, Simon said, "There's Harold." He pointed to the area of the park to the east of the stage and the carousel. "And he's alone."

"I'll bet they're meeting here." But as I searched the ferry terminal and the boardwalk, I didn't see Professor Russell.

"Wait a minute," Simon said. "Harold just sat down. It's looks like he's with those veggie heirloom women, Ramona and Rhonda, and Sandra and Martin Bennett, the artisanal cheese couple."

I groaned. "We won't learn much with them all together. We have to get the professor alone and confront him."

"Is that him?" Simon pointed to a man wearing a tan overcoat and rain hat, scurrying along the boardwalk.

"That's him."

We watched as Professor Russell entered the park and gazed around. "He must be looking for Harold," Simon guessed.

But as we tracked the professor moving toward the stage, all of the lights went out, and a voice spoke over the loudspeaker: "*Welcome to the East End Players' performance of* The Tempest. *Since the play takes place on a remote island in a storm, we thought it was the perfect choice to kick off the last weekend of the Maritime Festival—especially after today."* The crowd laughed. *"Now, sit back and enjoy!"*

The play was actually pretty good, but my mind wasn't on Prospero and his machinations, but on Jackson sitting in a cell in the Greenport jail, and what I needed to do to get him out. During intermission, we spotted Professor Russell with Harold, and once the play was over, we waited to see what he would do next.

We watched as Sandra and Martin said good-bye and walked away, and then, Ramona and Rhonda. Soon, it was just Harold and Professor Russell. But then the two men shook hands, and Professor Russell walked past us, back toward the boardwalk and the ferry terminal. "We need to catch up with him before he gets on that ferry," I said, grabbing the blanket.

We ran up the steps to the boardwalk. "Do you see him?"

"I think he's up there," Simon said.

We hit the boardwalk and threaded our way through the crowd of people who were leaving Mitchell Park, most at a leisurely pace, as they chatted about the performance. As I got closer, I spotted Professor Russell about a hundred yards from the end of the boardwalk and Third Street. "There he is," I said. "We need to run."

We picked up our pace and jogged through the crowd, trying to catch up with him. Just as he reached Third Street, Simon grabbed him by the arm. "We need to talk to you, Professor."

The professor blinked, looking only mildly surprised. "Certainly."

We walked with him up Third Street until we were outside the Blue Canoe, a restaurant close to the ferry terminal.

"Miss McQuade," Professor Russell said, smiling. "So nice to see you again. I'm sorry I haven't called, but I haven't heard back from Dr. Gillian yet."

"Cut the crap," Simon said. "We know what you're up to."

"Dr. Gillian is a fake," I said. "So we'd really like to know why you gave him our sword. The cops would like to know, too, for that matter. Where is it?"

"Dr. Gillian has it, and I don't appreciate you impugning my integrity—or his. Now, if you don't mind, I need to make my ferry." Cars began to drive onto the boat, filling it up.

"You can take the next one," Simon said. "Now tell us what is going on. Jackson Spade is in jail for Dr. White's murder, and we think you know something about it."

"For starters," I said, "what exactly is going on with you and Harold Spitz?"

"Nothing," he said. "We met at my talk at the Maritime Museum, and he's been helping me find nautical items for my house. Is that a crime?"

"It is if the items come from my garden."

"That is ridiculous and patently false."

A black SUV turned onto Third Street and parked on the other side of the road. Harold Spitz opened the driver's-side door and came over to us. "Are they bothering you, Professor? I saw these two running after you."

"He's fine," Simon said. "We want to know what is going on. Your friend Professor Russell gave the sword Jackson found to this fake Dr. Gillian."

"He's not a fake," Professor Russell said.

Simon ignored him. "And we think you two are working together to steal pirate treasure from Willow's garden."

"You two are really losing it," Harold said. "I'm a legitimate dealer. I don't have to listen to this, and neither do you, Albert. Come with me." He put his hand on the professor's arm.

"He stays here until we get some real answers." Simon grabbed the professor's other arm.

"Who do you think you are—the police?" Harold demanded. "He doesn't have to talk to you. Now let go of him."

Reluctantly, Simon did, and Harold hustled Professor Russell with him across the street to his car.

We walked back to Nature's Way and reviewed the events of the evening and what we'd learned, which wasn't much.

"So our next step is to go to the farmer's market in the morning?" Simon asked. "Not too early, I hope."

"Jackson's life is on the line. We need to go as early as possible."

"Okay, okay, so call me when you get up. Night." He gave me a kiss on the cheek and began to walk down the driveway next to Nature's Way to the parking lot behind it to get his car. But then he stopped and turned around. "Sure you're okay here by yourself tonight? I can stay if you need me to."

We were long past a time when Simon might use a situation like this to get close to me. So it felt good that he cared enough to ask. But I knew I'd be fine, so I said, "I'll be okay. Tony's here, and I have my dogs to protect me. But thanks, Simon. I really appreciate you asking."

"That's what friends are for, right? See you in the a.m." He threw me a wave and headed down the driveway. I turned and headed toward Nature's Way, but then I heard the faint sound of the garden gate creaking. "Tony, is that you?"

Simon answered, "I'm over here. What's up?"

"Hold on." I moved toward the garden gate and looked inside.

"I'm coming," Simon said. "Stay right there."

But instead of listening to him, I opened the garden gate. Once inside the garden, I took a few tentative steps and listened. Everything seemed normal. The sound of cicadas chirping filled the air, fireflies sparkled in the dark, and in a tree at the back of the property an owl hooted. But where was Tony?

Suddenly I heard shoes pounding on the garden path. Someone was headed in my direction, and before I could get out of the way, that someone pushed me hard. I landed with a thud, facedown in the dirt.

chapter twenty-eight

Willow McQuade's
Favorite Medicinal Plants

PASSIONFLOWER
Botanical name: *Passiflora spp.*, including
P. edulis (yellow passionflower), *P. incarnata*

Medicinal uses: An impressive perennial with purple and white flowers and twining vines, the passionflower is a calming herb, helping to quiet the central nervous system. Scientists think that passionflower works by increasing levels of GABA or gamma-aminobutyric acid in your brain.

Extracts of the flowers, leaves, and stems serve a variety of medicinal uses such as elevating mood, promoting peaceful sleep, clearing emotions, soothing trauma, quieting mental chatter, and easing chronic worry. Passionflower also helps to relieve anger, anxiety, irritability, and stress. Research shows that it can be as helpful as prescription antianxiety drugs in relieving anxiety. As a flower essence, passionflower

helps inspire the integration of spirituality into daily life.

"Willow? Willow?"

I could hear Simon calling and lifted my head up to answer him, but still dazed, I lay back down again. A few moments later, Simon ran up to me. "What happened? Are you okay?"

I brushed the dirt out of my eyes and my mouth while Simon helped me sit up. "Who did this to you?"

I glanced around. The intruder was gone. "I don't know. I didn't see his or her face. But now that I think about it, I did smell something, a fragrance, like patchouli . . . or sandalwood."

"So it was a woman."

"Not necessarily, but it was probably the same person or persons who have been in here all along. I just don't know where Tony is."

"I do. I saw him over there. He went back to his car to get new batteries for his flashlight, and then he got a call. I guess it was a case of bad timing."

"Or someone waited until he left, then took the opportunity to do some more digging. They haven't been able to get in here for days."

He helped me to my feet. "Forget about that for the moment. Are you hurt? Do you want to go to the hospital?"

I did a quick body scan. No serious damage, but I suspected I'd feel it in the morning. Thankfully, there was no reason to go to the emergency room. I brushed off my shirt and pants, and said, "I'll be fine, but more than that, I'm angry. I've had enough. Jackson is in jail, and whoever this is won't stop. Well, we've got to stop them. Tomorrow, we find some answers and end this thing."

Although my anger fueled my determination to find answers, it didn't do much to help me sleep—that and the fact that Jackson was lying on a cot over in the village jail. I did a quick check on the Internet that I should have done before; the sword we'd found was real and stolen from the East Hampton Historical Society, just as the fake Dr. Gillian had said. I also skimmed the books that Professor Russell lent me, hoping they would lull me to sleep, but after the revelation that Dr. Gillian was an impostor, I held little hope of finding anything truly useful.

Aunt Claire's journals, on the other hand, revealed a fascinating account of one woman's desire and determination to start a natural health store on the East End, many years before it was a popular—or even an accepted—thing to do. As I read, I could feel her speaking to me, and it felt comforting and reassuring and finally helped me drift off to sleep.

Saturday morning, I woke up a little after seven. I was covered in bruises, even though I'd taken a bath in Epsom salts and lavender before bed. But I knew the best cure for feeling stiff was activity, so I took the dogs for a quick walk, aware that this was normally Jackson's morning routine. After a restless night, it felt good to be outside, especially today, when the village was in Maritime Festival mode.

As we walked past Mitchell Park, I spotted two of the majestic tall ships, sails rippling in the breeze as they made port north of the ferry terminal. I'd toured the ships several times and found it amazing that dozens of men could live and work together in such small spaces.

The Saturday festivities included some of my favorites—the clam bake and clam chowder contest in Mitchell Park with various local bands playing, and the irony of ironies considering what had been happening, pirates performing. Since this was the closing weekend for the festival, all of the vendors were back on the south side of the street, although I didn't see Sandra and Martin at their artisanal cheese booth.

The first thing I did after I returned and fed the dogs was check in with Wallace. He was in the kitchen, heating up the commercial stove. "How is Jackson?" he asked.

"I haven't seen him. His lawyer says he's supposed to be out this afternoon."

"Let's hope so." He turned to the counter and stirred the contents of a large ceramic bowl. "Want some breakfast? I've already made the batter for strawberry buckwheat pancakes. The berries are in season now."

"Sure, I'll have some. Wallace, did Merrily call?"

He turned to me. "I know you won't be happy, but she isn't coming in today either." He put a large, flat skillet on the stovetop and added a few pats of butter.

"Did she say why?"

As the butter melted and began to sizzle, he poured the batter into the skillet, making five irregular circles.

"She says that Nate still isn't doing well, and she needs to take care of him. I told her that you understood all that but that we needed her here as well, not to mention that she was supposed to represent the store in the clam chowder contest. But she didn't want to hear it."

"It's just not like her to do this. She was always such a loyal and devoted employee." But, I thought, this was also what I'd been worried about, Merrily losing focus when she became involved with someone new. "I'm afraid I may have to let her go."

"I know. It's a tough decision to make."

"But what are we going to do about today? We need someone to work the booth out front and at least one other person to handle the store and café. I can't help much because I need to work with Simon to try and clear Jackson."

"I've already left a message with Lily, and yesterday Allie said that if Merrily didn't come in, she'd help out, too."

"But doesn't Allie have massage clients to see?"

"She knows the situation with Jackson. We'll make it work. We really just need one person inside and one outside." He used a spatula to flip the pancakes, which were now golden brown.

"Has anyone asked about the garden tours?"

"No, sorry."

"I guess everyone knows about Dr. White's murder by now. They're probably all afraid to come."

Wallace patted my shoulder. "Once you get this mystery solved, things will change for the better. You'll see."

"I hope you're right," I said, but I could hear the doubt in my words.

He put two of the pancakes on a plate, added a dollop of butter, and dribbled syrup on top. "Eat these. They'll give you the energy to find the answers you need."

Simon and I headed over to the farmer's market a little after 9 a.m. I hadn't bothered to call Kylie again, thinking it might be better to make a surprise visit and catch her off guard. Although, after my repeated calls, she probably expected me to show up.

When we arrived at the market, the parking lot behind the Presbyterian church was much more crowded than it had been the last time we were here. We found Kylie in the same place, behind the information table in the center of the action, her long brown hair in a glossy French braid. She was busy selling a young girl a T-shirt with the farmer's market logo. I waited until the girl left then went up to the table.

Kylie didn't seem surprised to see me. "Willow, I got your messages and I've been meaning to call you back, but I've been super busy. I had several cancellations and had to find replacement vendors, and it's just been a zoo since we opened this morning."

"That's okay. I just wanted to ask you a few questions."

She straightened out the brochures on the picnic table so they lined up neatly next to each other. "Ask away, but I don't know if I can help. Sandra told me she talked to you, and I don't know any more than she does."

"So you have no idea what Harold Spitz is up to?"

"None. Harold and I don't really talk. I'm not interested in antiques and he's not interested in veggies, I guess."

"But you joined with him to try and put me out of business?"

Kylie bit her lip and hesitated, as if weighing her words. "That was because of Arlene White."

"What's she got to do with it?" Simon asked.

"Arlene and her husband basically ran the village. Arlene used to be on the Southold Town Board, and they had not exactly friends, but allies in every department of local government and in every local organization. So if you wanted something done, or needed a permit to build or hold an event or anything, they could stop you if they wanted to."

"But Charles White is dead now," I said.

"Which just makes Arlene think that she's the one running the show. She called Harold and said she wanted you shut down, and Harold—who's always looking out for Harold—organized us into a group. None of us were willing to risk getting on Arlene's bad side. That's why we went along with it. I'm really sorry, Willow."

Me, too, I thought. I'd been so busy learning to run Nature's Way and solving murders that I'd somehow never paid attention to local politics. I never understood how Greenport really worked—that half the town was afraid of the Whites. Now, I felt naive and foolish.

"It's okay," I told her. "I understand. But who do you think might have wanted Dr. White dead?"

"That's a long list of people. Except for Joe Larson, I'm not sure he had any real friends. The truth is, Charles White was a selfish, manipulative power player who was also a bad surgeon. The only surprising thing is that it took so long before someone finally got rid of him."

Simon and I exchanged glances. I felt as if we were starting from scratch; nearly everyone in town was a suspect. "Are Ramona and Rhonda here?" I asked.

Kylie looked startled. "What, you think one of them did it?"

"Jackson is in jail. I have to consider everyone."

"I'm sorry, I didn't know." She shook her head. "I can't picture either one of them killing White. But if you want to talk to them, they're over there." She pointed to a booth in the back of the lot.

We thanked her and walked over to their heirloom stand. When they saw us coming, Ramona whispered something to Rhonda, who gave me an annoyed look. "Let me take the lead," Simon said. "Maybe I can find out something."

"Be my guest."

When we reached their booth, Simon gave them a charming grin and said, "Hi ladies. What's going on?"

"What does it look like?" Rhonda said stiffly. "We're selling our vegetables. This isn't a good time to talk."

"We just want to know what you were doing at Village Hall the other day," Simon said. "Good old Larry in the map room said you were down there asking questions. He also mentioned that some microfiche went missing. Can I ask what you were looking for?"

I leaned over to check out a beautiful heirloom tomato and as I did I caught a whiff of something, the same scent I'd smelled last night in the garden when I was shoved into the dirt.

"And did you find it?" I added. "Someone pushed me down in the garden last night when my guard stepped away. I think it was you."

"Don't be absurd," Rhonda said. She slid up the sleeves of her long-sleeved T-shirt, then reached down into a crate of lettuce heads on the ground and began arranging them in a basket on the table.

"You were in Willow's garden last night?" Ramona sounded incredulous.

"Of course not. Willow has a vivid imagination."

As she worked with the lettuce, I noticed that she had cuts and scratches all over her arms. "I don't think so. I think you got those scrapes from digging in my garden and pushing me down last night. And it probably wasn't the first time you've been in there searching for treasure."

"Treasure?" Ramona looked confused. "What is she talking about?"

"I have no idea," Rhonda said, turning to her partner. "It's nothing, you have to believe me." Then she stepped out from behind the table and came over to us. "I think you two should go."

"Why?" Simon asked. "Because you're afraid your partner will learn the truth about you?"

I put my hand on his arm. "We'll go," I said, "but I'll be telling the police my suspicions about you and what you did."

For the first time, Rhonda smiled. "You know what,

Willow, I'm not too worried about that. It's your word against mine, and I'm not the one who had a dead body in her garden."

"Well, I think Rhonda is definitely up to something," Simon said as we left the farmer's market.

"Yeah, I think she was the one in the garden last night, probably searching for treasure. Lily told us that she's having money problems. But I have to go with Kylie on this. I just don't see Rhonda as a killer."

"So you're *not* going to tell the police about her?"

"Not right now. I think telling the police would just keep me stuck answering questions instead of finding answers. We have to keep moving."

So we walked back into town, past Mitchell Park where the clam bake and clam chowder contest were under way and pirates were roaming around the green. Everyone seemed to be having a great time.

When we got back to Nature's Way, we found Lily staffing the booth out front. It had been stocked with fresh plants, T-shirts, and the rest of our merchandise, and she was handing a customer change. She gave me a thumbs-up as we walked by.

Inside, I found Wallace serving food in the café and Allie at the counter, ringing up a sale. They were all busy, and everything seemed to be working smoothly.

Allie waved to me and I went over to see her. She looked cute in the green apron, her red hair in pigtails. "You are so great to help out this way." I gave her a hug. "Thanks very much."

"That's what friends are for . . . So, is there any progress on the case?"

"Not yet. We need to regroup and figure out what to do next."

Simon walked up to us. "I've got our next move."

"And what is that?"

He held up his phone. "I just got a call from Juliette, the one at Dr. White's office. I left my number with her the other day in case she thought of something else that might help us, and she just did. Even though it's Saturday, she's working a half day and said we could meet her there."

chapter twenty-nine

Willow McQuade's
Favorite Medicinal Plants

PEPPERMINT OIL
Botanical name: *Mentha x piperita*

Medicinal uses: Often referred to as "a blast of green energy," peppermint is the go-to herb if you need to replenish, renew, and revitalize your body. A cross between two types of mint (water mint and spearmint), peppermint grows throughout Europe and North America. Peppermint oil has been used for a variety of digestive complaints including stomach cramping, nausea, and gas. It can also be used to ease headaches, bee stings, minor burns, and muscle and nerve pain. Research shows that peppermint oil may improve symptoms of irritable bowel syndrome, and that chewing peppermint gum or mints or inhaling peppermint essential oil can help to keep you alert when driving. You can try using fresh or dried peppermint leaves to make a delicious tea or to flavor foods.

We arrived back at the doctors' offices and headed inside to talk to Juliette, but we didn't get that far. That's because Arlene White and Joe Larson were on their way out. They took one look at us and stood directly in front of the door, blocking our way.

"The happy couple," Simon whispered.

Arlene wore a tightly fitted aqua-blue suit that accentuated all of her assets and a gold statement necklace. She held a slender Gucci clutch in one manicured hand. "What are you doing here?" she demanded.

I started to say something, but Simon interrupted me. "I came to see Juliette. We're dating. You know, like you and Joe here."

Joe's face turned a bright red.

"So it *is* true," I said.

"Don't talk to her, Joe," Arlene snapped.

"Why not tell her? It's no secret. Yes, we're dating. We've been friends for a long time."

"That gives you both a motive for wanting Dr. White dead," Simon noted in a triumphant tone.

Joe rolled his eyes. "If we conspired to kill Charles— and may I remind you he was my best friend—we'd hardly be openly dating."

"Willow's just trying to shift the blame," Arlene said. "Because her boyfriend killed my husband."

"Jackson didn't kill anyone," I told her.

"Then why is he in jail?"

"Because the police don't have anyone else for it," I said.

"She's right and we're going to prove it," Simon said. "Now, if you don't mind, we're going in." We moved toward the door, and Arlene and Joe stepped aside.

But as Simon opened the door, Arlene said, "I'm going to shut you and that garden of yours down, Ms. McQuade. Rest assured, I'm not done with you yet."

I turned to face her. "I know all about your power grabs in this town—you and your late husband's. But you don't scare me and you won't shut down my garden."

"We'll see about that."

"That's enough, Arlene. Let's go," Joe said, taking his keys from his pocket. One of them was an old-fashioned brass skeleton key with the number fifteen on it.

"That's an unusual key," I said, pointing to it.

Joe glanced down at it. "That's just the key to my locker at the men's club."

"I didn't get a locker," Simon said.

"The lockers are for *members only*, Mr. Lewis. We use them for our softball gear and other items. Maybe if you show your commitment to our club, you'll get one of your own someday."

"Oh goody, I can't wait."

"You're a real jerk, Lewis." Joe took Arlene by the arm. "We're going."

Simon flashed him a perfect white grin. "I do believe you're jealous."

"Of what?" Joe asked.

"Oh, maybe of the fact that I'm a Hollywood producer and I probably earn more in a year than you've made in your entire life."

Joe turned around to confront him, but this time Arlene said, "Joe, enough. Car. Now."

"Simon, stop taunting him," I said, pushing the door open. "We need to focus."

Inside, we found Juliette behind the reception desk, working on a computer. She looked up when we came in, then went back to what she was doing. "Be right with you two. Just have to finish this insurance form."

She hit a few more keys and said, "Done." Then she came around the desk and we sat together in the reception area, a small room with uncomfortable chairs, a worn carpet, and dog-eared copies of *WebMD* and *People* magazine.

"I'm glad you came by, Simon," Juliette said. "It's great to see you again."

He turned on his thousand-watt smile and said. "You, too, Juliette. We really appreciate your help. What's going on?"

"I don't know if it's really anything, but you said to call if I thought of something that was unusual or out of place and that maybe could help you solve the case. Have you two been up to Seaside Skilled Nursing, on North Road in Greenport?"

"No," Simon said. "Is there a reason we should go there?"

"Wait a minute," I said. "Fred Monsell, the artist who painted the cigar store, told us that Frank Fox was in a nursing home before he died. Do you think it's the same place?"

"I don't know Fred Monsell," Juliette said. "But last summer, Dr. White spent a lot of time at that nursing home, and as far as I know he only had one patient there, and that was Mr. Fox."

"And Frank Fox is the one who donated the lot that became the garden," Simon filled in for Juliette.

"What happened to Mr. Fox?" I said. "Why was he seeing an orthopedist like Dr. White?"

"He'd broken his leg in a fall and Dr. White had operated on him. But he recovered well. There weren't any complications or anything, so I began to wonder why Dr. White was going up there so often." She smiled tentatively. "I guess I read too many mysteries."

Simon took her hand. "You're doing great, Juliette. Is there anything else?"

"At first, I thought that maybe he was using the time to have an affair, but I never found any kind of indication of that." She made a face. "Really, who would want to date *him*?"

"But his wife was having an affair with Joe Larson, right?" Simon asked.

Juliette shook her head. "Those three had been friends for a really long time. But I think Arlene and Joe only started dating after Dr. White was dead."

"So they may or may not have wanted him dead," Simon concluded.

She took her hand away from Simon's. "I don't know anything about that."

"Why were they here this morning?" I asked.

Juliette shrugged. "Arlene never has enough money and wanted the new corporate credit card. I hope we can pay it." She put her hand over her mouth. "I shouldn't have told you that."

"The practice was having money problems?" I said.

"Yes, because of all the lawsuits and bad word of mouth. Also, Arlene is a compulsive spender. Dr. White was always complaining about that."

"Wait a minute," Simon said. "If White didn't have the money, how did he plan to build that hotel if they got the lot?"

"Joe Larson put together a group of investors, but when Dr. White didn't get the lot, the deal was off."

"How did Dr. White react?" I asked.

"He freaked out. It was awful around here. We were all glad when he started to leave early in the afternoons, although the other doctors complained about it."

"Where did he go when he left?" Simon asked.

She shook her head. "I have no idea."

"So what do you think we might find at the nursing home?" Simon said.

"Maybe you could find out what Dr. White was up to, and find out more about his relationship was with Mr. Fox. Maybe it had something to do with Dr. White's murder. It's a long shot, I know, but I thought it was strange and wanted to try and help you if I could."

"You're the best, Juliette," Simon said, smiling at her. "I owe you a dinner."

She beamed. "Simon, I'd love to."

As we walked back to the car, I said, "I thought you had a girlfriend, Simon. Remember Carly?"

"Just trying to get the answers we need," Simon said breezily. "It doesn't mean that I'll actually go out with Juliette."

I stared at him, outraged. "No, you owe Juliette a dinner, and it better be a nice one. But you'd also better explain everything to her once this is over. You can't just lead her on and use her for information."

Simon looked at me sheepishly. "Okay. I'll make it up to her, I promise." He thought for a moment and then said, "You know, Willow, I do believe that you're making me into a better human being."

"I try, Simon. I try," I said, and squeezed his arm.

Seaside Skilled Nursing was located about ten minutes east of Greenport. Ironically, the nursing home faced the cemetery across the road, but it did have a water view.

Simon found a parking spot in front and we went in to the reception desk. The lobby looked like it had recently been refurbished, with a fresh paint job, new floors, and potted ferns. To the left of the reception desk, I noticed a hallway that probably led to the patients' rooms in the back.

I let Simon take the lead again, and he asked to speak to the manager, a woman named Nancy Harrison. She came out of her office behind the reception desk a few minutes later. "How can I help you?" she asked.

Simon introduced us, then said, "We're looking for information about Dr. Charles White."

"Is one of your relatives in our care?"

"No, well sort of," he lied. "I knew Frank Fox and I know he stayed here."

"I'm afraid I can't confirm that. We can't discuss any of our patients or the doctors who treat them unless you're family, Mr. Lewis. However, you can call Dr.

White's office." She turned to the receptionist, a bored-looking twenty-something, and said. "Please give them Dr. White's office number." She turned back to us. "Talk to Juliette, his office manager."

"Okay, thanks." Simon took the number and we walked back toward the entrance. "Now what do we do, Sherlock?"

"We sneak in, Watson. When you were parking, I noticed other doors on the outside. Maybe we can get in through one of them. We need to talk to a nurse—preferably the one who took care of Frank Fox—and find out what his relationship was to Dr. White."

We exited and circled the red brick building until we came to the doors I'd spotted, which were adjacent to several beds of healthy, well-tended roses and a fountain with a cherub on top. I tried the doorknob and felt my heart speed up. "We're in luck," I whispered. "It's open."

Slowly, I opened the door and stuck my head in, checking for Ms. Harrison. "It's clear. Let's go. Act like you're here to visit someone."

"How do I do that?"

"Act casual, you know, relaxed but concerned."

We headed toward the nursing station, which was situated in the middle of a large atrium with rooms to the left and right. The nurse on duty was a pretty, petite blonde who wore green scrubs and was scribbling on a chart. "You take the lead again. Use your charm."

I watched as Simon went up to the desk, flashed her a smile, and began chatting her up. He really was ridiculously good at that. Sure enough, she smiled back and they talked for a few minutes, then he waved me over to them.

"Emily here was the nurse who usually looked after Frank Fox. His room was right there." He pointed to a room behind the nurse's desk. "Emily says that Dr. White was here often, and spent most of his time visiting Frank."

"What did they do?" I asked.

"Mostly, they talked," Emily said, "but sometimes they played board games."

"A doctor playing games with a patient?" I said.

"I know. It was unusual. Dr. White had operated on Mr. Fox when he broke his leg. It healed well and at first, none of us could figure out why Dr. White kept coming back to see him so often. I mean it was nice, but they weren't related or anything, and Frank was at least twenty years older than Dr. White. They weren't exactly friends, but they liked to talk about the history of the East End and about Frank's hobby. Dr. White seemed really interested in that."

"What kind of a hobby did Frank Fox have?" I asked, curious.

"He referred to himself as 'a digger,' and told me that years ago, he used to spend every weekend on the beaches and other places around the East End with his metal detector."

I looked at Simon and said, "Did he ever say he found anything?"

"Or mention pirate treasure?" Simon added.

Emily smiled. "It's funny that you should mention that. Frank had all kinds of books about Captain Kidd and other pirates. He told me that he was convinced that there was buried treasure out here somewhere, and it was his dream to find something like that. But I don't think he ever did."

"And Dr. White?" I said. "Was he interested in pirate treasure, too?"

"Maybe that's what they had in common," Simon said.

"You're right, he was. In fact, he used to ask Frank where he thought it might be buried, but Frank didn't tell him much. I think he wanted to keep that to himself. It got to the point where he didn't want Dr. White to visit because he kept bugging him about it."

"Did Frank ever mention anything about pirate treasure in Greenport?"

Emily hesitated. "I couldn't say for sure. He mentioned a lot of places. I honestly don't know if they were real, or if he was just trying to get Dr. White off of his back."

"Did anyone else come to visit Frank and ask about this kind of stuff? Like, maybe a guy named Joe Larson?" Simon said.

"Yes, Joe was another pretty regular visitor. But he and Frank just talked about the men's club and sports, that's all. I got the sense that Joe was a good friend to Frank."

"Did Frank have any relatives or any other friends?" I asked.

Emily squinted for a moment, thinking. "Frank told me that his wife died years ago. He had a stepson, but he moved away a long time ago, and both of Frank's brothers are gone."

"So it was mostly Joe and Dr. White who visited," Simon said. "Was there anyone else?"

The phone rang at the station and Emily said, "I have to get this." She answered the call then turned back to us. "I just thought of something. There was this young guy here that Frank became friendly with. He came to put in new rose beds as part of his course work at the Horticultural College in Riverhead."

"What was his name?" I got a funny feeling in my gut, as if I already knew what she was going to say next.

"I think it was Nate, Nate Marshall. Frank had been an avid gardener when he was younger so they talked about plants and stuff like that. It was really sweet to see them together." Another nurse, with a chart in her hand, approached the desk. "I have to go now," Emily said. "I hope I helped."

"You have," I said. "More than you know." We started to walk away and got halfway down the hall when Emily called to us. By the time we got back to the nursing station, the other nurse was gone, and Emily had placed a tattered cardboard carton on the desk.

"These are Frank's things. We tried to send them to the stepson but could never find an address or phone number for him. Dr. White wanted them, but I didn't think that was right because Frank didn't really like him. So I've been saving them, I don't know for what. There isn't anything of value inside—it's mostly old books—but maybe they'll mean something to you."

I could feel my heart begin to hammer with excitement. "Thank you," I said. "We'll take good care of them." I hoped they would help us solve this mystery.

chapter thirty

Willow McQuade's Favorite Medicinal Plants

ST. JOHN'S WORT
Botanical name: *Hypericum perforatum*

Medicinal uses: For over a thousand years, from the time of the ancient Greeks through the Middle Ages, St. John's wort has been used to treat mild to moderate depression. This hardy, sun-loving perennial is easy to grow and is traditionally gathered on a sunny afternoon, when the buds on the flowers are just about to open. You can make your own oil, salves, and liniment from these flowers, but when it comes to using St. John's wort to treat your depression, purchase standardized products from a health food store. This herb is also helpful in treating anxiety, stress, tension, and nerve damage, along with seasonal affective disorder (SAD). The oil when applied to the skin can help relieve pain, and speed healing from bruises, sprains, and burns.

Note: Do not take St. John's wort with prescription antidepressants. Remember, if depression is not adequately treated, it can become severe. See your health-care provider to get the help you need. There are many effective proven therapies available.

Simon and I headed back to Greenport and Nature's Way. For a while we were silent, mulling over what we had just learned. Finally, Simon said, "You know, when Emily first started talking about Frank and Dr. White, I thought the two of them might have been working together to find pirate treasure out here."

"Me, too," I said. "But after what she said, it's pretty clear that Frank didn't want Dr. White to know what he knew."

"Right, but White was too greedy—or dense—to catch on to what Frank was doing. So when Frank died last summer and White found out that he'd left a lot he owned in Greenport to the village, he must have figured that the most likely place to find something of value was right there," Simon said. "So he puts in a bid for the lot, to build the hotel and find the treasure, and Joe puts together investors for him."

"Between the hotel and the treasure, he must have thought it was his ticket to financial freedom," I said.

"But then you're awarded the lot. White must have been furious; first, because he didn't get the lot and the hotel deal fell through; and second, because now he had to work around you to get to the pirate treasure."

"There's something about all that that's not quite right," I said. "The sword was stolen, remember? And the earring is Victorian and no one got all that excited about the bronze goblet. So, though we've uncovered stuff in the garden, I don't think any of it was actually hidden there by pirates."

"Doesn't matter," Simon said. "Because White didn't know that. He seemed convinced that Fox knew of buried treasure there, and he was furious when he lost out on the lot. And, of course, Arlene was also counting on it as her ticket to wealth, so she, too, felt cheated when it went to you. Which explains her Garden of Death hate campaign, and her efforts to shut you down."

I thought about that. "Okay, maybe that explains why Dr. White was in the garden the night he died—and why he was killed. Someone must have known what he was searching for."

"We need to tell the police about all of this," Simon said.

"We need proof first." I looked at the box of stuff on the floor behind the seat. "Let's go back to Nature's Way and look at this. But first, please call Shawn and find out when they're releasing Jackson. I want him home."

Simon couldn't reach Shawn, so we swung by the police station on the way back to Nature's Way. The desk sergeant there had good news for us: Jackson had just been released. Moments later, I received a text message from Jackson, telling me that he was out and back at Nature's Way. I blew out a sigh of relief, then quickly texted him that we were on our way.

We couldn't get there fast enough, even though the store was less than five minutes from the police station. Jackson met us at the back door, pulled me inside, kissed me, and folded me into a hug. I began to tremble, and he pulled me even closer. "It's okay, it's okay," he repeated, until I began to calm down.

"They wouldn't let me see you," I said, tears forming in my eyes. "Are you okay?"

"I'm fine. It was Koren. He was playing hardball, but Shawn got him to release me. I'm just afraid they may pick me up again."

"Then we've got to solve this, so that doesn't happen," Simon said. "We've got a lot to tell you."

"Yes, I think we're getting close," I said, wiping away the tears.

"Good, what's that?" He pointed to the box that Simon was carrying.

"These are Frank Fox's effects from his stay at the nursing home," Simon said. "But we haven't had time to go through them yet."

"Let's get some lunch and take it outside, and we'll tell you everything."

A few minutes later, the three of us were sitting on the porch eating Gardenburgers, chips, and passion fruit iced teas with orange slices for lunch and reviewing what we'd learned so far.

"You two have covered a lot of territory," Jackson said. "I'm impressed."

"Thanks," I said. "But does it make sense?"

"I think it does. It's logical that if someone else was after the treasure, they may have run into Dr. White in the garden. They fought, and whoever it was, killed him. The question is, who?"

The door opened and Wallace came out, his face as white as the sheet of paper in his hand. "This just came in on the fax machine." He gave it to me, his hands trembling. "She didn't call in this morning, but I never thought . . ."

The piece of paper only had seven words, but it was enough to strike terror into my heart: *Find the treasure or Merrily is DEAD!* I sucked in a breath. "Oh my God."

"What is it, Willow?" Jackson said.

I handed him the paper, which he showed to Simon.

"Who do you think it's from?" Simon said. "Do you recognize the fax number, Willow?"

"No, I don't," I said. "But I'm calling Merrily right now." But she didn't answer and neither did Nate. "What do we do?"

"We'd better find that treasure fast," Simon said.

"Didn't we already find the treasure?" I asked. "Is there something else buried—or is this creep asking us to get the sword back from the fake Dr. Gillian? I don't even know where to start."

"First, we call the police," Jackson said.

I called the police and told the desk sergeant what had happened, that Merrily was missing, and what the note said. Unfortunately, among other things, there had been a multiple-car accident on the main road that demanded police attention, a boating accident, and a restaurant fire. Maritime Festival activities always stretched the police force thin, and this year was no exception.

There was also the fact, the sergeant said, that they usually didn't investigate missing persons until forty-eight hours had passed, and that the note could be a hoax or a practical joke. I said that I didn't think it was at all funny, and he said that someone would be over as soon as possible.

While we were waiting, I brought the box that Emily had given us into my office and put it on the coffee table. Simon came with me while Jackson said he wanted to check on the dogs and went upstairs. I really think he wanted time alone to process what had happened to him at the jail, but I didn't say anything.

"Let's go through it methodically, okay, Simon? I want to make sure that we don't miss anything."

I pulled several books out of the box that were about pirates on the East End of Long Island. "These look like the kind of books that Professor Russell lent me," I said as I began to page through the first one. "Let's check for any notes that Frank may have made."

Simon began looking through one of the other books. "What are we hoping to find exactly?"

"Anything that hints at buried treasure in Greenport—especially anything that refers to the area that's now the garden. I need to know if there's something else there. It would take us days to dig up that whole lot."

"I realize that, but I doubt that Frank would have put it in a book for anyone to see. If he actually had information like that, wouldn't he want a more secure place—especially with someone like Charles White coming around all the time?"

I sighed. "You're probably right, but let's check to make sure we haven't missed anything."

An hour and a half later, we'd carefully examined all six books and found nothing unusual. We'd just finished when Detective Coyle arrived, wearing baggy pants, a shirt with perspiration stains underneath the arms, and an awful purple tie with a bluefish on it. Wallace showed him into my office.

"I hear you have a missing person, Ms. McQuade. Want to tell me about it?"

I decided not to call Jackson and tell him Coyle had arrived, figuring he'd had enough of both him and Detective Koren in the past twenty-four hours. Instead, I went over to my desk, got the fax, and handed it to him.

"What's this bit about the treasure?" Coyle wanted to know.

"It's what we've been trying to tell you and Detective Koren about all along. Several people are looking for something in my garden—I think they think it's pirate treasure."

He laughed. "That again? C'mon. The important thing here is that someone is threatening to kill your employee."

"I know that, Detective, but it's because of the treasure, or whatever is out there, that this has happened."

Quickly, I explained what we'd learned at the nursing home. To his credit he did listen, and when I'd finished, he said, "I don't know about all this other stuff, but if your employee, and your friend, is in trouble, then you did the right thing by calling. I'll put out a BOLO, and we'll keep an eye out for her."

"A BOLO?" I asked.

"An all-points bulletin," Coyle explained. "It's an acronym for be on the lookout, so all officers in the county will be aware she's missing. Depending on what happens, we may need to bring the FBI in on this, too. Call us if this person contacts you again. Now, I have to go. I was on my way to that five-car pileup when you called. I'll update you later."

After he left, I told Jackson what happened. We agreed that now that I'd told the police what we knew, it was time to try to find Merrily ourselves. There was no way we could just sit there and wait for the phone to ring.

I asked Wallace to call me if another fax came through or if anyone, especially the kidnapper or the police, called, and we headed out to Merrily's house, where she lived with her mother. The three of us got into my Prius and Jackson drove while I called Merrily's cell again, and Nate's, but got no answer.

Next I tried her mother, Cheryl, who told me that she had seen Merrily last night before she left to go to Nate's. She said that Merrily did seem worried about something, but she wouldn't say what.

I told her that we wanted to stop over. I'd break the news about her kidnapping once we were there.

Merrily and her mother lived in a restored yellow Victorian home at the corner of Broad and First Street, with a neatly cut lawn and pretty flower beds filled with geraniums, nasturtiums, and marigolds. When Cheryl came to the door, she looked surprised to see all three of us and quickly knew that something was wrong.

"What is it? What's happened?"

"Can we come in?"

"Yes, of course."

We stepped into the foyer and she directed us into a sunny living room. Like Merrily, she liked to dress in a funky style. She was wearing a tie-dyed tunic and flip-flops.

Cheryl had worked as a production designer for films before she got married, moved to the North Fork, and had Merrily. Now she only worked occasionally on special projects.

"Is Merrily okay?" she asked.

"That's why we're here," I said. "We're not sure. We received this strange fax a little while ago."

She read the fax and started to cry. "Treasure? What treasure?"

I squeezed her hand as I briefly explained what had happened to Dr. White, why we thought it had happened, and what might be in the garden. "I've talked to the police and they are going to look for her, and maybe even contact the FBI, but we're ready to help right now. Let's start with when you saw her last night. Before she left, you said that she seemed troubled?"

Cheryl nodded. "Yes, she had something on her mind."

"Do you have any idea what it was?" Simon asked.

"I really don't." She reached for a tissue from the box on the coffee table and dabbed her eyes. "I need to call her father. We're divorced but he needs to know. He lives in the city, though, so it will take him time to get out here."

"Do you have any idea where she might be?"

She shrugged. "Nate's, I guess. But you've called there already, right?"

"Yes, but we'll stop by."

"Will you call me if you find her?"

"Of course we will."

"Cheryl," Jackson said, "we'll bring Merrily home. Don't worry."

Nate lived in a garage apartment in Arshmamoque, on the same road where Simon and I met with Joe Larson. His apartment was at the very end of the road, opposite Mill Creek and behind a ranch house that had peeling paint and a scruffy yard. No one was home but we parked on the road and walked down the driveway to the back.

The garage apartment was also in rough shape, with a roof that needed repair and cans overflowing with garbage. We peered through the windows. Inside, the place was a mess, dusty with dishes, magazines, and discarded clothing on the floor. Clearly, no one was home.

"How can he live like this?" I said. "I hate to think of Merrily spending time here. She deserves better."

"No argument there," Simon agreed. "This guy is a mess."

"He might be a lot worse than that," Jackson said, his voice grim.

"You think he took Merrily?" I'd had the same thought, of course, but hadn't wanted to verbalize it, to make it real.

Jackson nodded. "He seemed like an okay guy, even if he had an attitude. But what if he's turned into a kidnapper?"

chapter thirty-one

Willow McQuade's
Favorite Medicinal Plants

ROSEMARY
Botanical name: *Rosmarinus officinalis*

Medicinal uses: Ancient Greek scholars would wear laurels of rosemary on their heads to help them stay sharp and to keep their memories clear when taking examinations. I used it when I took my final exams at my naturopathic college.

An evergreen member of the mint family, with pale blue flowers, rosemary is also helpful for anxiety, fatigue, tension, and to improve energy levels and uplift spirits. In addition, rosemary is full of important nutrients including calcium, magnesium, potassium, phosphorus, and iron, and contains more than a dozen antioxidants. Because it improves digestion, circulation, and memory, it is an excellent herb for the elderly. In the bath or footbath, it rejuvenates

the body and mind and also helps relieve pain and sore muscles.

I've recommended rosemary flower essence to many of my customers as it encourages users to be less forgetful and more aware, more present in their body, and more conscious. It strengthens the heart and mind. In aromatherapy, rosemary essential oil eases stress and anxiety, whether you inhale eight to ten whiffs from the bottle or put oil in a diffuser and let it fill the room with this lovely scent.

It was well after six on Saturday night when we returned to Nature's Way. We'd checked out all the places that Merrily might be, including friends' houses and places she liked to hang out, shop, and eat, but didn't find her. By this time, Nature's Way was closed. Lily had brought in all of the unsold items from the booth, but there wasn't much left. She'd sold most of what we had, which was the only good news of late.

I called to check in with Detective Coyle and he confirmed that they had issued a BOLO. He also said that if Merrily didn't show up within the next day, they would contact the FBI and enlist their help.

He had also updated Merrily's mother and father, Andrew, who had just arrived from New York City, and assured them that everything was being done to help find their daughter.

Afterward, we sat at a table in the café and had a dinner of fresh tomato soup and Caesar salad while we tried to decide what to do next. We'd worked hard, yes, but we were no closer to finding Merrily or Dr. White's killer.

After I finished eating, I got up and went back into the office to continue going through the box of Frank Fox's stuff. Jackson and Simon followed me in.

"Willow," Jackson said, "what are you hoping to find?"

"I don't know, but I have to try to find something to help her."

At that moment, the fax machine began making noises. I got up and watched with dread as a new fax came in. I pulled it out and read it as my hands began to shake.

"Willow," Jackson said. "What does it say?"

I walked over to them and turned the sheet so they could read it: *You Have 24 Hours or Merrily is Dead!*

Jackson stood and pulled me into a hug, but I couldn't be comforted. I couldn't wrap my mind around any of this.

"Why is this happening? Merrily is such a sweet person. I know I've been a little aggravated with her lately, but I never could have made it through the first few months of taking over the store if she hadn't been with me." I began to sob. "We have to save her!"

"We will, we will," Jackson said, trying to soothe me. "But you need to call Detective Coyle and send him the fax. He needs to know about this. The police might want to set up camp here or at her mother's house."

He turned to Simon. "In the meantime, I think we need to start digging in the garden. We've got a little more daylight, and we can set up lamps after that. We could start in the places where we found the earring, the goblet, and the sword. I think we have to try."

"I agree," Simon said, handing me some tissues. "Let's go."

While Jackson and Simon went outside, I called Detective Coyle, who said he was assembling a task force to work on Merrily's disappearance and possible abduction. He said they would be setting up at Merrily's house. He would update me.

After that, I decided to finish going through the box of Frank Fox's stuff before heading outside to help. I just had a feeling that there might be something there—something that could cut through all of this confusion and lead us to what we needed to find.

But after going through the rest of the items—a watch, an old bottle of aftershave, a scarf, an Ace bandage, an alarm clock, a photo of his wife, and a small DVD player—I had come to yet another dead end.

In desperation, I returned to the beginning, to the books that Frank seemed to have treasured so much. This time I didn't look for notes but I examined the books themselves. The spines of the books appeared normal, so I opened each one and checked out the front and back.

When I came to the last book, a large coffee table book about the life of Captain Kidd, I found it. There, under the photo of Captain Kidd's ship on the inside back cover, was a raised area, one that prevented the book from closing properly. I ran my fingers over it but couldn't figure out what it was.

I went to my desk and got my scissors. Carefully, I used them to pierce the inside back cover right next to the object. It took several tries, but I finally managed to make an indentation right next to the object. Next, I drew the blade down to create an opening. Finally, I reached inside to pull out whatever was there.

It was a key, and not just any key. It looked very much like the skeleton key that Joe Larson had on his key chain.

The key had the number forty-nine on it—the same number that appeared in Roman numerals on the curb in Fred Monsell's painting of the old cigar shop. Then I remembered that it had been Frank Fox, a member of that same men's club, who had asked Monsell to put that number in the painting. Suddenly, I knew where we would find the information we needed to save Merrily.

"You do understand that this is breaking and entering?" Jackson asked as he used a set of lock picks to open the side door that led to the men's club.

"I know," I said. "But I think we've got the key to Frank Fox's locker—and maybe there's something inside that will tell us where the treasure is. If we can find it, we can save Merrily's life. We have to try."

Jackson jiggled the picks. "Let's just hope Koren and Coyle don't find out about this. It's all they'd need to put me away."

"It won't come to that," I said, praying I was right. Seconds later, the lock clicked open, and the two of us and Simon climbed the stairs to the club's main room. Simon flipped a light switch, turning on the overhead chandelier. The décor was dated, with dingy old-fashioned wallpaper, dusty lamps, and a threadbare rug.

Immediately, I went over to the painting of the men's club that Joe Larson had purchased and that now hung over the fireplace. "There it is," I said, pointing to the Roman numerals for forty-nine. "The exact same number that's on the key that Frank Fox hid in the book. And he's the one who had Fred Monsell put the Roman numerals in the painting. He must have been leaving some sort of message."

"Yeah, but he's been dead nearly a year," Simon pointed out. "Wouldn't the other club members have cleaned out his locker by now? Or one of the treasure hunters like Dr. White or Harold, since they're members?"

"Maybe not if this is the only key. Unless they broke in," I said. "Where are the lockers, Simon?"

"Up front." Simon led us into the next room, which overlooked the street and contained a small kitchen, a seating area, and a wall of antique lockers. "We'd better close these curtains."

"You two do that while I find locker forty-nine." I began looking; it didn't take long to find it. "I've got it." I pointed to a locker in the middle of the wall.

"Open it," Jackson said.

"This should be good," Simon added.

"Let's hope so." I inserted the key into the lock and tried to turn it. At first, it wouldn't budge. I tried again.

On the third try, there was a click and the door creaked opened. But there was nothing inside.

"Someone obviously got here first," Simon said, sounding disappointed.

"Someone with a key, since it doesn't look forced," Jackson said.

"Maybe one of the head honchos of the club, like Harold," Simon said.

"They'd have a key," Jackson said.

"Now what do we do?" Simon said, looking at me.

"Let me think." Instead of panicking, I forced myself to remain calm, then, moments later, I got an idea. "I need to look at the painting again." I left the room with Jackson and Simon following me.

"What are you doing?" Jackson said.

When I got to the fireplace, I said, "Look for another number. Maybe together with forty-nine it will add up to the right number and the right locker."

The three of us stood there in silence, reviewing every brushstroke. After five minutes, Simon said, "I don't see anything."

"Me either," Jackson said.

"Wait," I said, leaning in for a closer look. There, in the upstairs window of the building, a tiny book leaned against the sash. On the spine was the number VI. "Look, right here, another book, and another number."

"It's the number six," Simon said. "I don't need to look that one up."

"Forty-nine and six is fifty-five," I said.

"Right," Jackson said. "But what does it mean?"

"Let's check locker fifty-five and find out," I said.

The three of us ran back into the locker room and

searched for number fifty-five. After a few moments, we found it, on the very bottom shelf, three lockers from the end. I inserted the key and turned. This time it moved easily, like a knife through butter—Frank had probably visited this box in secret often before he died—and the door opened. I reached inside and pulled out an old metal box, which was embossed with strange symbols.

"Good job, McQuade," Jackson said, squeezing my arm.

"You're a genius Willow!" Simon said.

"Wow," I said, pretty amazed myself. "Let's see what's inside."

"Why don't you bring it over to the table and we can examine it?" Jackson suggested.

I carried the box over, put it down, and used a napkin that had been left on the table to wipe it off.

"It looks old," Simon said. "Maybe not pirate-treasure-old, but I'm guessing at least a hundred years."

"Luckily, it doesn't seem to have a lock," Jackson said.

I took a deep breath. "This has been a long road," I said. "So let's open it together. For Merrily."

"For Merrily," Jackson and Simon repeated.

Together, we pulled back the lid and looked inside. There was only one object in the box. "It's a piece of parchment paper," I said, carefully lifting it out.

"Maybe it's a map," Simon said. "Unfold it."

I did so, and put the oversized piece of paper on the table and smoothed it out. "It *is* a map."

"It's a map of the lot," Jackson said. "See, there's the boundary between your store and Frank Fox's lot."

"And there's Fox's old home," Simon added. "But where's the X to mark the spot?"

"Good question." I leaned over and carefully examined the map, which was old and tattered and had obviously been handled many times. After a few moments, I spotted it. "Right here. See?"

There was a tiny X in the middle of the lot, next to a drawing of a hedge. "The X is at the midpoint of his lot."

"Let's hope it marks the spot," Jackson said. "Let get back to Nature's Way and see what we find."

But when we headed back downstairs and peered through the window in the door, we saw a cop was patrolling the alley. "Can't go that way, at least not right now," Jackson said. "Is there another way out, Simon? "

"Yeah, you can go out the front, but we'd better check it first."

The three of us went back upstairs and into the front room. Jackson pulled back a section of the curtain and looked out. "We've got a problem here, too. There's a patrolman right in front of the store."

"What's with all the police?" Simon asked.

"There are a lot of people in town this weekend," Jackson said.

"There's a lot going on," I said. "There's the electric boat ride around the harbor, and another performance of *The Tempest* in Mitchell Park. Plus, there's the seafood restaurant crawl and a wine tasting from all the local vineyards at the Vine."

"No wonder it's so crowded," Simon said.

"The police need to keep an eye on things," Jackson said. "We'll just have to wait until they leave."

• • •

Unfortunately, the cop continued to patrol the alley and the other cop stayed out front. I wondered if there had been a tip about some possible crime in the area, or maybe they were looking all over town for Merrily. While we waited, I called Detective Coyle to get an update on the investigation into Merrily's disappearance. The police were searching all over the village, which might explain the cops in the area, but there was no word yet, and no more faxes. So, hopefully, whoever it was was honoring the deadline.

"The cop in front is walking away," Jackson finally said from the window. "But I can't tell who else is down there. Simon, go check things out okay?"

"On it." Moments later, Simon returned from his check of the street, the alley, and the boatyard. "No cops."

I looked at Simon, and then at Jackson. "Let's go find that pirate treasure and save Merrily."

chapter thirty-two

Willow McQuade's
Favorite Medicinal Plants

TURMERIC
Botanical Name: *Curcuma longa*

Medicinal uses: A shrub related to ginger, turmeric is grown throughout India, other parts of Asia, and Africa. Known for its warm, bitter taste and golden color, turmeric is commonly used in foods such as curry. Turmeric contains two natural compounds, curcumin and curcuminoids, that decrease inflammation naturally. A study in the medical journal *Arthritis and Rheumatism* in 2006 showed that turmeric is effective in helping to relieve symptoms of rheumatoid arthritis.

Turmeric's powerful healing properties also enable it to improve immune function, and cold and chest complaints. It aids digestion, cools off heartburn, improves liver function, and regulates men-

struation. Since turmeric is antibacterial, it is often applied directly to the skin for wound healing. Turmeric's fingerlike underground stems (rhizomes) are dried and taken by mouth as a powder or in capsules, teas, or liquid extracts. Add it to your favorite dishes for an immediate health boost.

We returned to the garden and found Tony standing guard at the front gate. "Anything happen while we were gone, Tony?" Jackson asked.

"Quiet tonight," Tony said. "Although there are a lot of people on the street. Had a couple of folks ask about the garden and if it would be open tomorrow."

"I hope so," I said.

Jackson opened the gate. "We've got something to do inside, so keep an eye out, okay?"

"Will do."

Simon and I trailed Jackson inside and down the path. Using my flashlight, we followed the map to the place that was marked. "It looks like we got lucky," I said, pointing to the path between two planting beds. "If this map is accurate, the treasure is buried here, which means we won't have to dig up all these beds, and will be able to get to the treasure quicker."

"Good," Jackson said, grabbing a shovel and digging it into the ground. He deposited the first shovelful in the path behind him.

Simon picked up the other shovel and joined him. Together, they made quick progress, and a hole soon took shape.

"I need the big clippers, Willow," Jackson said. "I'm hitting some pretty big roots here and I need to clear them if I'm going to go deeper."

"We need light, too," Simon said. "I can't see what I'm doing."

"I'll go get the clippers, and then I'll hold the flashlight for you."

Using the flashlight to guide me, I stepped along the path to the toolshed. The night was still and the garden was dark, and suddenly I felt unsettled being alone. I just wanted to get what they needed and get back to Jackson and Simon.

Opening the door, I stepped inside and used the flashlight to locate the large pair of clippers, which were on the floor at the back of the shed. But as I picked them up, I heard a voice behind me say, "Willow?"

"Merrily?" I turned around. Merrily stood in the doorway of the shed, shivering and looking frightened. But as I stepped toward her, Nate Marshall stepped between us and shoved a gun into my face. "Hi, boss."

Jackson had been right, even though I hadn't wanted to believe it. "I'm so sorry, Willow." Merrily started to cry. "He made me do it."

I fought to keep my voice calm. "It's okay, Merrily. What do you want, Nate?"

He used to the gun to motion me outside and grabbed the clippers with his other hand. "I want what I came here for."

"Which is—?"

"What do you think? Now move." Nate held the

gun on both of us and prodded us back toward Jackson and Simon.

Still concentrating on the hole he was digging, Jackson said, "Willow? Did you get the clippers?"

"Yes, and I found Merrily and Nate."

Jackson looked up. "That's great . . ." But then he saw Nate and the gun. Instantly, his voice became calm. "What are you doing, Nate? You don't want to hurt Merrily or Willow."

"So Jackson was right?" Simon said. "But how could you kidnap Merrily? She's your girlfriend. Why would you do this?"

Nate smiled. "So many questions. Well, here's my answer. Either you dig up the treasure or I'm going to kill your best employee."

Merrily started shaking and crying again. I went to put my arm around her, but Nate pushed me away. "Get back."

"I guess suing Willow wasn't enough," Jackson said. "You wanted more."

"Let's just say that a few gambling debts caught up with me, and the people I owe want their money now. I wanted the sword you found, but I know that you no longer have it, and that the goblet is in the bank. So we'll have to settle for what we find here. Keep digging."

Jackson and Simon began to shovel again while Nate stood to the side with his gun trained on Merrily and me. My phone was in my pocket, and I wondered if I could possibly call 911 without Nate noticing. Even if I couldn't talk into the phone, the 911 operator would pick up my location—and possibly overhear enough to send help to us.

To distract Nate, I started asking questions. "How did you find out about the treasure in the garden? Is that why you came to work here?"

He laughed. "Well, I did need some college credits, but searching for buried treasure trumped that."

"Frank Fox told you about it, didn't he?"

"Frank was quite a character. I actually liked spending time with him at the nursing home when I wasn't planting roses."

"It became even more interesting when he began talking about his love of history, in particular the adventures of Captain Kidd and other pirates, particularly on the East End. I'd heard the rumors all my life that pirate treasure might be out here, but it wasn't until I met Frank that I realized those rumors could really be true."

"What exactly did he tell you?" I asked, thinking that whatever it was, Frank Fox might have told the identical things to Charles White.

Nate shrugged. "Frank said there were several places on the East End where treasure might be buried and encouraged me to go after it. But I checked out all the other possibilities and found nothing. When Frank died and left this lot to the village, I knew it had to be here." He smiled at me. "So I applied for the job to work for you. It was just too convenient to pass up."

"How perfect," I muttered, and noticed that Jackson and Simon were digging but were also talking quietly to each other. They were probably trying to figure out a way to disarm Nate. I wondered if Jackson had tried to call Tony.

"So, Dr. White figured it out, too."

"Yes, we came to the same conclusion and unfortunately both of us came here last Friday night to look for it. Of course, I'd been searching for it while I was working, but I did my best work after hours."

"So you're the one who made all of those holes since then? You're the one who was all in black with the rucksack?"

"That was me. I did see someone else in here a couple of times, but I didn't catch his face. And I never found what I was looking for, so I had to resort to more desperate measures." He pointed the gun at Merrily, and she gave a little whimper of fear.

Then I realized why Nate was talking so freely: he wasn't worried about anyone spilling his secrets, because he was planning to kill us all. I tried to divert his attention. "Why did you kill Dr. White?"

He gave a casual shrug. "I never planned to kill him, but we got into a fight, and before I knew what I was doing, I'd hit him over the head with the shovel."

"You didn't plan it," Jackson said in a skeptical tone. "But you were wearing gloves. Which is why the police found my prints on the shovel."

"Correct, now get back to work." He pointed the pistol at him.

"No!" I yelled. "Don't hurt him."

"Chill, Nate," Simon said. "We'll get you what you want. Just don't do anything you'll regret."

"What I regret is having to waste all this time looking for whatever Frank Fox buried in this lot. That's why I took your employee here. So I could enlist all of you to help." He pointed the gun back at Merrily.

Merrily dabbed her eyes with the sleeve of her jacket. "Nate, please don't do this."

"Sorry, babe, I have to. What you and I had was fun, but there are some very bad people after me. Granted, this was a long shot, but I think it's about to pay off." He was looking at her when he spoke, and I slid my phone out of my back pocket. All I had to do was press the On button, slide to the first screen, and press Emergency. But first I had to press the button that turned off the sound, so Nate wouldn't hear it dialing 911. Unfortunately, pressing that button made a distinctive buzzing sound, which I couldn't risk.

He turned to me, and I quickly dropped the phone back into my pocket. "How did you figure out where to dig?" he demanded.

I explained what had happened at the nursing home, meeting Emily, the nurse, and her giving us the box of Frank's effects, and how I found the key, which led to finding the map.

"Aren't you the clever one?" Nate said, smiling. "I knew I sent that fax to the right person."

"I think we've got something," Jackson said. He used his shovel to strike the dirt and it made a metallic clang.

Nate moved closer to the hole and looked down at what they were doing. "That's it!" he said. "Keep digging."

Jackson and Simon used the shovels to dig most of the dirt out around whatever was there, and the edges of what looked like a box began to emerge in the dirt. Jackson brushed off the top and tried to move it, but it remained in the ground.

"Dig deeper!" Nate said. "You've got to get under it."

While Nate's attention was fixed on what they were doing, I noticed a small flash of light in the corner of the garden. Was it Tony?

Jackson and Simon dug around the bottom of the box some more. "I think we've got it now," Jackson finally said. He and Simon grabbed the box and pulled it from the earth. The box actually looked like an antique treasure chest. It had a domed lid and was covered with dozens of what looked like gems, and had a heavy clasp.

Jackson tried to open the latch. "It's locked."

"Stop," Nate said. "Bring it to me!"

He trained his gun on Jackson and Simon as the two of them lifted it, brought it over to him, and placed it on the ground at his feet.

Keeping an eye on Jackson and Simon, Nate leaned over and tried to open the chest. "It won't budge. We need a key."

Simon glanced at me and made a turning motion that Nate didn't see, and I realized what he was thinking: that the key to the locker at the men's club might also open the treasure chest.

Nate must have noticed something, because he whipped around and glared at me. "What? Do you know something? Do you have the key?" He pointed the gun at Merrily. "Give it to me or she dies."

"Don't do anything crazy, Nate," I said, and fished the key out of my pocket and handed it to him. "Here it is."

He grabbed the key and inserted it into the lock. There was a loud click and the clasp opened. "Got it!"

He pushed the lid open and it fell back with a clunk. "Give me that flashlight!"

I handed it to him and he trained it on the inside of the box. Over his shoulder, I could see dozens of items wrapped in plastic bags with tags. I wasn't sure if it was pirate treasure, but some of the items glittered in the light, and many looked old and valuable.

But Nate was not impressed. "What the hell is this?"

Nate was staring at the contents of the box, so Jackson seized the moment, took his shovel and swung it up and across, and knocked him on the side of the head. Nate slumped to the right and hit the ground, landing face first in the dirt. It was rough justice for a man who had done the same to Dr. White.

As if confirming his defeat, the annual fireworks show started moments later with pops and hisses. The dark night sky over the harbor was filled with a display of dazzling, sparkling colors.

"Thank God, Jackson!" I said.

Tony emerged from the shadows and ran over to us, gun drawn. "Is everyone okay? I was watching from over there and waiting to get the jump on that little creep."

"Do you think he's dead?" Simon said.

"Stand back, I want to get his weapon." Jackson put down his shovel and went over to Nate, who hadn't moved. He picked up the gun, checked it, and shoved it into his back waistband. "Then he checked Nate's pulse. "He's alive. And would you believe it, there were no bullets in his gun."

"So what his endgame?" Simon said. "He told us everything. That's a lot of witnesses to leave alive. But believe me, I'm not complaining."

Jackson took a look into the box. "He probably planned to use the treasure to disappear. Money can get you beyond the arm of justice."

Merrily slumped onto the ground with a groan and I went over to her. "Are you all right? Did he hurt you?"

"I think I'm okay."

"What happened? And where was he keeping you?"

"At first I thought we were going to have a weekend away, and I was really excited. But then all we did was go up to his friend's cabin on Mattituck Lake. Nate got a phone call, and after that, his whole personality seemed to change. He got so mean and nasty, and he wouldn't let me leave."

"That call must have been from the guys who were trying to collect on his gambling debts," Simon said.

"I don't know," Merrily said. "But after that call, he'd go out, but when he did, he'd tie me up and put me in the closet. All he kept talking about was this treasure."

"You poor thing." I held her and she began to cry. "It's okay, Merrily. You're safe now."

Simon had jumped back into the hole and resumed digging. Now he spoke up, his voice strained. "Guys, I found something else."

"What is it?" Jackson said.

Simon stood up, a horrified expression on his face. In his hand was a human skull.

chapter thirty-three

Willow McQuade's
Favorite Medicinal Plants

<u>VALERIAN</u>
Botanical name: *Valeriana spp.*, including *V. offici-nalis* family and Valerianaceae (Valerian family)

Medicinal uses: The early colonists brought valerian with them when they traveled to the New World, and it's a good thing they did, because this herb does wonders for stress, anxiety, tension, and insomnia. Valerian is a safe, powerful, and popular nervine, often prescribed by European doctors to soothe the nervous system and treat headaches and muscle aches and pains. In Germany it is more likely to be recommended than Xanax or Valium.

This nerve tonic works by depressing activity in the central nervous system thanks to two compounds, valerenic acids and valerenal. Valerian is sometimes referred to as a "daytime sedative" because it can improve performance, concentration, and memory during the day. It can also help you sleep better during the night and reduces the time needed to fall asleep. Take it as pills or capsules, as the taste is objectionable.

As a flower essence, valerian calms, encourages healthy sleep, and eases physical pain. It is helpful during convalescence from illness. If you didn't receive adequate love during childhood, it helps to lift the spirits and foster inner peace.

Note: If you are taking sedatives, antidepressants, or antianxiety medications, use valerian only under the guidance of a qualified health-care professional.

We all stared at the skull, crusted with dirt and decayed by the time it had spent in the earth. This was by far the most chilling thing that we could have ever found in my garden. Maybe it really was the Garden of Death after all. I found myself shivering.

"How did that get here?"

"I don't know," Jackson said. "But it's clearly been buried here for quite a while. We'd better call Koren and Coyle."

"We need to tell them about Merrily, too." I pulled out my phone and texted Koren:

Found Merrily & kidnapper. We R in garden. Come rt away!

Simon tried to hand the skull to me. "Can you please take this?"

I didn't want to. I shook my head. "I can't. Just put it on the ground."

But at that moment, Martin Bennett stepped out of the shadows, looking large and menacing. He, too, had a gun in his hand. Chances were good that his gun had bullets. Behind him was Sandra.

"I'll take that," Martin said.

I could not make sense of this—a guy who made artisanal cheeses waving a gun at us? "Martin? Sandra? What are you two doing here?"

He pointed his gun at Tony. "Drop your weapon, Tony. I know you carry. Tony and I belong to the Orient Gun Club, don't we?"

Tony gingerly placed the two pistols on the ground.

"Martin, this is crazy," I said, foolishly hoping I could appeal to reason. "What are you doing?"

"Cleaning up some loose ends and getting my own back."

"Don't tell me you're after the treasure, too." Jackson sounded positively weary.

"It's mine." Martin walked up to the treasure chest and looked inside. He crouched down and picked up several items and unwrapped them.

Sandra walked up behind him and looked over this shoulder. "This is amazing baby, just like you said."

"Told you so."

"What's in there?" I asked, wondering if he would tell us as much as Nate had.

Martin held up a small gold statue of Venus and an elaborate silver and jade necklace. "Things like this: antiques, jewelry, artifacts. I'm the one who buried them, but I guess my stepfather, Frank, found all this stuff after I left. I certainly didn't leave them all neatly put together in a treasure chest." Martin shook his head in amazement. "Frank was such a trip. He was always poking around with his metal detector. My mother used to complain about it when I'd call her. She said that he cared more about that thing than he did her."

"Wait a minute," I said, remembering that Emily had mentioned Frank having a stepson who moved away a long time ago. "Your stepdad was Frank Fox?"

Martin turned to me. "Yes, my real name is Ted, Ted Fox. I'm Frank's long-lost stepson." He continued to go through the items in the chest. When he'd finished, he glanced up at me, an angry look on this face. "Where is the sword? And the goblet and the diamond earrings?"

I looked at Jackson. "You were right. The pirates didn't bury any of the treasure. Martin did."

"I buried the stuff, Frank dug it up and buried it in this chest. But I don't see the sword or the goblet or the earrings. *Now where are they?*" he demanded, his voice louder. He stood and pointed the gun at me. Sandra took a few steps back.

I explained about Professor Russell and how we had given the sword to the fake Dr. Gillian and that the other items were in my safe-deposit box.

Martin nodded. "That's right. I remember that I wrapped some things in cloth. That's probably why Frank didn't find the sword or the goblet and earrings with his metal detector. Irregardless, I have to get that sword back. It's mine."

"Uh, it's regardless," Simon said. "Not irregardless."

Martin turned the gun on Simon, who was still in the hole. "Shut up."

"But Martin, I mean Ted, we don't know where the sword is."

"Maybe this Professor Russell does." He scowled at me. "Just call me Martin. It's easier."

"Aren't we forgetting something here?" Jackson said. "We just found a skull in this ditch. Do you know whose it is?"

Now Martin trained his gun on Jackson. "You, get back in the hole and keep digging. There's a body that belongs to this head, and I need it."

"*A body?*" I nearly shrieked. My garden was turning into a graveyard.

Martin gave me a bored look. "You want the story? Fine. I'll tell you, because you're not going to live long enough to repeat it. Consider it your last request."

"I grew up on this lot." Martin pointed to the north end of the piece of land. "There was a house there, and I lived in it with my father, Robert Fox, who was Frank Fox's older brother, and my mother, Denise.

"From the time I was ten, my not-so-loving father used to beat the tar out of me, and her. But he stopped when I was seventeen, because he knew I could take him. But he kept hitting my mother."

"That's awful," I said.

"Yes, it was. But he usually did it when I wasn't around. But one night twenty years ago, when I was nineteen, I was there when he went after her again. I'd had enough. We fought and I killed him."

"And you buried him in the backyard," Jackson said.

"That's right, I did. Keep digging."

"Then what happened?" I said.

"I hit the road and got as far away from here as I could. I think my mother may have suspected what I'd done, but if she did, she kept quiet. When I finally called her five years later, she'd married my father's younger brother, Frank Fox."

"Where did you go?" I said.

"California. I met Sandy when we were both working at an organic farm outside of San Francisco. She'd been away from the East End for over twenty years, too, and she wanted to move back here. I figured enough time had passed, so we moved back to the East End and started the dairy—after I had some plastic surgery done on my face and nose to hide my identity."

"See, Willow, I told you he'd had work done," Simon said.

"Shut up!" Martin said. "And get back to work!"

I looked at Sandra, who seemed completely nonplussed by Martin's story. "So Sandra knows about your father?"

Martin gave her a loving look. "Yes, and it didn't change her feelings for me."

"I always knew that you were gullible, Sandra, but this is extreme."

"I told you so," Simon said.

"Shut up and dig!" Martin brandished the weapon at Simon.

Sandra came up to Martin, took his hand, and looked at him adoringly. "I love him, and he takes care of me. That's all I need to know."

"Did you know about the treasure?"

"Yeah, of course. We tell each other everything, don't we, hon?"

"We sure do, sweetie." He leaned over and kissed her.

"Was she the one who told Harold and the others about it?"

He nodded. "She told Kylie, and Kylie let it slip to some of the others. I don't think Kylie thought it was true; she thought it was a goof. But everyone else sure believed it. Every time I'd try to break in here, to try to dig up the stuff I'd buried and find my father's body, I'd see Harold or this kid." He pointed to Nate, who was still lying unconscious on the ground. "It was like Grand Central Station in here some nights. Not to mention, Tony here."

"You say that Frank found the things in the box with his metal detector over the years, but where did those other things—the sword, goblet, and earring—come from?" I asked.

"All of it was stuff I stole when I was a teenager. I belonged to this gang. For kicks and cash, we used to knock over houses and the small local museums in the winter, when things were quiet out here. We sold what we could, but the other things that we knew would be recognized—like Captain Kidd's sword—I buried in the lot, to wait for time to pass."

"So it really was Captain Kidd's sword?" I said.

"Sure thing. We stole that from the East Hampton Historical Society."

"Did you see Frank before he died?" Jackson asked, taking a break from digging. There was already a mound of bones at the bottom of the hole where he and Simon were working. It was a grisly sight.

"No, by the time Sandy and I moved back to Cutchogue last fall, my mother and Frank were both dead."

"You must have been shocked when you found out that he donated the lot where you grew up to the village," Simon said.

"I was. That's when Sandy and I applied for the lot from the village. We could put the business here, and I could grab my lost artifacts and find my father's body before anyone else did."

"But it didn't work out that way," Simon said.

"No, it didn't. Ms. McQuade got the lot and I had to try and shut her down. Now, you two, get back to work!"

Jackson and Simon began digging again.

I continued talking to Martin, hoping that Detectives Koren and Coyle would show up. Where were they?

"So you were the one who painted on the fence and dug all the holes. Were you the one that Jackson almost caught that night?"

"No, that wasn't me. Must have been Harold or one of the others."

"Did you hit Nate?"

He nodded. "He was in my way."

"I knew that he hadn't fallen," I said. "And you're the one who broke into the store and ransacked my bedroom and office?"

Martin nodded, his eyes on the bones that were being excavated.

"Did Sandra know what you were doing?" I watched as the pile of bones got larger and larger. I could make curved ribs and the long bone of a femur. My stomach started to feel queasy.

"I tell Sandra what she needs to know."

At this, Sandra looked hurt; she had belied her statement that they told each other everything.

"Now I just need to clean up a few loose ends and I'll be free of the past and we'll have enough money to go anywhere we want." He threw a big duffel bag down into the hole. "Put the bones in here boys."

"So by taking these artifacts and digging up your father's bones you'll have a clean start—is that the plan?" Jackson said.

"Very good. You must have aced school," Martin said sarcastically.

"But you have six witnesses—Willow, Simon, Merrily, Nate, Tony, and me," Jackson pointed out. "You can't seriously be considering killing all of us?"

"You and Simon are going to finish digging up my father's body, and then all of us are going to take a trip out into the bay. There will be a fire and an explosion, and none of your bodies will ever be found."

"And once you find Professor Russell and the sword, you'll leave town with Sandy?" I guessed.

"Correct. I just have to do a little more research to find out the best place to fence these things. But I'll have plenty of leisure time for that. I hear Spain is nice."

"But most of these items probably are recognizable," Simon said. "It'll be hard to sell them, even on the black market."

"Don't you worry about that now. I have ways." He peered down into the ditch. "Do you have it all?"

Jackson and Simon looked around the ditch where they'd been working. "I think so," Jackson said. "We dug pretty deep and wide."

"Good, finish filling up the bag, then hand it to me."

They did as he asked. Martin pulled the bag toward his feet while keeping his gun trained on Jackson and Simon. "Now, fill it in."

About half an hour later, Jackson and Simon had filled the hole back in and, following Martin's directions, put new mulch on top to hide what they'd been doing.

It was nearly midnight when the eight of us walked across the village green in Mitchell Park, with Martin and Sandra at the rear. Before we'd left, he'd given Sandra a small revolver, and warned us if we said anything to anyone that he or she would shoot us on the spot. Nate was still out of it, but he could walk, and he leaned on Jackson, as if he were drunk. No one would suspect what had really happened to him.

The park was deserted, everyone having gone home after a busy day at the Maritime Festival. So we made our way across the green quickly and headed for the docks in the harbor behind it.

When we reached the docks, Martin motioned to the right and told us to keep walking, and instructed Sandy to run up ahead to watch everyone. At the next row of boats, we took a left. "Keep going," he said. "When you get to the boat named *Sandy,* stop and wait. No funny business."

But as we made our way down the wooden dock to the boat, Nate suddenly pulled away from Jackson and jumped into the inky black water below, dropping like a stone.

"What happened?" Sandra yelled.

"Nate jumped," Martin yelled back. "Stay where you are!" He walked over to the edge of the dock, put down the treasure chest and duffel bag, pulled out his flashlight, and aimed it and his gun at the water. "Where are you? Get back here, right now!" He stood there waiting, but Nate didn't surface. Merrily gasped as he fired several shots into the water. We all waited. But Nate didn't show himself. "Don't any of you get the same idea! Move it! Head for the boat!"

The six of us continued down the dock to the boat. In the harbor a Shelter Island ferry made another run back to the island. We met Sandra at their boat, a large white cabin cruiser with a dinghy powered by an outboard motor attached. I figured that he planned to light the boat on fire and then he and "Sandy" would escape in the dinghy.

"Drop your cell phones into the water before you get on," Martin said, pointing the gun at each of us in turn. "No funny business."

I did as he instructed and got onto the boat first, followed by Simon, Merrily, Tony, and Jackson. Martin put the duffel bag and treasure chest on the dock, then untied the boat from the dock, all the while keeping the gun trained on one of us. Sandra tried to keep a bead on us too, but moved her gun back and forth in a random fashion, and her hands trembled. She looked scared and out of her depth.

True, they both had guns, but she seemed inexperienced and scared. Plus we had five people on the good guys' team and they only had two on the bad guys' team. I just had to believe that we could get the jump on them.

"You go up first, I'll follow," Martin said. "Keep an eye on all of them."

Sandra nodded and climbed to the upper deck. When she got there, she turned around and trained her gun on us as we climbed up the ladder. Martin grabbed the treasure chest and duffel bag off of the dock and put them on the lower deck, then followed us. Once we were all on the upper deck, Martin positioned us in a half circle in front of him before he started the engine and pulled out from the dock.

The night was still and clear, and I knew sound carried across water. I wondered if anyone had heard the gunfire when he shot at Nate. Maybe someone would call the police. As for Koren and Coyle, they were probably in the garden, wondering where everyone had gone. Somehow I didn't have much faith in them finding us in time.

Martin maneuvered the boat out into the harbor and headed for Shelter Island, which was about three-quarters of a mile away as the crow flies. Jackson was on one side of me and Simon, the other. While Martin focused on piloting the boat, I tried to figure out what to do. Whatever it was, I'd also need to communicate it to Jackson and Simon.

As I stood there, I suddenly remembered that Shelter Island held its fireworks at midnight on the last Saturday night of the Maritime Festival. I felt my first glimmer of real hope. Maybe we could use this as a distraction to regain control of the situation from Martin. I glanced at my watch. There was still time.

I leaned closer to Jackson and tried to whisper this to him, but it was impossible to make myself heard over the sound of the boat's engine. Finally, when Martin glanced in the other direction, I pointed to Shelter Island and the sky and tried to pantomime fireworks. Jackson picked up on it immediately. Next, I found my moment and did the same with Simon and he shared it with Tony, who was to his right.

I glanced at my watch. It was nearly midnight. Jackson, Simon, and Tony were watching me, so when I pointed to the dial, they knew it was almost time.

When we heard the first little pop that indicated the fireworks were about to start, we prepared for action. Suddenly the sky lit up with the first geysers of golden light.

Startled, Martin looked up, and as he did, Tony tackled him from the left side. Jackson did the same from the right side, and they brought him to the ground. Martin made an *ooof!* sound and the gun he'd been holding skittered across the deck and landed underneath the captain's chair.

Sandy freaked out and ran over to him, but Simon intercepted her, pushing her against the railing on the starboard side, and then overboard. She landed with a splash below and began to scream for help.

"What did you do to her?" Martin yelled as he wrestled with Tony.

At the same time, Jackson scrambled across the deck. "Where's the gun?"

"It's over there!" I said. "It's under the captain's chair."

But Martin spotted it, too. He hit Tony, who went sliding toward the ladder. Tony landed with a nasty cracking sound and didn't get up.

Simon tried to tackle Martin, but the boat shifted and he tripped over a tackle box and went flying across the deck and landed on some life preservers.

"Should we do something?" Merrily asked, looking terrified.

"Not right now. We wait for our moment," I said, hoping it would come soon.

Jackson turned back from the gun and tackled Martin as he approached him. The two of them hit the deck hard, rolling as the boat shifted, now unmanned and unmoored, and Sandra continued to scream.

As the two of them wrestled, I began to make my way across the deck to the gun under the captain's chair. Then Martin managed to throw a punch that connected with Jackson's face, and he got up and scurried toward the gun, shoving me aside. I landed next to Simon on the deck.

"You okay?" Simon said.

"I'm okay. What should we do?"

"Get the gun, Jackson!" Simon yelled.

Tony was still unconscious, but Jackson slowly got up. From the boat lights, I could see he'd have quite a shiner. He looked dazed as he started across the deck to the captain's chair.

But before he could even get halfway across, the wake from one of the passing Shelter Island ferries hit us, rocking the boat. Martin managed to use the momentum to tackle Jackson. They fell again, this time right near the captain's chair. They both frantically grabbed for the gun. But Martin got there first.

"Okay, enough," he said as he used the chair to stand up. He dropped anchor while keeping the gun trained on us once more, then backed up to the railing on the starboard side where Sandra had fallen overboard, and yelled, "Sandy? Where are you? You okay?"

But Sandy didn't answer.

"Sandy? Sweetie? Sandy!"

No answer.

"Answer me!" He pulled out the flashlight and, while periodically checking on us, scanned the water all around the boat. "Sandy?" He seemed to be about to cry, but then switched emotions and became absolutely furious. "Where is my wife?"

We all looked at him with blank expressions on our faces. Finally, Jackson said, "I don't know, sorry, man."

"You should be sorry! This is all your fault! And you're going to pay for it! Everyone is going into the downstairs cabin until this is over. Let's go!"

Tony lifted his head and blinked. With help from Jackson and Simon he got to his feet, and we all headed back down the ladder, and Martin directed us into the downstairs cabin. He searched us for anything that could be used a weapon, and then used rope to bind our hands and feet.

He made us sit on the floor in the hold of the boat, between the bunks. I sat between Jackson and Simon with Tony and Merrily opposite me. We sat silently as Martin walked back up the stairs and closed the hatch. Moments later, the engine started up again, but the boat moved slowly, probably because Martin was look-ing for his wife.

"Start working on your ropes," Jackson said.

"There's got to be a knife in the kitchen area," I said.

"I've got a Swiss Army Knife in my shoe," Simon said.

"How James Bond of you," I said.

"I put it there when Nate had us start digging."

"Good thinking."

"Yes, that's very good news," Jackson said. "Now we just have to get everyone free and overboard before he blows it all up."

I scooted closer to Simon and reached one of my bound hands toward his shoe. "If I can get the knife, I can cut one of us free."

It took a bit of struggling and grunting, but I finally extracted Simon's knife from his shoe, got the blade open, and began sawing on the ropes that bound Jack-son's hands. Within ten minutes or so, we were all free again. Jackson went up the stairs, opened the hatch, and took a quick look around. When he came back he said, "Martin seems to be stopping again. I'm sure he'll probably check on us before he deploys the device to blow up the boat. I think you should all sit back on the floor and pretend you're still tied up."

"What are you going to do?" I asked.

"I'm going to get up top. When he opens the hatch and looks in, I'll knock him down."

"Sounds like a plan," Simon said. "Places, every-one."

We all did as Jackson suggested. Moments later, the engine began to slow even further and eventually stopped. By this time Jackson was already onboard waiting for Martin.

We heard Martin's footsteps on the ladder from the upper deck, heard him reach the lower deck, then walk across the lower deck toward the hatch. Moments later, he opened it and stepped in. He was carrying another black duffel bag, smaller than the one with his dead father's bones. "Is everyone comfy and cozy?" he asked.

"We're fine," I said. "Now, are you going to let us go?"

Martin continued down to the next step. "Oh, no. This is the fun part." He held up the bag. "I've just got to set the timer and you'll all go boom."

But before he could arm the device, Jackson stepped down and hit Martin on the head with the handle of an oar. Martin groaned, collapsed, and rolled down the stairs, landing with a hard thud.

Tony quickly snatched his gun, which had fallen to the deck of the cabin, while Jackson and Simon grabbed Martin and began to tie his hands and feet.

Once Martin was secured, Jackson grabbed a flare gun from the shelf. "I spotted this before. I'm going to shoot it off so the police can find us. Tony, can you watch the prisoner?"

"No problem."

Simon and I followed him up the steps and out on deck. Suddenly it seemed like a beautiful night, with cool breezes and calm seas. It felt good to be alive.

Jackson walked over to the middle of the deck and shot off the flare gun. We all watched as the flare shot up into the sky, leaving a red tail trailing behind it.

Simon smiled and put an arm around each of us. "We make quite a team."

"Like the Three Stooges?" Jackson suggested.

"No," I said. "We're definitely the Three Musketeers."

We spent most of Sunday telling Detectives Koren and Coyle exactly what had happened and signing statements. By the time we returned to Nature's Way, I was ready for a nice lavender bath and bed.

But the dogs had a different idea. They wanted to go for a walk. So we put on their leashes and headed down a now-deserted Front Street. For this year, the Maritime Festival was over. With everything that had happened, that seemed just fine with me.

When we returned to Nature's Way, we grabbed a quick dinner, and I took a long hot bath. By the time I came out, Jackson was asleep, with all of the dogs and cats surrounding him.

I, on the other hand, felt much too restless to sleep. The garden project that I'd envisioned has resulted in so many unforeseen, bad, and even evil consequences that I still wondered if it had been a mistake.

But there was part of me that still really wanted to use the garden to teach people about the medicinal qualities of plants and how they could improve the quality of their lives.

I wished that I could know what Aunt Claire would do if she were here, so once again, I began to go through her journals.

It was almost midnight, a full twenty-four hours since we'd been rescued from Martin Bennett's boat, when I found what I needed. In one of her journals, on the last page, Aunt Claire had written a list of ten things she'd hoped to accomplish in her business. For number one, she'd written: "Make Nature's Way a success by serving the community." When I came to number ten, she'd written: "Create a garden designed after the Chelsea Physic Garden in London to teach people about the value of plants."

Finally, I knew that I had Claire's seal of approval on the garden. It made me feel good to know that even now, I was helping to make her dreams come true.

epilogue

Two months later, at the beginning of August, we all gathered again to celebrate the opening of the teahouse in my medicinal garden. In the weeks after the capture and arrest of Nate Marshall, for the murder of Dr. White; Ted Fox, aka Martin Bennett, for the murder of his father and attempted murder of Nate and the rest of us; and Sandra, who had been rescued by the Coast Guard, for being his accomplice, the police had continued to be busy.

First, they tracked down Professor Albert Russell, who had been hiding out at his sister's house in Amagansett, and he surrendered Captain Kidd's sword. It was returned to its rightful place in the East Hampton Historical Society. Professor Russell gave up the fake Dr. Travis Gillian, and both were charged with receiving stolen goods.

Meanwhile, Jackson and I contacted the real Dr. Travis Gillian, who came over to examine what we'd found in Frank's treasure chest along with the goblet and the earring from the safe-deposit box at the bank.

All of the pieces had been stolen by Martin, and a few, like the goblet, were quite valuable. Dr. Gillian promised to help us identify their origins and, if possible, return them to their rightful owners.

Dr. Gillian also showed up with his staff to conduct a thorough examination of the entire lot with sophisticated sonar equipment. Although they didn't find any pirate treasure, they did uncover several bowls and crockery from the Colonial era, which we donated to the Floyd Memorial Library to put on display.

Once they'd ascertained that the lot was "treasure-free," Dr. Gillian released a statement to all the papers so that no one would come looking for anything valuable in the lot again. Visitors would have to settle for the myriad of medicinal plants that benefited body, mind, and spirit. Not a bad trade-off, in my mind.

In other news, Harold Spitz was never charged with trespassing in the garden or any vandalism, since we had no real proof. He was questioned regarding his relationship with Professor Russell, but that yielded nothing. His yard sale/antique business was still going strong. Unsuccessful treasure hunter Rhonda had to declare bankruptcy and she and Ramona sold the heirloom veggie business.

Joe Larson was thrown off the Village Board for colluding with Dr. White to get him my lot. When the mayor and the Village Board realized the power that the Whites had wielded over local business, Arlene was summarily dismissed from all committees and positions of power and authority.

Thankfully, since her husband's killer had been caught, she stopped her Garden of Death campaign.

Arlene and Joe got married in July on her yacht, *Lady White*.

In the best news of all, Detective Koren cleared Jackson of any wrongdoing and even begrudgingly acknowledged our help in catching Dr. White's killer. But I knew that he wasn't planning on stopping by for a chai tea at Nature's Way any time soon.

There were other benefits, too. Simon, spurred on by our adventure with pirate treasure, finished his screenplay just in time to send it to his agent before he went back to work on his new show in L.A. There was already interest from three big-time movie producers. He'd be back on the East End for Thanksgiving.

But for today, the weather was calm, bright, and beautiful—the perfect day to celebrate the completion of the teahouse and garden. It was the final piece of a yearlong project, although changes in plants and educational displays and tours would be ongoing.

All of our friends were on hand, including Allie, Wallace, Lily, Hector, and Aunt Claire's boyfriend, Nick, along with the mayor and trustees on the Village Board. Simon was needed on the set of his show, but he had sent a huge bouquet of flowers to celebrate our achievement.

But I was happiest about the fact that Merrily had joined us again. After a period of therapy, she seemed to be coming back into her own happy and productive self and was baking up a storm in the kitchen. Merrily's Marvelous Gluten-Free Pies had begun to attract attention and we had more requests from customers every day.

At 2 p.m., I went to the center of the patio, in front of a new portrait of Claire that Nick had painted. I'd placed it on an easel there, so everyone who visited would see it and be reminded of her.

"Thanks so much for coming to the opening of our new tea garden. Jackson has worked really hard to make this a reality." I gestured to him, and he made a small bow and smiled.

"I know that you're all going to enjoy sipping tea and eating Merrily's tasty pastries in such a serene place here, outside among the flowers." I smiled at Merrily and she gave me a thumbs-up. "I hope it becomes a sanctuary for all of you."

I took a breath and went on. "After what happened at the opening of this garden and the events that transpired afterward, I have to admit that I had my doubts about whether this garden was going to work." Jackson gave me a look as if to say *not this again.*

"This concerned me greatly," I explained, "because I love and miss my aunt, more than I can say, and I wanted to make her proud as I carried on her legacy." The day was calm, but at that moment, a strong breeze ruffled the trees. I paused for a moment and smiled.

"What I wanted most, I couldn't have, which was a heart-to-heart with Claire to see what she thought about what had transpired and her advice for the future. But I think I found the next best thing, her journal, in which she clearly stated her desire to create such a garden for the community. I'm happy to carry out her wishes today and every day that I can.

"And now, if Mayor Hobson would like to come up, he will open the teahouse."

The crowd applauded as the mayor walked over to me and shook my hand. "Thanks to everyone for coming here today to celebrate with us. And now, I'd like to declare the Claire Hagen Memorial Physic Garden and Teahouse officially open!" He reached over and cut the large red ribbon strung from the posts on the teahouse gate. "Enjoy!"

The guests clapped enthusiastically, and after a few moments moved onto the patio to get cups of tea and scones with cream and jam. Everyone looked like they were having a really good time.

As for me, I took a few steps back into the garden to take it all in. We *had* done a good job. It was a beautiful garden, teahouse and all, and I knew I'd always find it a place to soothe my soul.

Jackson walked up to me, took my hand, and gave me a kiss. "You did good, McQuade. How are you feeling?"

"I feel great, and I couldn't have done this without you. Thank you, Jackson." I hugged him, and suddenly my eyes began to well up with tears. "I just wish Claire were here."

Jackson hugged me back. "I know. But she is. She's here with you, with us, always."

I stepped back and gestured to the teahouse. "It's funny, you should say that. I felt her presence before when I was up there talking about the garden. It was so clear."

"What do you mean?"

"Remember after I said I wanted to continue her legacy, there was that sudden breeze?

"I didn't notice."

"I did, and as it ruffled the trees, I felt like she was saying that she loved me, and was proud of me, and would always be there for me." I turned to Jackson and smiled. "That's all I needed to know."

acknowledgments

No author is an island. Completing a book is a difficult task and it helps to have family and friends to lean on. In particular, I'd like to thank my mom, Marion Fiedler, my sister Val Boergesson, my nephews Jake and Alex, my friends Joann Tamin and Cindy Clifford, and, of course, my dachshunds Holmes and Wallander and my cats Tinker and Tuppence (all named after fictional sleuths!). For writing support, I'm especially grateful to Ellen Steiber, fellow cozy author Anne Canadeo, and my Killer Hobbies blog sisters: Tracey Webber, Linda Johnston, Monica Ferris, and Betty Hechtman. Thank you Ann Collette, of the Helen Rees Agency, for going the extra mile. Special thanks go to Natasha Simons, copy editor Faren Bachelis for making my book shine, and the rest of the team at Gallery Books for marketing and promoting my natural remedies mystery series. My gratitude also goes to my teachers in holistic health: Brigitte Mars, A.H.G., Jacob Teitelbaum, MD, Suzy Cohen, rPh, and Deborah Wiancek, ND. Finally, I'd like to thank all the readers who have enjoyed my books and told their friends, cozy blogs and websites, librarians, reviewers, and booksellers. If there was a real Nature's Way Market & Café, I'd have you all over for an organic smoothie!